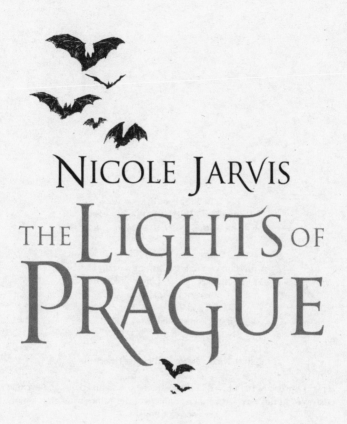

Nicole Jarvis

The Lights of Prague

TITAN BOOKS

The Lights of Prague
Print edition ISBN: 9781789093940
E-book edition ISBN: 9781789093964

Published by Titan Books
A division of Titan Publishing Group Ltd.
144 Southwark Street, London SE1 0UP
www.titanbooks.com

First Titan edition: May 2021
10 9 8 7 6 5 4 3 2 1

A CIP catalogue record for this title is available from the British Library.

Printed and bound by CPI Group (UK) Ltd, Croydon CR0 4YY.

To my mom, my first reader.

1

PRAGUE, 1868

Dark water reflected the line of gas lamps along the path, the rippling lights echoing the stars stretching overhead.

Fog twisted around the lamps behind Domek, the fire inside illuminating the mist like streams of smoke. The Old Town was quiet at this hour. Buildings were cramped and towering along the river, looking as though they might tip forward if not for their brothers holding them in place. Ahead, Charles Bridge arched over the Vltava toward the castle. After the recent storm, the river was swollen and heavy.

Domek nudged the next lever with the end of his pole, and a stream of gas flowed into the lamp. Flipping the pole, he used a match and red phosphorus block to strike the wad of cotton aflame and lifted the fire to the open glass casing.

He could tell the moment just before the flame touched gas, like a breath of anticipation.

After a moment of stillness, the first mantle ignited into blue flame. And then, with a series of small pops, the other three burst to life. The sudden light was a welcome visitor in the dark evening. Lingering for a moment, Domek watched the flames dance inside the glass lantern. Then, he pulled away his pole, blew out the small fire, and moved on.

Cobblestones gleamed underfoot from the rain earlier in the evening. Like a giant sated after a hearty meal, Prague after a storm was content and slow. Most of the citizens were tucked away in their homes and would stay there until dawn.

For Domek, though, the night was only beginning.

Domek stopped at the next lamppost and set the metal end of his pole to the gas valve, then froze when a scream pierced the night. High and shrill, it echoed across the river and cut off after a staccato burst.

It was what he had been waiting for. Leaving his pole behind, Domek moved forward into the darkness, feet light and swift on the uneven cobblestones. The lamps ahead were unlit, and only the light from the crescent moon overhead fell onto his path. Spying nothing along the river, he slid onto Charles Bridge where sandstone and copper statues of venerated saints lined the rails, a row of guardians black-stained and decaying from centuries of pollution. As he walked, holding his bag at his side to hide its rattle, he kept a careful watch on the looming statues. Some featured only one figure, others depicted a twisting group. In the night, any could hide a monster.

Finally, at the base of the statue of Saints Barbara, Margaret, and Elizabeth, he saw a still pair of figures intertwined in the shadows, a coarse mimicry of the statues above.

They were difficult to parse in the night, their edges blending with the darkness, but the moon caught on a woman's pale, slack face. A man stood behind her, one arm across her bosom to keep her pressed back against him, the other cradling her head to bare her neck.

Moving silently until he was only steps away, Domek barked, "Hey!"

The man jerked his head toward Domek.

And it was no man.

The creature's bloody mouth gaped like a wound across its face. It blinked at Domek, and bared fangs that glinted in the faint moonlight. These were not simply elongated canines, as on an alley cat, but a mouthful of thin, razor-sharp needles erupting from a vast jaw. It hissed, and the high, eerie sound grated on the quiet bridge. Horrible mouth smirking with triumph, it leaned back toward the woman.

Without hesitating, Domek pulled a hawthorn stake from his pocket and closed the distance between them before the pijavica could resume its meal. He grabbed the creature by its dark curly hair and jerked it away from the woman. Without its hold, she slumped to the ground, unconscious. Her neck was smeared with blood, a spreading shadow in the darkness.

Yanking the pijavica toward him, Domek aimed his stake at its heart, but the monster used the momentum to slide inside of Domek's reach. Its reflexes were unnaturally fast, and Domek had to drop to the ground to avoid having his head taken off by a snap of the creature's jaws.

His teacher would have told him to stab the pijavica immediately while it was distracted earlier, despite the risk to the victim.

Now it was his life on the line.

Even with his eclectic training, and even though he had at least two stone on the lithe creature, he was severely outmatched by a freshly fed pijavica. Without the element of surprise, his only advantage was that he understood what he faced. He knew the monster's many strengths, and its few weaknesses.

He dodged another swipe but caught a glancing fist to his ribs. It knocked him back against the stone railing. He tumbled to the ground, palms scraping against the stones. He panted, fighting for breath. The pijavica crouched over his chest, grinning with bloody teeth. "You shouldn't have interrupted me," the monster said, teasing its claws along Domek's throat. The sibilant words carried the stench of hot blood from its gaping mouth. "Fortunately for you, I have places to be tonight, so I can't drag this out."

Domek bucked but had no leverage against the creature. Taking a steadying breath, he twisted the stake in his hand inward along his forearm and bent his arm sharply. The carved hawthorn tip sliced through the fabric of his coat at his elbow, piercing his skin underneath.

At the smell of fresh blood, cloying and metallic on the damp air, the pijavica jerked its head sideways, pupils ballooning. It knocked the hawthorn stake from Domek's hand, sending it clattering on the cobblestones. Domek used his other hand to grab the monster and flip them both sideways so that Domek could move again. The pijavica, still distracted by the scent of his bloodied arm, didn't notice Domek pull out his second stake. It was slenderer than the hawthorn, made of a pale wood whittled from the trunk of a kalina bush.

Domek lunged and used both hands to ram the thin stake into the demon's chest, aim true from years of practice. The pijavica's eyes widened, and it fell back against the ground. They stared at each other for one brief, tense moment.

Then, the pijavica reached down to its chest and pulled

out the stake, slick from the blood of its victim. Its smile was triumphant and horrible, gaping from ear to ear.

Swearing, Domek scrambled away across the cobblestones. The monster leaped after him, tackling him to the ground. Domek twisted and rammed the fallen hawthorn stake into the pijavica's neck, feeling the sickening crunch of its spine.

There was a brief moment of suspense, like the catch of a lamp igniting, before the hawthorn did its job. One second, the monster was crouched over him, open mouth dripping venom and painted with blood. The next, it dissolved into dust, leaving its clothes to fall onto Domek's chest.

Domek resheathed the hawthorn, bundled the abandoned clothing in his blood-smeared arms, and stood. He wavered on his feet and blinked to focus. The clothes had been expensive— made of a better material than Domek's uniform—but torn and covered in the pijavica's dust they were now worthless. Worse, bloodied clothing without a body would raise questions that could lead ignorant authorities his way. He shoved the bundled clothes into his fallen satchel.

Something heavy fell from the pijavica's coat, and he fumbled to catch it before it hit the cobblestones. It felt like a small flask, just big enough for the palm of his hand, and was tightly wrapped in a dark cloth. Considering pijavice couldn't stomach human food or drink, it was likely filled with something even more suspicious than the abandoned clothing, so, despite his distaste, Domek put it into his satchel as well.

Domek retrieved the kalina stake from where it had been abandoned, glinting dark in the moonlight. Scowling, he chucked it over the bridge's railing, sending it spiraling toward the Vltava below.

He went over to the injured woman, who had regained her consciousness, if not her feet. He knelt and examined her wounded neck. The dark had made it seem worse than it was. Blood pricked from dozens of small points, but the fangs had not cut deep. Pijavice could bite their victims and barely leave a mark; the toxin in their teeth had a powerful anesthetic that impaired memory. If they could control themselves, a pijavica's victim would wake up none the wiser with only a spread of needle pricks on their neck and a slight headache. However, most pijavice lacked such control, and their extended jaws could rip a throat in half in one bite. Tonight's victim had been lucky.

"Are you all right, madam?" he asked.

"Someone attacked me," she said. Her hand shook when she went to check her neck, but Domek intercepted it. Feeling the blood would just make her panic. He grabbed the pijavica's shirt from his bag and wadded it into a makeshift bandage. "Hold this to your neck," he instructed, setting it carefully against the wound.

"Did you see where he went?" she asked. Her gaze was unfocused, her mind struggling against the numbing effects of the shock and the venom.

"He was gone by the time I arrived," Domek told her. "Are you missing any valuables?" He knew the answer before she patted down her pockets. The monster hadn't been interested in petty cash or false jewels.

"Is there somewhere I can take you?" he asked.

"No, no," the woman said. She allowed him to help pull her to her feet, but she stepped away without leaning on him.

There was a movement in his peripheral vision, and Domek whirled, stake in hand. There was a pale woman in the shadow of the looming tower at the base of the bridge, watching him with eyes like the night sky, the only disruption of a flawless white image.

She was floating a meter off the stone, her dress fluttering in an absent wind.

"My husband can help me," said the victim, diverting his attention away from the apparition.

"I can at least get you safe off the street," Domek said. He glanced back down the bridge, but the spirit was gone. Still clutching his stake, Domek focused on the other woman. "You shouldn't walk alone. You lost a lot of blood, and you were unconscious when I found you."

"I'm awake now," she replied, holding the bundle of cloth tightly to her neck. "I can handle these streets fine on my own. I'm not far from home."

"You're injured," Domek argued. "I won't be able to sleep unless I'm sure you've made it to safety."

The woman laughed, and then winced. "Haven't you heard? Nowhere is safe in this town."

2

There was something melancholic yet comforting about a silent library. So much knowledge sat unlearned. Books without readers were only paper.

Ora Fischerová sat on a plush, velvet-lined chair in front of a table piled with texts. By candlelight that night, she had immersed herself in a fascinating botanical treatise from a professor in Bologna in the original Italian. No doubt inspired by Charles Darwin's book published a few years earlier, the man had taken a similar approach to the evolution of flowers. It was impressive how dull the professor had made the subject sound. If anything should have contained some inherent romance or a touch of the sentimental, it should have been flowers.

She sighed and laid the book on the table. Academics were so intent on proving that their thoughts contained only mathematics and Latin that they could squash even the most interesting subjects into tedious boxes. Despite their dull approach, she was constantly amazed by the speed with which their scientific breakthroughs changed the world before her eyes. Acquiring such knowledge was worth slogging through a professor's written efforts to pat himself on the back.

Sometimes she wished she could spend all her time in the library, but then she could have become as dreadfully boring as the men whose work she read.

Ora was many things, but she refused to be dull.

She blew out her candles and stood, her skirts swishing loudly in the dark room. She frowned toward the windows, hesitating. The sky outside was a dark purple, already beginning to lighten to gray along the horizon. She'd been reading longer than she had thought. She had arrived well after midnight, restless after an orchestra concert and unwilling to hide in her home the rest of the night. The librarian was a friend, and would reshelf the books before the library opened for the day. He was fastidious in maintaining his illogical bibliographic system. Ora had learned it was easier to let him take on the extra work than attempting to return the books herself. By day the Charles University library would be filled with students far clumsier with the books than she.

She left the library through a service entrance, taking a staircase down, down below the city.

The tunnels beneath Prague were as much a feature of the city as its heavy fogs, cobblestone streets, and dark spires. Well before Ora's time, the Old Town had been nearly six meters lower than today's street level. When the regular flooding became too much for the citizens to bear, they began a century-long project to raise the city. Houses and streets were buried beneath a layer of earth, and the new city was built on top. The underground had been used for centuries as cellars and dungeons for the buildings above. The long-abandoned passages that connected Prague's basements were a secret city for those wishing to remain out of sight. The ground, a blend of forgotten streets and the interiors of abandoned homes, was made of rounded river pebbles, uneven beneath her slippers.

The remains of the underground not absorbed into modern basements were poorly maintained and notorious for cave-ins. The pale rock had withstood centuries of pressure, but nothing could last forever. There were stories of those who had been lost underground, having gotten disoriented, fallen into one of the deep, empty wells scattered throughout, or trapped behind a cave-in. However, for someone like Ora, the dark labyrinth under the city was worth the risks. Dawn would be cresting over the horizon now. Without the tunnels, Ora would have been trapped inside for half of her life.

Underground, everything was almost silent. Almost, but not entirely. The meters of dirt all around muffled the daylight world, but created an echo of anything within the tunnels. Every scratch of a rat's foot, every exhalation from hidden men, seemed louder and closer than they were in truth.

Her townhouse was across the river, so she'd need to traverse the entire city via the tunnels. If she had realized tonight was going to include such a long trek underground, she would have dressed for the occasion. Her evening gown had been lovely for her night at the orchestra, but the bell skirt made traversing the tunnels more difficult. She wished she'd brought a change of outfit so she could spend her morning somewhere closer—and less boring—than home. Unfortunately, she couldn't have her carriage wait for her overnight, despite the convenience. Her driver needed to sleep, even if she didn't.

There was a scuff on the ground ahead of her, and she froze. It was pitch black in the tunnels. The nearest exit, which was a set of stairs just ahead, led to the street directly, but a tightly sealed door prevented sunlight from seeping through. Even with her eyes, it was difficult to make out shapes in the darkness at a distance.

The scuffing resolved into unmistakable footsteps.

Ora wasn't the only one who used the tunnels. One lesson she had learned over the years was that those who spent their time underground rarely did so for the pleasure of stale air and mud. They needed the darkness.

She pressed against the side of the tunnel, wincing as she felt the slime at her back. The walls were coated in mold and damp this far below ground. Lina would have her head if she ruined another gown. She took a deep breath, and then cloaked herself in the darkness. Though she couldn't hold it indefinitely, she would seem invisible to anyone who passed. Her nature clung to the shadows.

The approaching footsteps were erratic. At moments, the other person in the tunnel broke into a sprint, and then subsided into a meandering, confused zigzag. They moved like a leaf in a storm wind, erratic and difficult to trace.

Soon, she could make out a hunched figure in the darkness. It stopped a few yards away. "I can smell you," he said softly.

Ora stiffened. Another pijavica. Humans couldn't smell someone at that distance, especially when the scent of her powders should have been masked by the tunnel's heavy dampness. A bubák could have detected her, but they had no physical form to scuff against the ground like that. No other creatures would lurk underground and confront one of her kind.

"Are you with them?" he asked. His eyes, glinting in the darkness, flickered over her hiding spot. "I'm n-not going back. I-I can't." He stuttered over his words, rushing over some and then lingering unexpectedly on others.

Uncloaking herself, Ora said, "I don't know what you're talking about."

The pijavica shuddered. "The cure *hurts*," he hissed. "I never wanted it."

Cautiously, Ora stepped forward. "I'm just moving past." She kept her voice calm and composed. Hopefully, if she designated herself as the authority in the situation, he'd let her by without lashing out. She wasn't dressed for a fight.

"I won't go back!" the pijavica snarled, and darted forward. Instead of attacking or taking the path beside her, he ducked into the side tunnel between them. He scrambled up the steps using both feet and hands to crawl toward the surface.

"Wait," she called, stepping forward but stopping short of following him upward. "It's dawn! You can't—"

It was too late. At the top of the steps, the pijavica opened the door. For a split second, she glimpsed the early morning light illuminate him, and then she ducked into the shadows. She pressed herself to the wall, panting though her body did not need the air. The morning light cast a spotlight on the tunnel wall across from her, and she saw the silhouette of the man just before the door slammed shut.

Gasping, Ora peeked back up the dark stairs. Had that man just committed suicide in front of her? Even pre-dawn light was enough to slay a pijavica in moments, and he'd just locked himself out of the tunnels.

He must have been mad. It happened far too often, especially with the newly turned. The bloodlust and the restrictions, the emptiness—it all weighed on the mind until it snapped.

Ora winced when she brushed the back of her hair and felt the dampness from the walls. Frowning, she stared up the stairs to the dark door above.

3

In the morning, Domek sat down with a bucket of water. He scrubbed his skin clean of blood and grime, and used the rest of the water to rinse his stake. Standing by the light of the window, he examined the bruise on his ribs. It had turned a sickly yellow, stretching across his skin. Hopefully it would heal on its own. After several years in the monster-hunting business, he had seen the effects of unstopped internal bleeding, and he had neither the funds nor the time to see a surgeon.

The flat Domek shared with his roommate Anton was large enough that they each had their own room. A luxury when some of his neighbors had to fit large families in a similarly sized space. Working as a lamplighter did not pay well, but with careful spending and the extra money Domek brought in with part-time tinkering they could just afford it.

The two lamplighters lived in a large gray tenement at the edge of Nové Město, the New Town that cupped the Old like a broad hand. Only alongside the ancient roots of Prague would a neighborhood five hundred years old be considered 'new.' The city had been steadily expanding around the central hill for longer than memory, an ancient metropolis as eternal as the river running through it.

Domek could tell as soon as he had woken that Anton wasn't home yet. His roommate's snores would have been audible even if the walls hadn't been paper-thin. Anton worked the second lamplighter shift, and often found somewhere else to pass his mornings. It was for the best—Anton would have overreacted to his injury.

Domek pulled on a shirt and then rattled around the kitchen for a quick breakfast before his busy day. Despite the pain in his side, he felt energetic. He had saved a woman last night, and—aha!—had the jar of honey his mother had brought him back from her visit to the countryside.

The fog from the night before lifted, leaving clear skies behind. The blue peeking over the orange rooftops was nearly blinding to his tired eyes, bright and vivid after days of rain. He ate the bread and honey on his way, savoring the sweet flavor as he dodged passersby and carriages on the winding streets. Prague was lively in the spring. Hooves clattered on the cobblestones, vendors called for customers, and tourists from Germany and France annoyed everyone by strolling four abreast toward the closest spa.

On Charles Bridge, the sunlight revealed hidden details. By night, the ominous statues were masked in shadow, but by day they were crowned with glints of warm gold: a cross, a crown, a sword. The metal was bright against the blackened stone. He paused by the statue of the lady Saints Barbara, Margaret, and

Elizabeth. In the late morning light, there was no indication that two people had nearly died there last night.

After he had finished igniting all the lamps on his route last night, keeping an eye on the darkness of the streets around him and an ear out for any disturbances, he had patrolled the long stretch along the river until his relief appeared. The church bells across the city had just tolled one in the morning, signaling the start of the graveyard shift with a single resounding tone. In early March, the nights were just starting to balance with the days, the great scales of time equalizing for a breath after a long winter. Three months ago, darkness had sat over the city from four in the afternoon until eight in the morning, but now the city's watchmen were able to work between the day's two six o'clock bells.

After telling the lamplighter on the second shift about the encounter on the bridge, Domek had trekked east back home and fallen into bed with the dust of the destroyed pijavica still coating his skin.

The path to Imrich Lanik's home was as familiar as his patrol route. As Domek crossed under the tower into the Lesser Town, or Malá Strana, he glimpsed the copper domes of St. Nicholas Church ahead, more gold glinting at the tops.

The inside of Imrich's apartment building was like a rabbit's warren: dark, warm, and full of unexpected branches and dozens of unseen inhabitants. The scent of boiled cabbage was heavy in the air, and children giggled behind closed doors.

Despite his age, Imrich lived on the top floor, sitting on top of the building like a hawk watching its domain. On his floor, the children were either silent or absent. Did Imrich have children or grandchildren? If so, Domek had never met them.

He was unsure if the old man had even ever married.

Domek rapped on the paint-chipped door. Though he hadn't sent Imrich a warning that he was coming, the elderly man answered the door almost immediately.

Imrich stared at him, his liver-spotted face unmoving beneath what remained of his hair, which was wispy and white as raw cotton.

"Oh, it's you," he said. His eyes ran over Domek as though assessing an undersized fish in the market before he stepped aside to let him in.

In sharp contrast to the familiar smells of cabbage and meat from the surrounding apartments, Imrich's home was filled with the astringent tang of chemicals and metals. For Domek though, entering Imrich's domain was the same as a child visiting a confectioner, if the store were run by an unamused authoritarian. Every inch of the small space not filled with books was covered in the detritus of Imrich's alchemical experiments.

There were beakers and coils scattered about, filled not just with the expected liquids, but also with moss, rocks, and small animal bones.

"I did not expect you back so soon." Imrich moved to sit in an armchair in between two towering stacks of books. The leather-bound columns gave the threadbare chair the gravity of a throne.

Due to Domek's mechanical background, the leader of the lamplighters had volunteered him as an unpaid, part-time assistant to the alchemist for the last four years. Paluska paid Imrich for consultations not with money, but with the promise of passing along any interesting artifacts or creatures the lamplighters found during their work. Some people—scholars, librarians—collected knowledge for the sake of knowledge. Imrich collected knowledge for the power it might provide him. He shared his field's eternal goal of finding immortality—though he would have settled for gold.

It was beneficial for the lamplighters to keep a man like Imrich around, but there was a reason he stayed on the outskirts of their organization. His experiments sometimes drifted close to witchcraft, and most of the lamplighters kept a healthy distance. Domek did not share his colleagues' fear of witches, but Imrich's prickly attitude did little to endear him.

Domek stepped closer to a machine on a table in the small open kitchen. Four glass bulbs were interlinked by metal tubing, all leading to a long copper candlestick. The candlestick held two pieces of whittled charcoal an inch apart. "Is this an arc light?" Domek asked. The design was distinct. When activated, the batteries would send blinding electricity sizzling between the pieces of charcoal, like contained lightning. As with all of Imrich's experiments, there was an unexpected element. Wires trailed from the copper base, ending in a metal circlet. The shape and size... "Tell me this isn't supposed to go on someone's head."

"Are you an alchemist now?"

"No, but trying to connect this type of power to—"

Imrich barreled over him. "Then do not tell me how to run my experiments. Sit down and explain why you're here outside our appointed time."

Domek sat. "I thought you'd want to know that I tested the kalina stake last night."

The old man leaned forward, suddenly eager. "And?"

"It didn't work."

"Are you sure?" Imrich raised one wispy eyebrow. "You might not have hit a fatal area."

Domek suppressed a sigh. "I stabbed it through the heart. It laughed and pulled it right back out. It didn't even flinch from the wound, and handled the stake with bare hands. Kalina is not a weakness for the demons."

Imrich hummed. "Where is it? I'll resharpen it and you can try again. You must have made a mistake. I've done the experiments—the properties of the wood should be the same."

"I threw it away," Domek said. "I can't go onto the streets with a weapon I know doesn't work. I couldn't risk accidentally using it again."

Imrich's scowl was like a thundercloud, sweeping over his face and casting it in darkness. "You can't abandon an experiment due to one failed test. Do you know how long I searched for a kalina bush with a large enough heart to create that stake? I don't know why Paluska sent me an idiotic thug like you to help me."

"The kalina doesn't work," Domek insisted, keeping his voice low. Compared to the frail old man, Domek often felt like an oversized oaf. "Lives are on the line. I would not have been the only person to die last night if I hadn't had the hawthorn on hand."

"There's no reason why the hawthorn should be the pijavice's only weakness. The kalina bush flowers just the same and produces its own fruit. The lamplighters are limited by the traditions of its past. We'll never evolve as a species if we never question common knowledge. Paluska assured me that you would be a helpful assistant."

"I understand that," Domek said through gritted teeth. "I'm here because I agree that there's still more for us to learn. But I can't risk innocent people for an experiment."

"Innovation requires risk," Imrich sneered. "I would not have thought a lamplighter would be so cowardly."

"I've been on the ground out there for almost ten years. People die when I make mistakes," Domek snapped. "I spend every night risking my life while you theorize, safe at home. You think *I'm* the coward here?"

Imrich pressed a hand to his chest. "Who do you think you are?" he demanded. "I should have a word with Paluska. He said you were the best they had. I'm not sure I believe it."

Would Paluska take Domek's side against the alchemist? The leader of the lamplighters was practical above all else— and with his knowledge of local history and the supernatural, Imrich was more valuable than Domek. Domek could be fired. "I apologize," he said finally. "It was a long night."

"Come back this weekend as planned." Imrich waved a hand, dismissing Domek. "I'm expecting a delivery of glass from Vienna you'll need to carry up, and I'll have a new stake for you to try. There are more flowering woods to test until I can find more usable kalina. This time, don't throw it away the moment you're met with opposition."

Domek nodded stiffly and left the old man's flat. He closed the door gently, though he longed to slam it hard enough to knock the delicate experiments from Imrich's tables and send them smashing onto the ground. If Domek had been the thug Imrich thought him, he would have.

Somehow, the high ground did not make him feel better.

One of the things Ora missed the most about mortality was sleep.

It was strange. While she'd been alive, it had seemed like an inconvenience. Having to shut down and recharge for hours every night took away from all the other things she could have been doing. Time had always felt so short during her hungry youth, and sleeping drained it away more quickly.

Now, with time stretching out endlessly in front of her, Ora just wanted to take a nap.

Some days, she pretended. Either at night while the rest of the household was boring and asleep, or during heavy golden afternoons when there was a drowsy sense of peace to the rumblings of carriages outside, Ora would lie still and watch dust float through the air.

Or times like now, when Ora simply wished for the clocks to stop.

Someone rapped against her door.

Ora did not move from her position on the chaise lounge. "Come in," she called.

The door opened and her maid, Lina, stepped into her sightline. Ora was draped on the chaise, staring at the velvet curtains nailed over the library's window. Her maid was wearing Ora's favorite dress of hers, made of a rich orange cotton that complemented her dark Romani hair and skin beautifully. Ora, who had inherited the criminally pale skin of her German ancestors and had become nearly porcelain after centuries without sunlight, longed for such bright colors.

"If you're trying to put me in a good mood, you could have brought up some breakfast," Ora said.

Lina huffed and crossed her arms. "I don't only wear this dress to cheer you up," she said, as though Ora had not learned her

27

tricks after watching her grow from a child. "Come downstairs if you want a drink. You've been in here all day. Mila said you sent a note to Sokol and then locked yourself away. It's midday and you're still in your robe."

"I'm sure it's been no more than a few hours. You'll wrinkle if you keep worrying all the time," Ora said. "Did you see the gown?"

"I'll be able to get the stain out," Lina said, waving a hand. Ora must have truly looked pitiful for Lina not to scold her. "What happened? You seemed to be…happy yesterday."

"I can't have one quiet morning without you sounding the alarms?"

"The last time you had a quiet morning like this, you stayed in your bedroom for two weeks. The mattress was permanently dented and we had to buy out the butcher's shop so you wouldn't starve," Lina said briskly. "I won't be letting that happen again."

"Lina," Ora said, voice cracking. "I watched a pijavica kill himself this morning." The concern in Lina's voice had shattered the shell Ora had hastily constructed overnight. Lina occupied an amorphous role in Ora's household: paid maid, part goddaughter, and part mother hen. Ora had been there for her birth, seen her wailing and bloody taking her first gulps of air. When had Lina grown so much? It seemed that if Ora blinked, Lina's mother could have been standing there instead.

Lina sat on the edge of the chaise and put a hand on Ora's arm. "Oh, Ora," she said.

"He was mad. He must have been." Ora sat up and rearranged her loose hair. Lina still watched her with those compassionate, anxious eyes. The window beyond the curtains loomed behind the maid, a siren's song. "I'm perfectly all right, Lina."

"You will be," Lina said. "Why don't you invite Lady Horáčková over for dinner tomorrow? She's good company."

"Anastazie was just over last week," Ora pointed out.

"And you never did confirm if you were going to the Beckers' ball next week," Lina pressed on. "You've been looking for a chance to wear that new dress in from Paris."

"The Beckers are horrible and you know it." Ora put her hand over Lina's and squeezed it. "Thank you, dear. You don't need to push me out the door. I promise I will be fine. I always am."

If Lina did not believe her, she was kind enough not to say.

4

As part of his training regime, Domek had often run up the long corridor of steps leading to Prague Castle. It was a steep trek, one most residents bore with reluctant grace. Though Domek no longer wheezed from taking the steps, the view from the top never failed to take his breath away. In the afternoon light, gold glinted like stars on top of the orange and pale green rooftops. The Vltava snaked through the center, and the twin spires of Týn Church were visible across the city.

The current resident of the castle was Ferdinand V, who had been emperor before his nephew had taken the throne in Vienna. Like Prague itself, the castle was a relic of a grander time. Though it was now used as a retirement home, it had once been the very center of Bohemia.

As with all old, beautiful cities, Prague drew in many tourists. Young Englishmen came through on their Grand Tour of Europe, frail French maidens and aging German lords traveled the long roads for their healing spas, and even the occasional American writer came through. The palace square was dense with sweating people waiting to enter the castle. Domek had been inside the sections open to visitors when he was younger, holding his mother's hand and gaping at the vast halls and the half-built cathedral at the center. Even in a city as steeped in beauty as Prague, the grandeur of the castle was undeniable.

Today, Domek passed the towering gates of the palace and went into the garden alongside instead. He was meeting a friend for an exhibit at an art gallery nearby, but with Imrich's quick dismissal, he had time to update his journal before his friend arrived, an indulgence he rarely had the time for. His handwriting, when sketches weren't enough, was painstaking and uncoordinated, but he needed the space to let his ideas take form. Like a tree in a clay pot, his mind could never hold all of his own questing roots.

He found an isolated spot in the garden overlooking the forested drop of the hill on the other side of the castle.

His journal had fallen to the bottom of his bag, and he had to dig past the pijavica's dusty jacket and pants. He would have to remember to add the spare clothes to the pile that the lamplighters collected to dispose of at their guildhall.

He reached deeper into the bag, and then hesitated when his hand closed over something unexpected. The pijavica's cloth-wrapped bundle. He had forgotten about it. Disgusted, he began to push it aside, but hesitated. Since last night, the cloth wrapping had loosened, revealing not the blood-filled flask he'd expected, but a clay jar. It was engraved with a delicate, swirling pattern, and had been fired without glaze.

Domek glanced around, ensuring he was still alone in the park, and then carefully loosened the lid and peered inside.

The jar was filled with fire.

The clay grew hot in his hands, as though he'd grabbed a poker from the hearth, but when he tried to drop it, he couldn't move his fingers. He jumped to his feet as the jar shuddered in his grasp. The ball of fire, which had seemed to burn inside the closed jar without kindling or air, drifted upward to float in front of him—a strange, flickering orb no bigger than an apple.

The fiery ball hovered over the path. Below, the dirt began to ripple, kicking up dust and fallen leaves which wriggled like worms before being drawn into the growing whirlwind. The fire was at the center of its own small storm, climbing into the sky.

It would be difficult to fight while he was trapped clutching the jar with frozen hands, but Domek braced his feet anyway. He didn't recognize the apparition. Was it some sort of spirit? Apart from the wraith-like bubáks that lurked in dark alleys, Domek's adversaries were generally corporeal.

The jar's heat dulled to a soft glow, like the small warmth of a gaslight. He was finally able to let go of the clay. Keeping hold of it with one hand, he reached for his stake with the other. Hawthorn didn't work on monsters apart from pijavice, but his silver blade had fallen with his bag to the ground. Did he dare look away to find it? His hair whipped around his face, and it felt as though invisible fingers grabbed at his clothes.

"What is this?" Domek murmured. He could hear the chatter of the tourists gathered nearby. How large would this windstorm grow? The devastation it could wreak would be immense. A twig whipped his face like a slap. "Stop!" Domek shouted, holding out his free hand.

Domek was stunned when the whirlwind died. He looked at his palm. It was seared with the symbols from the sides of the jar, though the pain had vanished with the heat. The brands had already healed into silvery scars that shone in the afternoon light. It was like nothing he'd ever seen before. The floating fire pulsed in the air like a man panting for breath after a run. "Stay still," Domek tried.

The orb stilled, though its flames continued to flicker under the sunlight. Daytime was supposed to be the sane part of his life. Part of him, the part that had once thought monsters were a fairy tale, wondered if the flame was some prank. Domek knew his reputation among the lamplighters. He was a bore, too serious about the things that mattered, and dismissive of the daily problems faced by his peers. There were several who would have been amused by his raving about a living flame to their leader, but none had the resources to pull off something like this. Domek's shaking hands were still branded with the jar's intricate, strange pattern.

Was it the scars that gave him power over this thing? It had reacted to his voice. Perhaps it was some new perversion of the pijavice, a mindless servant bound to its owner.

"Lift that stone," Domek said, pointing to a nearby rock. It had wobbled during the earlier whirlwind, but remained half-buried. The orb of fire pulsed brighter, and the stone rocketed into the air. It flew overhead, and clattered onto the roof of the castle. Domek swore. He should have known that any magical item belonging to the pijavice would be dangerous. There must be some method to control it. If Domek phrased his commands carefully, perhaps he could learn the extent of its abilities—and then its purpose.

He was contemplating an unequivocal way to phrase his next order when he heard a familiar voice from the garden entrance.

"Domek! There you are."

"Go back in the jar," he instructed. The light pulsed once, and then drifted back inside the clay jar. It glowed for a moment, as though fresh from the kiln, and then returned to its original dull brown. Domek quickly returned the jar to his bag and turned to the approaching man.

"Afternoon, Lord Bauer," Domek said.

"You know, most people wouldn't use a man's title to annoy him," Cord Bauer said, shaking Domek's hand and clasping his forearm. Domek winced, but the man's silk gloves prevented him from noticing Domek's strange new scars. Though nearing thirty, he appeared younger than the lamplighter. He wore only a mustache, rather than Domek's fuller beard, and kept his hair coiffed carefully below his hat. Dressed in a sleek gray suit with a starched white collar and a looming black top hat, he seemed to belong in the nearby castle.

"Most men wouldn't be annoyed by it. It'd be a shame to waste that. It's been a while, Cord. Where have you been?"

"Oh, you know. Horse races, dens of iniquity, and various other places my father thinks are draining my life away," he said. "I'm glad I could convince you to come out today. You need a bad influence in your life."

"Corrupting me with an art gallery," Domek said. "What will my mother say?"

"Your mother loves me," Cord said. He frowned at Domek. "You look as though you could use the break. Are you all right?"

Domek smoothed down his hair, which felt tousled under his fingers from the windstorm. "I had a meeting with Imrich before this," he said.

"Ah, of course. How is the old bastard?"

"Apparently now I'm a coward in addition to being a general idiot."

Cord shook his head. "He doesn't appreciate what he has in you. I still don't see why you need to waste your time on him when you have Zacharias."

"My uncle can't hire me full-time, and lamplighting isn't enough. Some of us need to work for our money."

"Well, maybe Imrich will leave you his business, but either way we'll raise a glass when he finally croaks. For now, distraction. Shall we?"

Sternberg Palace sat near the entrance to the castle. Many of Prague's most beautiful houses sat a stone's throw from the castle, built by lords eager to be near the emperor's influence. The National Gallery had purchased Sternberg Palace at the turn of the century from heirs too destitute to keep it functioning.

Above the grand white façade, dark statues lined the roof like oversized crows. Cord paid their fee, and they went through the ornate entry hall to where the base of a massive four-flight staircase emerged. A crowd of tourists and locals clogged the stairs toward the temporary exhibit halls, so Domek and Cord started with the ground floor.

As they passed a line of paintings, Cord regaled Domek with stories of his adventures. He described a Prague worlds apart from Domek's, full of ballrooms and gambling halls instead of dark nights and alchemist's labs.

On patrol a few years earlier, Domek had stumbled on a group of men beating another man in an alley behind a gambling hall. The men had been an entirely human sort of scum, but with odds of five against one, Domek hadn't hesitated before leaping to their victim's rescue.

He had stepped in and fought them off, nearly losing a finger to a knife in the process. Cord had bullied Domek into his carriage to get the slice on his finger stitched by a surgeon, and had been determined that they would become friends. Years later, even though Domek was often mistaken for Cord's servant rather than his companion, he had never regretted stepping into that alley.

On the first floor, paintings framed in ornate gold lined the walls: there was an early map sketch of Europe with Prague drawn in the center, and another where seven planets orbited the sun. This was the world the Bohemians had once imagined, with Prague at its heart and the heavens above.

"How much more is out there that we don't know?" Domek asked, staring at the swirling planets. His learning was firmly grounded, and the abyss of space disturbed him. It reminded him of the floating fire tucked at the bottom of his bag. There was so much hidden just on the streets of Prague, and worse in the monster-infested tunnels below. What dark secrets could lurk upon the moon or beyond?

Cord waved at him from the next staircase, which led up to the temporary exhibit they had come to see. "I doubt we'll ever know everything," he said, shrugging.

Domek sighed and followed.

There was a dark ocean in Ora's chest. It teemed with sharp teeth and gaping maws and spiked tentacles. Most days, she floated on top in a small rowboat, parasol on her shoulder, refusing to look into the abyss. If she fell in, she was quite sure she would drown.

Despite her inner turmoil, it was a lovely spring day, and the sun was casting its deadly rays over the city unimpeded by clouds. Draped in a hooded velvet cloak, wearing gloves that reached her elbows under her dress, she stepped down from her carriage and was guided to the museum's entrance by Lina. She had lost her ability to sweat when she had lost her tears and blood, but the heat was still uncomfortable.

"Was this really worth the risk of coming before sundown?" Lina asked as she led her through the halls. Unfortunately, most of the museum was populated by broad windows, and Ora could only watch the tile beneath her slippers.

"You did request that I not lock myself in forever," Ora pointed out. "This exhibit is supposed to be lovely."

"I'm sure you could find a way to have the doors unlocked for you if we came back tonight," Lina said. "This seesaw between sloth and recklessness is going to give me gray hairs. If you are going to risk your life, I would prefer if you didn't bring me along."

"I've been doing this for more than two hundred years." Carefully, she followed Lina's shoes up the steps. "I know how to avoid the sun."

Lina hushed her, though the stairwell was so crowded with museumgoers that none would have been able to hear her. "Discretion would be advised, my lady."

"By whom?" Ora asked. "Come, Lina. You know boredom is far worse a danger to me."

"This was not what I meant earlier and you are well aware. I'm just saying, my lady, it wouldn't kill you to slow down."

"Slowing down is dangerous, my dear. I'm incapable of slowing without freezing."

"Except in Mělník," Lina said.

Quietly, Ora said, "You're overstepping."

"Apologies, my lady," Lina said, though she didn't sound

apologetic in the slightest. She had never been afraid of offending Ora. They walked through a curtain, and the ambient sunlight was replaced by a dull orange glow. "You can remove your hood, but please be careful."

Ora looked up to find the promised exhibit spread before her. The space had been transformed since her last visit, during which she had mingled with the city's artistic patrons with an empty wine goblet in hand. Ornate tapestries from India had made the long boat journey to Prague and had been strung along the walls. The windows in this exhibit were curtained and the halls lit with candlelight to protect the line of ancient fabric from the harsh glare of the sun.

The tapestries were a riot of color, the blues and reds and yellows bright even in the candlelight. Ora stopped before the first tapestry of a man and woman in a carriage drawn by four horses. In only mustard yellow, dark red, cream, and black, the artist conveyed the lush chaos of the scene. Ora took a deep breath, searching for some hint of the spice, marigold, and jasmine scents that had characterized her time in India. It had been many decades ago, just after she had fled Lord Czernin's estate in the countryside. Her memories of the beautiful country were marred by the shadow of terror that had filled her, the way she had skittered across the sub-continent like a rat in a storeroom, body tense for the fall of the farmer's ax.

The museum smelled only of dust and the combined sweat of a hundred humans.

"Even you have to appreciate the detail of this," a man was saying to his companion, a calloused finger tracing the air just over a pattern of threads in one circular tapestry.

Ora turned, drawn to that familiar, deep voice like a drunkard to a pub. "If it isn't Mister Myska," she declared, a smile unfurling as she strolled over to interrupt the conversation.

Domek Myska turned, curiosity and surprise brightening his dark eyes. Those eyes, his square jaw shadowed with a closely trimmed beard, and curly, untamed brown hair may have had some influence in her interest in him. He was tall and broad as an oak tree. She sometimes forgot how raw and delectable he looked. His name—which meant mouse—could not have been less apt. "It's nice to see you again, Lady Fischerová." He nodded to her maid as well. "I hope you're doing well, Lina."

"I am," Lina said, abruptly.

Lina may not have liked Domek because of his callouses, but Ora appreciated that he always made the effort to acknowledge her maid. Lina's Romani heritage meant she was scorned or ignored by many of the people Ora had flirted with over the years, and was therefore a sure test of who was worth spending time on. There were few things she found less appetizing in a person than rudeness to her friends.

"It's always a delight to run into you, Mister Myska," Ora said.

"Ah, the famous Lady Fischerová," said the other man. Ora had been uncertain if they were visiting the gallery together, as Domek did not seem the type to associate with a man in tailcoats and a top hat. "I am Lord Cord Bauer, since my friend seems to have forgotten his manners." He brushed a kiss above her gloved knuckles. Bauer. That was the name of one of the men in Parliament, head of one of the wealthiest families in the city.

"How do you know my mechanic?" Ora asked.

"It was all very dashing and heroic, but it's a story for another time," Bauer said. "I'm much more curious to hear how *you* came to know our dear Domek."

"He's a genius with his hands," Ora said. She could smell the blush rushing to Domek's face, though the color was hidden by the candlelight and his beard. His scent was of sweet honey and the tang of metal, both of which seemed to have seeped into his lifeblood. "My pocket watch broke last year, and I feared it was beyond repair. Mister Myska and his uncle took care of it. Since then, our paths simply seem meant to cross."

"We've seen each other at a handful of events in the city," Domek said, angling his body between them as though to shoulder his friend from the conversation. Was he so eager to speak with her, or only embarrassed of what his companion would think of their long flirtation? Ora knew her charms, but Domek had never pushed their coy conversations further. She hoped it was simple shyness, but there were men uninterested in any charms offered by a widow. Sometimes, he seemed like the sun: powerful, pure... and beyond her reach. "There was an outdoor concert last winter by the Old Town Hall we found one another at."

"Mister Myska tracked down some mulled wine for us to drink." She had stealthily poured it on the cobblestones when he had been distracted, trusting the general mess of the streets to cover it up. She had felt a tad guilty, as she doubted he had the money to waste, but mortal fare twisted her stomach horribly. "It was very kind of him."

"It was a cold night," Domek demurred. "Are you enjoying the exhibit?"

"It's very impressive. I've been looking forward to seeing it. I'm a member of the Society of Patriotic Friends of the Arts, of course, but am more of an uninvolved supporter. When I learned about this exhibit, I knew I must come. I spent some time in India in my youth."

"Did you?" Domek said. Finally, he seemed to forget the amused, watchful eyes of Lord Bauer. "What was it like?"

"Warm. Ornate. Beautiful. You must go when you can."

"I'm not sure I'm fit for travel." He flushed again, but this time it had the unpleasant stink of shame. "I've never even left Prague."

"Everyone is fit for travel," Ora insisted. "Some of us are simply layabouts who can afford the time to swan off across the ocean. That's the benefit of exhibits like this, for hardworking men such as yourself." Beside her, Lina made a pained face.

"A fellow layabout," Bauer said. "I assume I've met a kindred spirit who gets a perverse pleasure from Domek's disapproval. There's something invigorating about spending time with an honest man, isn't there? We were going to eat lunch nearby after this. You should join us."

"Oh, I wish I could," Ora said, and the truth of it surprised her. After her morning, she had not expected to want any companionship. Around Domek, she felt alive and grounded in a way her melancholy morning and spontaneous decision to risk the sunlight had lacked. She wished she could go to lunch and dissect these men's unusual friendship, to sit in the sunlight by the Vltava and drink a glass of wine. To experience the life she had never had, even before her baptism in blood. She searched for a lie, and hated the ease with which it fell from her tongue. Domek Myska deserved better than her. "I promised the curator I would meet with him after I finished looking through the exhibit about another project. Next time I'll take you up on the offer."

"Another time, then," Bauer said.

"Enjoy the rest of the exhibit," Domek said. He cleared his throat. "I hope I'll see you again soon."

"I'm sure you will," Ora said. She thrust her hand to him, leaving him no choice but to kiss it. She could feel a pulse of heat from his lips as they grazed her glove. The hair of his beard pricked the silk, dragging slightly.

She kept her eyes on Domek through Lord Bauer's farewell, and watched the unlikely pair until they reached the end of the hall.

"Was that your version of flirting? Come on, man." A human would not have heard Lord Bauer's hissed comment as the men walked through the curtain, but Ora's supernatural hearing had the occasional benefits.

"You like him," Lina said.

Ora lost the thud of Domek's heartbeat in the crowd and turned to her maid. "What was that look for earlier?"

Lina sighed, walking beside Ora as they took in the next tapestry. "He's a mechanic. He's a good, solid Czech worker. You won't impress a man like that by reminding him about how indolently wealthy you are."

"I'm clearly not the only useless noble he spends time with," Ora pointed out.

Lina shook her head. "His friend would be more appropriate for you, anyway."

"His friend is not my type. Besides, I'm not looking to get married again, Lina. Just having a bit of fun." Ora moved on to the next tapestry, examining the ornate but anatomically atrocious tiger in one corner. She could feel Lina still watching her.

"It's been a long time since I've seen you light up like that talking to someone," she said carefully. "I did not think I'd see you act that way after this morning."

"He smells nice and he's kind," Ora said. "Why should it be anything more than that?"

5

After lunch with Cord, Domek traveled back down the hill for his afternoon meeting, taking the stairs twice as fast as he had on the way up. The spring day was clear around him, the bright blue soaring endlessly over the city's orange rooftops.

Compared to some of the city's more ancient guilds—the first, the tailors' guild, had been formed in 1318—the lamplighters were mayflies. Just twenty years ago, the Old Town had made history as the first area of the city to be lit entirely by gaslight. Domek had been just a boy, so his memories of the day slipped through his mind like fog, but his mother assured him that he'd been there for the celebration. It was strange now to think that there had been a time that even central Prague had been shrouded in darkness through the night. For Domek, the gas lamps were his job, and his assurance that there were people in the world who wanted to make things better. For centuries, Prague after dark had belonged to those who fed on fear and uncertainty.

Pijavice, of course, were the deadliest of the predators, but there were other monsters as well. Even worse, there were humans using the shadows as a mask as they pickpocketed, mugged, and murdered anyone unlucky—or unintelligent—enough to be out after sundown.

Once the seat of the Holy Roman Empire, Prague had fallen in status since its dissolution, though it remained the capital of the Kingdom of Bohemia. Emperor Franz Joseph I, based hundreds of miles away in Vienna, had bigger issues to worry about than the churnings of Prague. The war with Prussia and Italy was only two years past, and maintaining the Dual Monarchy was like attempting to direct a hundred arrogant toddlers. Prague was on its own.

Locals mixed with German immigrants who came from the north on the Dresden road, along with the thousands of tourists who visited the art galleries and health spas in the city. Together, they crammed an impressive amount of people in the city south of the castle, clustering around the Vltava. Attempting to stop crime in a city so densely populated was like stopping water slipping from a cupped hand.

Before the gas lamps were installed along the main streets, those who wanted to venture out into the dark could hire link boys to light their way, but they were just as likely to set you up to be robbed as they were to help you to your final destination safely. With the gas lamps came the lamplighters to patrol and protect their routes, fighting back against the shadows of Prague.

Rather than one of the historic buildings filled with the archives of centuries of work, the lamplighters met in a converted church in Malá Strana, just down the street from the bakery of the very first lamplighter, Jakub Salzmann. It was functional and small, just like their guild.

There were occasionally men who asked to join the lamplighters without knowing their secret responsibilities. It seemed, from the outside, to have less risk than working the docks or slaughterhouses. They would have realized their mistake if they ever made it through the guildhall's front doors.

A splinter of hawthorn wood and an ornate silver dagger sat on a table near the entrance, where there once would have been a holy water font. A lamplighter named Svoboda stood beside it, greeting everyone who entered. Domek rolled up his sleeves—fortunately, they were not required to wear their uniforms with their cufflinks to daytime meetings—and presented his forearms to the lamplighter. "Afternoon, Svoboda," Domek said, keeping his branded palms facing the floor. "Did you see anything else last night?" Svoboda was Domek's replacement for the second shift alongside the Vltava.

"It was all quiet. You must have taken care of the worst of it," Svoboda said. He lifted the weapons and pressed the edge of the wood and the flat of the dagger against Domek's skin. He held them in place for a long moment, and then lifted them away. As always, the skin of Domek's arms was unmarred by the contact.

Svoboda nodded him forward, and Domek went deeper into the guildhall. The interior of the church had been filled with long tables and lines of benches replacing the customary pews. As usual, someone had tapped a barrel of pilsner for the meeting, and mugs lined the scarred wooden surfaces.

The dais was empty, and there was no sight of their leader, Kuba Paluska. Domek had hoped to find him alone before the meeting to tell him about the mysterious jar of floating fire. Without Cord or the beautiful Ora to distract him, Domek knew he had to decide how to handle the strange entity. Paluska would likely know just what it was, along with the best way to destroy it.

But Paluska had never mentioned anything of the sort before. Domek had not known it was possible to capture an element, nor for one to wield control over the wind. It seemed fantastical even when compared to the wonders and horrors Domek had seen. And if he did not know what it was, there was only one person Paluska would trust to figure it out: Imrich.

After Imrich's insults that morning, the thought of handing over the unique find was galling. Domek didn't need the alchemist's help to test the fire. He was as smart as Imrich, no matter what the old man thought. If Domek could learn the fire's secrets on his own, both Imrich and Paluska would have to acknowledge his intelligence. After years of Imrich's snide remarks, Domek would have the chance to earn recognition for his mind.

Domek took a seat on a bench in the corner of the room with two men he was friendly with. One of them, a Jewish man named Abrahams, patted Domek roughly on the shoulder in greeting. The movement jostled his bruised ribs, making him wince.

"What happened to you?" Abrahams asked, peering at him. Though Jews had gained their citizenship twenty years earlier, Josefov, the old Jewish ghetto, was still one of the most difficult lamplighter routes, with its decrepit buildings and winding streets.

"Fought a pijavica on Charles Bridge last night," Domek told him. "It had its teeth in a woman on my route."

"On Charles Bridge?" asked the other, a burly German named Webber. He must have arrived early, since he was down to the dregs of his pilsner. "Lord, Myska, you've got the worst luck. The last few nests I've found have been empty before I even get to them. Your area was supposed to be cleaned up ages ago. That's one of the easier routes, unless you run into a vodník from the river, but they don't usually wash in."

"Apparently someone missed that message," Domek said. "There are still dark corners in the city." He hesitated, and then admitted, "I think I saw something else while I was out there. A strange woman. I thought she was floating. She disappeared before I could get a closer look."

"A ghost?" Webber asked, leaning into the table. "Was she horrible? I saw one once that scared the shit out of me. Transparent like light, but cold as ice. Skeletal face and long black hair like weeds."

"Sure it wasn't just your mother?" Abrahams asked.

Webber shoved him. "Piss off, Abrahams."

Domek shook his head. "She was more solid than a ghost. And she was wearing white."

"You think it was the White Lady? Next you'll tell me you saw the golem," Abrahams said. Even for the lamplighters, the white-clad spirit that wailed through the castle's halls was more myth than reality, like the legendary Jewish golem.

"I've heard that she's real. Rumor says she does come out sometimes," Webber said. "Soldiers said they saw her when the Swedes were storming the castle a few years ago. She shows up to warn people about death."

Abrahams laughed. "If that were true, she'd be out in this city every night."

"Maybe she can only be seen by the person who is going to die," Webber suggested.

"Thanks," Domek said dryly.

"Not that you're—"

Abrahams was interrupted by another man sliding onto the bench beside them. Domek's roommate, Anton Beran, was as lithe as Domek was broad, with a dark narrow mustache sitting like a nosebleed on his lip. A thin cigarette hung from his mouth, the smoke curling toward the ceiling. "Isn't there any beer that doesn't taste like piss in this town?" he asked in greeting.

"Not that they'll give us." Abrahams sighed, staring down into his own drink. "They save the real stuff for the rich assholes."

"Domek was just telling us that he had to take out a pijavica on Charles Bridge last night. He probably nearly had a heart attack just from the surprise. He's supposed to have the easiest route," Webber said.

"You all right?" Anton asked. They had been friends since they were children growing up as neighbors in the north of the city. Domek had spent long afternoons avoiding his flat by exploring along the river with Anton and his friend's younger sister, Evka. Evka Beran had been Domek's first kiss, much to Anton's despair. There was a soft, warm glow to Domek's memories of the younger Beran. They had remained friends after their youthful dalliance had waned. Nine years ago, before her wedding to a local blacksmith, she had asked Domek and Anton to spend one last day with her along the river, further north where the bustle of the city gave way to quiet forest.

They had been laughing and splashing in the river when Evka had been dragged beneath the water.

The strange creature lurking beneath the surface had been

like nothing Domek had ever seen, some vicious monster from a dark fairy tale. The vodník's face was painted in cartoons around the city, sitting on logs and jovially playing the fiddle, but the reality was a horrific grimace distorted by the churning water. It had pulled her down toward the muddy riverbed. Domek had splashed toward her, cutting his foot on something sharp in the mud, and together with Anton had managed to pull Evka away from the water sprite, but it had been too late.

She had been limp in Domek's arms as they had fought their way back to the riverbank.

Later, Domek had learned that a vodník's lair was littered not just with bones, but with clay jars which captured the souls of its victims. Without Domek and Anton there, Evka would not only have been consumed by the vodník, but her soul would have been stolen from heaven to rest instead among the demon's perverse collection.

Anton had never forgotten why they had started working as lamplighters and tracked Domek's injuries with more attention than he would ever admit to.

"I'm fine," Domek assured him. "It barely touched me. I found it taking a bite out of a woman. She was lucky someone came along."

"I bet she was very grateful," Anton said with a wink, and the other two men laughed. He patted Domek on the back as though confirming he was still solid beneath his hand.

Domek rolled his eyes, but didn't shrug off the gesture. "She was very unconscious."

"You won't ever get a wife if you don't start trying," Anton groaned. "You get the perfect situations handed to you on a platter and then you escort them politely home. You're hopeless."

"I ran into Lady Fischerová again today," Domek blurted.

Anton raised his mug. "Another perfect situation, from what I've seen."

"A *lady*," Abrahams repeated, raising his eyebrows.

"It's nothing. Don't be crass. She's a widow."

"She's rich and unmarried," Anton said. "That's all the more reason to take your chances with her."

"I don't know why I even told you guys," Domek said, crossing his arms.

"Because you get butterflies in your gut every time you think about her?" Anton teased. "Come on, Myska, I've known you since before your jewels dropped. You've been interested in Ora Fischerová for a year at least."

Domek rapped his knuckles on the scarred wooden table. "She's far out of my class."

Anton shook his head. "Well, when it happens, don't be too shy to tell me just because you know I'll brag about being right! I'll want to hear everything."

"I'll tell you as soon as Prague rules the Empire again," Domek muttered.

"You were right, Anton," Webber said. "He's never going to get a wife."

Fortunately for Domek, the meeting began before his friends could continue ribbing him. Paluska had finally stepped onto the dais and cleared his throat. The leader of the lamplighters was in his mid-fifties, slightly older than the rest of the room, but could likely have won any fight thrown at him. He was lean and hard, leathered by the sun, and deadly as an adder.

"Settle down," Paluska called, voice clear despite the noise of the room. His accent, smooth in some places and rough in others, was a testament to his journey across the continent in his youth. After spending decades volunteering to fight in wars around Europe, from the War of Schleswig to one of the Italian Wars for Independence, he had ended back up in Prague and taken charge of the lamplighters' organization when Jakub Salzmann retired. Under his guidance for the last several years, the group's initiative to bring light—and safety—to the streets of the city had grown more and more successful. "I'll make this quick. We didn't lose a single citizen to the evil this week." He waited for the cheers to die down. "That doesn't mean that we can take time off. Evil never sleeps, and neither can we. We must remain vigilant. One instant, one drink too many, one slip of the foot, you may not be here to cheer next week."

"I've heard this speech before," muttered Webber, too quiet for anyone beyond the table to hear.

Anton hushed him, kicking him beneath the table.

After Evka's funeral, Anton and Domek had gone to a nearby pub. Anton, tongue loose from the absinthe, had ranted to the room about the monster in the river, and had then picked a fight with a group of sailors. Domek had jumped into the brawl, and by the time it had ended, Anton had a loose tooth and Domek had two black eyes.

It was in that sorry state Kuba Paluska had found them slumped against the wall outside the pub. Despite the pain, despite the grief, despite the haze of drunkenness, Domek and Anton had listened with rapt attention to the older man's story of an organization that protected the city from monsters like the one who had killed Evka.

Paluska continued for another few minutes about the training schedule that week and updated the group on upcoming events that would impact patrol routes. With the gas lamps came an increased level of security at night, but also more people venturing onto the streets. For the general populace of Prague, 'safer' meant 'safe enough.' The factories along the city walls were open later, ladies left balls without a full escort, and river sailors wandered the streets too drunk to walk in a straight line. For the lamplighters, the city's giddy, bold trust in the night meant more work.

"The ministry has passed along a new task for us," Paluska said. There was a wave of booing from the gathered group, and he let it pass before he continued. "They want to discover the mechanics of the pijavice. They asked if we could take some prisoners for them to study. They want us to restrain them and take them in to their scientists."

There was a tense silence in the room. Simply killing a pijavica was difficult enough; in the last three months alone they'd lost two lamplighters. Trying to restrain one would be suicide.

Then Paluska laughed. "I told them to go jump in a river."

The lamplighters cheered.

"They can go talk to Vienna if they have a problem with it. Prague is an ashes-only city," Paluska said.

Domek leaned back in his chair. Paluska was right, as he always was. Let the ministry fret about why the monsters did what they did. Prague had enough to worry about without stepping deeper into the shadows. The lamplighters were funded by the government and overseen by a local ministry of bloated bureaucrats and retired soldiers so dedicated to secrecy they left the lamplighters fighting on the streets with half the information they needed. While Paluska and Domek's team were working overtime to save Prague, the ministry spent its time playing politics with the Imperial Council in Vienna for money the lamplighters never saw.

After the meeting, Domek lingered by his bench as everyone else stood and filed out, watching Paluska having an intense conversation with a lamplighter who worked in the Old Town Square. He was a general with his soldiers. No matter how the ministry devalued their work, Paluska was running a war on the streets of Prague.

Domek rested a hand on his satchel. If he were going to tell Paluska about the strange jar, he should do it now.

"Are you coming, Domek?" Anton asked, waiting beside the bench.

Domek hesitated. The fire had only made a small whirlwind. Was Domek truly prepared to lose a chance to prove himself to Imrich and Paluska? It was an opportunity he had been waiting years to find.

"Sorry," he said, turning to Anton. "Let's go."

6

Over the course of her life, Ora had learned a great many lessons.

She had studied a half-dozen languages, none of which stayed in her head for longer than a decade. She had learned the importance of carrying spare cash tucked in her bosom while traveling, since many pickpockets could work so lightly that even Ora couldn't detect them. She knew the rules of dozens of card and dice sports, and had suffered through an equal number of tedious parlor games.

One rule had served her best over the last decade: people would overlook an extraordinary amount of eccentricities when enough money was thrown about.

As a widow, Ora had rights and privileges that single and married ladies, both poor and titled, did not. She could associate with whom she wished, had inherited an estate, and was invited to the best art events Prague had to offer. However, her odd behavior would still likely not have been overlooked if she hadn't been able to distract people by smoothing her path with a steady flow of money.

It also helped that Ora rarely gave a damn what anyone thought of her.

Her townhouse was in Malá Strana under the shadow of the large castle on the hill. She was only two streets from Charles Bridge, which was enough of a convenience that she could excuse the tourists the area drew. The main arterial road off the bridge split off into capillaries, creating a complex system. Ora's townhouse sat at the split of two of the smaller streets, like the fork of a stream. The façade was painted a soft yellow, and bright orange shutters framed the curtained windows. Ivy had been carefully encouraged to grow along one wall.

The interior of Ora's house, which had been mostly designed by Lina's mother back when she had been Ora's primary maid, was a show of theater that few would ever appreciate. The front room was well-lit and perfectly maintained, though Ora never set foot in it before dark. There was a fully functional kitchen and dining room, though Ora never ate. There was even a master bedroom with a large bed she had never slept on.

Not all of Ora's eclectic friends knew what she was, and she was wiser than to betray her secret lightly. There were forces beyond her control dedicated to keeping the existence of monsters in the shadows.

When not entertaining guests, Ora spent most of her time either in her study, her painting studio, or the kitchens, watching her employees mill around. A household such as hers was expected to spend a certain amount at the local grocers, after all, and Ora had learned early on that keeping her staff well-fed earned more loyalty than a smile ever could.

Ora's friends, when they visited, took advantage of it as well.

"I can't believe you spend so much on food you can't even eat," said Sokol, plucking another canapé off the tray. Sokol cast an absurd figure in Ora's lace-decorated sitting room. A lieutenant in the emperor-king's army during the Seven Weeks' War, Karel Sokol was broad and powerful. He dwarfed any piece of furniture he sat on, and the hors d'oeuvres looked like crumbs in his massive hands. They had already finished dinner—Ora had sipped on an opaque goblet filled with pig blood—but the men were insatiable. Her cook, prepared for the men's hunger, had already laid a platter of bread garnished decoratively with pickles, cheese, and tomatoes, along with a tray of Russian eggs. "Does the cook ever get mad that it all goes to waste?" he asked, licking his fingers. "All *you* need is a liquid diet and raw meat."

While serving as a foot soldier, Sokol had been violently introduced to the existence of pijavice on a bloody battlefield. Though he wasn't forthcoming on all the details, Ora gathered that his experience had qualified him for his current position on the mysterious Prague ministry concerning supernatural activity.

Sokol's job required him to consider pijavice a threat, so Ora had made it a mission to befriend him thoroughly. She never could resist a challenge. It helped that she avoided all talk of his work, and not just for his sake; she resisted politics like an allergy.

"It's not going to waste," Ora pointed out. "If you're not here to eat me out of house and home, she takes the extras back to her family."

"I just mean that it's all so fancy," Sokol said. "Luxury finger foods like this are supposed to end up in ladies' stomachs, not feeding the emperor's men."

"You're not supposed to talk about ladies' stomachs," Válka said, elbowing Sokol sharply. He was a recent addition to Ora's collection of friends, and still balked at spending time in her polished townhouse. Válka—Ora had never learned his first name—was as lean as Sokol was broad, with a scar on his cheek he had earned on some battlefield. He was several years older than Sokol, but the two had become unexpectedly close friends when Válka had been stationed at the Prague army headquarters to help train new recruits. When Sokol introduced them, Ora had appreciated his self-deprecating humor and thoughtful nature, which were hard qualities to find in a military man.

Sokol scoffed. "Ora's not your average lady."

"I'm genuinely not sure whether you're trying to flatter or insult, and whether the target would be me or other ladies," Ora said. "You're both right, though. Sokol, never mention a woman's stomach. Válka, in this case Sokol does know that I won't actually take offense to anything he says. After all, I take the fact that the two of you are sitting here for dinner with me instead of shoving a hawthorn stake into my heart to be a sign of dear friendship."

Válka winced. "I'm not sure I can be as cavalier as the two of you."

"About my stomach or about my species?"

Sokol chortled. "You're going to send him into hysterics," he said. "Válka is used to me being absurd. Even after the last few months, he still thinks you're some sort of lady. I think he thinks the pijavica bit is just a phase."

"I try not to make assumptions about others based on their sex or…diet," Válka said. "There's a reason Sokol trusted me to learn your secret, Lady Fischerová. I know what most of your kind is like, but I've met other exceptions."

"So you keep hinting," Ora said. "I'd still love to know who you've met." Ora had avoided other pijavice since leaving her master's family, though she knew there must have been others like her.

Válka just shook his head and changed the subject. "Thank you for having us over. Tell the cook that we appreciate the food, even if the lady of the house can't enjoy it."

"It's not as fancy as you're making it out to be." When Ora had traveled abroad, though stuck with said liquid diet, she had become fascinated with the more delicate pastries served in places like Paris and Mumbai, and had come back to Prague with firm ideas about what her parties would look like. It had taken a combined effort from her cook and her friends to convince her to serve local fare at meals.

"There's *garnish* on these," Sokol argued, eating another.

"Let me spoil you. To quote the Buddha: 'If you knew what I know about the power of giving you would not let a single meal pass without sharing it in some way.'"

He laughed. "Of course you wouldn't reference the Bible like a normal Czech."

"I'd burst into flames," she deadpanned. Common folklore suggested that pijavice were as allergic to Christianity as they were to hawthorn and sunlight. Ora didn't mind Christianity for the most part—they had created some beautiful art—but she preferred borrowing from various religions to cobble together a version that felt right. Traditional religions were rigid, while nothing about Ora had ever been. She was quite sure Jesus, Buddha, and all the other holy men would not approve of her. "I'm sure you're just glad to be away from army rations."

Válka shrugged. "They need to give us a reason to want to come home." He had served with Sokol in the Seven Weeks' War two years before but had been kept busy since then with the recent absorption of Hungary into the Austrian Empire. Before returning to Prague, he'd been sent around the continent to quell offshoot rebellions sparked by the changes. If his shadowed eyes were anything to go by, Válka needed time away from the battlefield.

"I hope you're here to stay. The local offices would be lucky to have you."

Sokol nodded, his expression sobering. "There's far too much going on in Prague to have time to focus anywhere else these days," he said. "Speaking of... Ora, the note you sent this morning was quite interesting."

"Was it?" she asked. After her afternoon flirting with Domek Myska and walking through the museum, she had nearly managed to bury the upsetting event under a layer of honey-metal blood and delicate tapestry threads. "If you're interested in the ravings of madmen, I'm sure you can find your fill in this city."

"Have you heard from any of your brethren here lately? Other than the mad ones in tunnels?"

"Not when I can help it," she replied shortly. "Like I said, they're mostly uncivilized."

"You're friends with Sokol," Válka pointed out mildly.

"His brand of uncivilized I like," Ora said. "It doesn't involve murder or cannibalism." To most pijavice, devouring humans was akin to eating beef, but Ora did not agree with that sentiment. One did not have conversations over a meal with cattle. Or marry them. She turned back to Sokol. "Why do you ask?"

Sokol cleared his throat and sat up, moving his attention fully from the snacks to Ora. "There have been some interesting rumors. Your encounter this morning has given them some weight in my mind."

"What kind of rumors?"

Sokol and Válka exchanged a glance. "The kind about a cure for the transformation. The pijavica transformation," Sokol said.

Ora laughed. "I've heard that one. It takes a sunny day and a hawthorn stake to the heart. *Voilà.* Cured."

"It's no joke," Sokol said.

"There is no cure for the change," Ora said more seriously. "No more than there's a cure for death." The thought was too tempting to think about. If there were a magic ritual Ora could perform to regain her mortality, to be able to eat, and drink, and sleep, and walk in the sun, she'd do it without hesitation. "Once you've burned a piece of firewood, you can't reverse the process."

"That's what we thought too," Sokol said. "We're starting to suspect that we were wrong. A source told us that there are reports of pijavice walking in the daylight. You said that the pijavica you saw this morning ran right out of the tunnels."

"He died," Ora said, waving her hand. "It was suicide."

"Are you sure?" Sokol asked. "Did you see him die?"

"He was in sunlight. I wasn't going to risk my own life to watch it happen," Ora said. "It was inevitable. He went outside. He's gone. That's the way of things."

"He must not have thought so."

"Or he was mad, or eager for death, or both," Ora said. "There is no cure, Sokol. I shouldn't have even sent you the note. I was shaken by the encounter, and I thought you'd…add it to an archive, or something. This isn't worth an investigation."

"Your story isn't the only source. Pijavice have been disappearing from their usual haunts, outside of the usual killing patterns. A source told us that they heard whispers that those pijavice were going to receive a cure."

Ora folded her arms. "What source?"

Sokol shrugged, lips quirking in anticipation of her response. "Guttman."

"Guttman lives under a bridge and eats rats," Ora exclaimed. "He lost his mind centuries ago. I didn't even know you consulted him."

"We don't have many options," Sokol said. "Guttman hears things. He's involved with the underground. People talk around him without expecting him to understand."

"That's because he doesn't," Ora said. "Honestly, Sokol, I'd have expected this from your superiors, but I always thought you were smarter than them. No information is better than misinformation."

"This is my job, Ora. I look for the larger patterns of the pijavice in the city, and I make sure they're not getting out of hand. I have to look into these rumors."

"Isn't that what those lamplighters are for?"

"They're doing as much as they can, but they don't have the resources to follow up on insubstantial leads like this," Sokol said.

"And you do?"

"Not as much as I'd like. You know my funding comes from the Ministry of Security, and they pinch every coin they can. For the most part, as long as monsters stick with attacking the lower classes, and do it quietly, the police and military will stay uninvolved. The minutia of life outside of Vienna is not deemed *worthy* of the emperor's attention, and there are always more human rebellions to be repressed." He and Válka exchanged a knowing look, and Válka sighed. Sokol took another slice of egg but held it loosely in his hand instead of eating it. "Peasants kill each other more often than they're taken as snacks for local monsters. My superiors told me that it's too much effort with no quantifiable reward to dedicate too many forces to protecting them."

"It's hard to get glory fighting a war no one knows about," Ora said.

Sokol nodded. "I've had to be creative. I was hoping I'd find some outside help here."

Ora froze, watching him cautiously. "You're not implying what I think you're implying."

Sokol leaned forward, resting his elbows on his knees. "Ora. You must have seen this coming."

He was wrong. She'd thought their friendship had developed enough that Sokol didn't see her just as a bloodsucker.

"I'm not involved in pijavica politics," she said, and then snapped at Válka, "Stop flinching every time someone mentions pijavice. I know you work with Sokol. I know you kill pijavice for a living. Pretending that all three of us are not just what we are is useless."

Válka held up his hands. "I know full well what you are."

"I'm starting to see that," Ora said.

"Ora, we're coming to you because we trust you," Sokol said.

"You're coming to me because you're desperate for an insider who won't turn around and rip your throat out."

"Precisely," Sokol said with a shrug.

"Sokol and I talked about this at length," Válka said. "We didn't bring it up to the larger ministry yet. We know that you want to stay away from others of your kind as much as you can, but there's no other way to figure out the truth."

Ora stood up. Válka flinched slightly, just a blink, but Sokol was unmoved as she started pacing. "You haven't thought this through. First of all, the entire idea of a cure for the transformation is absurd. Finding someone to go sneak around to prove this insane theory wrong is a waste of resources. Secondly," she continued, interrupting Sokol when he started to speak, "I'm not sure I see the trouble with a cure, if there were one. Doesn't that solve all your problems? A pijavica without their additions is just…human. I was your average girl before my transformation."

Sokol leveled her with a long look, making her think he could hear the wistfulness that covered her heart like a fog. "We need more information. What *is* the cure? Is there a contingent of pijavice looking to regain their humanity and leave all aspects of the demonic abilities behind? Or are they looking for a way to simply break the normal laws so that they can expand their hunt to daylight hours?"

"The pijavica in the tunnel still smelled like one of us. Even if it was immune to sunlight, it was no human."

"Then maybe it had not taken the cure yet, or only thought it had. It might not be a voluntary choice on the pijavica's part, either," Válka pointed out. "From your description, that pijavica was mad. Maybe a human found the cure and has started implementing it to stop the pijavica problem on their own. They could be clearing out the nests by force."

"And if that's the case, I assume the Empire will soon be funding it?" Ora asked.

"Don't be stroppy," Sokol said. "Of course we'd fund it. Once you start thinking clearly, you'll come to the same conclusion."

Válka cleared his throat. "Maybe try for some delicacy," he suggested to Sokol.

"You hate that your brethren treat human like prey as much as we do, despite the side you fall down on," Sokol pressed. "You can't blame us for trying to stop them. This is our fight."

"That's your fight," Ora said. "I'm not on either side. I'm not one of the pijavice you're afraid of."

"But you could help us stop them. I'm not asking for much. Just ask some questions, poke around where we can't. We've been friends for years now, Ora, and this is the first favor I've asked of you. Help us find out what's happening. That's all I'm asking."

Ora sighed and leaned against the fireplace. "I suppose I can ask around and see what I can find out," she said finally. "As a personal favor. You won't convince me to don your uniform and join the good fight."

"They're not your best colors anyway," Sokol said breezily.

Ora made a sour face at him, and he returned it.

"Thank you, Lady Fischerová. We'll be with you every step of the way," Válka interjected.

"In spirit," Sokol corrected. "We can't send men in with you, not where you'll be going."

Ora shook her head. "I can always rely on you, Sokol, to not sugarcoat these things. I'm not making any promises. Something like this—a cure, and a concentrated effort to administer it—is more than the average sewer rat could manage. Any pijavica worth its teeth knows that I don't associate with them anymore. Those who know me won't speak to me, and those who don't won't trust me. And that's *if* anyone I talk to knows anything worth talking about."

"And if they do know something?" Sokol asked. "If you find out something that could give the government a way to reverse the affliction, would you tell us?"

"If you don't trust me, why are we having this conversation?" Ora asked. When Sokol just raised his eyebrows, she said, "If there is a cure, I want to know about it. You can trust that." She straightened up. "Let's discuss the details over cards. I'm filled with the sudden urge to take every krejcar you two have."

7

The sun sank low over the hill, illuminating the spires of St. Vitus behind Domek as he crossed the river. There had been a time he could walk all day and night without tiredness, but now his feet ached in step with his heartbeat. He was not yet thirty, but his body had begun to protest the years of patrolling, training, and brawling.

Lamplighting was a new job, but there had been people fighting against the shadows since the beginning of history. Those who survived to retire were often spat out scarred and battered. Many moved on to work as priests or cemetery watchmen, watching for threats until the day they died. None left the work and found peace. What were his other options? The men sent deep into the copper mines outside the city walls lived no longer, and, more importantly to Domek, made no difference while they lived.

Domek's destination was a squat building on the upper edge of the city beyond where the Vltava whipped suddenly to the east, near Štvanice Island. When he walked into the flat, he felt some of the tension slide out of his body. He was greeted by the smell of goulash from the kitchen: beef, onion, garlic, tomatoes. It was warm and hearty, triggering an instinct to settle down and relax.

"Maminka?" he called.

"In here, Domek," his mother responded. She put a lid over the pot she had been stirring and wiped her hands on a towel. Domek had inherited his height and bulk from his father, but his coloring from his mother. Her dark, curly hair was streaked with threads of white, obvious even when pulled back from her kind, lined face. She was thinner than he would have liked. "I'm finishing up dinner now. You're just in time."

He breathed in the scent of home. "It smells great. I've missed your cooking."

"You wouldn't have to if you visited more often," she said.

"I know, Maminka. I've been very busy," he said, wincing.

"So you always say." She set the bowl in front of him and he waited until she had her own bowl to dig in eagerly. It was a mix of dumplings and a few bits of gamey meat, all thinned out with water to last longer.

"So," she said as they ate, "has some sweet young girl caught your eye yet?"

"Maminka." Domek sighed. "I promise to tell you if I begin courting someone." What would his mother think of Lady Fischerová? No one would meet the vivacious lady and accuse her of being a 'sweet young girl.' Besides, despite her youthful face, she had been widowed for nearly a decade. She must have been Domek's age, if not older. Wealth was more powerful than youth, and longer lasting.

If his mother wanted a soft daughter-in-law to take under her wing, she would be disappointed by Ora Fischerová.

It did not matter—Ora was both achingly vivid, and perfect and distant as the moon. There was no hope of Domek ever wedding her.

His mother hummed. "I don't believe that. You keep your secrets close to your chest until you're sure about them. I had to hear about you and Evka from Anton's mother."

"I was twelve," Domek protested, ignoring the pang in his chest at the mention of Anton's sister.

"You know, if you were a woman, you would already have two or three children by now," she said. "Men can afford to wait longer to get married."

"Not if their mothers have any say," Domek laughed, and moved the conversation to her neighbors, who were always embroiled in some drama or other. Domek had not lived in the apartment building for nearly ten years but had been kept abreast of the gossip by his mother.

The sun was setting outside by the time they finished eating, painting the sky in bright orange and yellow. He would need to leave for his patrol soon. As he returned from cleaning their bowls, his boot connected with the edge of his satchel, clunking against the jar within. He bent down and lifted the bag. "I found something strange yesterday," he told her. "I've been trying to figure out what it could be. Maybe you can help."

It was easy for Domek to forget his mother's past. She was a quiet woman, so reserved that the first time a young Domek had heard her talk about her life before his birth, he had felt deeply betrayed. It had taken many years for him to slowly unravel the hidden threads of her youth. Her childhood friends had dabbled in local traditions such as looking for the name of their future husband in the boughs of an apple tree, but had left them behind over time. His mother, unable to abandon the promise of glimpsing the future, had become adept with divination through a Tarot deck. During those years, she had flung herself into Prague's occult world, only to eventually find herself strangled by his father's leash. The Tarot deck, if it had survived, was nowhere to be found in her flat.

"I can try," she said. She straightened the napkin on her lap. "You know I wish you would work with your uncle instead. What you do is a dangerous business."

"Zacharias can't afford a full-time shop assistant," Domek pointed out. "The work I do is important." The bloodier side of lamplighting was kept secret from the citizens of Prague, but his mother, who had in her day known the unauthorized organization that predated the lamplighter guild, had known about his work since the day Paluska had recruited him. "You did something similar once."

"Once," she said. "It's long since behind me."

"You know," Domek said quietly, "Father is dead now. You could go back to it."

"It's dangerous to be a Tarot reader when there is one among the dead who would have you join him," she said with a wry smile. "Those doors should remain closed, brouček."

"Maminka," he said, throat tight.

She patted his hand. "It's okay, my love. I could use a few more visits a month from my only child, but I'm not unhappy. It's a quiet life I lead, but I've earned that after all these years. I'm settled."

"I'm glad," Domek said, holding her hand. "I just wish I could do more for you."

"Stop worrying so much," she said. "I'm easy to please. Make me some grandchildren. Now, show me this mystery."

He dug out the jar, holding it between his scarred hands. "Come out," he instructed. "Do not harm anyone or break anything here." The flame floated from the jar, brighter than the sunset outside.

"My goodness," his mother breathed, leaning forward. "Where did you find this?"

"Don't touch it," he warned, pulling back. He shifted a hand to show her the silver brands on his palms, and she hissed in sympathy. "It seems to follow my orders, though it's fickle. Do you know what it is?"

"Well, I've never seen one bound before, but that is a will-o'-the-wisp."

The name was familiar. He recalled stories he'd heard from hunters who had visited the city from the countryside. One man had mentioned a phenomenon he'd seen in the dark forest: malignant, floating lights that attempted to lure him and his wife to their deaths in the marshlands. He examined the warm jar in his hands. The symbols on the clay were strange and alien in their intricacy. "I've never heard of anyone finding a wisp in a container like this before. I thought they roamed free. They're forest spirits, aren't they?"

"They are," she said. "I haven't seen one in many years, especially not in the center of Prague. The first time I saw one, I was visiting the forests near Hýskov. Fortunately, I was traveling with another practitioner who warned me away from following the light."

"I thought wisps were simple things. I've seen this one create a small storm from nothing, and lift stones from a meter away."

"They are powerful creatures, despite their appearances. Not only can they control light, but they're able to transform objects. The person following them believes they're still on solid ground, but the grass in front of them turns out to be a pond when their foot touches it. I've heard of them controlling sticks or even traveler's bags, animating them to float away. Clever, too. They can linger near a camp until they learn your name, and then call it back to you from the other side of a sinkhole."

"It can speak?" Domek asked, watching the floating flame. It hovered before them, small and humble in his mother's kitchen. "It's been silent since I found it."

"I'm not sure," his mother admitted. "It could be a form of mimicry."

Feeling slightly foolish, Domek ordered, "Speak, if you're able."

There was a moment of quiet before a voice spoke. "What shall I say?" It sounded as insubstantial as the crackling fire, smooth and staccato at once.

"My God," his mother murmured.

"Tell me why you're here," Domek said, heart thudding. Now he could speak with the creature, he could learn more about its origins. He had no need for Imrich.

"You carried me here."

"Answer truthfully—what brings you here?"

"My spirit is tied to that jar, and my powers to your will. I'm bound to your whim. I assure you," it said, voice dripping with poison, "I would not be here if not for that."

He remembered his mother's story about the demon attempting to trick her deeper into the forest. Though the spirit was bonded to him, there was no guarantee of its benevolence, particularly considering how he had discovered the jar. "What were you doing with the pijavica? Were you conspiring with it?"

"I was conspiring with nobody."

"Then what was it doing with you?"

"I was not informed of his plans."

But surely there had been one. For the pijavica to be interested, there must have been some dark power still hidden. Domek sensed that he had only brushed the edge of the wisp's potential. "And now I have you," Domek mused.

"You shouldn't. You're not the one who brought me to this city," the wisp said. "Before now, you knew not what I was. You have no clue how to use my abilities."

"I can learn," Domek said.

The flame sparked. An ember sizzled through the air, disappearing before it hit the ground. "Free me."

It was an easy conclusion to this. Domek hadn't meant to pick up the wisp's container. If he let it go, he could continue with his week as though this strange interlude hadn't happened.

What would an unbound wisp do, though? If it was as powerful as his mother believed, it could use those powers to hurt those in his city if it were let loose. He had instructed the wisp to be truthful, but had no guarantee it had worked. If the spirit had been allies with the pijavice, it would surely find a way back to them. Domek had something dangerous under his power right now. He could not lose that control.

"I can't free you," Domek told it.

Another spark shot from the wisp, falling toward the kitchen table before again sizzling into air. "Free me, or you will regret it. You and your dear maminka."

Beside him, his mother flinched.

Domek was suddenly very aware that he had brought a strange occult creature into his mother's home. His confidence that his control of the creature would protect her seemed foolish in light of the threat. Domek would never forgive himself if his actions harmed his mother.

"Go back in the jar and stay there. Now," Domek snapped.

There was a rush of warm air around the kitchen as the wisp poured back into the container, creating a strong wind that ruffled his hair and sent the curtains waving. Sparks of color sprayed out like drops from a living watercolor painting, casting the room in a rainbow glow. Then, everything stilled.

Domek shook the jar, making sure the lid was tightly shut. There was no reaction from inside. Carefully, he set the jar back into his bag and closed the flap. Only then did he allow himself to take a deep, shuddering breath.

"You should free that thing," his mother said. Her voice was weak, warbling like a bird. "Take it somewhere far away and leave it behind."

"There must be a way to control it," Domek said. Surely the pijavica would have had a way. Imrich would have found a way.

"I don't care. It will try its hardest to undermine and destroy you. You can't take the risk."

"If I can just learn to understand it—"

"Domek," she said, grabbing his hand. She turned his palms to examine the scars again, the silver dulled in the fading light. "This is already hurting you. Your job is already so terrifying for me. Please don't chase this. Don't create new dangers out of curiosity."

After Sokol and Válka left, Ora paced around the upper hall of her home.

A cure. A reversal of the affliction that had kept her hungry, thirsty, awake, for centuries. She could go into the sunshine. She could *sleep*. Did Sokol know what a cruel taunt the idea was? If pijavice were searching for a way to undo their curse, who could blame them?

But to investigate the mystery by insinuating herself among the city's other pijavice pushed the line of what Ora was willing to do.

Pijavice were as diverse as humans, some lingering near the cemetery mud they burst from, some building empires of wealth and influence. Tonight, Ora would search for some of the former. They were the more palatable.

Ora had been transformed by a monster in a cold, ancient palace on a hill, and had stayed under his rule for more than a century. The idea of walking back into Lord Czernin's grasp, even for a chance at the mortality he had stolen from her, made her stomach twist. She hoped it would not come to that.

"I want to go to the bookstore," Ora announced, throwing open the door to the kitchen.

"Tonight?" Lina asked. She had eaten dinner with the rest of the staff while Ora had entertained the two soldiers, and was talking with the cook over cups of coffee.

"Come, Lina. I'll let you sleep in tomorrow if you'll come with me on this one last adventure. It won't take long—the store is sure to close soon. I'm in desperate need of a distraction."

Ora prodded Lina into the carriage while the girl yawned pointedly. "If I had known this would be the result of forcing you from bed this morning, I might have let you waste away."

"Yes, yes," Ora said, climbing in behind her. Having a mortal maid could be so dull.

The Emporium was the city's largest, and only secular, bookstore. It was located only a block from the Old Town Square, surrounded by pastry shops and pubs meant to draw in the city's visitors. Comprised of a main showroom, which featured new novels and texts from around the Empire, and an open back room for weekly salons, the Emporium was one of Ora's favorite buildings in Prague.

She paused to look at a collection of poetry set at the edge of a table. The poet wasn't one she recognized, but she flipped through it anyway.

Mister Novy, bookseller and proprietor of the Emporium, was near the back wall, speaking with a customer over a heavy text. "…should have the tale in question. Will-o'-the-wisps are a bit of folklore seen across Europe, you know. It's a beautifully written work. You can read German?"

"Ah, no. Only Czech." With that delectable low rumble, Ora recognized Domek Myska's honey and metal scent woven beneath the ink and paper all around. It had, again, the bitter scent of shame.

Mister Novy hummed. "You know there aren't as many interesting texts in Czech. You won't find a good book of fairy tales you can understand. If you're going to frequent this store, you should learn to read German."

Ora could remember a time before the lower classes had gained literacy. The education programs of recent decades had the charming effect of encouraging the mass printing of the newest novels in both Czech and German, and filled the bookstore with the most interesting people. The Czech revival was still nascent, only just emerging from the peasant class into the national conversation. She strode across the room, her bustle nearly knocking over a stack of new books. She leaned into the conversation. "Why, hello," she said.

Both men jumped, and she smiled wider.

"Back again so soon, Lady Fischerová?" Novy said, shuffling to accommodate her and turning his shoulder to Domek in the process. "Thank you for coming to last week's literary reception, by the way. Everyone always appreciates your fantastic insight."

"Thank you for hosting us. Now, I couldn't help but overhear your conversation," she said. "Is it possible, Mister Novy, that you're forgetting the work of Professor Andel? If this man is looking for a book of fairy tales in Czech, surely Andel's book is the perfect fit."

"You're a literary maven, Lady Fischerová," he said, leaning closer. "Surely you know that the Czech translations degrade the original text. It's a coarse language."

"I'm sure that's what the Russian author said about the German translation in the first place," Ora said, smile not faltering. "Do you not carry Professor Andel's translations? I know that Charles University supports your store. I'm surprised that you would not carry their professors' recent works."

Novy swallowed. "We have one copy."

"Oh, lovely. Could you find it? It seems this man is looking to purchase it. I'm sure, after all, that you are not deliberately attempting to alienate any of your customers. My friends don't want to host readings where they may not be welcome."

"Of course, Lady Fischerová," Novy said. "You are always—"

"So, go fetch the book for Mister Myska." Ora raised her eyebrows until Novy bowed and scurried to a nearby stack to collect the text in question. It was a slender tome, bound in a dark leather and stamped with gold. Novy apologized profusely to Ora, not giving Domek a glance after dropping the book into his hands. Ora impatiently shooed him on his way.

Once Novy was gone, Domek cleared his throat. "Thank you, Lady Fischerová."

"Please don't think of it. Did you come here hoping to see me? You know this is my favorite shop. I didn't mean to break your heart so very badly in skipping lunch."

"No, no," Domek said.

She pouted. His eyes fell to her lips. "You didn't come here for me?"

"I… That is, I was here to find a book. It is always a pleasure to run into you."

Ora stepped forward to inspect the book in his hands. It was only partially an excuse to get closer to him. "I hope you enjoy my recommendation. I didn't know you liked fairy tales. Did you know that the first records of those stories are from the twelfth century?"

"Is that so?" He stroked the book with one finger, and her eyes traced the breadth of his hands. "You've read them?"

"I have." Ora tapped her chin, and was gratified to see Domek's eyes flick over her lips. "They're delightfully bloody. You would think that people would learn early on to stop interfering with beings they don't understand, but humans keep making terrible decisions and paying the price. I think you'll enjoy them."

Domek smiled weakly. "I'm sure I will."

"You'll have to let me know what you think," she pressed.

"Of course," he said, but his gaze was distant.

The conversation was slipping away from her. She leaned back out of his space, though she lost some of his honey and metal scent when she did. "I'll stop taking up your time," she said. "You've already seen me twice in one day. I'm sure that's twice too many for most."

"I'm sorry," he said, focusing on her again. "I have a lot on my mind."

"That's not an affliction I'm burdened by," Ora said, waving her hand.

He shook his head. Now that she'd redrawn his attention, his gaze was intent. She felt as though perhaps now he was seeing more than she'd wanted him to. "I don't believe that. You're too clever for someone with nothing on their mind."

She grinned at him. "Say," she said, leaning closer again, "I have two tickets for the opera tomorrow night. Would you like to come with me?" It had been barely twelve hours since she'd watched the pijavica in the tunnels fling himself into the sunlight, but there was a thrum of *life* in her veins as she plied reactions from this man. Ora's very existence demanded sacrifice, and her recent decades would never wash the blood from her teeth, but flirting with Domek was simple and gentle.

"The opera? Tomorrow?" he repeated. Ora could smell the blood rising to his cheeks, the metal in his scent intensifying. "With me?"

"With you. My original plans fell through, and I'd hate to go alone. I know you like art. Do you like music?"

"I love music," he said, the words slipping from his lips like breath.

"Excellent. Read up before then. We'll talk about your favorite stories. Pick one of the tragedies—they're always more fun."

He looked down at the book in his hands, and some of the warmth left his face. "Of course," he said. "I'm sorry. I've kept you from your shopping. I should go." Ora was about to protest when he smiled at her. "I'll see you tomorrow."

He bowed toward both her and Lina—not the most practiced she'd seen, but a genuine effort—and then left toward the front of the shop to purchase his book. Lina moved to stand beside her, but Ora didn't speak.

"He's not good enough for you," she said quietly.

With a sigh, Ora said, "I think that he might be too good, actually." Shaking her head, she said, "No matter. Come on. I'd still like to find a new book, and then I need to find some tickets for an opera tomorrow."

Domek was out of sight, but she could hear the steady thud of his boots and heart. His scent lingered like incense.

8

Words were not easy for Domek. He'd only been formally schooled until he was twelve, and since then he'd learned in practice. He found books worth the effort, but each sentence was a journey, and a commitment.

The tome Ora had secured for him was thin, but the interior had large text and beautiful line drawings of trees, rivers, and monsters.

After he finished lighting the lamps on his route, he sat beneath one and flipped through the text, squinting in the blue light to read the story about the wisp. He would need to return to his patrol shortly, but the thin book was irresistible. He could never let a puzzle lie.

The book was one of children's fairy tales, and the story followed a boy named Hans as he wandered through the forest. Domek mouthed along as he read, frowning. There was a long section about Hans's father, a blacksmith who often scolded the boy for his laziness.

He skipped forward to try to search for information he could use, and found the end of the story.

"Come to me, and you may eat this roast chicken and more." The roasted chicken floated in the mist, and the boy's mouth watered.

"But how will I cross this canyon?" asked the boy. He was so hungry.

The will-o'-the-wisp said, "The mist is a magical mist. It allows the chicken to fly, and will let you fly too."

And the boy jumped and broke his neck.

The blacksmith later found the boy's body, and regretted his harsh words. Several years later, he remarried and had a pair of sons, who were warned away from the forest. After the blacksmith died, they inherited his forge, and made the king's swords.

An inauspicious ending. He flipped through the book, searching for other stories about the will-o'-the-wisp. He stopped at a page near the front. A vodník stared up at him, grinning around a pipe. Its expression belonged more to a kindly grandfather sitting at a café than the beast Domek had once watched kill his childhood sweetheart. Disgusted, he closed the book and put it back in his bag. His purse was substantially lighter, and he was no closer to answers.

His mother had warned him away from the demon, but Domek had hoped to find the key to unlocking its cooperation. It had powerful magic and was bound to his will. Perhaps Domek could do good in Prague with its help.

Unfortunately, if the fairy tale could be believed, the wisp's power was not in its magic, but in its manipulation. Domek was intelligent and clever with machinery, but he was not prepared for a war of words. He could barely keep his tongue functioning when faced with the beautiful Lady Fischerová, and reading always took him considerable time. He was sure to lose his wits when trying to outsmart the fire demon.

He wouldn't be able to learn about this demon from a book—especially not the one in his bag. If Domek could plan both the situation and his commands for the wisp in advance, he could avoid being thrown from his path by tricky words, as poor Hans had been.

He needed to find out what the wisp was capable of—and if Domek was capable of managing its power on his own. If he had the chance, he could prove his worth to Imrich and Paluska. Giving up now and admitting he was too afraid to learn more would reduce him to being Imrich's oafish assistant for the rest of his life.

Domek stared out over the dark river, watching ripples reflect the crescent moon overhead. He needed a controlled experiment, one that wouldn't hurt him nor any innocent bystander. He would approach the task like it was the inner workings of a pocket watch rather than a riddle, play to his strengths rather than his weaknesses.

After years of patrolling the twisting streets of the city, Domek knew exactly where to go.

The monster at the back of the alley pulsed and rippled, a living darkness. Even at noon, this corner of the city would be swathed in blackness. At midnight, its power was at its zenith. Malice and horror emanated from the darkness like a poison, clogging the air and making it difficult to draw a full breath.

Adults passed the alley without looking twice. Children, however, knew there was something more inside. They told their parents there was a monster lurking there, and no amount of cajoling or reassurance could dampen their fear.

Deep in the shadows, the monster fed on that fear, billowing larger with each frightened gasp.

Bubáks were mysterious creatures that lurked in the shadows around humanity, feeding not on blood or spirits, but on fear itself. Some found their ways into homes, settling under the beds of the children who felt their presence most strongly. Others found alleys like this, claiming their territory and then settling down to soak in the fears of a city.

Domek stepped inside the alley and felt the bubák's aura nipping at his flesh, raising goosebumps along his arms. He reached into his bag and grabbed the jar. He opened the lid, and the wisp appeared before him. This close, the feel and smell of it felt like standing on the bank of the Vltava before a storm—like air itself had become his enemy, charged with power.

It was smaller than he remembered. After reading the unsettling fairy tale, details of the mysterious creature had conflated into something more terrifying in his mind. In reality, the wisp was insubstantial. Compared to the murky, pulsing blackness of the bubák, it was like a sandcastle in front of an oncoming wave.

"Wisp, obey my order," he said in a clear, loud voice that seemed misplaced in the darkness. "Clear this alley."

For a moment, the wisp pulsed unmoving, a small ball of fire hovering in front of him. But then, the pulsing grew brighter. The flame became blinding, bleeding from orange to white. The wisp floated forward as though on a breeze, and every meter it covered down the alley was scourged clean in its light. As the small spirit approached the living darkness, it appeared outmatched, but it did not hesitate.

It pressed forward into the bubák's space with its steady, unrelenting light, and the bubák writhed. The shadows throbbed, sending out pulses of poisonous energy. A wave of sheer terror gripped Domek, freezing his muscles and turning the air in his lungs to ice. It was overwhelming, like drowning while standing still.

When the wisp's light reached the center of the bubák's dark heart, there was a high, quiet shriek as the bubák lost control of its form.

The mass of collected terror burst and disappeared.

Though the wisp had no face, he had the sense of it turning back toward him. Then, the strap of Domek's bag tightened. He had just a moment for alarm before the strap lurched up and wrapped around his throat.

As though it were being held by a giant's fist, the strap hoisted him up off the ground, leaving him dangling over the cobblestones by the tightening strip of leather. He grappled at his throat, trying to push his hands between his skin and the strap to gain some traction against the strangulation.

"Stop," he croaked with the last of his breath.

The strap slackened, the force holding it up disappearing completely. Domek fell. Dazed from the attack, he could not catch himself, and hit the stone hard enough to bruise his leg. The bag fell heavily onto his lap, still strapped around his chest.

The wisp just hovered in front of him. "You did tell me to clear the alley." Its quiet voice was smug.

Domek reached into his belt and pulled out his silver blade. It had been foolish not to do so from the moment the wisp had manifested that morning.

"You don't need to attack me," the wisp reminded him. The shadows in the alley flickered as its pulsing light darted back slightly. "This was all your mistake."

"You nearly killed me. You threatened my mother. Tell me why I shouldn't find a way to destroy you right now," Domek said, adjusting his grip on the weapon.

"I didn't hunt you down," the wisp pointed out. From its tone, it seemed torn between placating him and insulting him. "You're the one attempting to wield a power you don't understand. Free me, or I'll continue to make this difficult for you."

"This was me wielding you?" Domek demanded, pointing to his neck.

"It's my power; I decide how it manifests. You were in the alley too. If you want to use me, you'd better be smarter about it."

"It was a simple order."

"Laughably so. You can't outsmart me," it spat, a spark flying from its heart. "If you let me free, you won't have to worry about your words. I can tell that wit is not your strong suit. Don't play this game with me."

"Under my control, the only actions you can take are the ones I let you—if I can make sure there's not room for you to misinterpret them. If I let you go, you'll be able to use that power as maliciously as you want."

"I may not want to," the wisp countered.

"Right. And I'd take your word for it." Domek shook his head and rubbed at his throat. "This was a test. I wanted to see what you could do, if you were worth saving." To see if Domek had a chance at controlling its power.

"Were you impressed? I did rescue you handily."

"I could have gotten rid of the bubák without your help," he said. "We have a map of each one in the city. They stay in one place and don't really hurt people, not the way the other monsters we deal with do. They're not usually worth our effort.

I wanted to understand your power—and I believe I do now. In the book I was reading today—"

"You can read?" The wisp's voice was skeptical. "Your hands are calloused from work. Are they teaching just anyone their letters these days?"

"What does a will-o'-the-wisp know of books?" Domek asked. He shook his head. "The point is that you are powerful, and you're dangerous. If you were freed, you would be a liability."

"I'm a liability in your possession too," the wisp said. "You're the one who can end this. It will be easier for both of us. Smash that jar, and I'll leave you alone. I'll leave this place entirely."

"And if I don't?" He adjusted his grip on his dagger.

"There's no need to kill me," the wisp said. "I'm not attacking you. I have to obey your orders. You brought me here, and you can make me leave." When Domek hesitated, it added, "Look at your hands. We bonded the moment you opened the jar, and will stay that way until you dismiss me, kill me…or perish." The wisp drifted closer. Domek could understand the men who had followed its soft light through the woods, searching for salvation and finding only death. "Free me. You didn't want this. You can stop this."

"You'll be relieved to hear that I don't want to deal with you either," Domek said. "But I'm not reckless enough to let you loose on the city. You should have a new master by the end of the night. It's what I should have done from the start."

"Planning on dying so soon?"

"You were right," Domek said. "I'd be too easy for you. Nothing you can offer me is going to be worth the risk of attempting to outwit you every time I open my mouth. Working with you wouldn't be worth it. Even if it benefited me, I couldn't be sure it wouldn't hurt someone else."

"A man whose honor outweighs his greed. That's unusual to find." The wisp's form flickered. "Tell me. The person you're handing me over to—are they as noble as you? Are you sure that they won't use my powers for the very things you're afraid I'd do on my own?"

Domek wanted to argue the point, but he held his tongue. Any more discussion with the wisp put him—and Prague—at risk. "I suppose we'll find out. Back in the jar until you're summoned again."

The wisp faded into mist and disappeared.

9

For the second time in two nights, Ora found herself underneath Prague. The bookstore would be long closed, Domek Myska tucked in some bed far away, while she journeyed through dark tunnels.

She had dressed for the occasion in her sturdiest boots and a lightweight riding gown. She had been careful picking the outfit; instead of going to the library or a pub with friends, she was sniffing out a nest of pijavice. Lina had begrudgingly helped her change again, too tired by the long day to argue.

She stepped over a puddle of what she hoped was water, and nearly slipped on the uneven path. Her transformation had given her strength and reflexes that humans couldn't hope for, and her eyes allowed her to make out most of the shapes in the darkness, but there was still something uncivilized and unnerving about wandering below the city.

It wasn't just pijavice and bubáks who had staked out the

tunnels and rooms underground for use. From the amount of oyster shells and empty bottles that lined some of the tunnels, Ora expected a great number of Prague's most desperate had wound up hiding there over the centuries. The winding paths of the forgotten town beneath the surface were easy to get lost in, both for its residents and any authorities from above. In some corners, she could smell the remains of humans who had fallen into a monster's grip: desiccated corpses that had stumbled into a bubák's lair and had starved in a mindless, terrified fugue, organs and bones left behind by roaming pijavice, and more.

When Ora had to sniff out other pijavice, she did so literally. Similarly to humans, who were rife with smells from their various organs and bodily functions, pijavice had a distinct scent. After their rebirth, their bodies were in stasis, propelled forward by the blood and flesh stolen from others. Rather than the scent of life, they smelled of the blood they stole and the magic that kept them moving, a potent mix of poison and lightning that lingered on the tongue.

Most pijavice passing in polite society like Ora used various perfumes to cover the smell, like potpourri in a coffin. However, the pijavice of the underground did not bother to hide themselves, nor the scents that came along with their residency. Blood was not uncommon in Prague. Butchers, tanners, surgeons, fighting rings—blood was spilled across the city every day; a red Vltava. Finding the subtle poison of the pijavice was like finding one raindrop in a storm. Luckily, in addition to her sharp nose, Ora had experience on her side.

She backtracked from two dead ends, and then nearly stumbled on a homeless family looking for a place to sleep. She hesitated around the corner, listening to the mother murmuring to her child. She took a step forward to warn them away, but where could they go? Nowhere in the city was safe, and Ora had a mission. She turned away, hoping the small family would find their way out of the tunnels before something else found them.

Finally, Ora found what she had been looking for.

The nest consisted of four pijavice in a filthy stone room at the bottom of a long set of steep stairs. 'Nest' was a misleading term, if only because it was used as commonly for baby birds as it was for pest infestations. These pijavice were the latter.

'Nest' was the human term for the pijavica groups that spawned underground, bound together either by a creator or a desire for mutual protection. Ora had been taught a different word for that bond—'blood families.' It was a callous joke. The only blood shared among the families was that of their victims. In fact, pijavice were driven by a mindless bloodlust targeting their own family bloodline. The first sign of a pijavica was often hearing whispers of a massacre inside a home, wiping out three generations of a family. After that, the only family left to them were the monsters who had created them.

Though not as deranged as Guttman, these were not the type of creatures Ora would have willingly spent time with even if they had been human. Ora was not selective when it came to the class of her friends, but she valued certain things that these pijavice lacked: decency, cleverness, and hygiene being chief among them.

If they had been humans, these pijavice were the type of men who sat in pubs all day, complaining about the money and women that hadn't fallen into their laps. Ora had never met these particular specimens before, but she knew the type. She could see it in their hungry eyes when she ducked into the nest.

The bare room could have passed for a lion's den. Blood, both fresh and rotten, caked the floor beside a pit in the corner of the room. Once a well, it seemed to now serve for disposal of the pijavice's victims. Ora listened carefully, but the pit was silent. That was a relief. Ora would not have been able to leave a human in these monsters' care, and she had not dressed for a fight.

"What do we have here?" one of them hissed. All four of them had discarded their human façades, mouths split wide to show dark fangs.

"A tasty treat," said another, a broad man with a surprisingly ruddy face for a pijavica. He must have fed recently.

Another one, so skinny that he could have passed for a sapling, punched him in the arm. "Smell her. She's one of us," he said.

The other man shrugged. "There are all different types of treats."

"I'm no one's 'treat,'" Ora said, moving into the room. The tension made her nails sharpen to vicious points, and her jaw unhinged to reveal her second, sharper set of teeth.

From the corner, a pijavica with hooded eyes and blood-stained sleeves drawled, "All dressed up for us. Be a shame to let it go to waste."

"I was transformed before any of you were even born. I'll be asking the questions here."

The first pijavica who had spoken got to his feet with disconcerting speed considering his size. He towered over the room like an oak in a field of wheat. "The only question left is who gets you first."

In a blink, he charged her. Ora didn't hesitate. Using his momentum against him, she ducked and heaved, sending him flying headfirst into the stone wall behind them. He crumpled to the ground, splashing in a rancid puddle. Before he could find his feet again, she landed on top of him. She drove her claws under his ribs, punching through his tough skin to reach his poisoned heart. She plucked it from the arteries it dangled from, and held it aloft. It dissolved in her hand, along with the body beneath her.

She stood, flicking blood from her hand. "Let's start this over," she hissed, the words elongating with her altered jaw. "I'm here to ask some questions. No one will touch me, so no one else will get hurt. I'm not looking for another fight—I'd prefer answers before your deaths. I've faced pijavice far more experienced and numerous than you."

For a moment, she stayed tense, waiting for the rest of the pijavice to avenge their friend. Instead, the skinny one chuckled. "Horan always picked fights he couldn't win."

Crossing her arms, Ora said, "I could do the same to each of you." Her claws pricked through the fabric of her sleeves like thorns.

"I'd enjoy that," he said. The single candle that lit their hovel illuminated the strands of saliva dripping from his own needle-sharp fangs. "What are you offering? If you're not here for fun, that is. I assume you're not wanting to take our spot."

Ora looked around the room. It reeked of offal and dirty pijavice. "Decidedly not." She reluctantly took another breath— she needed the air for speech, if not for the oxygen. "I can offer your lives."

"For all we know, you'll kill us in the end anyway," he said.

"I don't kill for fun. Answer my questions, or I'll make sure someone less nice than me finds their way to your hovel."

There was a quiet conversation among the group. "All right," the skinny one said. "What do you want to know?"

"Excellent. How much do you know about the other pijavice in Prague?"

The pijavica, who seemed to have taken the role of leader after Horan's loss, said, "We fight them for territory and blood when it comes down to it. With the lamplighters popping up everywhere, it's getting harder to keep territory. We're being kept underground. One killed a friend of ours in the Jewish Quarter last week. That neighborhood has gotten harder and harder to hunt in now that the ghetto has been opened."

"Tragic. Have you heard any rumors about anything… strange going on?" Ora was already losing hope in finding answers here. This was akin to asking a pack of rabid dogs whether they'd heard the news about local city politics.

"The butcher down on Botolph Lane started carrying venison," the pijavica said. "Not as good as fresh flesh and blood, but it keeps you alive during a slow week when there's no human or pork."

"I actually prefer venison to pork," Ora commented, and then shook her head. This was getting her nowhere. "Interesting, but irrelevant. I'm speaking of bigger whispers. Whispers about…a cure."

"A cure for what?"

"The type of cure that sends you back into the sunlight. Something that undoes the pijavica curse and makes you mortal again."

The pijavica recoiled. "That exists?"

"That's what I'm trying to figure out."

"Terrible."

"I don't know," Ora said thoughtfully. "I don't mind the idea." She couldn't remember what the sun felt like, but she remembered its warm scent. The way it bathed everything in richness and made the whole world more vivid. It had glinted off the gold accents around the city. Every church and statue in Prague was tipped with gold, an incorruptible substance on top of blackened sandstone and corroded copper. At night, it all looked the same. Gold was for the living.

The pijavica nudged its nearest companion. "What do you think, Stiven? Would you give up everything to get back in the sun?"

"And lose the power? Not on your life," Stiven said. "Why be a sheep when you can be a wolf?"

Ora glanced around the hovel again. The pijavice reminded her more of maggots than wolves, but she was still trying to find answers. Insulting them would just lead to more fighting, and she already was concerned about the state of her dress. "So, none of you have heard anything."

The skinny pijavica shook his head. "If there were something big stirring up, we wouldn't be the ones to know, would we? You should be talking to the Zizkovs. I'm surprised you didn't go there first, with your fancy gown."

"You mean the little group over in Smichov?" Ora asked. "They're small time, self-contained. They take care of themselves."

"Where have you been?" he asked incredulously. "The Zizkov family moved out of Smichov and are in Kampa Island now. They have money, and they have an enforcer who works for them that can rip a man in half without trying."

"The Zizkovs? You can't be serious. They're just thugs. I've never heard of them doing anything relevant at all."

If someone was creating a cure, they'd need some scientific guidance. Ora had been listening to gossip for years, and there was little to no legitimate scholarship about her race. Any experimentation, whether run by humans or other pijavice, had usually been so gruesome that they couldn't sustain themselves. There was little appreciation for the sanctity of pijavica life, and they would need extravagant resources and manpower to test any sort of cure. A group of common criminals who had gotten to the top of the power wheel by sheer luck wouldn't have the brains.

"I don't know anything about all that," he said. "All I can tell you is that if you're looking for information in Prague beyond where to find the sweetest blood, the Zizkovs are the place to start. They're in control in this city."

"You almost sound impressed. Why haven't you gone begging to join their family yet instead of living down here?"

"You're joking. They're half the reason we're hiding down here. When they're around, pijavice disappear. I don't want any of their business—or yours."

Ora tapped her fingers on her chin. She hadn't seen a family strike fear in the hearts of sewer rats since her time with Lord Czernin. If the Zizkovs had managed to bring the lower predators to heel while keeping their activities quiet from both Sokol and Ora, they were more competent than she'd expected. "If they come by, don't tell them I was here."

The pijavica shrugged, a sharp, jittery motion. "Hopefully they won't ask."

Domek tugged at the scarf around his neck as he walked down the streets of Prague. He could feel bruises forming in his soft flesh. It seemed unfair that he had to continue with his patrol after nearly being strangled by the wisp, but he had a duty. At the end of his shift, he would take the wisp to Paluska, but he could not leave the streets unattended until then. A steady drizzle coated the world in a layer of water without the satisfaction of a real storm. Domek was tempted to go back to the nearest lamp and turn up the gas to create a flame with real heat he could rest in for a moment.

He resisted the urge. In the twenty years since gas lamps had been introduced to Prague, the inventors had been working on ways to make the system safer, but there were still the occasional explosions. Most of them were from simple human error, or an accidental gas leak. Some, including one Domek had been involved in the year before, were only *reported* as accidents; gas explosions were a quick method to exterminate monsters when there were no other options. The tunnels beneath Prague were impossible to monitor and patrol: narrow, labyrinthine, and far from the sun. But nothing could survive obliteration.

Around him, the trees planted along the rail by the river shook with a passing wind. To his right, the fountain at the center of the small Park of National Awakening stood taller than the trees. Domek remembered when the fountain had been completed nearly two decades ago. With its intricate spire and collected statues, it nearly seemed as though it could have always been there, but the sandstone was still mostly pale rather than blackened with age like its companions on Charles Bridge. The water inside burbled quietly, barely audible over the nearby river.

The bridge arched ahead, and Domek rubbed absently at the healing cut on his inner arm that had saved him from the attack. His branded palm seemed silver in the lamplight. When he had run to save the woman, he never could have predicted the strange events to follow.

Stepping around a bench by the river, Domek nearly slipped on the wet path. His boots had had solid traction when he'd first gotten them, but years of use had left the bottoms dangerously slick. He caught himself on the back of the bench, but the moment of distraction cost him.

Movement flickered in the corner of his eye, and then arms clamped tight around him. One covered his mouth, muffling his instinctive shout, and the other wrapped around his waist to pull him with superhuman speed across the street into the Park of National Awakening. Mud splattered around his boots as his feet dragged against the ground.

"Were you the man on patrol in this area last night?" The voice that hissed in his ear had a polished accent, crisp as an apple. Domek thought it was appropriate to try to bite the creature, but the hand over his mouth moved before he made contact.

"Let me go," Domek snarled.

"You or one of your colleagues was here last night. They had a run-in with a friend of ours," the pijavica continued. "A woman told us that a lamplighter saved her."

"What did you do to her?" he demanded, struggling to get loose.

"You should be more worried about what we're going to do to you," said a voice behind them. It came from another man with a similarly posh accent.

Domek tried to reach into his pocket for his stake, but the pijavica jerked his arms behind his body. Domek's wrists ground together, trapped in a vise.

"Your 'friend' deserved what he got," Domek spat.

"I'm sure he did," the second pijavica said mildly before

jerking on Domek's satchel. For a moment, the leather dug painfully into his shoulder—a strange echo of the night's earlier struggle in the alley—before sliding free.

They were going after the will-o'-the-wisp. Domek should have gotten rid of the jar as soon as he'd found it. He struggled to get loose, but the pijavica was able to keep his wrists together without effort. This was exactly the sort of situation Paluska and the other veteran monster fighters told them to avoid. Pijavice were stronger than humans in every physical sense. Lamplighters relied on the element of surprise to win their fights. These two had been waiting for Domek, seeming to know what to expect.

He was only still alive because they would need to interrogate him if they couldn't find the wisp on him. As soon as the pijavica found the jar at the bottom of his satchel, Domek would be dead. He wondered if the brand on his hands would fade after death, magic and life draining out with his last breath.

He shouldn't have been so quick to tell the wisp that he didn't need its help. It had gotten rid of the bubák in moments—could it do the same to his current assailants? With it tucked inside the bag, he would never know.

Domek's brow furrowed. He had assumed that he would need to be holding the jar in order to access the wisp's powers, but if that was the case, what was the point of the bond? Why were his hands branded if the wisp was only his when the container was in his grasp?

One of the lessons Paluska drilled into their heads since the first day of training was to take advantage of any opportunity that presented itself. Waiting to weigh each idea was dangerous when fighting creatures with five times the reaction speed of humans. No matter how much he had fumbled his last attempt to instruct the wisp, he couldn't let his embarrassment lead to his death.

Domek clasped his hands behind his back. The scars pressed together, warm to the touch. "Wis—" he began to call, but the pijavica holding him was too fast. It clocked him across the head with enough force to daze him, and then wrapped a cold hand over his mouth again like a vise.

Domek jerked and struggled, fighting the haze from the blow to his head.

The other pijavica ignored the scuffle, digging through Domek's bag with focused efficiency. Domek's lamplighting tools clattered to the cobblestones. Any moment, the pijavica would close its hands on the jar and this would be over.

Then, between one blink and the next, there was another figure in the park.

Despite the speed of her arrival, the pale woman stood for a moment as though she had been there all night. Even though the wind had died, her long, white hair drifted in a breeze Domek could not feel. As Domek had thought in his brief glimpse of her last night, she was a wall of white. A long, frilled nightgown swept toward the ground, but did not touch the grass. It was impossible to tell her age from her expressionless face, which was blurred as though he were viewing it from a hundred meters away rather than two.

She was silent, watching them with dark eyes that stood out like coal scattered on a snowdrift. The pijavica holding Domek had noticed her as well, if its sudden stillness was any indication, while the other remained oblivious. It made a triumphant noise when it reached the bottom of the bag.

The White Lady's serene face contorted into a silent scream. Though her lips were as pale as the rest of her, the inside of her mouth was a vivid, dark red.

The pijavica holding Domek took a breath as if about to speak, but the White Lady was already across the park. She grabbed the pijavica holding Domek's bag and threw it as easily as someone tearing a weed from their garden. The pijavica hit the fountain with a grotesque smack, destroying one of the stone figures, and fell into the water with a splash. Domek's bag dropped to the grass.

Domek used the distraction to wrest himself free, using the monster's weight to knock it off-balance. He stumbled away, anticipating a fresh assault, but the pijavica was focused on the White Lady.

She was standing over the pijavica in the fountain, mouth still contorted in its silent scream. She lifted her pale hands and seemed to grasp the air in front of her. When she suddenly twisted her hands in opposing directions, the pijavica jerked, and then subsided into dust. His clothes sank into the water, empty.

The White Lady turned to Domek and the second pijavica. The monster turned and sprinted away, moving with supernatural speed toward a side street. Unfortunately for it, even the pijavica's speed wasn't enough to combat this spirit.

There was another blur, and the White Lady was upon it. Domek left it to its fate in favor of scrambling on the ground for his fallen stakes. No one in the lamplighters had ever fought the castle's White Lady. According to Paluska, she never left the walkways of the castle, and was no threat to the city.

Clearly, Paluska didn't know as much as Domek had once believed.

Domek recovered one of his two stakes and jumped back to his feet, holding it at the ready. Silver was a better weapon against spirits than hawthorn, but he couldn't afford to be particular.

The second pijavica was already dust, its clothes strewn on the cobblestones as though it had been killed while still running. The White Lady stood facing Domek, her palms open by her sides. Her mouth was closed, and her gaze darted around the park.

Domek kept his stake at his side and held up a placating hand. "I—" he began. The word rang loudly, making Domek realize how quiet the fight had been.

She lunged toward him, fast as thought. He stumbled backward, slashing toward her face with his stake. The hawthorn passed through her as though she were only a memory, but the hand that collided with his cheek was solid enough.

Domek was lucky he had already been ducking, or the blow would have been enough to snap his neck. As it was, he tumbled back through the grass, hands scraping against the dirt. The stakes would be useless, but he was not weaponless. "Wisp," he shouted, clapping his bloodied hands together. "Come here!"

The White Lady jolted, startled. Her dark red mouth opened again, a horrified, violent wail. By the time the wisp finished its sparkling light show emerging from his fallen bag, she was gone.

Domek blinked and looked around, expecting to find her lurking behind him, but she had left as quickly as she had arrived. He waited for another few seconds, but the night was quiet.

The wisp floated in the dark, illuminating the scattered clothes of the fallen pijavica. "You called?"

"Back in the jar," Domek panted.

The wisp dissolved again with a disgruntled hiss. Domek quickly returned his now muddied belongings to the bag, awkwardly keeping his stake in one hand. The wisp's jar was still safely tucked at the bottom, protected from the fall by the leather bag.

Once he had his belongings, he left the park and its piles of ashes behind.

The pijavice had figured out that Domek had taken the wisp's jar. The chances that the first pijavica hadn't known what he had been carrying were dwindling fast. Why would a pijavica need a will-o'-the-wisp? They were already faster and stronger than humans, and functionally immortal. If the two races of demons teamed up, humanity was in danger.

It was becoming increasingly obvious that he was entirely out of his depth, like a swimmer who stepped into a lake without realizing a vodník was waiting to pull him to his death. There was no time to finish his patrol, not with so many forces out to harm him.

He needed to step away before someone got killed.

10

Domek spent the walk through the Old Town on edge, watching the shadows for another pijavica. A crouching figure peered at him through the darkness, and he jolted in alarm before realizing it was a stray dog. He tore a strip of dried meat from a wrapped bundle in his satchel and tossed it to the dog before moving on.

The leader of the lamplighters lived near the Powder Tower in a modest, narrow house squeezed between two nearly identical structures, all beige with the same architecture, as though a printing error had produced three duplicate pages in a row. His neighbors had added to their homes with bright paint on their shutters and flowers popping from windowsills, but Paluska's residence was as somber as the man.

Every lamplighter knew the address, even though Domek had only been once. The lamplighters were spread thin, and Paluska thought it was important to have a place they could report any emergencies in person. Though Domek, unlike some of his fellows, was literate, there was some information too sensitive for a messenger. In tonight's case, some of the information was simply too difficult to summarize.

Like his subordinates, Paluska kept late hours, so Domek only had to wait a few moments after knocking for the door to open. Paluska's valet, an elderly man browned and wrinkled like an apple set out in the sun for too long, greeted him and led him inside.

Paluska had committed a large amount of his own money toward the lamplighter initiative. There was a shadowy branch of the government aware of their actions, but the responsibility and management belonged to Paluska. Given the amount of his own money that went into weaponry and recruitment, it was no wonder his home was impressive. Though modest in size, the fact that he had a full building to himself was enough to awe Domek. Inside the old city walls, space was difficult to come by.

Domek was left in Paluska's study to wait. Three of the walls were sparsely decorated with paintings, ranging from portraits of austere strangers to landscapes of foreign locales. The effect all together was of glimpsing flashes of memory laid bare. The fourth wall, in a glinting, ornate counterpoint, showcased a large collection of weapons. In addition to the expected swords and daggers, there were several rifles as well. While waiting for the lamplighter master, Domek occupied himself examining the hanging swords. Each was unique: some had carvings etched on bare blade; others were rustic and functional, like something a farmer in the outskirts would have picked up to defend his home. All had worn handles and sharp blades.

"Admiring my collection?" Paluska asked, coming into the

room. "I've gathered them from around the world."

"They're impressive," Domek said.

"I've always found swords to be a useful weapon when hunting what we do," Paluska said. "These are all dipped in silver and then rubbed with hawthorn ash once a month. With most modern swords made of steel, our prey rarely expects to meet the kiss of death at the edge of a blade. There's an element of surprise, and an elegance not found in the up-close nature of the stake."

"What about the guns? Imrich refuses to work with them."

"For good reason. I tried, in my earlier days, but they're a clumsy weapon. Unless you drop the monster with your first shot before it notices you, you're dead. But you're not here to talk about my collection."

"I'm not," Domek agreed.

Paluska went behind his desk to take a seat, gesturing for Domek to sit down as well. The desk seemed to be mostly for show. Other than a thick journal and a battered fountain pen, the surface was empty. It was as though the room was meant to showcase his wall décor, and the desk was an afterthought. Domek was not surprised that Paluska had not settled into a sedentary life. Despite his age, he was a warrior at heart, and would always choose to be on the streets rather than sitting with a pen and paper.

"We haven't had a chance to speak one-on-one very often, Myska," he said. "I'm glad you're here. I've thought for a while that you're a strong asset for this organization. Your friend, Anton, has a lot of positive things to say about you. I'm grateful to have you on our side. You're not here looking for Anton, are you? His training ended, and he's out on patrol by now."

"No. I'm here to talk to you."

"All right. What brings you here in the middle of the night, Myska?"

Domek took a deep breath. "You told us to come talk to you if we found anything...unusual."

Paluska leaned forward, raising his eyebrows. "You've encountered something."

Domek nodded. "A will-o'-the-wisp."

"That's not so unusual. They're rare in the city—they prefer the countryside—but not unheard of."

"This one had been bound somehow. I found it in a jar."

"Bound?"

"Or so it says. It obeyed my orders."

"I didn't know wisps could speak," Paluska said.

His mother had known. How much did Paluska truly understand about creatures beyond the usual demons of Prague? "This one could."

Paluska tapped his chin. "Humans can't control wisps. We don't have the power. That's very unusual magic. You don't know how it was captured?"

"I don't. I tried not to talk to it for long," Domek said. "A pijavica I killed last night was carrying it. I assumed it was the creator."

"It seems beyond a pijavica's skills, unless they learned something we don't know. If they have, we're in trouble. Either way, it's disturbing that they had it at all. I don't know what they would use its power for, but it's certainly not good."

"Do you think they were allies?" Domek asked.

"Who can know the minds of monsters? Do they have allies? It seems unlikely the pijavica was ignorant of what it had, whether it was planning a partnership or to use it as a servant. We need to find out what they were planning. This can't bode well."

"Why would a pijavica need a wisp? I've been wondering and can't come up with any reason. They have their own powers."

"Not like this demon might have. Capturing creatures can change their nature. It may be more powerful with your will to guide it than it was when it was free. Their powers bring instability, so outside will can shape it into something more precise, like an arrow. We can use this to our advantage. We could change the tide of this endless battle."

"But it's a monster. It nearly killed me tonight."

Gaze sharpening, Paluska said, "You said it obeyed your orders."

"It did," Domek said. "I…made a mistake. It was looking for an excuse to attack me. We can't trust its powers."

"We would be more careful," Paluska said. "Understanding something is the key to controlling it. Imrich will have an idea. We would be cautious, of course, but a potential weapon like this doesn't fall into our laps every day. The pijavice were planning on using it. We can't afford to stand on principle and give away such a powerful tool. You're part of this team. You can help us make the decisions. You are the one who found it, after all."

"It doesn't want to be used. It would be dangerous."

"Our lives are a study in risk," Paluska said. "I have faith that together we could handle one will-o'-the-wisp. I'm sure Imrich will know what to do. Where is it? Do you have it with you?"

If Domek handed it over now, he'd be giving the wisp a new master, a new team of masters. The more people who knew it existed, the more people who had access to its power, the more likely it was that someone would give into the temptation to use it like Domek had—and doom themselves and everyone around them.

Was it arrogance that made Domek want to keep the wisp to himself, or was it reasonable caution? He could look for a way to safely get rid of it, if he had the time. There was no cause for anyone to use it.

When Domek had been a child, his mother had always noted his tendency toward introspection with both amusement and concern. She used to say that he could think himself in or out of anything if he put the time in. He was a solemn, awkward child, with an attraction to mechanics that he didn't inherit from either parent. He had never understood her concern. Making decisions without all the facts invited mistakes.

Paluska, it seemed, had few of the facts. He had never heard of a captured wisp, knew less about them than Domek's mother, had told them all not to fear the White Lady, and now he wanted to use the wisp even after hearing that Domek had nearly been killed.

"I don't," Domek lied, carefully not looking at his satchel. "I had patrol duty tonight. I didn't want to risk carrying it around. I came here straight after to tell you what I'd found."

"Smart, very smart," Paluska said. "You have a level head, Myska. You're doing the right thing, handing it over. Not many people would be able to resist the temptation to use it for themselves. Where is it now?"

"It's safe," Domek said. "I thought I should warn you in advance so you can plan ways to keep it secure."

"The lamplighters are Prague's best protectors," Paluska said. "I'm sure we can defend one jar."

"Even from each other?"

Paluska frowned. "This is a brotherhood, Myska. You need to trust your fellows."

"Would you?" Domek asked. "Even with unlimited power? You, I trust. Anton too, of course. But the others? Men who would protect this city from monsters aren't immune to other temptations, especially one we don't understand."

Paluska leaned back in his chair. "I hate to admit it, but you're right. Maybe I was too tempted by the idea. This isn't something we can spread widely, unless we want to end up with an extra smile carved into our throats. Who else knows about this?"

"Only you," Domek said. "And any other pijavica who knew the one I attacked last night was carrying it." He nearly mentioned the attack he'd fended off earlier that night, but it would have given Paluska more reason to demand the wisp from him.

"Good. Keep it safe for now," Paluska said. "This could change the tide of our fight."

Domek nodded, pressing his leg against his satchel. "Yes, sir."

By the time Domek left Paluska's house, it was nearly two in the morning and his exhaustion felt like lead boots dragging down his feet. In his bag, the jar seemed to weigh a stone—or was it the guilt? Paluska placed more trust in Domek than he deserved. He had tested the wisp earlier that night, and then had tried to call for its help against the pijavice and the White Lady. What right did he have to decide the wisp's fate?

He looked back over his shoulder at the front door he'd just left. Perhaps he had made a mistake.

"Hey."

Domek whirled around, stake in hand. There was a lithe figure standing in the shadows at the corner.

"Slow down," the man said. "No need to stab anyone." He stepped forward, face half-illuminated by the streetlamp nearby. He was close to Domek's age, clean-shaven and well-dressed, with curly hair under a top hat.

"If you don't want to get stabbed, you shouldn't startle strangers at night," Domek said, lowering his stake but keeping a hold of it.

"I've been waiting for you to come out," he said. "I have an offer for you."

Domek sighed. After the last day, an aggressive grifter on the street was nearly a relief. "I'm not interested," he said, giving him a short nod and starting up the street.

"I saw you fighting off that bubák," he called after him, voice laconic and far too loud.

"I don't know what you mean," Domek said, turning around. This wasn't a conversation he wanted to be having in public, no matter how late the hour. If the man had seen the bubák, that meant he'd almost certainly seen the wisp.

"Don't play dumb. I've worked on these streets at least as long as you have. I don't close my eyes to what's hiding in the shadows, and neither do you. Now, you'll want to hear my offer."

"You're not a lamplighter," Domek said.

"How did you guess?" the man drawled. "The name's Bazil. I'm the proprietor of The Pigeon Hole."

"Honest business, is it?" Domek asked, looking up and down the street again. The man was too slick. There was no sign of his backup, but that didn't mean he didn't have any. Even with the gas lamps lighting the street, there were always places to hide.

"Is there any such thing?" he drawled. "Now, I have a

proposition for you. You've made my night very exciting. I've been trying to confirm rumors about the possibility of containing and controlling spirits for years. When I saw the fire you wielded, I could hardly believe my eyes. It took me a minute to recognize it. I've never seen anything like it. A wisp in a jar. I didn't know that was possible." He took a step forward, smiling brightly. "I'm so curious about it."

Domek stepped back in tandem. "It's mine. And I don't enjoy being followed."

"Yes, so I gathered from that," he said, nodding toward Domek's stake. "I'm no fang, though."

"And you know about pijavice as well," Domek said.

"And ghosts and the others. Most people like to pretend they're just a story. A fiction created by drunk farmers to give us something more interesting to fear than other humans," he said. "The government encourages that misconception. If I weren't on the streets every day, maybe I'd believe that too. I know what they're capable of, and turning a blind eye has never been one of my strong suits. I like to know what's happening around me, even when everyone else would rather pretend it's not there. My job is to know what's happening."

"Are you part of one of the old groups? Do you hunt the monsters too?" The man was thin, but muscle could hide on all bodies. Before the lamplighters had taken their sanctioned role as watchmen, there had been a long line of other groups trying to protect Prague. Some had been loved for their secret efforts, some reviled for seeming to be at the heart of all trouble.

"God, no. Pijavice are half my business—they pay for private space at my club to do what they will, and are always curious about the information I can offer them. They're not cooperative at returning that favor, though. That's why I'm interested in what you've found."

A business that catered to pijavice. What was the world coming to? "You help pijavice and you still believe I'd listen to a word you have to say? You're a traitor to humanity."

"You're making a mistake. I have information you need. Resources you don't. I'm a good man to have on your side, Domek Myska."

"We have different understandings of what makes a good man."

"Clearly."

"Stop following me. You know I have the power to take care of myself." He held up the stake. He had never wielded it against a human, but Bazil did not know that. "Get out of my sight."

Bazil tipped his hat to him. "You'll regret this," he warned, but turned away.

Domek watched until the man was out of sight before he started on a winding route to his next destination. As he walked, he kept one hand on the hawthorn stake in his pocket and the other inside his satchel, resting against the warm jar.

Just in case.

Once Domek was sure that he wasn't being followed by Bazil, he paused at a corner and changed directions. This late, the streets were eerily quiet. A handful of people passed, all tucked into their coats as though they could disappear if they didn't show their faces. Domek wondered what they had been doing, and whether they knew the dangers of staying out so late. Though Domek knew the type of criminals that hid in the darkness, he also knew that innocents were caught outside after sunset. People made mistakes and rash decisions—inadvisable romances, drinking a few pints too many, or just working on a ship that didn't make it to port until the middle of the night. When Domek had first started working as a lamplighter, he had been frustrated by all the people who continued to venture into the night. Didn't they realize the danger? If everyone stayed home, Domek wouldn't have to risk his life to protect them.

Over time, though, he realized that life couldn't be contained to daylight hours. For every human or pijavica that used the dark to prey on passersby, there were a dozen people just trying to make it home. Prague belonged to all of them, and Domek would be damned if they would be made unsafe in their own city.

Domek cut down a side street. An iron gate was set into a tall stone wall, covered with vines and pointed leaves. Putting his satchel across his body to keep it secure, Domek deftly scaled the gate, using a low, solid tree branch that jutted out near the iron bars to hoist himself high enough. As a child, Domek had scaled innumerable fences to escape his father. Scraped hands were better than the alternative.

The small garden was lit only by the waxing moon and dim starlight peeking through passing clouds. The grasses seemed silver, as delicate and beautiful as the gilded altars in the town's churches. Hedges sprawled onto the stone pathways, untrimmed for years. A fountain at the center of the small space featured a quartet of women with instruments, their delicate faces dark with mold.

To an outside eye, the layers of Prague, built on top of each other for centuries, seemed to preclude the possibility of privacy. Every moment of solitude was guaranteed to be interrupted by a group of French tourists visiting the health spas or a class of students flocking past. Even at night, when the humans moved inside and darker things prowled, ever-present windows stared down at the streets. However, each city dweller found their own pockets of secret quiet, even if it were only a rock shaded by a tree on Petřín Hill.

Domek had stumbled onto the abandoned garden near his flat one night after patrol. After asking some neighbors, he learned that the broad, pistachio green home had been owned by a man with no children. After his death three years earlier, the estate had become tangled in a legal battle as his nephews fought for ownership. In the meantime, the vast building and garden went to waste, slowly reclaimed by nature.

The stink of the city, the sour musk of too many humans in close proximity, never left the air, but here the grass beneath his feet was fresh and green, and white flowers bloomed on several trees that lined the garden. He leaned against a wide oak tree, the bark scratching against his shirt, and pulled the jar from his bag.

He had spent the whole day trying to find answers, but he hadn't asked the only being who had them. It was time to change that. There were pijavice and thieves after the wisp, all of whom could use its powers to hurt the lamplighters and the innocents of the city. Domek needed to understand precisely what they were hunting. There was no doubt in Domek's mind that if Paluska had the wisp, he would find a way to use it. Giving it to Paluska would keep it safe from outsiders, but the lamplighters weren't the most patient group. If one of the brasher members got a hold of the jar, they could be corrupted by the temptation.

If Domek could not trust the wisp to his own people, he would be obligated to destroy it. And though it had done nothing but threaten him, something in Domek recoiled at the idea of killing a creature bound to his care.

Domek placed his branded palms against the jar. "Come out, but be silent."

The wisp appeared before him. Its fiery form glowed in the dark, but the wall and home would likely block any peering eyes. Ignoring him, the wisp turned as though looking toward the night sky. The clouds parted for just a moment, like an eye blinking, to reveal a patch of star-strewn sky overhead. Infinity stretched over them for a breath, and then the clouds closed back together like storm water swirling in the river, swallowing anything that dropped into its currents.

"Hello," Domek said, taking a fortifying breath.

The wisp was silent.

"You said before that you would follow my orders, correct? That's where I went wrong earlier. I wasn't clear enough."

Impassive, the wisp did not move.

"Then take note. You cannot harm me, or any other human, no matter what you believe I've ordered you to do," Domek said, speaking the orders he'd been carefully phrasing for the last hour. "Now you can speak."

"Where's the new master you promised me?"

Domek ignored the question. "Tell me about your previous master."

"You tell me," the wisp said. "I still don't know how you acquired me."

"A pijavica had your jar. I killed it," Domek said. "Was it the one who put you in there? Have pijavice figured out a way to capture your kind?"

The wisp hesitated, and then said, "No. It wasn't the pijavica who trapped me. It was a vodník."

"A vodník?" Domek looked at the jar in his hands. If he had looked more closely at the jars stuck in the mud beneath Evka's killer, would he have found the same pattern carved into their clay? "I didn't realize vodníks could capture other spirits."

"Neither did I. But what am I but a soul? It trapped me in that cold, dark place for countless years, smothering my essence. I knew that if I did burst free from the jar, I would be immediately destroyed by the pond's water."

"Then how did the pijavice find you? What did they want with you?"

"I don't know their minds."

Domek ran a hand through his hair as he thought. "Water would kill you? Is that the only way wisps die?"

"There are other ways," the wisp told him. "Why, do you plan on trying?"

There was something unsettling about the fact that Domek could make the creature betray its own weaknesses just by asking. Guilt clenched his guts in a fist. Finding the jar and getting bound to the wisp had felt like a curse on Domek. He was starting to wonder now if the wisp saw it the same way. "If I weren't to kill you, how would I get rid of you?"

"You could die," it said. "You can gift the jar to someone else, though the bond won't break until someone else holds it and summons me. Someone could steal it from you and take ownership. Or you could free me."

Domek leaned back against the tree. "Do you have a name?"

"I do," said the wisp.

"Tell me."

"I've gone by Kája."

"Kája," Domek repeated. A Czech name. Somehow, Domek had expected something more unusual. "I'm Domek Myska."

"I don't care."

"Why are you so determined to work against me?" Domek asked. "You're malicious, but you don't seem evil. You could have killed me in that alley. The more I think about it, the more I think you were trying to scare me into freeing you. Why go through all the trouble when you could just work with me?"

"You? The man who controls my spirit against my will? I have no reason to trust you. Most men are selfish, disgusting creatures," the wisp said. "They will lie, steal, cheat, and murder to get ahead. When they're suddenly given the power to change the world, nearly all of them immediately use it for self-gain, no matter the cost."

"Not all men, though," Domek said.

"Majority rules in this world," Kája said. "Even men who exist under everyone's notice for years, following the rules they were given, lose all sight of their values when someone tells them that they're exempt from normal laws. You say 'not all men,' but you're the same. The moment you ran into trouble, you called me forward to win your battles."

"I told you that was a test," Domek pointed out.

"Are you saying that if you ran into trouble again that you wouldn't summon me immediately? You would die before calling me to aid you?"

It was right. Domek had tried to summon it not three hours after the last time. If the White Lady had not fled, he would have used it to overcome her. He threw up his hands. "Fine, you're right. Of course you're right. When it comes to life or death, I'll use whatever resources I have."

"Even if that resource is a slave you got by killing someone else," the wisp said.

"You're not a—" Domek cut himself off mid-sentence. Was declaring that the wisp wasn't a slave enough to constitute wishing him free? "I killed it to save someone else. It was just a pijavica."

"And you're just a human."

"Do you not realize that pijavice kill innocents?"

"So do humans. So do you. From what I saw earlier, pijavice simply do it with more skill than you."

"I'm not a murderer. I've spent my life trying to protect people," Domek said, twisting the grass beneath his fingers. "I've risked death for years trying to make these streets safer for innocents to live in. It's my job."

"Give men weapons and tell them they have a righteous war, and they'll do anything."

"I don't want to battle you and control you," Domek pressed. "I want you to work with me voluntarily against the monsters. People should be able to live without fear. It *is* a righteous war, one that's worth fighting."

"I could. I won't, unless you force me to."

Fuming, Domek said, "Back in the jar. Don't come out again until I summon you."

"As you wish, Master," Kája said before dematerializing. Though Domek had instructed the wisp to stay quiet, he had left another flaw for Kája to exploit. On its way back into the jar, the wisp glowed so brightly that it seemed like a beacon to all Prague, flashing bright sparks of every color imaginable. The fireworks lasted a long, breathtaking moment, illuminating the overgrown garden. By the time it disappeared, Domek was blinking away lingering stains on his eyes.

11

After leaving her meeting with the pijavice underground, all Ora wanted was a few hours alone in her home to rest from the world. However, Sokol was waiting for her report in a nearby government office. The building was unobtrusive, overshadowed by the towering castle just behind it, painted a dull gold and unmarked aside from a small plaque etched with the Empire's double-headed eagle. The road outside cut at a steep angle, building toward the castle. From the name on the office's doorplate, Sokol was borrowing the space overnight. Like his prey, Sokol kept nocturnal hours. She told him what she had learned; namely that the nest hadn't been any help on their case whatsoever, but that there was a new pijavica family in power. He perked up at the mention of the Zizkovs like a dog spotting a choice scrap of meat.

"We need to find out more about them," he said. Despite his familiarity with the night shift, he still looked tired. Perhaps it was the job, rather than the hour. It was as strange to see his bulky form in a stale government office as it was to see him in her sitting room. Was there anywhere outside a battlefield where this man looked comfortable? "I had also heard that pijavice were going missing. If these Zizkovs are behind that, they may be behind this alleged cure as well."

"Not bad for a night's work. Are we done?"

"We still don't know what they're doing, or how they're doing it. I can't send my men into a situation with so little information. What if all these missing pijavice are waiting for them inside the Zizkovs' door?"

"I'm sure you and your brilliant team will figure it out," Ora said. "I gave you their name and their new neighborhood. Put a man to watch every door until he sees someone licking blood from their lips."

He shook his head. "This is pijavica power politics. From what you heard, it's a complicated mess. These Zizkovs are playing games. Even the others are scared of them for some reason."

"I've already shaken some answers out of some sewer scum. They won't know much more, even if I find another flavor. There's nothing I can do that you can't. You're the professional, Sokol. You're good at this."

A smile twitched at his mouth—he was not immune to her flattery. His eyes were intense on her face, gaze lingering for a moment on her lips. It wasn't the first time. Ora was never quite sure whether he was envisioning her fangs or…something else. She was distracted enough by the heat in his stare that it took her a moment to wrap her mind around his next statement. "You could ask the expert of pijavica politics."

"Oh, no," Ora said, blinking. "Not a chance."

"You have access to the man who has played every pijavica throughout the Empire like a puppet master pulling strings for centuries," Sokol said. "Instead of interrogating the whole city, you could ask one man and answer all our questions."

"If he's cared to learn anything," Ora said. "It sounded as though these Zizkovs are new. Lord Czernin plays the long game. He wins chess matches before they're started. He won't waste his resources on pawns."

"We won't know if they're pawns unless we learn more," Sokol said. "If there is a nest of pijavice who learn how to cure themselves, we need to know. Why would pijavice be trying to rid themselves of their powers? You said yourself that the pijavice in the sewer were horrified by the idea. You're the only one I've met who wasn't salivating for more power, not less. Pijavice bleed everything dry—there's a reason they're named for leeches."

"Thank you."

He ignored her. "I need to know what they're doing. If they truly are looking for a cure, if they've found a way to eliminate the poison that causes the bloodlust, I would move mountains to make sure it was administered to every pijavica on the continent. If they have some darker ulterior motive, I need to know that too. This isn't what I've been trained to handle. That's why I need your help."

Her help. As though requesting she walk back into Lord Czernin's grasp were as simple as asking to borrow a few hundred crowns. "I don't like seeing my friends hurt, but there's a reason you don't see me prowling the streets at night trying to save every victim in sight. I don't *care* to, Sokol. I have a life that I've clawed into place, and I won't throw that away by getting involved in the mess of pijavica politics again for your sake. I'm not a spy or a soldier. I'm just a widow with an unfortunate taste in friends."

"Perhaps it's my taste in friends that's in question," Sokol shot back. "If there's a way to rid our streets of an entire breed of predators, we have to try. But we need information, the kind of information we can't get on our own. By not helping us, you're hurting us. You hide while innocent people die. Do you not care if I'm next?"

"Mortals die. That's what they do. I've done this song and dance before. I've lived…a long time. I can't fight every day."

"Just one more favor," Sokol said. "I wouldn't ask if I didn't believe it was important."

"You know that I haven't spoken to Lord Czernin in years. There's a reason I left him. I despise him. What I've told you, it wasn't everything. You don't know him."

"The ministry has been around far longer than the lamplighters. Our very first records mention Czernin, though by previous names. He's a myth, but you've told me that he is real. If anyone will know what is happening, it's him."

Ora clenched her fingers, watching her skin shift with the bones. "If you've read stories, you know what he's capable of. You have to understand what you're asking of me."

"I do. And I'm still asking."

So, after pretending to take a nap until a reasonable hour, Ora was stuck getting dressed for another adventure.

"You want the feathers *and* the pearls in your hair?" Lina asked, standing behind her as Ora went through her closet. She had woken with the dawn, just in time to help. Lina's expression was still fuzzy with sleepiness and a cup of tea steamed on the dresser, but she was giving Ora's wardrobe her full attention.

"You think it's too much?" Ora asked as she moved another day dress aside. Over the years, she'd collected outfits for all sorts of occasions, but none of them seemed right today. Some of the dresses in her closet were decades out of style by now. Why had she ever thought that this particular shade of yellow would look good on her?

Lina cleared her throat. "I do, actually."

Ora bit her lip and moved past another gown. Too frilly. The gowns she had shipped in from Paris were all drowning in ruffles these days. "None of my dresses are interesting enough," she said. "Besides, head ornamentation is in fashion in London. I'll bring it to Prague."

"Ease them into it," Lina said. "Here, what about the gray muslin?" She pulled out a dress with a simple silhouette in a soft, dove gray. There was a layer of lace over the bodice that flared over the hips, adding an element of sophistication.

"Gray?" Ora asked. "I'd look as though I'm still in mourning."

"Unless we add that pink belt I saw in here the other day," Lina said, digging through one of the accessory boxes. "Gray and pink look lovely together, especially with your red hair. With pink feathers, and no pearls, it would be the height of class."

Ora frowned at the dress. "You're sure?"

"It will be perfect," Lina insisted. "After all, you don't want to look like you're trying too hard. Not for *them*."

"Absolutely not," Ora agreed.

The horizon was gray by the time Domek trudged up the stairs to his flat, the promise of the sun slowly staining the clouds. He'd spent the rest of the night walking along the Vltava, lost in his thoughts. The clouds that had been lurking overhead all night had opened up again on his way back, raining just enough to make him feel damp and heavy, but not enough to justify stopping his journey until it cleared. It felt like the river had come to life, drifting across the city in miniscule droplets to explore beyond its shores. Shaking the dew from his hair, he unlocked the door and entered the flat.

And then stopped.

The flat had been ransacked. The contents of the drawers were strewn across the counters, the pillows on the couch had been sliced open and de-feathered, and the window in the kitchen was shattered. He ran to his bedroom and found his bed shredded and flipped, his closet upended, and torn pages of his journal scattered on the floor. It was as though a feral animal had been let loose, tearing and destroying everything it could reach.

"There you are," said Anton, coming into the bedroom behind him.

"What happened here?" Domek demanded.

His roommate looked exhausted, shadows like the clouds outside lurking under his eyes. "It was like this when I got home. I was getting worried about you. Where were you all night? Your shift ended hours ago."

"I had things to take care of," Domek said, looking around. "What did they take?"

"Not much, from what I can tell," Anton said. "They picked the wrong apartment to rob, didn't they? All I have of value is my stash of coins, and they didn't find it. Are you missing anything?"

Domek ran a hand over his face. "I'll have to look around," he said, but his mind was racing. He had been so relieved when Bazil hadn't followed him to the garden, he hadn't stopped to consider where the man would go after their conversation. Domek should have known better than to trust someone like the mysterious stranger to take no for an answer, but he'd been distracted by Kája.

He fingered the cotton shreds that poked out from his torn mattress. It might not have even been the thieves, he admitted to himself. The pijavice too were on the hunt for the wisp. The pair that had attacked him in the Park of National Awakening might have had more allies. When they hadn't returned, their friends might have sent someone to his flat to try to find the jar there.

The spirit was putting everyone in danger. Maybe it was time to weigh the jar down with bricks and then throw it in the Vltava.

A small voice inside him balked at the idea, twisting his heart with shame. Would the wisp eventually die after enough time without a vodník's magic protecting it underwater? Or would it simply be trapped in its jar until someone dredged the river? And which option was crueler?

He pushed the thought aside. Either way, someone knew where he lived. Domek knew he only had one object of real value in his possession, and this burglary could not have been a coincidence. "I'm sorry," he said, turning to Anton.

"I think they came in through the kitchen window," he said. "Looks like it was broken so they could get to the lock. Someone must have realized we're never home at night."

"Right," Domek said. He looked around the room again. "This is a mess."

Anton shook his head. "They're just lucky they *didn't* come while one of us was here. We'd have shown them what a mistake they were making. You don't work at your uncle's shop today, right? And I know you're not on shift on the streets tonight. You can stick around here, see if anyone comes knocking again."

Domek rolled his shoulders, the idea of a fight making his fingers ache. He felt so *helpless*. He would have welcomed the chance to defend his home with his fists. "I doubt they'll be back during the day. We'll need to repair the window first," he said. "Then we move on to fixing the rest."

"With what money?" Anton asked. "Would your friend Cord help?"

"You know I don't ask him for money."

"He could spare it. It's not his, anyway. It's his father's. He wastes it."

"That doesn't mean I'm going to ask him for help."

"You're too noble for your own good. Cord owes us for his soft, spoiled life. We hunt monsters on the streets for barely a krejcar while he's going to parties. People like him are sitting alongside the demons who have been hoarding money for centuries to cover their crimes, and don't even notice because they're all the same."

"Anton, he's my friend," Domek said. It was a familiar argument. "He's not a monster, and he doesn't pay us to do our job. We need to focus on the flat."

Anton ran a hand through his hair. "I don't understand. Why did they target us?"

"I...I don't know," Domek said.

"No ideas?" Anton prompted. "Not even a suspect?"

He had never been a good liar, and he had been friends with Anton since they were children, but Anton was overprotective. He would not understand Domek's decision to keep the wisp.

He had never truly recovered from Evka's death. Even when he had found his calling as a lamplighter, he had spent the first several months showing up late and drunk to shifts, bruised from reckless bar fights. Though he'd steadied out over the years, like a boat settling into the river, the fear was ever-present.

Domek turned back to him. "No," he said, keeping his voice level. "Do you?"

"It's just that you were out all night," Anton said. "That's not usual for you." He put a hand on Domek's shoulder. "If there's something going on, you can tell me. Maybe I can help."

And put his friend at risk? "There's nothing," he said. "I'm not staying here. I'll help clean, but I need somewhere that hasn't been pillaged to sleep for the day." He pulled a string of fluff free from his ruined bed and tossed it aside. "Do you have somewhere you can stay today?"

"I can find somewhere. There's always a willing lady to be found. Where will you be going? I may be able to find a lady with a friend who wouldn't mind the company," Anton said.

Domek shook his head as he pulled a set of fresh clothes from his closet to add to his satchel. "Don't worry. I've got somewhere in mind."

12

Lord Czernin lived in a palace by the Berounka River, a lazy waterway that would eventually meet the Vltava before it flowed through Prague. The palace looked down over the small villages in the valley below, so old it seemed part of the natural landscape. The dark heavy stone stacked to create intertwined buildings and towers roofed with orange tile. There were no windows. A great wall surrounded the estate, with a single gate connecting to the road from beyond. Unseen below was a realm of secrets: layers of tunnels carved deep into the hill, a respite in the hot summers and a warren of death.

The trip took nearly three hours from Prague, so it was past noon when the carriage made its way slowly up the steep hill. With the curtains tied closed to protect Ora from the morning sun, the small box of the carriage, with its wood frame, lush fabrics, and stale scent, felt like a coffin. Lina had spent the entire ride valiantly trying to take Ora's mind off the impending meeting, but Ora's fangs threatened to rip free from the tension.

Lina's forced cheer faltered when the horses stopped. "Are you sure about this, my lady?" she asked. She had fallen back on using Ora's title, which either meant she was irritated or anxious. In this case, probably both. "It's not too late for us to turn around. Sokol is asking too much of you. Again." Ora did not talk often about her time with Lord Czernin, but Lina had known her long enough to read her distress.

"I'm fine," Ora said. "He's right; this situation is worth getting to the bottom of, and if anyone knows something about these Zizkovs, it'll be Lord Czernin." She forced a smile until it felt genuine. "It's fine, Lina. I can handle this."

Lina huffed a sigh. "We'll see if *I* can. You don't need me with you."

"But I'd miss your company," Ora told her with a smile.

Lina left the carriage to announce their presence. Lord Czernin's estate was built for the nocturnally inclined, which meant that the carriage had pulled inside the enclosed courtyard. She had heard the creak of the gate opening and closing, returning the palace to its artificial night. Without the sunlight to stop her, Ora could have gone on her own, but she appreciated the extra minute to compose herself. By the time Lina returned to lead her up to the door, Ora had her chin lifted and her gaze steady.

A valet was waiting at the door to collect her cloak, which she had worn from the carriage as a matter of habit. She could tell at a glance that he was a human, one of the staff sourced from the local villages. A palace like Czernin's, with all the maids, gardeners, artisans, cooks, and other servants necessary for self-sufficiency, was expected to have a staff of at least fifty. No one outside the grounds knew how few of those jobs were necessary. Working for Lord Czernin was an honor many parents from the villages hoped their children would achieve. When a person was hired for the palace, money would flow back to their family.

The servant rarely returned home again.

The valet was pale—undoubtedly a combination of life inside the windowless palace and some level of blood loss. Good servants in Czernin's employment were kept alive until they either grew too old to be of use or were selected for immortality. The latter was used as an incentive for many of the humans, though it was rarely granted.

Bad servants did not last very long at all.

All humans on the property were used as a steady stream of blood for the inhabitants, but Czernin carefully controlled the lives and deaths of his servants. Accidental deaths were harshly punished. Czernin had lived in the palace for a very, very long time, and the pijavica who threatened to reveal his nature to the locals with their bloodlust was quickly eliminated.

She had spent more than one hundred years as part of Czernin's family, draped in lace and soaked in blood. It had been as long again since Ora had walked the dark halls, but the memories swept through her mind in a vivid rush. If only long life came with short memory. Rather than the silks that Lina's mother had used to decorate Ora's home in the modern style, Lord Czernin's theme was heavy velvet and wood. Ancient frescoes adorned the panels along the walls, portraying birds, fruits, hops, fish, and Czernin's house crest in a classic style. The coat of arms, which Ora was certain Czernin had designed himself, showed a row of black spikes on top of a red field, all topped with a golden crown.

Ora expected to be led into the parlor, the opulent meeting place for the noble humans Czernin occasionally permitted beyond the gate. Instead, they turned left down a familiar hallway, and Ora glanced quickly toward Lina. She was looking around the lush interior with cautious interest, dark eyes wide. She could not know what waited at the end of this hallway.

Ora never should have brought her along.

"Do you have anything for mortal stomachs?" Ora asked, stepping forward to walk alongside the valet. "My maid, Lina, would love some tea and honey cakes."

"Lady Fischerová—" Lina protested quietly.

"Of course," the valet said. The cooks in the palace worked exclusively to feed the staff.

"Maybe you could show her to the kitchens while I wait for Lord Czernin?" Ora prompted.

The valet nodded. "Of course, my lady."

Lina looked between them, uncomfortable being put under the spotlight of attention, before murmuring, "I can wait in the carriage if you don't want me here."

"Don't be difficult," Ora said. Sending Lina away now would show Ora's concern. It was dangerous to admit the value of anything in Czernin's domain. "Hackett is watering the horses right now, and it's stuffy in here. Besides, I heard your stomach growling on the trip."

Lina frowned at her. She disliked reminders that Ora, who was free of most bodily limitations, was acutely aware of the humans around her. "Very well," she said before turning to the valet. "I would appreciate a snack." After a beat, she added, "I have no desire to become a snack. I'll scream if necessary."

"And I'll come running," Ora assured her. "I'm sure Lord

Czernin can imagine how upset it would make me for his hospitality to be so compromised."

"Of course," the valet said with studied neutrality. "Let me first show you to where you will wait."

"I know where we were going," Ora said. "No need to waste your time." If Lina saw their destination, the scent of her fear would draw every pijavica in residence.

"I can take Lady Hahn from here," said a cool voice from down the hall. A woman approached them, gliding over the stone floors like a tiger prowling the jungle. She was wearing a simple gown, outdated in style. Beside her, Ora would look like a peacock. Her dark hair was swept away from her face in a loose knot, and her cheeks were hollow. In the one hundred and fifty years Ora had known her, she had never seen Darina Belanova appear so homely.

The valet bowed and gestured for Lina to follow. She looked between Ora and Darina, but trailed after the valet down the hall without another word. Ora sent a thought blessing her for her discretion. Darina watched her go with sharp eyes, like a hawk over a field.

"It has not been long enough," Ora said pleasantly, stepping forward and intercepting her gaze.

"I couldn't agree more," Darina said, and turned to lead her forward. Ora's attention stayed with the familiar thud of Lina's heart slowly moving away.

They walked down the precise halls Ora had expected, passing the same paintings that had hung there for centuries. The drapes had likely been replaced at some point, as even without sunlight fabric would begin to fade, but Ora could not tell for certain. Every inch of the palace was kept in its original condition, seemingly immune to the passage of time outside. It was a mausoleum, a stagnant testament to a death that hadn't happened.

Finally, they arrived in their destination.

Ossuaries were usually reserved for churches. There, the use of bones in the walls of the building served two purposes: to save room for more burials, and as a *memento mori*—a reminder to the visitors that death would come for them all one day, and to make peace with God now rather than later.

Lord Czernin's ossuary was a *memento mori* as well, though the peace in question was to be made with the lord of the palace.

The room was a pale contrast to the dark décor of the rest of the building. The circular room was built of bones from floor to ceiling—humeri and tibias on the floor, their knobs like river stones underfoot, skulls stacked in hollow-eyed columns, a chandelier dangling from the center of the room with jawbone chain links and dangling femurs. Even the chairs were bone, delicate and yellowed, though the seats were accented with embroidered cushions. No thought but for the comfort of his guests, that was Czernin.

"I was surprised when the valet began to lead me here," Ora admitted. "The ossuary? Really? Has Czernin forgotten how to greet his guests?"

"Does it bother you?" Darina asked. Her smile was as beautiful as ever, bright white teeth behind dark lips, green eyes pale beneath long lashes. "I thought you'd want to see the new additions." She gestured at the wall, where Czernin's coat of arms had been painstakingly arranged with a variety of bones, large and small. A skull sat on top of the crown as a final touch. "After all, you helped build this place, when you lived here."

"Where's Czernin?"

"You're not going to ask how I've been?" Darina's lips stretched a touch wider, wider than a human's could have. "It's been nearly one hundred years."

Ora hummed, looking around the room. "I don't see why that would possibly interest me. You know I don't care for boring stories."

"You've always thought you were so clever. You've missed so much since you've been gone. You thought Czernin would greet you in the sitting room, possibly bring out a tray of venison for you to snack on while you caught up. You have no idea how things have changed." Darina tilted her head. "You're not going to ask after me. But are you not curious about Otto? Or Agnes? They were once your friends."

Frowning, Ora tilted her head and sniffed the air again. When she had come in, she had been distracted by the many ways the palace had remained the same. Beyond the scent of ancient wood and bone, Ora could detect the sweat of a few dozen humans, and only three pijavice. Czernin's scent was one she could have given shape to in her dreams, and Darina was the same. The third took a moment to place, though she should have remembered it at once. Jan Zdražil had been Lord Czernin's personal butler in life and beyond, and was his sharp, unforgiving eyes that monitored the palace when Czernin's attention was drawn beyond. Any other scents had long since gone stale.

Once, the palace had held more than a dozen pijavice.

"Where is everyone?" Czernin often sent his family out of the palace on missions across Europe. Ora had negotiated on his behalf as far abroad as Amsterdam, though she had spent most of her time helping him against the waves of hunters in Prague.

"Dead. Not in here, of course," she added, tapping a nail

against a skull. "No bones left behind when they turned to dust."

"Even Agnes? She was the strongest of us. How did it happen?"

"Oh, now you care? Now you think to wonder about your family?"

When Ora had escaped Czernin's hold, she had tried not to think of the pijavice she had left behind. She had expected them to live in stasis inside the dark palace for eternity, preserved in amber without Ora's presence.

"If you thought our master was paranoid during your time here, that is only because you did not see him after you left," Darina told her. "He has culled down the family to those he can be sure he can trust."

It was not unusual for Czernin to kill members of his own family. He had encouraged in-fighting, as anyone weak enough to die at the hand of one of the other family members could not be trusted to represent him outside the palace, and had slain anyone not meeting his expectations. Ora had lived in fear of losing the man's favor.

But the entire family? Otto had been with Czernin since the early 1200s, if rumor was to be believed. Czernin's authority came from maintaining a group of the strongest pijavice on the continent. Was Ora to believe that he was down to two? "Why you?" Ora asked. "I smell Jan. He makes sense. But you were turned after me. Czernin had no special affection for you."

Darina's smile grew a bit too wide, stretching toward her ears like a feline. "No need to sound so disappointed. You would miss hating me."

Ora's long relationship with Darina had been complex. They had been bitter rivals, both too ambitious and bold to speak without trying to tear each other into shreds. In the end, though,

Ora had preferred the rival she respected to the enemies she didn't. When they fought, the palace shook. When they fell into bed together—or, more often, slammed each other into walls and tables and floors—stone cracked. When they cooperated, they had devastated entire cities.

"Mostly, I stay out of his way," Darina continued. "An approach I thought you had finally learned."

"There you are."

The voice made both of them straighten and turn toward the door. Ora had been so focused on Darina that she had missed the rasp of the approaching shoes. Lord Emil Czernin was a slight man, feline in movement and structure. Golden hair was slicked against his head like a perfect crown on top of his perfectly tailored clothing. The style of the cut had been popular centuries before Ora's birth, so long that they now seemed traditional rather than dated. He strolled into the room, eyes intent on Ora.

"Think about what I said," Darina said.

"Ora Hahn," Czernin greeted. He did not bother to watch Darina leave.

Reluctantly, she allowed him to kiss her gloved hand. "It's Lady Fischerová now," she reminded him.

"Of course," he said. "How could I forget?" He looked around and sighed to himself. "I was wrong. This is not the place for us to meet. Come with me. We'll go somewhere more interesting to talk. Unless you'd rather stay here?"

"No preference," Ora said with a smile that could have been carved in stone.

"I assume the valet offered you food and drink. Should we find him?" He would still be with Lina. Ora itched to check on her maid, alone in this house with an unseen Darina and Jan, but keeping Czernin away from her was the best way to keep her safe.

"I'm not hungry at the moment."

Czernin looked her over, from the feathers in her hair to the hem of her gown. As always, he seemed to be looking straight through her. "No. You wouldn't be."

They left the crypt and walked through the palace. Czernin strode forward without fear, though Ora was close to his back. Did he not believe she could be there for revenge, or was he so confident he could beat her in combat? He had been the bogeyman over her shoulder for her last century of traveling the world. For the first several decades, she had lived with the certainty that he would come for her on one dark night, either to kill her or—worse—drag her back to the palace by her hair. When she finally felt sure he was going to let her leave without punishment, she spent every action defying the person he had made her become. He had molded her, changed the very blood in her veins and the thoughts in her head. Her hands tightened into fists as she watched his blond hair shine in the candlelight, and she could feel the prick of her nails against her palms. It was only with intense focus that she kept the nails blunt.

They emerged into one of the covered courtyards near the back of the palace. If she had not been so focused on controlling her emotions, she would have known where they were headed. In her time, this courtyard had been designated for laundry, but that had changed at some point. It was a relief, somehow, that not all of the palace was unchanged. Being back in the same halls, Ora had begun to wonder if she was also unchanged, despite the distance of decades.

Birdsong lilted through the courtyard, high trilling mixing with low hooting, and the scent of feathers, flesh, and feces was heavy in the air. White doves sat on an opposite doorframe. Small gray birds with bright orange beaks hopped on the ground, eating what seemed to be seeds strewn across the stone floor. Flashes of blue and red darted past on swift wings. Despite the number of birds, the room was surprisingly clean. Several of the human staff must have spent hours a day scrubbing the droppings and fallen feathers from the ground.

"An aviary?" Ora asked, looking up toward the ceiling. There were only candles on the ground, so the upper reaches were difficult to see even with her enhanced eyesight. The fluttering wings there seemed a part of the shadows.

"It's convenient," he said. He stepped further into the room. The birds nearest hopped a few feet away, but seemed unafraid of the monster in their midst. He looked back at Ora, eyes glinting in the candlelight. "I didn't think you'd come back so soon."

Czernin had a skewed sense of time that came with the endless stretch of immortality. She had left his home more than a century ago. "But you knew I'd come back?" *Ora* hadn't known she'd be back. She turned to examine a magpie. Its feathers had lost some of the species' usual gloss, dulled by captivity. How long had the birds been here?

"You couldn't stay away forever," Czernin said. "For us, forever is a long time. You've been living in Prague, is that right?"

Ora didn't bother to ask whether or not he'd been keeping track of her. Czernin made it his habit to know everything—that was why she'd traveled out to him today. He sat like a spider in a web, plying each gossamer thread for information. "I am. I enjoy the cultural stimulation. Country life is so dull in comparison."

"We find ways to entertain ourselves out here," Czernin said. "You used to be one of us, not long ago."

"It *was* long ago, if you go by mortal standards," she pointed out. "A lifetime or more."

"I don't mean when you lived *here*, my dove. I mean your dalliance with domestic life over in Mělník."

Ora looked toward the ceiling again. "Right." What had Czernin thought when he had learned of Ora settling down with a human so close to Prague? How quickly had he learned? The thought of his agents watching their home in the fields made her skin itch.

"So, have you finally gotten over that phase?" Czernin asked. "Your mourning period went on for an entirely unreasonable length of time." His eyes lingered on her pink belt. "I assume you're back here because you realized that mortals have nothing to offer us. I knew you'd be back." He repeated the phrase like a mantra.

"They have plenty to offer," Ora snarled, meeting his gaze. "And my mourning is none of your business."

Czernin clicked his tongue chidingly. "Still so sensitive. It's been over a decade."

"You're the one who always said that for our kind, decades pass like blinks and centuries like sighs," Ora said. "It's been no time at all."

"Ah, but you've been living on mortal time," he pointed out. "If your husband had survived, he'd have grown so old at this point that you'd be running back into my family. Mortals are so very weak."

"You don't get to talk about him. Franz was ten times the man you are, even before you turned to stone."

Czernin shook his head, not rising to meet her. "Still so defensive. If I'd known you'd go this weak over a human, I'd never had turned you in the first place. You must have hidden that delicacy better when you were younger. You were never so fluttery over Darina."

"What we had was not love. We needed an outlet outside of a battle to the death. I was surprised to find her still here."

"Not all of my family are as disloyal as you."

Loyalty had never been one of Darina's strengths, no matter how well she pretended. "I noticed how small your family has become. And there has been no one new?"

"No one has impressed me enough for me to give them the gift of immortality for many years now. I do not need them. They were poor company, and humans are simpler to command."

"The gift," she repeated, shaking her head. "I only let you transform me because you convinced me that eternal life was worth the sacrifices. I didn't stop to wonder whether eternal life was a sacrifice itself."

"You were young, but you were not naïve to the costs. I remember how easily you killed your first meal," he said.

During the transformation, the pijavica curse corrupted and consumed the living blood inside the body. When the painful throes of the conversion were complete, the pijavica needed the blood of others to survive—and was drawn, inexorably, toward the blood most similar to that they had lost. Whether born from the grave or created with an exchange of blood-drinking, pijavice were sent into a frenzy when they smelled anyone of their own bloodline. Even if they had the will to resist drinking blood of most other humans, as Ora had for the last several decades, the bloodline curse was unconquerable. If rumors were to be believed, Czernin had bathed in the blood of everyone from his own parents to his child niece when he had first been turned centuries before.

Ora's parents had died when she was only fifteen, leaving her an untethered kite, adrift in the world. She had been living on her own for more than a decade by the time Czernin had lured her in with promises of power and eternity. As a human, his warning about the bloodline frenzy had been distant, hypothetical—laughable, even. If she had not been so alone, would she have been begging for him to take her away? Her only living relative, a kind but sickly uncle, lived in Salzburg and had not been to Prague in years. Though he had adored Ora, his health prevented him from doing anything but sending the occasional letter for his niece.

When she'd finished the painful transformation to stop her heart and fill her veins with poison, she'd had no energy to be surprised to find Czernin had collected her last living relative and bound him in chains. She'd only been so very thirsty.

Afterward, the memory of his pleading screams had haunted her endless days. She'd learned she didn't need sleep to experience nightmares.

"Your viciousness masked the weakness of your mind."

Ora's gaze snapped back to him. His tone had been sharper than before, an emotional outburst he rarely allowed. "You believe it was *weakness* that gave me the courage to flee this place?"

"I should have known," Czernin continued. "It's the Bohemian blood now. It's been watered down. Worse, you were a peasant before I found you. The lowest of the low. After they lost the

Battle of White Mountain, the entire country chose to live as victims. Failure is in their hearts, now, and there's no cleansing it. We used to be the capital of a kingdom. Now this place is unimportant, overshadowed by others."

"Wars are lost sometimes, Lord Czernin," Ora said. "It's not so intrinsic as you believe."

"Isn't it? Prague has gone from being the center of Europe to losing nearly every war it entered. It's a lesser state of the new empire, barely relevant beside Vienna. It's grown soft."

Ora hummed. "You think Prague has grown soft when you had one family member run away and then threw a hundred-year temper tantrum and refused to make any more?"

Czernin met her eyes, and then his hand darted sideways to catch a dove swooping past. The ancient pijavica had always had more control over his monstrous form than anyone else. In one moment, he seemed nearly human. In the next, his jaws were extended, and the dove was gone. It was so quick, so merciless, that only the birds closest to them fluttered away in alarm. The rest of the aviary continued to peck at the seeds on the ground and fly in circles around each other. His mouth fell back to human dimensions as he swallowed, and the lips curled into a smile.

As though nothing had happened, Czernin said with measured calmness, "I turned pijavice to maintain control of this region. Now no one is fighting for Prague, and most pijavice would be more trouble than they are worth. Better to have none at all. My human spies are enough for the sorry state the city is in. There are no golems to fight, no clever German pijavica lords encroaching. What's the point of maintaining a family?"

There were four doors into the courtyard, though only one Ora knew to be unlocked. If she had to run from Czernin, it would already be too late. She had had several indulgent decades, and he, clearly, was as fast as ever. "Well, then I won't waste your time on a family member past. I need your help on a professional matter. You still keep track of all the up-and-coming families in the region, don't you?"

"You know I like information," Czernin said, examining his left hand. He plucked a feather from his cuff and let it float to the floor. "I don't limit myself to our brethren born of Bohemian waters. There are others like the pijavice throughout Europe, though they have their own names and customs. I keep an eye on everything." He shrugged. "It's rarely as interesting as I'd hope. You're here for gossip? I can tell you a hundred stories."

"I don't have that kind of time to spare on you," Ora said shortly. "I'm looking for information on a certain family based in Prague. The Zizkovs. What do you know?"

"Now, you know I don't trade information for free."

Ora had seen Czernin's deals. "I have nothing I'm willing to offer you."

"You thought I'd see your pretty face and just tell you what you wanted to know?"

"I thought you'd jump at the chance to be relevant again."

She regretted her sharp words to this new, more volatile Czernin, but a slow smile spread over his lips instead. It made her nervous. She'd seen that look before many times. It was normally followed by a spray of arterial blood. "I don't need much," he said. "Information for information. Every question you ask, I can ask one of my own. How does that sound?"

"I suppose. Just be brief, if you can," she said, affecting nonchalance with all the conviction she could muster. "I'm expected for dinner back in Prague."

Czernin's smile grew bigger. "So, what are your questions, *Maus*?" The pet name—mouse—had grown no less condescending over the years. Ora did not mind, however. She was going to the opera with a Mister Mouse tonight, though in Czech rather than German. Domek Myska had certainly never let the name limit him. Perhaps to Czernin, Ora was a mouse. She would be the type with sharp teeth, slicing claws, and a trail of devastation in her silent wake.

"Tell me what you know about the Zizkovs," Ora said.

"That's not a question." He waited, but she stayed silent. "Let's see. The Zizkovs are barely worth noticing. They have a dozen members, maybe fewer. They're street trash with delusions of grandeur." That followed what Ora had known about them. "The current leader, Mayer, was common-born, and is so new to his fangs that he probably still slurs. He has aspirations, though, and he moved them from their Zizkov hideout to a nicer address, west of the river. They're involved in some sort of smuggling scheme for the humans and made a commendable amount of money. Enough to buy a house, if not a title or property. I assume they're looking to become important. Not that they'll succeed, of course. They're not even a speck on the international scene, much less taking any sort of place of influence. Prague is their playground, and as I said, that is nothing now."

Ora tapped her fingers on her opposite wrist. She had hoped for something more damning. It wasn't unusual for families to grab for power when the bigger players were sequestered away. With timelines like those Lord Czernin worked on, it wasn't unusual for there to be a few slow decades in big cities where power was up for grabs. The Zizkovs would lose any status they'd acquired the moment a pijavica with power and influence moved back to town. Despite what Czernin asserted, Ora knew Prague was not invisible yet. There was an ebb and flow to power that only an eye to history could reveal. "Are there any scientists in their family?"

"I don't have a list of professions," Czernin said. "From what I've heard, they used to rely more on brawn when it comes down to business than brains, but their new leader has changed that. He came in from nowhere, took over their territory, then replaced nearly every pijavica in the family with new blood. In the last few years, they've brought in some professors from the local university. Not a common choice, but I'm sure Mayer thinks he has a plan. I haven't wasted much of my attention on them. Most of the big moves they've made have involved clearing up some of the worst scum from the tunnels. They're not a threat, and they keep the biggest risks to our secrets from getting out of hand in the city."

"There was a time you knew every movement in the city."

"Prague was once the magical heart of an empire. The threats there were dangerous to all of us. You, however, never seemed to care. I could hardly convince you to leave this estate, no matter how important the work. I would think the Zizkovs would be under your notice. Why are you asking?"

Ora turned to him. "Waste of a question. A friend of mine wanted me to find out some information for him."

"Your friend Karel Sokol, I assume."

Bristling, Ora said, "You've been looking into Sokol?"

"I've been looking into *you*," Czernin said. "Prague is of little interest, but you. You're quite the social butterfly. It's interesting to see the types of humans you have coming in and out of your home at all hours."

He had been spying on her house. Though she'd known that he would have been keeping an ear on her activities, the implication that he had someone watching her regularly twisted Ora's stomach. Was it Darina, or some human informant? Her home was meant to be her safe haven in Prague, far away from Czernin's controlling, seeking tendrils. "Perhaps you've forgotten what it's like to have friends."

He ignored her. "If he's asking for your help with his little ministry, either he's an idiot, or he's just trying to convince you he is. How could a ministry created solely to keep track of internal threats to the Empire overlook an expanding family like Zizkov? I would have expected that the ministry had an eye on them from the start, especially since they've turned a few people of note in the city, people who would have been missed."

Raising an eyebrow, Ora asked, "If he already knew that, he wouldn't have gotten me involved. Why would he bother trying to make me think he knows less than he does?"

"Maybe you should ask him that. I still have two questions—you should be careful adding more."

"Fine—go ahead."

"Why do you spend so much time on humans, Lady Fischerová? Have you become addicted to having life blood all around you? I understand that compulsion."

"No. They're so changeable. It's fascinating. Sometimes..."

"Yes?"

"Sometimes I miss being human," she said, shrugging helplessly. "It's nice to be around the living."

"It's such a shame," Czernin said. "You're like an eagle who dreams of being a fish."

Another bird, this specimen one of the small gray balls of fluff Ora had thought were cute. It chirped quietly in protest before there was another single bite.

"I thought I was a mouse," Ora said, keeping her voice steady. "Ask your last question. I'll need to be heading back to Prague soon."

Czernin took a step closer. Ora wanted to retreat on instinct. He smiled slowly, like honey pouring into a mug. His fangs were hidden again, but his blunt teeth were just as fierce. "Why didn't you turn your husband into one of us? How much of this grief has been an act? You had the power to save him."

Ora's heart had not beat in many years. Still, it seemed to stop. "That's more than one question," she said, mouth numb.

"Don't play semantics with me, girl."

"I'm leaving."

"You still owe me an answer," he said, coming closer again. "I want to know. Why not offer him the chance? Why let him die?"

"I can't," she said, backing away. Birds hopped to get out of her way. Grief, rage, and guilt warred in her stomach, a maelstrom worse than any of Czernin's intimidation attempts could have caused. "I'm done here." She turned toward the door.

There was a shift of a heel against stone, too quick to be casual. Ora whirled around and found Czernin lunging toward her, jaw fully extended and fangs bared. His pale eyes were bright and glinting. Startled, Ora stumbled backward, tripping over one of the cobblestones. She was slower than she had once been, and they both knew it. The fire of the hunt was alight in Czernin's eyes, vicious and hungry. He slammed her shoulders into the stone, claws ripping through the fabric of her dress to pierce her skin.

"Did you think I would let you go again?" Czernin snarled.

Ora twisted, making the claws dig in more deeply. "Fuck you," she spat.

"Your blood is all prey animal now," Czernin told her. "You've let weakness into your veins."

"Let me go," she said, voice wavering.

He rattled her shoulders, knocking her head against the stone. His claws were deep enough to pierce bone. This was not the controlled violence he had used to toy with his family. He was going to kill her.

She screamed.

He jerked her again, and then inhaled deeply. His pupils had vanished beneath an expanse of black. Poison welled from the tips of his fangs, dripping onto her face. "I should have done this before you left."

"Lord Czernin."

Czernin turned to look at Darina, but Ora kept trying to break from his hold. She could not die here, not like this. Not after fighting so hard to escape.

"This human has been making a fuss looking for her mistress. What shall we do with her?"

Lina. Ora finally managed to free one hand and drive it into Czernin's stomach, dislodging him. She scrambled away, nearly flying across the aviary to her maid's side. She was standing slightly behind Darina, wide eyes on Czernin.

"Ah, thank you, Darina," Ora said. Her voice was shaking. The other pijavica would be able to smell the terror on her skin. "I'm still training manners into her." Lina gaped at the chill in her tone, but Ora just turned back to Czernin. "We'll be going now." She tried to sound firm. If Czernin ordered Darina to help him kill Ora and Lina, they would be dead before either of them could escape the aviary.

Czernin climbed to his feet in a smooth motion. His claws and fangs had retracted as though they had never existed, though his fingertips were still stained with her blood. The feral creature that had knocked her to the ground was nowhere to be seen. He straightened his disheveled cuffs. The mania was still in his eyes, but he had pulled on a mask of his old self. "I'll see you in another few decades, then, Lady Fischerová."

She left him in the dark aviary, the unknowing birds fluttering at his feet.

Darina walked them to the front door. It was a testament to how shaken Ora was that she found her old enemy's presence a comfort. The loudest sound in the empty hallways was the thudding of Lina's heartbeat. Ora expected to hear Czernin's pursuit, but it did not come.

"I told you," Darina said simply, her hand on the door handle.

How long had Czernin been so volatile? He had always been brutal, but with an iron grip on his control. While Ora had been traveling the world, seeing the mountains of China, the art of Paris, and then falling in love, Darina had been stuck inside this dark palace with the unraveling Czernin. "Darina…"

"I know you're not sorry for leaving. Don't waste your breath. You were a fool for coming back, much less with a bite like that," she said, waving at Lina. "Go."

Ora wanted to linger, to tell Darina her advice for fleeing Czernin's reach, but Jan or Czernin could appear at any moment. Czernin had taught her all her tricks, including how to mask their presence in shadow. Darkness had ears in this estate.

Ora nodded once, and then ushered Lina toward the carriage.

She could feel Darina's eyes following her until the door was safely closed between them.

"I can't believe you left me alone in there," Lina burst as the carriage lurched into motion.

The curtained windows stopped her from being able to see the courtyard beyond, so Ora's ears and nose were sharp. Darina was still nearby, but the stone dampened the activity inside the palace.

When Ora did not respond, Lina pressed, "That woman came and collected me. I didn't know where she was taking me. Until I saw you on the ground, I thought she was going to kill me. She wouldn't tell me where we were going."

"She thinks it's fun to scare people," Ora said. They had finally passed through the front gate onto the dirt road outside, if the rattle of the carriage wheels was any indication.

"She succeeded," Lina snapped, shrill. "I thought you were going to stay with me. You sent me away to get watered like I was one of the horses."

"I couldn't," Ora said. "They couldn't know you were important to me."

"Am I? You dragged me into a viper pit without thinking twice," Lina said.

"Damn it, Lina, I barely got us out of there alive." Czernin's last question pounded in her head to the throb of pain in her bloodied shoulders. *Why did you let your husband die?* Today, Lina had nearly joined the long list of mortals Ora had loved and lost.

"You should never have let Sokol convince you to go. He manipulated you for his own reasons, just like I said he would. I knew you've been feeling reckless, but we could have both died today."

"Lina!" Ora snarled. "Leave me alone!" Her rage shuddered through her, and she turned and punched the wall of the carriage. She screamed, shrill and keening, when her fist crunched through the wood paneling and stretched into the sunlight beyond. She jerked her hand back into the carriage and leaped to the opposite seat, pressing herself against the front of the carriage. Her hand was blackened and withered. In another few seconds, she would have lost it completely.

Lina silently moved to the other bench and sat against the side wall of the carriage, body twisted awkwardly to press her back against the hole and block the caustic light. She shuffled for a moment, and then lifted her feet onto the bench, wrapped her arms around her knees, and rested her head against the back of the carriage.

Ora opened her mouth, but Lina's eyes were closed tightly. Her heart, which had only just begun to slow after they had left the palace, was rabbit-fast again.

They sat in silence for the duration of the ride back to Prague, leaving Ora to nurse her burnt hand and her bitter thoughts.

13

Domek wandered through the streets in a circuitous route after leaving his ruined flat, satchel securely slung over his shoulder. The sky was clear and bright overhead, free from clouds. Years of nightly patrols had made each street familiar beneath his boots, a home as beautiful as it was deadly. On one street, he had shyly kissed Bina Laska when he was sixteen. On the next, he had held an elderly woman in his arms as life drained from her body, blood pooling onto the cobblestones like rainwater. Prague did not know Domek, did not need him, but his life was overlaid on the ancient streets in watercolor, the patterns sheer and impermanent.

He passed Prague Station where it sat half inside, half outside the old city walls, filled with the heaving sighs of steam engines. A train's sharp whistle clawed the air. He allowed himself to be lost in a crowd of tourists speaking a quick, foreign tongue before slipping through the other side.

Thanks to the lull in the spring rain, the streets were crowded in the city center. The Old Town Square was the heart of Prague. At this time of day, it pulsed with activity. Vendors stood along the edges, selling sausages in the summer, mulled wine in the winter, and hand-carved puppets and trinkets year-round. The grand square sat in the shadow of Týn Church, a four-hundred-year-old structure with dark, pointed towers that shot toward the sky like spears. Around it, pastel façades clustered like flowers, their uniform orange roofs creating a bright, jagged horizon in every direction.

He went north and wandered through the winding streets of the Jewish Quarter. Broad synagogues sat on street corners, the six-pointed star carved into their thresholds. Many people had moved out of the ghetto when the Jews had been granted their citizenship two decades earlier, but there were still some who refused to leave their homes. Older men with locks of hair curling by their temples from under black hats talked in cafés while women in multicolored headscarves looked through the wares of the street vendors. Called by the warm scent, Domek stopped by a bakery Abrahams had shown him when he had asked for help eliminating a nest of pijavice living under an apartment building. Abrahams was a talented lamplighter, dedicated to keeping his home safe, and was humble enough to bring in reinforcements when necessary.

What would Abrahams think of Domek's decision to keep the wisp instead of handing it to Paluska? Domek shook his head. Abrahams wasn't the one who had had the wisp's jar dropped into his hands, and he was doing the best he could to keep everyone safe. He bought a braided loaf of challah and tucked it under his arm as he walked along the river the rest of the way.

By the time he made it to his mother's flat, he was sure he was not being followed.

"Hi, Maminka." He handed her the challah, which she took with an appreciative sniff. "Sorry for just dropping by again. Do you mind if I sleep on the floor here today?"

"Has something happened? You're always welcome, but you haven't done this before," she said. "Did you and Anton get into a fight? I never thought he was the right roommate for you. Cord is so much more charming."

"Too charming," Domek said, rolling his eyes. "Anton and I are fine. It's nothing to worry about."

"You can take my bed. I won't need it until sundown. No reason for you to sleep on the floor. Besides, I'm not sure my legs could survive having to step over you to get around the flat all day." The flat was small, but he knew it was an excuse to make him agree. His mother had always been selfless to a fault—something his father had taken advantage of his whole life.

"Thanks, Maminka." He hesitated. "About the wisp…"

"Did you free it?"

"No. I couldn't. I don't know what it would do to the people in this city. My question is—do you know how to kill one?"

"Domek," she said, putting a hand to her chest. "Is that truly your first thought?"

"It threatened to kill you," Domek pointed out. "It's dangerous. I can't free it, but I can't keep it."

"Everything is dangerous," she said.

"Not like this. It's my job to keep this city safe."

"And this is what that job has convinced you. To eradicate anything you don't understand. There are solutions to problems outside of violence," his mother said. "I had hoped I had taught you that."

No, his mother had never resorted to violence, but nor had he seen her manage a threat. Her faith in eventual peace had only ever come about by luck. If his father's heart had not failed him, Domek may have killed a man before his twentieth birthday. His mother's attempts to appease him had certainly never worked. "Right," he said, smile tense. "Of course, Maminka."

"You're so conflicted, my love." She frowned at him. "Sit down at the table."

He sat, staring at his hands. The wisp's jar was tucked in the satchel by his side, but he felt the malice pouring from it. It had only led to trouble. Soon, he would have to make a decision.

His mother came back into the kitchen with a small wooden box in her hands. She sat across from him and opened it with shaking hands. "Maminka..." he began, worried, but fell silent when the contents were revealed. A deck of yellowed cards.

"I've been thinking about what you said. I've been afraid for so long, but you were right. If I can help you, I must." She was pale, but her mouth was set in a firm line.

He remembered the way his father had demonized his mother for her occult past, the way she had begged him for a forgiveness she did not need. How much of her light was still shuttered by his long-dead father? She had thrown herself onto too many pyres for Domek. "You don't have to."

She put her hand over his. "If I can help bring you some clarity, I would do anything."

With stiff movements, she shuffled the deck. After a few moments, she found a rhythm. The cards jumped at her command. She closed her eyes, as though listening to music he could not hear.

Finally, she laid out three worn cards in the center of the table. "This is a three-card spread. I knew other methods, but this is the simplest. I'm out of practice," she said. She twisted her wrists, thin fingers fluttering. "I've asked for insight into what you should do. The first card establishes your past." She glanced up at him. "Let's see if I still remember what I'm doing."

She flipped the card, revealing a woodcut illustration of a man on a horse, a sword drawn and ready. "The Knight of Swords. Of course. My brave Domek."

"What does it mean?"

"He's a straightforward fellow. Dedicated to action and defending his values. If any card could summarize your journey, it's this." She traced the image's curly hair, and then moved to the next.

The second card looked like any seen in a standard card game. Red and blue lines arced toward each other, with a pair of yellow swords overlapping on top.

"The Ten of Swords," she murmured. "It urges you to protect yourself, and to lay low until the turmoil ends."

"Not bad advice."

His mother tapped on the table. "But it's a complicated card, Domek. There are layers to all of these, and alternate meanings for each. It could also mean defeat is already upon you. Or… that you'll soon be betrayed."

"How do we know which meaning is true?"

"It's an art. I know which I would prefer for it to mean, but nothing in life is ever clear except in hindsight. I was hoping I'd be helping you. I'm only raising questions."

"I didn't expect encouragement," he assured her when she continued to stare at the card. "I know I'm in trouble. It's not your fault."

"I wish I could bring you comfort," she said. She rested a hand over the final card. "This one will show your future. If not comfort, perhaps it will bring you guidance." Still, she hesitated.

"I need to know," he said.

"My knight," she said, and turned the card.

A yellow skeleton stood hunched in the center of the image, a scythe sweeping from its hand. The field below its bone feet was littered with body parts: a head, a hand, a bare heart.

Domek swallowed. "I've never read Tarot, but I can make a guess what that means." He tried for levity, but his voice fell flat.

"The Death card does not have to mean an actual death," his mother said weakly. "It can be the end of an era, a time to leave aside what you know and embrace the new. We all have to change, Domek."

"But it *can* mean death," Domek said. His mouth was dry. "Is there a way to stop the future from happening?"

She spread her hands. "That's a question I can't answer." She took a deep breath and then gathered the cards from the table, sliding them back into her deck. Once they were tucked safely away, she clicked the box closed as though it would erase what they had seen.

"Would it have to mean my death?" Domek pressed. "Death surrounds me every night, Maminka. This doesn't have to mean my doom. Could it be a sign I should kill the wisp?"

"There are other signs for the death of an enemy. This death, metaphorical or not, will not be a triumph. I'm sorry, my love. I shouldn't have tried this. I should never have kept these cards."

"No, no," he said. "It's better to know the truth, even if it hurts."

"You're always sweet to me," she said. "Don't dwell on the final card. It's the present that matters now. Keep your head down. Stay safe. Don't rush into any decisions."

"And if it did mean betrayal?"

She reached out to straighten his collar, patting his chest twice. "Keep your eyes open, but your heart as well. Betrayal says more about the other person than you. I hope it does not come to that, but don't change who you are to avoid the possibility. You're a knight, Domek. You fight for what's right."

After he woke from a restless sleep on his mother's small cot, he went down the street to his uncle's shop—both to occupy himself and to give his mother some space. She had watched him as though he had already died, and she had killed him herself. He had given her a kiss on the forehead and told her not to worry, but knew the words would not help.

He carried his satchel slung over his shoulder, one hand holding onto the flap like a child's blanket. He had unpacked the extra clothes he had brought, but wanted to keep his stakes and the wisp's jar close by.

When Domek walked in through the shop door, a bell clanged overhead to announce his entrance. Though he knew the sound well, he still jumped, on edge. A shout echoed from the back room: "I'll be with you in a moment!"

"It's just me, Uncle Zach," he called back.

"Domek? Come on back here. I need your help with this clock."

His uncle Zacharias owned a repair shop only a few blocks away from his mother's flat, close to the river. Always eccentric, he had allowed Domek to play in the shop when he had been a child and his parents had been working their long hours. Domek had immediately loved the work. Tinkering with gears, testing mechanics, peering through a lens to do delicate work, and fixing things that were broken; it all had appealed to a child who had craved control and order.

Though his uncle couldn't afford to take him on as a full-time assistant, Domek worked in the shop at least twice a week— more or less depending on how often Zacharias could spare a day's wages from the shop's intake. Compared to Imrich, who paid him nothing and disparaged his work, the few days with Zacharias were a balm. His uncle did not know the truth about Domek's night job, so with him, he was able to simply be Domek.

The back room of the repair shop consistently had the appearance of a recent explosion—sometimes literally. There were so many gears, springs, half-built machines, and tools, that the tabletops were barely visible. His uncle was always working on at least four projects at once, unable to slow down for long enough to dedicate himself to one task. Somehow, considering his pell-mell approach, Zacharias was a very skillful mechanic. He was a magpie, clever and curious, but easily distracted by the next shiny object.

"Come hold this lid back while I fix this gear into place," Zacharias said, both hands deep in the bowels of a grandfather clock that took up most of one of his worktables. Zacharias was of a height with Domek's mother, making him far shorter than Domek. He kept his thinning hair cropped tightly to his skull but rarely bothered to trim his beard, leaving him with more hair on his chin than on his head. He worked with a grease-stained apron tied over his plump stomach and a pair of spectacles perched on top of his head for easy access.

Domek followed his instructions, allowing him to work on the innards of the clock without worrying about the lid slamming shut on his fingers. His uncle worked in silence until he fixed the problem, seemingly forgetting that his nephew had shown up at all. Finally, once the clock's gear was settled back into place, he straightened and grinned at Domek. "We didn't say you'd work today, did we?" he asked suddenly.

"No. I was in the area and wanted something to do, if that's all right. We can swap out the day I was planning later this week."

"No, no, stick around if you have the time. I've been swamped this week. There's something over on the other table back there that I think you'll be interested in."

The table in question was covered from one end to the other with matches, some in boxes, but most loose. Most had come from Vienna, their labels in German block letters, but Domek spotted a few written in scripts from other languages. One pile contained only the red phosphorus blocks that most of the matches needed to be struck against to ignite.

Domek examined the table, frowning. "What are these?" he asked, picking up a strange match from a jumbled pile of its brothers. It had a ball of chemicals on each end, one white, one red.

"Ah," Zacharias said, plucking the match from his grasp. "These are French. This is a clever one. With these, you don't need to buy a separate striking paper. They'd make your job much faster." He snapped the matchstick in half, and then vigorously rubbed the two heads together. With a sizzling flash, the white end ignited, flaring up and blazing fiercely. The harsh smell of sulfur and burning wood filled the air, acrid and bright.

Zacharias beamed, and then quickly dropped the short halves into a pail of water before they could reach his fingertips. The pail was filled with half-burnt sticks.

"You have these just thrown in a pile?" Domek demanded, staring at the collection of two-headed matches in horror. "What if the wrong heads rub against each other and set the whole table on fire?"

Zacharias opened his mouth, and then frowned. "I didn't think of that."

Domek began carefully plucking the matches from the bundle and lining them in a row at the edge of the table. "Do you not remember the lucifer incident of 1859?" Zacharias's previous experimentations with matches had resulted in an explosion that had required the rebuilding of half a room of the repair shop. His uncle's eyebrows were still patchy and uneven from the burns. "This is why my mother worries about you."

"Innovation always comes with some danger! I do keep the pail nearby," Zacharias said.

"None of these are white phosphorous, are they? You know that's dangerous. There have been rumors about people's jawbones being eaten from the inside by that poison."

"Yes, nephew, I'm aware," Zacharias said. "I am an expert in this. I'm using red only. Don't be such a worrywart. Don't you want to hear what I'm trying to do? Or can you guess?"

Despite his reasonable concern, Domek couldn't suppress a grin at the challenge. He looked over the collected matches with renewed interest, noting the prototypes Zacharias had started crafting along the left edge of the table.

"You're trying to include the striking pad with the matches," Domek said finally, picking up a prototype. It was a cannibalized matchbox with what looked like English written on the flap. Half of the box was filled with regular matches, and the other half had a miniature striking pad tucked inside.

"The modern world is searching for convenience. Who can keep track of their matchbox and striking pad, especially when they're just trying to light a cigar?" He grabbed one of the two-headed matches Domek had half-sorted and held it up. "This is a start, but it's risky. Who wants to break their match sticks in half? We've all had enough singed fingers." He picked up the bastardized matchbox again. "This one isn't good enough. The striking area is too small—you can't get enough friction against it before you run out of room."

"This is a great idea," Domek said. It reminded him of the alchemic arc light experiment he'd seen in Imrich's apartment, which had also brazenly wielded combustive compounds in the hopes of bringing light. There was a race between flame and electricity. There were some engineers who believed that the gas lamps only just spread throughout Prague would be replaced by some form of electricity in the next hundred years, while others—like Zacharias—saw fire as the eternal tool of man. Working with Zacharias, Domek could succeed where Imrich failed.

"If I can get it to work. Take some of these with you and think about it. This way you can waste them without having to explain the experiment to your bosses. If we can patent a portable combined form, we'll be rich! Return Prague to the glory of the Empire!"

Domek took a handful of matches and a red phosphorous pad, setting them in opposite pockets so he wouldn't risk accidental sparks. He didn't want to know what might happen to the wisp's jar if it caught on fire. "Thanks," Domek said.

"Now, come on. I have a double-action revolver in need of touching up before the owner comes by tonight. This gentleman managed to completely cock up the cock, if you can believe it. People shouldn't be wielding guns if they don't know a bolt from a spring."

This was just what he needed. He would have to make a decision about the wisp soon, but for now, it was just his hands and the simple act of creating and repairing. Tucking his satchel under his worktable, close enough to touch, he began to work.

By the time Ora arrived back at her home, her hand had begun to heal. It would take a long time, possibly weeks, to be normal again. Once, on a ship to China, Ora had opened the wrong door and had been confronted with the full force of the noonday sun. She had crawled back to her cabin, half-blind and scorched to the bone, and had not moved again until the ship had docked two weeks later.

One of her maids, a young girl named Mila, greeted them at the door. Lina slid past her and took the stairs beyond. Ora watched her go, wishing there were words to fix what she had broken.

Mila was twisting her hands anxiously when Ora looked back to her. "Lady Fischerová, you have a guest. Nedda," the cook, "has given her tea and pastries in the sitting room."

Ora frowned. "You let someone in when I was out?" She kept a small staff, just enough to maintain the house and appearances. With Lina and Ora out for the day, Mila and Nedda had the run of the house, and they kept it well in order. Though Mila, being young and still awed by Ora's wealth, was shy, Nedda was a brusque older woman who normally had no compunctions about standing her ground. After two years in Ora's service, Nedda had uncovered her mistress's unusual appetite. Instead of alarm, she'd only yelled at her for a half-hour about all of the food she'd wasted by having Nedda prepare meals anyway, and had designed a plan to continue masking her grocery purchases without needing to send any food to the trash. Even better, Nedda had briskly taken over the collection of blood for the household, managing a deal with the butcher for it as easily as she haggled for vegetable prices at the market.

Nedda and Lina were key allies in keeping her secret from the rest of the servants. To them, Ora was just an eccentric widow with a deep fear of the wrinkles any time in the sun might cause.

"She wouldn't take no for an answer. I told her you would be out for an unknown amount of time, but she was determined to wait for you." Mila cleared her throat. "It's your sister-in-law. She said that you'd been avoiding her."

Ora swore quietly. This was the last encounter she needed today.

Quickly, she darted upstairs to pull on a shawl over her bloodied dress and found a pair of purple gloves to hide her burnt hand. Then, Ora sniffed the air, and realized the back of her dress had been smeared with bird droppings when Czernin had tackled her to the ground. Lina was nowhere to be found, so Ora found the jacket of her riding habit and pulled it on. It was stiff with disuse—Ora did not ride horses, and had bought the outfit to complete her closet—and did not match the fabric of her dress, but any longer and her guest would be suspicious. Ora patted her hair, plucking out feathers of both Lina's placement and from Czernin's attack.

She took a moment to open a drawer and place a hand over her pocket watch, a gift from Franz. The metal was cool under her touch, ticking steadily into the future. Then, she went downstairs.

The woman perched in the sitting room, sipping her cup of tea quietly, had hair whiter than the first snowfall. Her wrinkled face was nearly the same color, suffused with a pale pink that stayed uniform even at her lips, though her cheeks were slashed with heavy blush. Instead of making her look younger, the effect was funereal. Or maybe that was just Ora's mood.

"There you are, Ora," Lady Alena Nováková said, setting down the porcelain cup. It clattered slightly as it hit the saucer, betraying the tremor in her hands. "I was starting to wonder if you were going to keep hiding upstairs. I know how quiet you can be."

"I just got in," Ora said. "You should have told me you were coming." She bent to brush a quick kiss across her withered cheek. She smelled of lavender powder and sugared plums, with the same underlying scent as an aging tome on a back shelf of the university library. Decay.

"If I had, then you would most definitely have been hiding," Alena said. The half-smile that stole onto her lips was the same as always. "You've been avoiding me, and you can be creative when you're determined. You might have shut the entire neighborhood down if you'd had to. Sit down. Don't make me look up at you."

Ora sat. "I haven't been avoiding you, Alena. I've been busy."

"You lie as beautifully as ever," Alena said. "Your face hasn't changed, my dear. Your tells are the same ones I learned at twenty-five. Now, I want to hear about how you've been."

"There's a beautiful art gallery at Sternberg Palace. Have you been? Probably not—you've always thought art was boring. I'd also rather read a good book or go to a lecture any day, but you always can meet the most interesting people at galleries." Ora chatted about the exhibit for several minutes, and then slipped into recounting a discussion she'd had with the new theology professor at Charles University. If she talked enough, perhaps they could get through this whole visit like a stroll through a meadow, surrounding themselves with sweet-smelling things and not lingering in any shadows.

Alena let her chatter while she finished her tea, laughing at the right moments and adding comments when Ora let her. Alena had never cared about academia the way Ora did. Before she'd gotten married, the only thing that could interest Alena was horses. After her marriage, she'd learned how to gossip with the best of Prague, but she'd never developed a taste for culture. She'd always said that if she needed a dose of pretension, she could just go visit Ora and her husband at Mělník.

Alena had always loved to tease her older brother.

When Ora paused to accept a tray of slivers of raw venison from Nedda, Alena finally interrupted her. "I did come to see how you were doing. I think you've answered my question." She sighed. "You're still sad."

Nedda left the room, closing the door firmly behind her.

"Not everyone sees salons and lectures as torture," Ora reminded her airily. She ate the venison ravenously, unworried about decorum in front of her sister-in-law. Her body was screaming for replenishment to heal her burnt hand.

"Ora, I've known you since I was practically a child. You can't bluster your way around me." She waved a hand. "I thought you might have started to settle by now."

"No one comes to Prague to settle," Ora pointed out, waving a slice of raw meat at her.

"I did," Alena said. "It might not be Mělník, but that doesn't mean you can't find stability here. That you can't find happiness here."

"Alena, you can't think to tell me what happiness is."

"I didn't know you before you met Franz, but I saw how he changed you. You loved each other deeply. The home you built together was full of the steadiest love I've seen. In the early days, before he proposed, I thought you were like a dandelion seed that would be caught on the wind forever. But you made roots with him. You were a better country wife than I think even you thought you could be."

Ora laughed. The sound was bright and harsh. She'd met Franz in Vienna. At that point, she'd thought she'd never go back to Prague. It was the city she'd been born in, the city where she'd met Czernin and fallen into his tangled web. She had been traveling the world since she'd fled Czernin's decadent estate, and Vienna was the closest she'd gotten to Bohemia in decades. When she'd met the shy but charming Lord Fischer, she'd dallied with flirtation, but told him during the first night that she would never move to his estate and play the good wife. She'd had brief love affairs across the world, as delectable and thrilling and empty as the dregs of a honey wine: Herman in Oslo, Vihaan in Bombay, Clara in Paris. She was not interested in settling with someone from her homeland.

Within three months, she'd fallen hard, and found herself with a ring on her finger and a house in the country.

If Ora were a moon, she had waxed during her time with Franz, full and bright, and had been waning ever since.

Alena shook her head. "Art galleries, the friends you have flitting in and out, your trips to the theater—do you *talk* to anyone, Ora?"

"Some would say I talk their ears off," Ora said.

"I don't have time for you to dance around me," Alena

snapped, showing some of her old temper. She'd mellowed in the years since her own husband had died. For her, it had been nearly twenty years, and though she'd gotten along with him, there had been no great love between them. Her husband had left her with a title, an expensive home just down the road, and eight children who had already moved on.

"You know I have no interest in slowing down," Ora said. "I've been this way for nearly a decade now, Alena. There's no reason to change it now."

"But there is," Alena said quietly. "I want to know that I'm not leaving you suffering."

Ora clenched her fists. "Don't talk like that."

"I'm old, Ora. We both know it. Nothing will make this easier. Let me at least try to make sure I'm not leaving you completely alone." They sat in silence for a long moment. Ora couldn't meet her eyes. "I know it killed you when Franz died."

"It didn't kill me," Ora said. "I kept on living, and I'll keep on living long after you follow him."

"For your definition of living," Alena allowed. "I miss him too. But you can find happiness again."

"I loved Franz more than I've ever loved anyone," Ora said. "I traveled for half a century before I met him. I saw India and Russia and England and China. But none of those places compared to the home I made with him. I would have given up a lifetime of exploring the world for another day with him. He was the soul I lost when I was turned into what I am. But now he is gone, and I have to find a version of happy I can live with. I'm sorry it doesn't look how you want it to."

"It doesn't look like happiness at all. Franz wouldn't want you to be alone," Alena said.

"Then he shouldn't have died," Ora replied.

"Franz knew about our eternal life in heaven. I know you must be frustrated he left you behind, but you can't begrudge him his peace with God. You may be damned, but he wasn't. He had to move on." Her voice was gentle, comforting, despite the words. Ora stared into her kind eyes and saw Czernin again. *Why let him die?*

"He wanted to become a pijavica," Ora blurted. "He *begged* me for the change. He wanted to be with me forever. He wouldn't have chosen some unknown heaven over the life we had together. He *loved* me."

"There was a reason he chose not to become a demon in the end," Alena insisted, hands clasped tightly in her lap. "If all of that is true, there's still a reason you didn't turn him. And why you haven't offered to turn me. You loved him back. I know you did. You wanted to save him."

"We wanted to save *you*," Ora said. "When he got sick, I had to tell him my final secret. The pijavice are more demon than you know—we're drawn to our own bloodline like rabid dogs. When we first turn, we can't rest until all our living relatives are dead and the blood that used to be in our veins is eradicated. I knew he wouldn't take the change knowing that. I loved you like a sister. The thought of him killing you, of both of us living with that, sickened us. But I gave him the option anyway because I *knew* this would happen. I knew that someday, you'd grow old and die, and then I would have an eternity alone without either of you. Killing you would have haunted us forever. It was the right choice. But now it's all for nothing anyway. Watching you die has been the slowest torture of my life."

Alena's hands were clasped over her mouth in horror, frail fingers shaking.

Ora felt her stomach twist. Her outburst had been poison in her mouth, roiling out of her. "Alena..." She scrubbed her hands over her face, wincing when her blackened hand rubbed against the inside of her glove. She felt too large for her body, as though her fangs had spread into her blood and were trying to burst through her skin.

"I should go," Alena said weakly, finding her feet. She stumbled slightly, and pulled away when Ora reached to steady her.

"I'm sorry," Ora said, stepping back. "I was never going to tell you."

"That," Alena said, voice more fragile than Ora had ever heard, "does not make it better. I need to leave."

Ora reached out a hand as she left, but did not call to her. She waited, alone in the sitting room, until the front door closed.

Alena's heartbeat, the ticking clock that marked the final era of her life, faded into the distance.

Ora picked up a vase and flung it at the wall. The crystal shattered like frost on a lake, dissolving into dust with a ringing crash. A shard bounced back across the room toward her and sliced the skin of her cheek. Monster that she was, it healed over before she reached up to wipe the blood away.

Destruction was all Ora knew how to do.

14

After the gun was fixed, Zacharias seemed to forget about Domek's presence, absorbed again in testing the stacks of matches on his table. Hoping he would not hear the sound of an explosion, Domek moved to his station at the front of the small room.

As Imrich laughed at Domek's ideas, he kept his small experiments tucked away in his uncle's shop. Though the kalina stake had not worked against the pijavica on the bridge, Domek thought Imrich's idea to test beyond the traditional weapons had weight. Why did pijavica blood reject hawthorn wood and no other? Why were spirits only vulnerable to silver? New silver alloys were being tested every day—at what point would the iron content overwhelm the silver heart and make the weapons useless?

He picked up his box of silver shavings, salvaged during years of work with Zacharias. Paluska helped keep the lamplighters stocked with silver weapons, despite the ministry's reluctance to give the poor watchmen the precious metal, but Domek was on his own for his experiments.

The pure silver glinted in the low light of the shop. If he poured the metal directly into the clay jar, would the wisp survive? The flame would have no way to escape the poisonous metal. He could end it now.

His mother's horrified face flashed in his mind, and he put the silver back on the shelf.

Instead, he threw himself into repairing a sewing machine, putting on a pair of magnifying spectacles and losing himself in the intricate work.

When Domek was on patrol, he was always alert. He had a method for scanning the surrounding area so that nothing was overlooked. On his own time as well, Domek was methodical and absorbed in whatever activity he put his mind to. It was one of the reasons he enjoyed tinkering. Slowing down had always been easier for Domek than it seemed to be for others.

The bell over the door rang out, and Domek blinked back to awareness. Across the room, his uncle was doing the same. If Domek looked as dazed and startled as he did, the shop's client would likely turn right around to find a more aware repairman.

"One moment!" Zacharias called.

Wiping his hands on a rag, Domek poked his head out of the back room to check on the guest. He shook his head. "Don't worry about it, Uncle Zach. I'll handle this one."

"My God, it's so musty in here," Cord said in greeting. He would have looked out of place if he hadn't had a casual, confident air that made him seem welcome everywhere. Dressed in buckskins and a green riding jacket, accented with a purple cravat, he stood out in the shop like a drake surrounded by hens.

"That's the smell of men who actually work for a living," Domek said, clapping Cord's shoulder. He led him over to the front counter where Zacharias kept his cluttered mess of receipts and bills so that their conversation wouldn't interrupt his uncle's work in the back room. From the sounds back there, he had already forgotten there was a potential customer in the front. "What are you doing here?"

"I thought I might find you here. Anton said that you went missing. I couldn't believe what happened to your flat."

"You talked to Anton?" Though they were technically friends through Domek, Cord and Anton had never gotten along. Domek had been grateful for them tolerating each other for his sake, but had given up hope that they'd enjoy each other's company. Domek hoped Anton hadn't gone behind his back to ask for money.

Cord shrugged. "He was asking for you. Thought that I might have given you a room for the day. I guess he didn't think that you might have gone home; he's not the family type. I figured if you hadn't told him, you didn't want him to know."

"It's not that," Domek said. "I'm just trying to...lay low."

With a low whistle, Cord said, "Just what have you gotten yourself into?"

"Nothing."

Cord just raised an eyebrow. "As an expert in getting into disasters, I can spot someone else in one from a town away. You, Domek, are in trouble. You were acting strange at the museum as well. I've been worried about you. Are you in debt?"

Surprised by the blunt question—though he shouldn't have been—Domek spluttered, "No, no, nothing like that."

"Because if you were, you know I have a weekly allowance that's bigger than your monthly pay," Cord continued.

"Yes, I'm aware," Domek said tensely.

Cord pressed on. "You've had my back for years. You know I'd give you a loan if you needed it."

"I'm not in debt," Domek said. "You know me. I'm careful with my money."

"True," Cord said. "I'd believe it more if it were Anton. He was acting guilty too, but it was probably because he was knocking on my door before noon. He knows I don't wake up that early. So, there was another reason someone decided to bust into your place."

Domek flattened his hands on the counter. "Drop it, Cord."

"I'm not trying to be overbearing," Cord pointed out. "I'm trying to be a friend."

"Not all your friends want you for your money," Domek said quietly. "I'm not your pet."

Cord frowned. "I never said you were. If anything, I'm yours. Like a silly dog you give attention to when you're bored."

"Cord," Domek said, irritated and hurt.

Cord shrugged. "Look, I'll stop nagging. But if something is wrong that I can help fix, tell me. I don't have many of those not-money-grubbing friends, and I'd like to keep the ones I do have alive. Now, let's go out tonight. Thursdays are your night off, right?"

"I can't. I'm going to a...thing." When Cord raised an eyebrow, Domek clarified, "An opera."

Cord grinned. "You're still sniffing around Lady Fischerová's skirts. You would never go to a show like that on your own, and I know I'm not the one dragging you. When did you have time to make your move? Did you find her again after the museum? I hope you did a better job at seducing her."

"It's not like that," Domek hedged.

He wished he had been the one to take the first step, but he had been dazzled by Ora from the first time they'd met.

When Ora Fischerová had walked into Zacharias's shop a year ago, it had been as though a bell had been struck inside of Domek's chest. Ora's presence radiated in every room she entered. Eyes were drawn to her like a fireworks display on a cloudless night. It was not only her appearance, though Domek could still remember the hue of the low-cut gown she'd worn that day, her moon-pale skin, and her soft red hair. She carried an indefinable energy like a shawl.

She had brought in a gorgeous old pocket watch with an ornate bronze shell. Though, as they discovered when they cracked it open, its gears were meticulously polished, one of the springs had been knocked out of place. Zacharias was already salivating over the craftsmanship while Domek had reassured Lady Ora Fischerová that they'd repair it for her.

She'd given him a small, intimate smile. "I did my research. I trust you," she'd said, and Domek hadn't been able to look away since.

Cord grinned at him, laughter sparking in his eyes. "Then can I come?"

"No."

"It's not as though I'm a threat between you and your lady," Cord reminded him. "I want to get to know the woman who has you panting after her. You barely give women the time of day. Besides, from what I saw yesterday, you need the help. I'll make sure you don't stutter too much."

"Between the two of you, I think I'd be ribbed mercilessly. But there can't be anything between us."

"I can't imagine anything you could say next that would make me believe that," Cord drawled.

"She's a lady, Cord. I'm a lamplighter. She doesn't know what I do, but she knows I work. There's no reason to start something between us," Domek said. "I couldn't survive in her circles." And if he kept spending time with her, she might not survive his.

"She came up to us yesterday. She asked you to the opera. It's not as though she's afraid to be seen with you," Cord pointed out. "Besides, my family name is older than the one she married into, and you and I are friends."

"That's different."

"She's an eccentric, wealthy widow. She doesn't have to answer to anyone. If she wants to spend her time with you, that's her decision. Not society's, and not yours. Don't tell her what's best for her. From what you've told me, she's well able to decide for herself."

"We'll see," Domek hedged.

Cord sighed and shook his head. "Someday you'll realize how excellent my advice is. Now, if you're not free later tonight, what about dinner before? It's almost time for Zacharias to close up the shop, if he's noticed the passage of time at all. My cook is making something delicious tonight. It'd be a shame to eat it all on my own. Besides, you should be staying with me until your flat gets fixed, and not bothering your poor mother. She barely has enough room as it is, and I have too much."

Domek shook his head. "I couldn't do that."

"Let's argue about it over dinner," Cord suggested.

Hesitating, Domek rested a hand on the bag at his hip. If

he wanted to keep the wisp safe, Cord's was as good a place as any. His mother was distressed after the reading, and, with a full-time butler, Cord's security was better than Domek's flat would ever have.

"Go on," Zacharias said, coming into the front of the shop. "You've done enough for the day. I'll see you for your real shift on Monday."

Domek nodded to his uncle. "Thanks for letting me pass some time here." He turned to Cord. "Let's see what that delicious dinner looks like."

It looked, it turned out, like more food than any one man should have ever planned to eat on his own.

There was duck that had been roasted so perfectly the crisp skin practically crackled off the tender meat. The vegetables on the table could have come directly from a farm to the cook's pans—they were as bright and fresh as any Domek had seen. Apricot dumplings sat artfully in the center of oversized platters, drenched in melted butter and shredded cheese.

As Domek ate, not even trying for delicacy as he shoved food into his mouth, he asked, "When did you hire a chef like this for the flat?"

"The new cook is a fellow from Paris. A friend of a friend put us in touch when he moved here. Not my type, but he's a master in the kitchen. France is missing out."

Cord's dog, a whip-smart brindled mongrel, sat on the floor beside him, staring up at every motion of Domek's hands. He whined and tapped his claws on the floor. "Sorry, pup. Not for you." He looked back at Cord and waved a hand at the table.

"Does your father not still have you on a strict budget?" Cord's father, who was part of the Bohemian parliament, was one of the most powerful men in Prague. The last emperor, who had retired and still lived in the palace, saw him as a mentee, and had been giving him preferential treatment for years. Cord, a wild son, had been placed under some restrictions, but was left mostly to his own devices. "This all seems a bit beyond even your standards."

"I had a bit of a gambling windfall a few weeks ago. I've been using it to supplement my allowance," Cord said. "Besides, I keep a small staff. I'd prefer one great chef and my butler to an entire household."

Discussing finance with Cord was often an exercise in translation. As he had grown up with wealth and did not work, Cord seemed to view money as a fickle but mostly reliable friend, rather than something to scrounge and fight for.

With his monthly allowance from his father, Cord had purchased a vast flat on the south end of the city, close to the Francis I Chain Bridge, which stretched precariously over Střelecký Island toward the west bank. The island, wild and wooded, famously served as a training area for men practicing with longbows or crossbows. Cord had joked that with the current state of the local militia, he would need to trek north for Charles Bridge at the risk of being shot while on his morning constitutional. The flat was on the top floor of a narrow building the color of rich butter with elaborate cornices over each window. Bursting from between a garden and a plain white building, its grand design reflected its occupant.

Domek took another bite of duck. "I'll agree on the cook," he said. Cord's butler had disliked Domek from the moment he'd set his low-class boot in the door years before. Proving the butler right, Domek gave into the beseeching eyes beside him and slipped Cord's dog a bite of duck.

Domek wondered if there were any leftovers in the kitchen that he could wrap up and take over to his mother tomorrow as an apology. She was likely eating the challah from that morning.

"Are you going to tell me about what happened to your flat?" Cord asked while they sipped plum brandy after their plates were scraped clean. Though his flat had several rooms for the purpose, they lingered in the dining room. Once Domek stood up, he would need to prepare for his night at the opera, and he wanted to draw out his evening with his friend slightly longer. After the chaos around the wisp, it was comforting to be with someone familiar.

"I wasn't planning on it," Domek admitted.

Cord hummed. He was lazily petting his dog's head. After wolfing down the duck, the disloyal beast had moved back to sit by his owner. "You said it wasn't about money. Should I assume that it's related to your...job?"

"Why do you say that like you mean something else?" Domek asked.

Cord raised an eyebrow. "You can't really think I don't know what you really do after all these years. Remember how we met?"

"I'm a lamplighter," Domek said. "Part of that job is keeping the streets safe. We're watchmen as much as we are mechanics."

"But you're not just protecting us from humans," Cord said.

Domek put down his glass. "You know?"

"About the demons? Yes."

"How long? Why have you never said anything?"

"I knew that you were probably tasked with keeping the secret," Cord said. "I know something about that, and I didn't want to put you in a sticky situation if one of your bosses found out I knew. Besides, you never seemed to want to talk about it. But if the problem is starting to follow you home…"

"I'm handling it," Domek said. "How did you find out about them? Did I let something slip?"

"I've known since before we met," Cord said. "Those who operate in Prague's underground tend to run into one another, whether we're looking for the same thing or not. I learned early that you need to be careful who you take up on an offer to be sucked in a back room."

"Cord!"

"Don't be a prude," Cord said, waving a hand.

"It's not that," Domek said. Cord had always been blasé about the laws against sodomy—the harsh punishments of the past had been reduced to jail time in recent decades, which he could buy his way free from—and Domek trusted him to know his wants. "You're putting yourself at risk. What sort of men are you associating with that you can't tell a pijavica from a man?"

"It's not as easy as you might think," Cord said. "I'm sure you've walked past a dozen in tailcoats and never looked twice."

"I know there are pijavice who have wormed their way into power, but I'm sure I would recognize them if I saw them. There's no hiding evil. You need to be more careful about who you trust. They're monsters."

"Don't worry. I've taken up with an entirely human sort of degenerate," Cord assured him. "I'm not picking up anyone new right now."

"It's that serious?" Domek asked, distracted. In their years of friendship, Cord had never settled down with anyone.

Cord knocked back the rest of his brandy. "I'll give you all of the gossip later, Myska. Right now, you have your own love life to worry about. If you don't get going soon, you'll be late. Come on. Let's see if there's anything in my closet you can borrow for it that won't be ripped to shreds by that chest of yours."

15

After her day with Lord Czernin then Alena, Ora was tempted to cancel her plans and spend the night wandering the streets, working out her roiling anger on anything in her path. She wanted to crush something in her hands until she was no longer the most broken thing in the city.

Why did her past continue to drag at her heels like a hound running a fox to ground? Would she spend eternity picking up more sorrows to haunt her? Perhaps it was what she deserved. Today, she had hurt two of the only living humans who gave a damn about her.

Late in the afternoon, Lina had turned up at her door with a flat expression. Without speaking, she had carefully sponged the blood and dirt from Ora's skin, squeezed her into a new gown, and curled her hair in an elaborate modern style. Every time Ora opened her mouth to apologize or to announce she was canceling her date, the oppressive silence had kept her quiet. They had avoided eye contact as Lina worked, and Ora did not complain when Lina tugged on her knotted hair too hard.

Hackett drove her alone across the river, and she waited outside of the Provisional Theater, adjusting her white silk gloves. The massive building was a study in classic lines, with a pointed roof and two tiers of columns lining the front. The small plaza before the theater had a clear view of the castle on the hill, lit with candles in the many windows. The rain last night brought a crispness to the air, reminding the city that winter hadn't quite loosened its claws.

"Lady Fischerová!"

Ah, yes. There was another reason Ora had wanted to avoid the opera tonight. As she spent more of her time in society at literary salons and lectures than at galas, the opera was one of the few places she ran into the more overbearing ladies. Most days, she could make conversation with anyone, but tonight she had little patience. "Lady Enge," she greeted, turning to the other woman, who had dragged Lord Enge along with her.

They were new money, accumulated from an empire of coal mining that neither had ever touched. Lady Enge had been cold to Ora when she had first arrived back in Prague ten years ago, excluding the brash newcomer. Over the years, as Ora had become a settled figure and other, more vulnerable new people had arrived, Lady Enge had changed her tune.

"You look as radiant as ever," Lady Enge said, not giving her husband time to add his own greeting. "I swear you haven't aged a day since I met you. What *is* your secret?"

"I used to drink virgin blood, but that was unsustainable," she said coolly.

Lord Enge laughed. "Now, if that were true, we could bottle it and make millions!"

"It only works when taken straight from the vein," said a new voice.

Ora whirled to find that in the overwhelming mix of scents from the surrounding crowd, Darina Belanova had snuck up on her. She was wearing the same serviceable gown from Czernin's palace earlier and a vicious smile.

"I don't believe we've met," Lady Enge said, looking between Ora and Darina.

"We haven't," Darina said. "Ora—we need to talk."

Ora gave the Enges a tight smile and then grabbed Darina's elbow. "What are you doing here?" she hissed, leading her away from the press of the crowd toward the edge of the river.

"Is this what you've been doing? Going to the opera and letting grubby mortals treat you like you're one of them?" Darina asked. "You should be running this city. Instead, they'll be laughing at you as soon as they have the chance." She glanced back toward Lady Enge. "Have you ever thought that if Czernin were a woman, he could never have sat in that palace for so long? A line of identical male heirs doesn't draw attention, but a line of ladies inheriting a palace would have the villagers loading their rifles. You must have to move every few years to stop people from catching on to you."

"Did you follow me?"

"No, I had a sudden horrible hankering for droning orchestral music," Darina drawled. "Czernin sent me. He wanted me to keep an eye on you. I was supposed to follow you around the city without you noticing."

"Well, you're doing an excellent job," Ora said.

Darina shrugged. "Czernin is not here."

"He'd kill you if he found out you were working against him," Ora said. She brushed her unburnt hand over one of her shoulders, feeling the healing claw wounds under her dress.

"He may kill me anyway. He doesn't know what he wants. You saw him, what he's become. I'm not such a fool as to follow his orders blindly anymore."

"Then leave Prague," Ora said. "You helped me earlier, but that doesn't mean you're welcome in my city. The people here have done nothing to deserve you or Czernin."

Ora tilted her head when she caught a familiar scent on the air. It was warm and metal-bright, laced with charred chemicals, honey, and the promising smell of a storm boiling on a horizon. It was an intoxicating mix that stood out as authentic in a crowd of men and women doused in pomades, cologne, and the heavy must of burnt tobacco. She turned to follow the trail.

Domek Myska was walking through the crowd toward her. Though he was broader than any other man there, he didn't use his bulk to push people aside. Instead, he slipped and wove his way through, like a bird flitting among the steeples of the city.

"We'll talk later," Darina murmured. Ora turned back to her, but she was already slipping away. She wanted to call her back, demand more answers, but this was a poor place for a confrontation.

Domek stopped in front of her and bowed. He was nearly an entire head taller than her with broad shoulders and a trim waist that came from manual work. His dark hair curled over his collar, slightly longer than was fashionable. Though his pants were of his usual work-hewn variety, an expensive, modern overcoat was wrapped around his shoulders. It was tight on him, but it did give her a fantastic view of his chest and arms. She wished she were in the mood to appreciate it. "Evening, Lady Fischerová. I hope you weren't waiting long."

"Mister Myska," she said, forcing herself to smile. It felt unnatural on her lips, the grimace of a skull. "I was worried you wouldn't show up."

"I said I would," he said, as though it were as simple as that. Perhaps to someone like him, it was.

Domek was solid, dependable. Ora, as much as she'd tried, wasn't. Her husband used to tease her for it. In many ways—most ways—he and Domek were opposites. Franz had been slender and delicate, prone to sickness. Part of Bohemian nobility, he had been privileged all of his life. Their horses had been his only brush with physical labor, and even that he managed mostly through the force of his gentling personality. One look from him and a horse would *want* to be better. Ora had felt the same way.

Ora looked past the mechanic. The Provisional Theater was set at the back of the land purchased for the city's new National Theater, which was being designed by Prague's greatest architects after the last had burned down. The location had a perfect view of the castle on the hill, with the spires of the eternally half-finished St. Vitus stretching into the sky, and the river that cut between them. At night, the river was visible more for its absence than its presence, a dark line in a city that was more and more brightly lit.

Was Domek's steady personality part of what had attracted Ora in the first place? Though he had more physical strength, and his background could not have been more contrary, Domek had the same soothing nature as Franz. Perhaps she had been searching for someone with the same stability as her lost love unaware. Maybe Lord Czernin was right. No one could escape the mistakes of their pasts. Even Ora, by convincing herself that going to his estate was the best way forward, was falling back into her own bitter patterns.

"Are you all right?" Domek asked.

Ora turned back from the river. "Fine," she said with a bright smile.

He didn't match her expression. "You seem distracted." He glanced down at his borrowed overcoat skeptically. "You're sure you'd like to go inside? We could leave."

She sighed. "Mister Myska," she said, taking his arm and dragging him toward the opera's entrance. "Does it ever seem pointless to you? The uphill battles people seem to constantly be fighting? You don't suppose Sisyphus ever just…let the boulder fall? Look at this theater. It's an entire structure that's simply a stopgap to the next. Who's to say the next building won't simply burn down again once it's built, starting the entire process over?"

He gave the question solemn consideration. "I've never been the type to stop trying," he said finally. "Some challenges are more difficult than others. Sometimes, sleeping would be the easiest option. But if you don't keep pushing forward, what's the point of…anything?"

"Exactly," Ora said.

"That *is* the point," he said. "Hopeless or not, life keeps moving. I don't intend to let it move on past me."

"Seize the moment and hope everything works out in the future?" Ora prompted.

"Something like that," he said. "There are days when it seems like no matter what happens, everything stays the same. Maybe on a grand scale, it does. That doesn't mean that every minute in someone's life can't be important too."

Ora looked up at him, swaying closer. "That was practically romantic," she said. She was ready to move past this serious conversation and into her distraction for the night. "I didn't peg you as a romantic type. Broody, thoughtful," a tad awkward, "and quiet, yes, but not romantic. Do you read poetry, Mister Myska?"

"Rarely," he said stiffly, taking a step back. If they had been somewhere more private pressed so closely together, it would have been entirely inappropriate. Even in a lobby full of people all pushing their way toward their seats, a charged intimacy sparked between them.

"That's more than most. I hope you're as strong as you look. I may swoon."

"You're teasing me," he said.

She couldn't tell whether or not he was pleased by that realization. "I only tease people I like," she assured him. "Thanks for escorting me to this show. Not many would have been up to the task."

"It's not a hardship to listen to music," he said.

"I'm being serious. I'm not the most traditional of women. There are men who would have run screaming at the thought of an evening alone with me."

"I like that you're not traditional," Domek said. "If you were traditional, you wouldn't be speaking with me at all."

Ora wanted to argue, but knew it was true. "That would be my loss," she told him. "You're a delightful conversationalist, you let ladies lure you to operas, and you're good with your hands. What's not to like?"

Ora led him up to their seats on the balcony, which pressed

close to the railing. Since she'd only bought the tickets yesterday evening, they had ended up in seats tucked in the middle of a row, leaving them crammed in by the murmuring crush of humanity on either side. Still, she knew it was likely better seats than he'd ever sat in before. With worker's wages, he would have been in the standing room section below, if he'd come at all.

Disgust for herself and those surrounding them washed over Ora. Domek was a good man—solid and shy. What made these people, most of whom inherited their wealth, better than him? Ora had been a peasant in her first life, and it had been the judging looks from the wealthy which had sent her careening into Czernin's grasp. She had longed for power, for respect. How could Domek seem so unaffected?

A woman looked twice at the secondhand overcoat stretching over Domek's shoulders, and Ora sneered at her before considering it may have been an appreciative glance instead of condescending.

"Have you been to the opera before?" Ora asked, if only to get out of her own thoughts for a moment.

Domek shook his head. "I enjoy music, but haven't been here," he said.

"You'll like this," Ora decided. She leaned closer to him. His honey and metal scent helped drown out the river of perfume surrounding them. "I wish the National Theater would be finished more quickly. It's on track to be the most beautiful building in the city. Did you know that they plan to fold this design into the final structure? I presume the architect was feeling fussy about putting effort into something so blatantly called the Provisional Theater."

"I can't blame him," Domek said. "It's difficult to believe this is simply a placeholder. It's magnificent."

"Music is for the ear, but opera is a full sensory production. The scenery is as important as the singers. Tonight, we're seeing *The Bartered Bride*, which was written by the principal conductor. This theater was actually opened with one of his operas, but they didn't give him the job conducting until four years later. Politics. You'd think you'd get to avoid them in the arts, but they're worse there than anywhere. This show is supposed to be very German, but should still be enjoyable."

The orchestra began to tune their instruments, adding a layer of cacophony on top of the muttering, shuffling crowd. Ora was tempted to cover her ears to try to muffle some of it, but knew that would barely help—and would worry her companion for the evening. As charming as Domek was, Ora was sure coming tonight had been a mistake. She was able to distract herself while teasing him, but sitting silent among the crowd threatened to shatter her composure. She felt like a spring being pressed and pressed until her energy threatened to defy suppression.

When the first song faded and the soprano stepped forward for her first aria, the sensation grew worse.

Music was pleasant, but Ora's tastes had always leaned toward physical art and academia. Her thoughts worked too quickly for a single mode of engagement. She needed conversation to supplement her enjoyment, or a story to compel her. In opera, the story was done in broad, predictable strokes, making it accessible to all languages and intellects. There was nothing to distract from her fear and shame. How was Alena coping with the horrible revelation Ora had thrown at her? What was Darina doing in her city? Would Lina forgive her for her temper?

She needed to get out of there. She couldn't sit through an entire opera tonight, not even with the delectable Domek Myska for company. This was a night for running along the Vltava, finding a disposable book and shredding it to pieces with her hands, for trying to find something in her house that could break her skin and—

She turned to Domek, ready to tell him that they were going to leave.

He was enraptured by the performance. Leaning forward slightly, he stared down at the stage with a slight, awed smile on his lips. As the soprano soared to a new height, his chest lifted with it, as though his soul were trying to escape his body. The music had cast a spell upon him, transporting him from their cramped conditions and sending him somewhere Ora couldn't follow.

He noticed her gaze and, carefully, reached over to clasp her hand in his. She leaned back, closed her eyes, and focused her attention on the gorgeous music. Not the singing on the stage below, but the steady pulse of his heartbeat.

At the first intermission, the normally stoic man chattered like a schoolboy about the show. It was charming—more charming than a man of his bulk should have been. Ora was grateful to be there with him for this experience. She wasn't arrogant enough to give herself credit for it, but it warmed her to know that when he thought back to this night, she'd be there in his memories alongside the singers on stage.

Using his breathing as a regulator, Ora made it through another act before she finally caved to the instinct to flee. She leaned over to Domek at the next break, enjoying the excuse to whisper in his ear. There was a near imperceptible tremor that ran through him when her breath hit his skin. "It's getting late. I should head home. Would you care to escort me? If you don't mind leaving the show slightly early."

He cleared his throat and turned to her. "You don't have a carriage?"

"There's a carriage. I live halfway across the city, and my slippers wouldn't be able to handle the cobblestones for so long without shredding. It's a long way to the door, though, and then the footman has to retrieve the carriage. I'd be lonely without company."

Domek nodded. "I believe I've had enough of the opera for the night." She took his arm and they slipped out of their seats and retreated toward the exit. There were a few other people milling about in the main lobby, getting drinks and stretching their legs. The opera could last more than four hours. Half of the building's business came from selling the fuel to get the audience through to the final bows.

"They really did put quite a bit of money into a building designed to become redundant, didn't they?" Ora commented, brushing a hand along the intricate gold filigree lining the threshold as they walked. "Do you think the gilding is spreading? Like a fungus?"

"Careful," Domek said. "If it is, you don't want to touch it. You might end up covered."

Ora laughed, delighted that he was joking with her. "And then you by way of me," she said. "Your chivalry leading me out of this place would be your downfall. I'll avoid any more brushes. I'm not sure gold is the right metal for your complexion."

"Much appreciated," Domek said.

She paid one of the loitering footmen a krejcar to fetch her carriage—her driver, Hackett, would be parked down the street to avoid the crush at the entrance of the theater—and then she and Domek stood on the steps in front of the theater to wait. They were the only ones outside.

Overhead, the night sky was cloudy, but free of rain. It felt like a sign, an opportunity.

Checking that the footman was still gone and the door behind them was closed, she moved in closer. Now that she had fresh air in her lungs, she felt sharper, more alive. His scent was almost overwhelming. She could hear the steady pulse of his heartbeat. "Why don't you escort me all the way home?" she asked. "The carriage ride will be so lonely by myself."

His eyes grew wide and he faltered, so she took the opportunity to strike. Ora was a predator at heart. She knew when to press an advantage.

Standing up on her tiptoes, she pressed her lips against his. Placing a hand on the side of his face, she kissed him as beguilingly as she knew how. Over the centuries, Ora had kissed many people. Men, women, pijavice, humans—she had learned the taste and touch of them all. There was an art to kissing, and after she had left Czernin's estate, she had found a vicious thrill in using her mouth for pleasure rather than pain. If she had her way, Domek would not be able to stand in the wake of her onslaught. Domek tasted the same way he smelled, honey-sweet and strong. His lips were soft against hers, even as his beard scratched her skin.

After a moment of hesitation where Ora coaxed and pleaded silently, he kissed her back. One of his hands landed on her waist and the other cradled the base of her skull. His hands were broad, spreading wide over her smaller frame. She felt encircled, safe as a bird in a nest. He kissed with the same methodical, contained focus with which he spoke, tempting her with what could come next. He was learning her with careful movements, testing and prying to unravel her secrets the way he had once fixed her pocket watch.

So methodical. Ora wanted to make him lose control.

One hand tangled into his curls, holding him close, and the other drifted down his back to explore its planes. He was broad and solid, sturdy as a mountain. Making sure her second set of teeth were still concealed—arousal of all kinds activated her predatory senses—she bit his lower lip and tugged.

Immediately, he stepped back, moving his hands to her shoulders to keep her apart from him. She had to release his hair, much to her regret. His lips were reddened from her attentions, giving him a deliciously mussed appearance.

"That's the opposite of what I was hoping for," Ora complained, trying to move closer again.

"What are you doing?" His accent was rougher than before, his voice slightly raspy.

"I would have hoped that would be obvious." She hooked a finger in his lapel. The fabric was expensive, and smelled of another man. Domek must have borrowed the jacket from a friend for tonight. She found the thought endearing, and wanted to tug him back down.

He glanced around the quiet street, and back at the closed doors at the front of the theater. There was another couple walking along the river, arm in arm. A carriage clattered nearby. "My lady," he said firmly, "you can't kiss me."

"I clearly can," Ora said. When he didn't move, she asked, "Do you not *want* to kiss me?"

"This isn't appropriate, Lady Fischerová."

"We just kissed. You may call me Ora. I'm a widow, *Domek*. My virtue is no longer in question. No one cares with whom I spend my time."

"They may not be able to complain, but they'll care if they see you with me. I may not be in your circles, but I know that much. You haven't thought this through."

Ora frowned, narrowing her eyes. "I hope you're not implying that I can't make my own decisions. Is this about—"

There was a shout from down the street. It was silenced abruptly, but Ora and Domek jumped apart and turned toward it. Her ears were sharp, but there were no further sounds. "Where is the footman?" she asked slowly.

Domek was already taking the steps two at a time, running toward the source of the noise. Ora sighed and followed.

16

Ora hurried after him, grabbing her skirts to free her legs. Up the street, she could hear the sound of a scuffle. As they got closer, she identified the scent of the footman—and his spilled blood—and the grave dust smell of a poltergeist.

At her side, Domek seemed ready to jump into the fray. She wanted to pull him back, step in front of him, protect him from the threat he would have no idea how to handle. It was a noble impulse for him to leap in to protect the poor footman, but also alarmingly rash for such a stoic man.

The footman had been dragged into the tight space between two of the street's buildings, out of sight of the main road. The thin alley was large enough for no more than two men standing abreast, blocked by buildings on either side, with a walkway connecting the two in an arch across the middle. The space was oddly illuminated by the thin green glow emanating from his attacker. Sharp bones had scored across the boy's face and chest, leaving vicious, bleeding lines. Behind him, the dark eye sockets and hanging jaw of the glowing skeleton seemed to laugh.

Death was not the end. In addition to the pijavice, whose mortal bodies were twisted by hatred into an undead existence, the souls of anyone unsettled by death tended to linger. The most common were the ghosts, faded impressions left by the spirits of those unable to untangle themselves from the patterns of life. Others, the poltergeists, were haunted by their sins, stripped down to their skeletons and searching the city for a redemption that would never come. There were stories of a greedy loan shark in Malá Strana who was seen hobbling through the alleys with a coin sack over his shoulder, hunched and alone for all time.

More malicious were those who had known occult power in life, which let them manifest into powerful, tormented beings like the White Lady in the castle on the hill.

The footman's attacker was a poltergeist, though Ora had never seen one attacking a mortal like a wild animal. The skeletons that wandered the city in the dead of night tended to pass unnoticed, too trapped in their own sins to bother with the mortal world. For a reaction such as this, the footman must have pissed on the poltergeist's grave. She winced when it lashed out again, slicing the boy's neck and drawing a spray of blood.

"We should call for help," Ora said when they paused at the mouth of the alley. If she could get Domek to leave, she could jump in to save the weakening boy.

"Go back," Domek instructed. "Now."

"Not without you," she said.

In response, Domek pulled a silver dagger from his satchel. "Run, Ora."

Vaguely, she thought she should feel excited about his use of her Christian name. Instead, her mind was stuck on the object in his hands. Silver. Since when did her normal, humble Mister Myska walk around Prague ready to kill spirits?

Before either of them could react, a dark figure dropped from the rooftop overhead and landed heavily on the skeleton. The footman collapsed to the ground as the poltergeist lashed out against the newcomer. Ora's eyes, unaffected by darkness, saw Darina laugh before tearing the skull from the spindly neck.

Domek bit off a curse, as though Ora would not know the end of the word, and dropped the dagger. It clattered against the cobblestones as he reached into his satchel and instead removed a pair of stakes. Ora could feel the poisonous pulse of the hawthorn from a meter away.

He had had those in his bag while they *kissed*.

Darina saw the stakes and hissed, her teeth a spot of white in the dark alley. She turned and scaled the wall, claws punching through the brick as she skittered toward the roof again.

Domek took a step toward a nearby ladder, but Ora stepped in his path. "Stop the bleeding," Ora instructed, pointing at the fallen boy. "I'll get help."

"Be careful," he said. "I'll…I'll explain later."

He must have expected her to swoon from the sight of the demons. The fool. "Just save him," Ora said, and darted from the alley back to the street.

She waited until she was sure Domek had not followed her, and then searched for a way up the building's front façade to chase down Darina. Even if her half-healed shoulders were not still aching, her scorched hand prevented her from using Darina's method. The street was quiet, with everyone either inside the opera house or tucked away asleep. She swore quietly. Darina was nowhere to be seen, the boy's lifeblood was spilling in the alley behind her, she had spent her night holding hands with a lamplighter, and Ora was no help to anyone.

With one last glance toward the rooftops, she turned and ran for her carriage.

This was his fault.

The poltergeist and pijavica must have been there for him. He didn't know how they had found him again. It was a miracle the demon had not attacked Ora.

Cursing himself, Domek ran toward the footman and crouched beside him. He pulled off his jacket and pressed it to the worst of the wounds he could see, the deep gash on the boy's neck. Somehow, the poltergeist's fingers had not hit an artery, but blood was pooling on the alley floor.

The boy was even younger than Domek had thought, likely not yet out of his teens, and seemed even younger in his pale stillness. Blood soaked through the cloth, leaving Domek's hands slick. The scent, copper and pain, was thick in the air.

Was Domek pressing on the right wound? The blood seemed to be everywhere. The nearest gas lamp was on the road beyond, so the alley was as dark as the night.

"Wisp," he called. "Come to me."

The flame drifted up from his satchel, flickering and sending an orange glow over the alley. Compared to the sickly green of the poltergeist, the familiar hue was comforting. In the light, Domek could see that the boy had been sliced across his face and chest as well. His uniform was dark with blood. Domek searched for his pulse, and found only a weak flutter beneath his fingertips.

"He's dying," the wisp said, voice like the crackle of tinder. As always, its scent was that of a storm on the horizon, powerful and raw.

Over the years, Domek had seen many final breaths. Each time was its own small horror, an anticlimax as a living person became only a body. Would the footman's soul reach heaven, or would he be trapped to repeat the doomed steps of the poltergeist that had killed him?

"Order me to save him."

Domek turned his head to look at the wisp. There was no expression to read, no tone to dissect. The last time Domek had tried to give the wisp an order, it had nearly killed him. Perhaps this was a trick, and Domek's words would be twisted to hurt the boy worse. But was there a worse fate than bleeding out in this alley?

"I can do it on my own, but my power is stronger with your energy directing it. Don't let him die for your pride."

"Save him," Domek breathed.

The wisp pulsed and drifted closer to the footman. As with the bubák, the wisp seemed to grow impossibly bright. Energy thrummed in the air like a thunderstorm, building and building pressure inside Domek's ears. Like the first time Domek had summoned the wisp, wind began to whip around them. An old newspaper fluttered and lifted from the ground, swirling up into the air.

Under the wisp's magic, the boy's wounds began to heal. It was a slow process, nearly indecipherable under all the blood. The slashes on the footman's throat closed first, the skin slowly scarring over. Finally, the cuts sealed. Blood still smeared his pale skin, but the wounds were gone.

The scratches on his face were next, though they seemed to close more slowly. It was like watching a puddle evaporate on a sunny afternoon, the edges slowly receding toward the center. The gashes had been deep and bled profusely, but after a minute they seemed like they had been healing for weeks.

The pressure in the air began to fade. Domek squinted to see the boy's face more clearly, and realized that the wisp's flame had dimmed to barely a flicker. It could have been the fire from one of the matches in Domek's pocket, small and temporary.

"What's happening to you?"

"I'm nearly...out of energy," the wisp told him. Its voice was fading into a whisper.

"Stop," Domek told it, sitting up. "You've stabilized him. We'll take him to a doctor. You've done enough."

The pressure in the air receded entirely, and the wisp seemed smaller for it. Without its power, it was nothing but an insubstantial glow in the night.

"Will you survive?" Domek asked.

"I need to...rest."

"Go back in the jar," Domek said. He hesitated, and added, "You did a good thing this night."

The flame fluttered and drifted down to his bag, seeming to collapse into it.

Domek barely had time to check the boy's wounds again before a man in tailored livery appeared in the alleyway beside him. When he didn't scream at the sight of them, Domek assumed it was Ora's driver. "I'll carry him," the man said. It was no wonder Ora seemed so confident traveling Prague alone—her driver was nearly double Domek's width, with arms as large as most men's thighs. There was a revolver strapped to his belt, its ornate silver barrel glinting in the dim light.

"Where's Lady Fischerová?" Domek asked. "Is she okay?"

"She's in the carriage," he replied gruffly. With little effort, the man lifted the footman in his arms. Domek followed, keeping the bloodied jacket in place. Though his neck and face were healed, the wounds on his chest were still deep. They maneuvered awkwardly out of the alley, careful not to jostle the unconscious boy too much.

Ora opened the carriage door when they approached. Her expression was composed once again, despite the situation. Her curls had fallen out of their bundle on top of her head, and her lip rouge was smeared. Or had Domek done that during their kiss? It seemed long ago. "Get in," she said briskly, and then moved to the opposite bench so Domek and the driver could leverage the injured footman inside.

Domek followed her inside while the driver moved to the front of the carriage, and then crouched on the floor by the pale boy to keep pressure on his chest.

The carriage began clattering forward. Domek nearly fell, but Ora's firm hand on his shoulder steadied him before he could lose his grip on the boy. It was lucky that the boy had fallen unconscious. The shake and rattle of the carriage was enough to jar Domek's teeth, and it would have been far more painful with the footman's injury.

"How far away do you live?" Domek asked.

"Less than ten minutes, if Hackett keeps up this pace."

Domek nodded, and settled in for the ride.

Ora rushed up the stairs to open the front door for Domek while Hackett whipped the horses forward again to go collect Dr. Roth. Domek carried the footman carefully, taking the steps with a slow efficiency that made Ora want to scream. If she had just left him behind like she had considered, she could have had the boy inside the house already. Instead, she had to play the simpering human who couldn't have lifted both Domek and the boy with one arm.

"Lina!" she shouted. The rest of her staff lived outside the home, so that she did not need to feign sleep for an ignorant team of useless servants, but Lina's room was on the ground floor. She ushered Domek into the dining room. She swept aside the tablecloth and candelabra with one deft motion, ignoring the clatter they made as they hit the floor. "On here," she directed, stepping back.

Domek set the footman onto the table, careful to keep one hand on the wound while not jarring the boy's body. "He's still unconscious," he said.

Lina stumbled into the room in her nightgown and a robe, her hair braided over her shoulder. She scowled at Ora, and then her expression slackened as she took in the tableau. "What in heaven's name…?"

"Lina, take Domek to the linen closet. Domek, grab as many as you can carry and then come back. Lina, heat up a bucket of hot water. The surgeon will need it when he arrives. Go, now!"

They both hurried from the room, and Ora tore off a new piece of her gown to press against the boy's chest. She had been worried the boy's neck had been cut, but it seemed his chest was the worst of his injuries. She had wanted to stay close enough to monitor the footman's fluttering heartbeat, but a rush of dread flooded her chest as soon as she was alone.

The smell of blood was horrifically appealing, coppery and bright.

The idea of harming this injured child turned her stomach, but her jaw twitched at the heady scent. Her horror at her own reaction soured and swirled with her predatory instincts, making her feel sick and weak. A sudden vision of her own mouth striking the hot wound overwhelmed her, and she closed her eyes.

What darkness was inside of her that it surged to the surface even when her heart and mind found it so horrific? Even as she fought to save this boy, was that instinct inside of her proof that she could never truly overcome the drive built by biology and a past of cruel indulgence?

The footman groaned, and his eyes fluttered open. From the way his breath hitched, Ora thought it would have been a mercy if he had stayed unconscious. Her hands slick with his blood, she leaned down so he could see her face. "Hush," she told him. "You're safe. We're getting you patched up. Hold on." The boy's mouth opened, but no words came out. His throat flexed beneath her hands, and she shushed him again. "Just breathe. It will be okay."

Domek returned before Lina, carrying a stack of crisp, white linen. He noticed that the footman was awake as soon as he stepped through the door, and he hurried to the boy's side. "My name is Domek," he told the boy as he deftly moved Ora's makeshift bandage aside and replaced it with the clean linen. "We're going to take care of you, okay?" His deep voice was soothing and confident.

Ora flinched back when their hands brushed, unable to reconcile Domek's softness with the revelation about his true nature. How could a man like Domek be a hunter by night? This was not a man she would have thought could kill. How many pijavice had the broad hands pressing against the boy's wound murdered? Was there a bloodlust lurking inside of him, just as it was inside of her?

Ora felt betrayed by the new knowledge. If they had met in a dark street, they would have been mortal enemies. The mild-mannered mechanic she thought she knew had a double life.

Ora circled the room, lighting the candles in the wall sconces. With her drapes in place, it was a wonder that Lina and Domek had even been able to follow her voice. The candles' dim light made the scene worse. In the darkness, her vision was flat and monotone. The light added violent color. Red. So much red.

She glanced up at Domek, wringing her hands as though she could flick away the blood still smearing her pale skin. "Did you see who attacked him?" she asked.

His eyes flicked up at her, and then he looked back at the boy. "It was dark."

She supposed he could not reveal the existence of the monsters in the shadows in front of the boy even if he had wanted to tell her, but she didn't think he would have brought her in on his secret either way. There were depths to Domek, slow-moving currents invisible at first.

He glanced back up at her, eyes sharp. "Could *you* tell?"

She shook her head and moved to open the heavy curtain over the dining room window to see if Hackett was close. The streets outside were empty.

The boy groaned again. Had he realized what was attacking him? In her experience, victims often were too turned around by the darkness and the speed of the attack to comprehend that it was fangs or bone sinking into their flesh rather than blades.

If Hackett did not hurry up, it would not matter if the boy had potentially seen a poltergeist and pijavica that night. Blood was staining the fresh linen like a horrific sunrise, and he needed medical help to survive.

Lina came into the dining room, hefting a heavy pail from which steam swirled. Though stronger than her slender frame suggested, Lina still needed to hold the handle with both hands. Ora crossed the space to help her, taking the bucket from her and setting it on the edge of the table where the boy would not accidentally kick it.

Domek was still murmuring reassurances to the boy. Ora could smell his sticky lifeblood and weak heartbeat, but Domek's voice was so confident and gentle it was impossible not to believe him.

Perhaps Ora was wrong to doubt Domek. Though he was clearly capable of violence, he was not a man predisposed to it. Sokol could not have been so gentle with an injured boy, not with the instinct inside him clawing for him to solve his problems with fists, guns, and blades. There was no urgency in Domek's voice, no fear, though Ora could hear the worried pounding of his heart.

Lina did not have the same composure. "What is happening?" she hissed to Ora, giving the table a wide berth.

The front door opened, and Ora's head lifted a moment before Lina or Domek noticed the noise. "That's the doctor. I'll collect him," she said as she left the room.

Dr. Ludwig Roth was frowning beside the looming form of Hackett just inside her door, cravat loose around his neck and hair rumpled with sleep. Though his crooked fingers were spotted with age, they were still clever and nimble. He was a transplant from Vienna, and only spoke German despite having lived in Prague for nearly forty years. "I'm too old to learn a new language now," he'd said early in their acquaintance. Ora herself, of course, never needed medical care, but she and the doctor attended some of the same scientific salons, and she'd hired him twice before: once when Lina had scalded her leg on the boiler, and another time when Nedda, her cook, had sliced a bloody chunk from her own thumb.

"*Gute Nacht*, Dr. Roth," Ora greeted him before sending Hackett to care for the horses. "Thank you for coming over so late."

"Your man was quite insistent, Lady Fischer," Dr. Roth said.

"It's an urgent matter," Ora explained as they entered the dining room. "We're in need of your expertise quite desperately."

"*Mein Gott*," the doctor said when he saw the tableau. He immediately opened his case of instruments on the table and leaned forward. "What happened here?"

"A mugging gone wrong, I believe," Ora said. "We found him on the street. Can you save him?"

Dr. Roth pushed Domek aside so he could inspect the wound, and the larger man conceded gracefully. The doctor hissed through his teeth when the still-bleeding gash was revealed. "This is a nasty wound, though it could have been worse. He seems to have been grazed on his face as well. I will do my best."

"How can we help?" Ora asked.

"You can give me my space," he said. "There are too many eyes on me right now. Get out, and let me work."

"I don't know much German," Domek said quietly, coming up beside Ora. "What's he saying?"

"He wants us gone," Ora said.

"Tell him I can help," Domek said. "I'm strong. He'll need another set of hands."

"Not a set that can't understand his instructions," Ora pointed out, and Domek flinched. Though nearly everyone spoke Czech due to the recent revival of the native tongue within Prague, German remained a standard of the upper classes. Domek, from his rough hands, would likely have never been given the chance to learn it.

"I'll stay," Lina said quietly. "In case he needs something."

"No. I will," Ora said.

"My lady, it's not proper."

"I don't give a fuck about propriety," Ora snapped.

Lina tapped her own cheekbone in warning.

Damn. Ora turned away and took a deep breath to collect herself. Now that Lina had alerted her, she realized that her face was still on the verge of ripping back into her monstrous form. The first step, the pupil dilation that stained her irises black, must have already begun. Her skin crawled from the effort of resisting the change provoked by the stink of fear and blood in the air. How obvious was it, if Lina had noticed? Domek, trained to hunt pijavice, would not remain oblivious for long.

"You'll tell us if you need more hands," Ora ordered both Lina and Dr. Roth.

The doctor ignored her, already wiping blood from the wound. The boy whimpered, a pained, terrified sound that made the hair on Ora's arms rise. Lina nodded. "I left extra hot water in the kitchen. You can get tea, if you need it." Ora didn't drink tea, so the implicit 'if you need something to do' rang loudly.

"Good luck, doctor," Ora said, and then forced herself to leave the room.

17

Domek leaned against the wall outside the living room, a cup of cold tea in his hand. He and Ora had retreated to the kitchen in a tense silence while the doctor had begun his work, and had returned to wait outside the door without needing to consult about it.

Ora, who had not even sipped from her teacup, stared at the door. The doctor and Ora's servant were quiet on the other side. The boy had whimpered for a while, but had fallen silent. Had he slipped back into unconsciousness, or had the surgery failed? Domek prayed it was the former.

When he had seen how much the wound had continued to bleed under the candlelight in Ora's dining room, he had been certain they would lose the boy despite the wisp's efforts. Even as he had held his hand and comforted him, Domek had been sure he was giving false promises.

The smell of the blood was cloying and bitter.

"Maybe you should go to bed," Domek said finally, a hoarse croak in the silent hallway.

"There is not the slightest possibility of that happening," Ora said crisply. "Perhaps you should leave."

Domek didn't move. They lapsed into silence again.

"I know you're scared," he said. "It's okay."

"I'm not scared."

"He'll make it."

"I don't need false platitudes, Domek. Don't waste your breath on me." She was resting her head against the wall, arms folded over her knees.

"I'm sorry," he said. "When you followed me into that alley…I was terrified for you. I thought you would end up like that boy in there, and the thought was more than I could bear. You're right. I can't promise things will work out. But I would die to keep you safe."

She laughed, tipping her head back to look at the ceiling and exposing her long, pale throat. "How are you real?"

He had never seen her like this, jagged as a glass shoved off a table. He had never been good with words. He reached out his hand, leaving it palm-up on the floor between them. Slowly, without looking at him, Ora slid her hand into his.

Finally, the doctor emerged from the room, and they both stood to greet him. His ancient form was slow and uneven, as though the work had sapped more life from his bones. He said something to Ora in German, his body language unreadable.

Ora murmured something in another language—something guttural that was not German nor Czech—and then slumped against the wall and let out a shaky breath.

"He'll be okay?" Domek asked. She nodded, and he felt the

tension sap from his shoulders like a physical blow. "Thank God."

Ora thanked the doctor—a German phrase even Domek knew—and paid him his fee before seeing him to the door. Domek slipped into the dining room on quiet feet, holding his breath. The boy was pale, and his eyes were closed, but his bandaged chest rose and fell steadily.

They had saved him. The *wisp* had saved him. If Domek had gone through with his plan to kill Kája, the boy would have died. He had nearly rejected the wisp's help, and even with it, the doctor had barely been able to stop the chest wounds from bleeding. The gashes Kája had closed on his throat had been far deadlier—the boy would have had no chance.

"He's asleep," Lina told him softly from by the boy's bedside. She brushed a wet cloth across his brow. "It's for the best. It was all too much for him, especially with the brandy I gave him."

"Are you all right?" Domek asked. Ora's maid was pale, and the sleeves of her robe were soaked in blood.

She looked away. "I'll be fine."

"You helped save a boy tonight," Domek told her softly.

Ora returned, brushing a curl of pale red hair from her face. Her up-do, which had been so perfectly coiffed at the start of their night, had fallen entirely. "Lina, go to sleep. Domek, help me carry the boy to a guest room. I'm not leaving him on the table overnight."

Domek nodded and carefully cradled the boy to his chest. Thick gauze covered his wounds, and Domek ignored the urge to peel back the bandages and reassure himself that the gashes in his chest were closed. He had to trust that the doctor was competent, and believe in the slow breathing from the frail body in his arms.

Ora took a candle and led him up the stairs to a small bedroom, which was in pristine order. Domek set the boy on top of the plush quilt and stepped back. "Someone should stay with him."

"I'll hear if he wakes up," Ora said confidently. She ushered him out of the room and shut the door. She looked up at him, and her fingers gently enclosed his wrist. "Come with me."

Domek allowed Ora to pull him down the hallway, away from the stairs, and into another bedroom. By candlelight the fabrics on the vast bed were lush and inviting, suggesting softness and luxury—along with other, more active, pursuits. This bedroom was larger than the guest room, but just as pristine. Ora's maids must have worked constantly to keep the rooms looking so untouched. Ora set the candle on a dresser while Domek looked around to find what she had wanted to show him. Carefully, she untied her shawl and spread it across the bed.

She prowled across the room back toward him, her eyes dark and hungry. She put a hand in the center of his chest, forcing him back until he was pressed against the wall. "Ora," he breathed. His body flushed with heat, chasing away the lingering chill of the night's events.

"Who are you, Domek Myska?" she asked. "You did not need to follow me home to make sure he survived, but you did anyway. How can someone be so prepared to fight and still be so soft with the victim?"

"I fight *for* the victims," Domek said. He spoke roughly—her hand was on his torso, yet he felt as though there were a grip around his throat.

"You," she said, running her hand down his stomach, "are so damned noble, aren't you? What are you doing here with me?"

It was a good question. Ora was alive and eager in his arms, but they were only just down the hallway from the evidence of how quickly that could change. What was he doing? He was dangerous to be around, especially with the wisp hidden in his bag. Ora was vibrant and beautiful, and the thought of carrying her limp body in a desperate bid to find a surgeon chilled him.

"We shouldn't," Domek murmured, turning his head away from her inviting, pale skin.

She huffed a sigh that he could feel against his neck. "Hang up the nobility for just this night, Domek." She put her hand on his cheek to lure him back down.

"I can't," he told her. "I'm sorry." He took her hand and kissed her knuckles, and then moved it away from his face. "We can't."

"You want me," she said, unwavering. "Don't deny it." When he didn't answer, she pressed closer, aggressive. "I can't believe I thought the fact that you are absolutely no fun was endearing. Perhaps instead of telling me how I should behave, instead of protecting me from myself, you could do what we both want to do."

"There are things you don't know about me."

"I know everything I need to." She shook her head and took a step back. "The next time, it could be you or I on the brink of death. I hope you don't regret this."

Instead of answering, Domek leaned forward to capture her lips. She gasped into his mouth, and then surged against him like a storm cloud bursting over the city. Caving to the instinct he had resisted before, he threaded his fingers through her soft hair to cup the back of her head. Gone was the teasing hesitance they'd entertained in front of the opera house. He was lost in the sensations, and she seemed eager to drown with him.

Her skin was cool to the touch, enticingly so. He felt overheated, flushed, and pulling her closer seemed the only cure. He dragged his mouth from hers so he could explore the rest of her face, kissing those high cheekbones, tugging on her small ears with his teeth, and then pressing his lips in a trail down her neck.

"Domek," she murmured, tilting her head encouragingly. One hand still in her hair to keep her where he wanted her, he teased the thin skin of her neck. She reacted with small gasps and pleased sighs, pressing herself into him.

The heady, blurry pleasure of her lips against his and the desperate grasping of her hands was a sharp contrast to the vivid fear of the last few hours. There was nothing to worry about beyond the feel of her lithe body against his.

There was no world beyond the touch of her hands and the taste of her mouth.

Ora was dancing with fire, and could not resist sticking both of her hands into its deadly core.

The man in her arms was a hunter, and she was his prey. Tonight, she had hunted him, and now she had him where she wanted him.

He kissed down her neck as his hands roamed over her body. His beard scratched against her collarbone, and she wished for the downy soft skin of her youth. She wanted to have marks to feel tomorrow. The veil of caution he hid behind had lifted. His hand was firm on her waist, dragging slowly upward. He unlaced the ribbon at the back of her dress, and her neckline loosened. His questing lips moved toward her shoulders, and Ora had just enough of her mind left to realize it would be dangerous to let him feel the wounds still healing from Czernin's attack.

Instead, she tugged at his curls until he kissed her mouth again, and ushered him back toward the bed. She pushed him onto it, leaned over to blow out the candle, and then crawled on top of him.

She helped him strip her from her clothes. She wanted to feel the heat of his hands on her skin. Ora had done nothing but make mistakes for days—for centuries—but feeling Domek beneath her was *right*.

She pulled off his shirt and explored the body hidden beneath.

Ora had been with many lovers over her long life. Darina had been as hard and slender as a steel cable, with jagged edges which could tear Ora to pieces. Vihaan had been in his fifties, still far younger than Ora's true age but more settled into his skin than her other lovers. Clara had been as soft and powdered as the beignets she had adored. Franz had been gentle, and had only grown frailer with age. She had needed to be careful with him, plucking and teasing out the reactions she wanted.

Domek was as solid as a mountain. The trimmed black beard on his face was matched by the sparse, unruly patches on his chest and arms. He was stoic under her ministrations at first, but she made it her mission to break him.

Finally, he surged up and twisted them over. She let him secure her beneath him, raising her arms over her head and luxuriating under his heavy heat. Finally, he continued the trail of kisses he had begun against the door, tracing from her neck to her collarbone to her breasts. By the time he made his way between her legs, she was certain she would shake out of her skin before he began in earnest. He was firm but methodical, and Ora was too fragile to be teased tonight.

"Domek," she said. She tried to find the words to express what she needed, but her mind was a haze. "Please."

He took mercy on her, moving back up to kiss her mouth. She spread her legs like a flower blooming, and they moved together.

The fire she had been bathing in all night now burned her from the inside.

She dragged her nails down his back and he groaned, kissing her again. He was a risk, but so solid and unmoving that she could throw herself at him and be as sure he would catch her as would the ground.

They moved together like a sunrise, slow and subtle before growing into an all-encompassing, blinding phenomenon. She closed her eyes against it. Ora felt scalded and protected at once, torn open only to have her dark abscesses filled with the softest silk. *Life* was all around her, from the pounding of the blood in Domek's veins to the pleasure blooming through her body. In Domek's arms, she was someone new, someone worth loving. He was tearing down her walls, taking her apart—and would piece her back together.

She let herself shatter.

"Ora," Domek murmured as they collapsed down onto the bed together. He felt loose-limbed and content. It had been years since he had last bedded a woman, and had never felt so enraptured. Sweat warmed his skin, and he could not stop running his hand through her hair. "You're so beautiful."

She blinked her eyes open and turned to him.

He shouted and lurched backward, nearly falling off the edge of the bed. "Your eyes," he breathed, standing up on unsteady legs. Vast pupils reflected bright green in the darkness, more feline than human. More monstrous than human.

Domek stumbled away and flung open the closest curtain, ripping the nails from the wall. The gas lamp outside spread a faint blue glow across the room.

Ora reached up to her face. Her claws touched her distended cheek. The sting in Domek's back from her nails resolved into a more vicious ache. "Domek," she breathed. Her fangs glinted.

He dove for his satchel and the hawthorn stakes inside. A pijavica. This had been an unusual way to catch a lamplighter unawares, but Domek cursed himself for being fooled. Heat turned to ice in his veins. "I suppose now I know why a lady wanted a lamplighter to escort her home," he said. The stakes were a familiar weight in his palms. "I'm surprised you didn't just snap my neck and steal it in the alley when your friend showed up."

"It's not what you think."

"You're a pijavica!" he accused. "Are you going to deny it? I can see your fangs. I've fought enough of you to know."

"And you're a pijavica hunter," Ora shot back. "How do you think I felt realizing I've been flirting with someone who kills for a living?"

"I kill those who kill us," Domek argued. He wished he weren't nude. "And I hopped into your carriage like a fool. What was your plan? Is the footman still alive?"

"Of course he is." He scoffed, and she glared at him. "Lord, I wanted to fuck you, Myska, not kill you."

He readjusted the grip on his weapons. "I have trouble believing that."

"Then that's on you. I've never lied to you. I haven't told you everything, but obviously neither did you," Ora said.

"What did I have to tell you? I thought I was protecting you. I didn't know you were the monster."

She stood up from the bed, leaving the sheet behind. Had he never noticed how truly pale she was? He had never seen her in the sunlight—their meetings had been in gaslit shops and deep into the night. She had shown up at the museum and the bookstore and acted as though it had been fate. How long had she been following him? Was she part of the cabal that was searching for the wisp? He glanced back down at the satchel at his feet. He had abandoned the weakened wisp and its jar without a thought as soon as she had kissed him.

Slowly, inexorably, like the moon rising in the night sky, she approached him. In the dim light, there was something entrancing about the too-wide stretch of her lips and her gleaming eyes. She held up a hand toward his wrist. "You know me, Domek."

She smiled gently and began to push his wrist aside, and he moved his other stake up to press against her ribs.

She went unnaturally still. She was no longer breathing.

"You won't have the chance to fool me again," he told her.

Suddenly, she fell backward, leaving his stake to jab into the air. She twisted and ducked beneath the blow, red curls flashing. Slamming her forearm into the back of his calves, she knocked his legs from under him.

Domek fell to the hardwood floor, barely avoiding landing on his own weapon. Ora straddled his torso and pinned his hands to the floor. She squeezed the bones in his wrists until the stakes clattered from his grasp. "I tried to do this kindly," she snarled.

"You're not capable of kindness."

She flinched, and he used the momentary lapse in her strength to flip them over. It was disturbingly reminiscent of their bedplay. He managed to pin her arms by leaning his full weight onto one hand, and scrabbled for one of the fallen stakes with the other.

"I would never have hurt you," Ora told him.

Domek held the stake to the base of her jaw. In one movement, he would be able to sever her spine. That quick laugh and broad smile would be turned to dust. Why hadn't she killed him earlier? Why play with his heart, why let him see her vulnerable, if she were going to murder him and take the wisp for herself? Ora was a mischievous person. Perhaps their entire relationship had been a perversity, like a cat batting about its prey.

She stared up at him, and she was as beautiful as ever.

He tightened his grip on the stake, but his muscles were locked like the gears of a broken watch. She had taunted him, teased him, but his emotions—those had been real.

"I don't want to see you again," Domek said lowly. "Whatever game you were playing, it's over." He moved the stake away and climbed to his feet. She stayed on the ground, hair sprawling like a sunburst. "Stay across the room. I'm leaving. I'm going to regret this, but I can't do it like this. Don't believe I'm soft, though. The next time we meet, I'll know that you're the enemy."

Ora looked away. "I suppose if that happens, then I'll know you're mine."

Domek walked backward out the door, grabbing his satchel as he went and holding it close. In the hallway outside, he waited for her to burst through the door after him, but the house was still.

And he was still naked.

Body tensed for an attack, he went to the guest room, pulled a robe from a hook on the wall—from the scent and silk, it belonged to Ora—and then pulled the footman from the bed. The boy groaned in protest, but Domek could not leave him in the house with a pijavica. Fortunately, the boy was dazed enough not to protest, but aware enough to stumble alongside Domek down the stairs.

Finally, Domek dragged him to the street and hailed a hack. Before the driver drove away, Domek looked back one last time.

The house was preternaturally still behind them, a mausoleum waiting for new corpses.

18

Ora stared up at the ceiling.

There was a new injury to add to the day's collection. She could feel the phantom press of the hawthorn in a blister on her stomach.

Once she heard the front door close, she levered herself to her feet. She found a clean dressing gown, washed her hands and face, gathered Domek's abandoned clothes, and went downstairs. She went into the sitting room, threw her bundle of cloth onto the hearth, and searched the mantle for a match.

She smelled Lina's approach, and did not jump when she commented, "Mister Myska isn't staying?"

"You should be asleep," Ora said, staring at the dark fireplace. "It's been a long day."

"I couldn't."

Ora abandoned the clothes and went into the parlor. With a clink that echoed in the quiet house, she poured several fingers of brandy from a crystal decanter.

Lina trailed after. "My lady, you know what alcohol does to your system."

"I do," Ora said. "This is for you."

Lina accepted the glass and took a bracing sip. Her hands were shaking slightly, and blood streaked the back of her forearm where she had missed a spot cleaning up.

"I'm sorry," Ora said, remaining by the liquor cabinet. She traced a finger over a crystal glass. "I'm sorry about everything. You should not have seen any of the things you saw today—my own actions included. Are you all right?"

"Part of me wants to say yes just so we don't have to have this conversation," Lina said. "But I'm not."

"I know," Ora said softly. "I appreciate your honesty."

"That wasn't a mugging that did that, like you told the surgeon," Lina said. "It was…"

"A poltergeist," Ora said.

"One of you."

Ora turned around to look at her long-time maid. "You're frightened. Of me."

Lina slammed down her glass on a table. With only her human strength, the crystal stayed intact. "I'm angry. I'm angry that someone with your power attacked that poor boy and nearly killed him. I'm even angrier that pijavice like your old master are still out there running estates full of human cattle. And of course I'm terrified. What if it was me bleeding out on the dining room table?"

"I was trying to stop that from happening. If I had hovered over you while we were there, Czernin would have known that you were my weakness. And you are that, Lina. You're very important to me." She hesitated, but forced herself to keep going. "But if you decide you want to leave, I'll write you the most glowing recommendation in Prague."

Lina sighed. "I'm not scared of you, Ora. Mama told me what you were when I was growing up. You were a lady, you were a gadji, and you were a pijavica. In every sense, you were different from me. In all those ways, you had power that I couldn't dream of."

"I never wanted your mother or you to feel that way." Like Ora, Lina's parents had been wanderers before they'd joined her in Mělník, part of a migrant group that had only been supposed to stop in Bohemia for a few months. Instead, Lina's mother had broken from their group to live with Franz and Ora in their country house. Her husband had died—she had never said how—and her pregnancy had been a difficult one.

She had stayed with Ora for fifteen years. She was as gifted with horses as Franz had been, and her light touch with the household management had suited both Franz and Ora's personalities well. Through Franz's long illness, she had helped Ora search for new cures, and then, near the end, palliative medicines.

Though she had followed Ora to Prague afterward, city life was too much for her wandering sensibilities. She needed fresh air, space away from the press of the crowds. She had left after a year, finding another caravan to join. By that point, Lina had been sixteen, and had made her own decision to stay with Ora rather than searching for a new life.

"You know my mama loves you," Lina said. "What I'm trying to say is that you have the ability in so many ways to hurt my family. But you never have."

"I nearly did today."

"If you had really tried, you wouldn't be the one who had gotten hurt," Lina pointed out, nodding to Ora's burnt hand. "If there are monsters like Czernin out in the world, your side seems to be the safest place to be."

"I'd protect you and your family with my existence," Ora assured her.

"I know," Lina said. "So, thank you for the brandy, but stop trying to politely get rid of me. You couldn't survive without me even if you wanted me gone."

Ora smiled. "I adore you."

"Repay me by letting me sleep until noon tomorrow," Lina said, knocking back the rest of the brandy.

The doorbell rang, and Ora frowned. Had Domek changed his mind? And if he had, was he back to apologize or to kill her? She sniffed the air, and her frown only deepened. "Go to bed, Lina," she said. "I'll deal with this."

Darina slouched inside as soon as Ora opened the door. She took one look at Ora's dressing gown and laughed. "Between this and the half-naked man I just saw getting into a hack outside your house, I'm assuming your night did not go well. I waited to hear any screams or breaking glass, but I decided you were either handling it well or dead."

Ora resisted the urge to tie her dressing gown more tightly closed. "Your contribution earlier did not help. Have you forgotten the art of subtlety?" Ora hesitated—the dining room would still smell of fresh blood, but she did not want to let Darina deeper into her house. Finally, she led her back to the sitting room.

"That was always your strength. I saved that boy. I didn't need to interfere," Darina said.

"Then why did you? Selflessness on you makes me nervous."

"I'm trying to prove to you that I'm here to be on your side. You would be thanking me if that human hadn't soured your mood." She picked up Lina's empty brandy glass and sniffed. "I never thought I was your true love, but I'm a bit offended in hindsight if he's to your taste."

"Is this the sort of gossip you'll be taking back to Czernin?" Ora asked.

"Czernin isn't as innocent in all this as he made you believe," Darina said. "He sent me to be sure you're not interfering with his plans. He's been in contact with the Zizkov coven. You think their new leader, Mayer, would have had the mental capacity as a newly turned to build such a strategic family? Czernin has been guiding him, nudging him in the right direction."

"Why?"

"I don't know the details. You saw Czernin—he doesn't trust anyone."

"But he trusts this Mayer?"

"He created Mayer. Not with his venom, but with his shaping. He nudged him into position. He stopped trusting his own family—now he's creating followers without giving them his teeth. Mayer was turned by the Zizkovs. Czernin can wash his hands of this if it turns sour."

"And you don't know what they're planning?"

"I'm sure it's nothing you would approve of. You're domestic now. Czernin's games would ruin your fun, no matter his aim. I've seen the spies' reports about you and your little human pets, for all that they can be believed. They've been running circles around him for years now, you know. Thieves and liars, the lot."

"Even if that's true—why are you telling me?" Ora asked. "You've never been interested in being 'on my side' before."

"Czernin is losing his grip on reality. He's been in Prague since there has been a castle on that hill. Prague's golden era is behind us now, and so is Czernin's. I took the gift of immortality because I wanted a long life. Being trapped in that dark hell with a mad old monster and his butler was never part of the offer. Undermine his work here, start to loosen the threads of his hold around this country, and maybe one day we will both be free."

"I'm already free," Ora pointed out, crossing her arms.

Darina's eyes went to her bare hand, blackened from the sun. "Are you?"

"How am I meant to stop Czernin when I know nothing of the Zizkovs' plans? There have been rumors of some type of cure—I assume, if Czernin is involved, it would send the pijavice back into the sun without altering our other abilities."

"What other type of cure is there?"

"The type where we become human again."

Darina laughed. "You really have grown soft."

"It doesn't matter," Ora said, waving a hand. "The entire premise is impossible. What's done can't be undone. We have our weaknesses. Death changes everything, even us."

"You're so sure?" Darina asked.

"It's never been done before," Ora pointed out.

"And we all know tradition is the only reliable source of information. I thought you were more creative than that. Aren't you curious to see what they believe they can do?" She pulled an envelope from her sleeve and set it on the mantle. "The Zizkov family is looking for new members. They're hosting a party at their home tomorrow to meet some pijavice in town.

It's no masquerade ball, but I'm sure they'll bring out whatever impressive bits they can. They're new money, but they're desperate to seem established. Czernin told them he would be sending me. Go in my place and tell them I sent you."

"If you're trying to help me stop Czernin, why wouldn't you go?" Ora asked. "Any pijavica with an ear in Prague knows that Ora Fischerová is not interested in their squabbles."

"Pick another name. I, certainly, have better things to be doing with my time," Darina said. "And if this cabal of pijavice gets intercepted by that soldier friend of yours, it won't be my neck on the line."

It had been a century since Ora had seen Darina, and the woman had not changed at all. As mutable as the mortal world was, Ora's old life seemed set in stone. "It's been a long time since we worked together. Me heading into danger while you sit back feels quite familiar."

"It's how we work best," Darina said with a wicked smile. "Prague should gird its loins."

The next afternoon, Domek found Cord in his study, scribbling a note at his oversized mahogany desk with his dog asleep at his feet. With so much of Cord's apartment sitting at the cutting edge of style, Domek could always tell which decorative pieces had been directly influenced by Cord's family. He may have thought himself separate from his father, but the man's traditional influence lingered in the places where Cord wanted to show his seriousness. In contrast, Cord's outfit today, which had enough bright colors to mimic the early spring flowers that were blooming in squares around the city, was all himself.

Cord grinned. "You're no longer allowed to mock me for sleeping in," he declared. "It's past noon."

Domek ran a hand through his disheveled hair. He had settled the injured boy at a hospital, emptying his pockets to afford the bed, and then had stumbled into Cord's apartment to sleep the rest of the night. He'd left Ora's purple dressing gown spread across the floor like a puddle. "I have reasons beyond drinking until dawn."

Cord laughed, unfazed by the caustic tone. "Reasons, you say? I hope this is a sign that your date went spectacularly. I wasn't sure you'd be back last night at all, to be honest."

Domek sat in the chair across from the desk and picked up a decorative glass paperweight. "She's a demon, Cord."

"Hm, then perhaps it did not go so well," Cord said.

"A pijavica," Domek clarified, examining the twin blue rivers twisting through the glass orb. "A bloodthirsty monster."

"Lady Fischerová is a pijavica? You're sure?"

"The fangs gave it away," Domek said. "She was right in front of me. There was no mistaking it." He sighed. "Cord, I let her live. What kind of fool am I?"

"The kind who does not kill the woman who had just paid for his opera ticket," Cord suggested.

Domek turned to glare at him. "This is serious, Cord. I'm a lamplighter. It's my duty to protect Prague, and I let a demon slip through my fingers. I had her under my stake, and I left."

"And she let you leave?"

"I had won the fight. She knew she could not win if she pursued me."

"The Lady Fischerová I met did not seem the type to fear anything. Have you considered that she had no plans to kill you? I told you, I've met pijavice before. The ones who operate in the upper echelon have had to learn restraint."

"Or so you believe. I always thought I'd know a pijavica whenever I saw one. I've fought enough. We all know there are rich pijavice, but we're lamplighters—we can't break into a palace and kill a nobleman, no matter how many people they've killed."

"I can't speak for what goes on behind their closed doors, but they're more rational than you give them credit for. Surely they can't all be bathing in blood."

"You're as rich as anyone, Cord. You know well that you get away with more than any poor man ever could. Money makes a difference. It can hide evil."

"It can. I've seen the worst of men from all social strata. But Ora didn't seem like one of them. What if you're wrong about her?"

"I saw her eyes. I know what she is."

"But do you know *who* she is?"

"What do you suggest? That I look away and hope that she's not killing innocent people in her parlor every night? That there are some monsters who are different?"

"I'm not a lamplighter. I don't make life or death decisions. I prefer choosing the wine with dinner," Cord said. "If you want to know my opinion, then, well. You know where she lives. Watch her. See if you were right about her. Why rush and make a decision you may regret? You've never been a rash man. Why start today?"

Cord's butler cleared his throat from the doorway. "Anton Beran is back," he announced. "Shall I let him in?"

"You told him yesterday you didn't know where I was, didn't you?" Domek asked.

Cord nodded, standing up and stretching his arms over his head. "He probably realized I'd be able to track you down. Saved him the effort—I know that's his favorite thing. Or he just assumed I was lying. He's never trusted me."

Domek shrugged. "He's probably wanting to ask if I've started cleaning the flat yet," he said. "I doubt it's occurred to him that he could be the one to have the window fixed."

"Are you sure you want to see him?" Cord asked. "I can have Hollas send him away, tell him we're not in."

"I have the speech well-memorized," the butler said dryly.

Shaking his head, Domek said, "I'm not avoiding him. He can keep quiet about where I am."

"I hope you're not in more trouble than you think," Cord said.

Hollas led Anton into the sitting room, where Cord had perched at his piano, tapping keys with one hand and sipping an afternoon brandy with the other. Domek sat in the embroidered armchair, ignoring the glass Cord had poured him.

Anton's eyes lit up when he saw Domek. "I knew you'd be here," he said triumphantly. "I could tell Cord was lying yesterday."

"I wasn't lying," Cord said. As he crawled his hand along the ivory, he deliberately pinged the wrong key. The discordant note echoed around the room like a bullet. "At that point, I didn't know yet."

"Then where have you been, Domek?"

"I was off-duty last night," Domek reminded him.

"I know, but I still didn't hear from you for twenty-four hours. I told Paluska about the break-in, and he said he wants to talk to you."

"Does he?" Domek asked, careful not to betray his lack of surprise to Anton. After telling Paluska about the wisp, and assuring him it was safe, Domek had fallen out of touch for a full day and night. He might have assumed from Anton's story that the wisp had been stolen during the break-in, and would be looking for confirmation.

Undoubtedly, he would take the incident as a sign that Domek wasn't qualified to keep the wisp safe. The next time he went to see Paluska, he would need to hand it over to his keeping. Imrich would lord it over Domek's head until the old bastard died.

After the wisp's intervention last night, perhaps Domek could trust it to aid the lamplighters, despite its initial reluctance. Domek was feeling less confident in his ability to judge character—he had trusted Ora until he had seen her eyes reflecting in the darkness. Was the wisp fooling him as well?

"Paluska was mad at me for letting you swan off on your own right after our break-in," Anton said. "We're supposed to look out for each other. When I realized I didn't know where you'd ended up yesterday, I started to worry." He glared at Cord, who ignored him in favor of tapping out a simple melody on the piano.

"I'm fine," Domek said. He gestured around them. "I landed on my feet."

"I can see that. Nicer than where I ended up," Anton admitted. "So, should we go see Paluska now?"

Domek hesitated. "I can't today," he said.

"Too busy playing piano and drinking?"

"I…"

"We have plans," Cord interrupted. "I'm showing Domek the town. I made him promise. You know how he is about his vows."

Anton frowned at Domek, crossing his arms. "I thought the lamplighter vow was the most important to you. You believe in what we do. In our job." He glanced over at Cord. He didn't know that the aristocrat knew about the pijavice, which worked in Domek's favor. Anton couldn't press the issue with Cord present.

"I do," Domek protested.

"Imrich was with Paluska. He seemed eager to see you as well. He said you have something of his? Something important?" Of course Paluska had told the alchemist about the wisp. Imrich would be apoplectic with rage that Domek had access to such rare magic and would be itching to dissect the wisp.

"He thinks everything I own is his," Domek said. "I'll go by Paluska's tonight after my patrol. I just have something to do first."

"You don't have to do everything alone," Anton said, somewhere between irritated and wounded.

"He's not alone," Cord said, leaning on the keys to stand up. The dissonant noise rang through the room, grating against Domek's bones. Across the room, the dog huffed his annoyance. "We should get ready," he said to Domek. To Anton, he continued, "Satisfied that I've kept him alive?"

Anton held up his hands. "I didn't mean to offend you. I was just worried," he said. "Domek, go by tonight before Paluska has a heart attack, all right? I'll tell him that my message has been passed along."

"Thanks, Anton," Domek said, clapping him on the shoulder. "Don't let him bully you. I'll explain everything when I see him." As soon as Domek decided what to do.

After Hollas ushered Anton out the door, Cord sighed. "You're a terrible liar," he said. "Next time, let me know if I'm going to need to cover for you. Shall I come up with plans for us to do today? I'm sure I can keep you busy."

"No, but thank you for that," Domek said. "I won't string them along much longer. I have some things I need to handle."

"It's odd seeing Anton act as anyone's messenger. He's never been one for authority figures," Cord added.

"He respects the lamplighter leader," Domek said.

"And you don't?"

"I do," Domek hedged. "But I trust myself more."

"In that, I agree with you," Cord said. "Come on. Have some brandy and keep me company while I finish that letter. You'll want to wait a few minutes before heading out just in case Anton is waiting to ambush you anyway. After the night you had, it's the least you deserve."

Domek sighed and picked up his glass. "It can hardly make things worse."

19

Clouds hung heavy overhead, blocking the afternoon sun and smothering Prague under a low sky.

Domek's career was about helping people. Even when he failed, he was assured that he was doing good work for the world. After last night, though, he felt at a loss. The wisp in his bag, which had seemed an evil, chaotic force, had tried to save the footman. Ora, who had pulled him into her bed, had turned out to be his worst enemy.

Domek was frustrated by his own passivity. It was time to stop letting things happen to him. Waiting around for the next person to attack him and those around him would only put more innocents in danger. He needed answers.

In addition to housing the lamplighter's guildhall, the tangle of buildings in the dip below the castle was home to a collection of the most active gentlemen's establishments in Prague.

The small building was tucked in between a tailor's shop and an auction house. He had asked around; it was one of the area's premiere gambling halls, exclusive to members. It would have been innocuous if not for the sign proclaiming it The Pigeon Hole over the door—and the two men standing guard. They frowned when Domek stopped in front of them. "I'm looking for Bazil," he said.

"What business do you have with him?"

"He'll want to see me. Tell him Domek Myska is here."

They didn't budge. Both were close to Domek's size, broad-shouldered and scarred from years of brawls.

"Don't worry, gents. I've got this one." A girl stepped away from the wall, tossing aside an apple core. She was dressed in more layers than were needed for the spring afternoon, and had a cap pulled low over dark curls. "Follow me."

"Who are you?"

She was young to be working at a gambling hall, but Domek had seen how quickly difficult times could land on the shoulders of children. No girl should have been working at a place like this, but at least she had protection.

Left on the streets, she would have been easy prey for monsters.

The transformation into a pijavica was difficult enough for a sturdy adult, and youths were more quickly driven mad by the bloodlust. It was a sight Domek never wanted to see again. A child's face split open by teeth, ravenous. Their family dead around them.

"I work with Bazil. He told me to keep an eye out for you. Knew you couldn't stay away. You were lucky I was taking a break. Even a bruiser like you couldn't get past those two."

They went through the alley around the back which smelled of sewage and mud. Domek scanned the shadows, cautious of walking into a trap. No one leaped out at them, however, and a whispered password at the door allowed them into the back of the club.

The girl led him through a series of dark hallways until they emerged blinking into a small, velvet-lined room. A group of six men were playing cards, despite the early hour. Cheroot smoke was thick in the air, creating a slight haze near the ornate ceiling. Though clearly in the middle of a hand, the occupants of the table noticed their entry. Bazil, with the smallest pile of chips in front of him, waved at the others after they finished the hand, dismissing them from the room. They went without complaint, carrying their tokens to play with elsewhere in the gambling hall.

"Domek Myska," Bazil greeted once the room was cleared. He wore a simple dark suit, and the vest beneath was patterned with organic shapes and colors like a turtle's shell. And like a shell, the effect was an impressive camouflage of a respectable man. He could have blended with society easily. "I was hoping you'd come to see me." He flicked a coin across the room, which the girl caught in midair. She tucked it in her belt and left. Bazil turned to Domek, grinning. "She's not allowed to gamble."

"Because she's too young?" Domek asked.

"Because she takes everyone's money, and my clients are usually bitter losers," Bazil said. "Take a seat, Mister Myska. We have a lot to discuss."

Domek remained standing. "You're right. You told me you have information I need. But to start, I'd like an apology."

Bazil raised his eyebrows. "For what?"

"Don't play stupid," Domek said. "You had your criminals ransack my apartment the other night. I'm here to learn what you know, but I haven't forgotten that."

"You think I had you robbed after I extended an invitation for us to work together," Bazil said, "and you decided it was wise to show up here anyway?"

"I've faced more frightening things than you," Domek said coolly.

"I'm sure you think you have," Bazil said, shuffling the stack of cards methodically. "Luckily, we won't have to test it. We didn't have anything to do with a break-in—at your home, that is. I'm looking to work with you, not against you."

"Why should I believe that?" Domek asked. "I know you're not on the right side of the law. It's not a stretch to assume that after I refused your invitation to meet, you thought to try to take what you wanted by force."

"Ah, but that's where your logic fails," Bazil said. "I don't want what you've got. I have enough trouble in my life without taking something like that wisp on." When Domek faltered, he continued, "Now, take a seat, Mister Myska, so we can talk."

Finally, Domek sat.

"Do you play cards?"

"No."

"Shame," Bazil said. "I guess you're as much of a bore as you look. Both in the sense that you are boorish and boring. Don't you know better than to come into a man's space and accuse him of thievery?"

Domek folded his arms. "I've worked in the city long enough to know someone on the wrong side of the law. The secret passage into your underground gambling rooms gave it away."

"Fair point. The fact remains that I'm more honest than my profession would make one think. After what I saw in the alley the other night, I knew I needed a chance to talk with you. I know what you are, even without the wisp to help you fight. If

I *had* tried to rob you, I wouldn't have let you come here into my space. I prefer not to get into fights I can't win, and you're trained for enemies far stronger than me."

The problem was that Bazil *appeared* imminently trustworthy. His eyes were bright and curious, and he spoke as though he and Domek already shared some childhood pact of intimacy. If they hadn't been in a private room at a gambling hall, having been united by Bazil stalking him, Domek would have been tempted to open up to him. It was a dangerous impulse, one that Bazil had undoubtedly taken advantage of over the years. "Then talk."

"I've been following up on a variety of whispers," Bazil said. "After I saw you in the alley, I've been questioning my contacts. It turns out that yours is not the only wisp in the city. I heard from a friend of mine in the smuggling business that there's a certain fanged demographic currently on the hunt for vodníks—and the unique soul jars some of them have."

"Pijavice have been hunting vodníks? How do you know?"

"They've been pillaging vodník dens for soul jars across the countryside. As for how I found out about it, that's easy. Once they've found what they're looking for, they have to bring back the jars somehow. Dock workers see things, especially such unusual trinkets, and they tell me."

Domek sighed. "If you don't want the wisp for yourself, why bother chasing me down?"

"Information is as valuable as coin," Bazil said, picking up a token from the table and rolling it across the velvet toward Domek. "Knowledge is the most powerful weapon I have. If I'm going to keep my men safe, I need to know what's out there." He leaned forward in his chair. "Do you remember the first time you encountered a monster? That moment when you realized that the world wasn't what you thought it was?" Domek nodded. "I hate that feeling. I like to preempt it wherever I can."

"Why don't you want the wisp for yourself?"

"I know better than to trust deals that seem too good to be true. They never turn out to be worth the hassle," Bazil said. "It sounds like you're learning that lesson too. The bubák in the alley, the break-in—I don't imagine things are going the way you planned."

Domek had come to Bazil to get information. He'd not expected such insight, but would take advantage while it was on offer. "I didn't plan any of this," Domek admitted. "I found the jar by accident."

Bazil nodded. "After talking to you, I thought that might be the case. I was hoping that since a lamplighter got their hands on one that it meant your men were on top of this. None of you had any idea this was happening?"

"Most of the pijavice I run into are more focused on their next meal than conspiracies," Domek pointed out. "They're sewer rats, nothing more. I don't look for larger secrets."

Though, he remembered, all the pijavice who had attempted to take the wisp from him so far had been dressed like lords.

The type of pijavica Ora likely invited to her house to drink blood from crystal goblets.

"Hm. I suppose it's like asking a bird watcher about astronomy," Bazil mused.

"Have you heard of a pijavica named Ora Fischerová?" Domek asked, pulse thudding in his ears.

Bazil shrugged. "I may have."

"Is she involved in this hunt for the wisps?"

"You're still focused too much on the details. You'll never have any idea of the bigger picture if you're only focusing on what's around you."

"I save lives," Domek said. "That is the bigger picture for me."

"Take a moment to think about why pijavice might be collecting wisps," Bazil said, tapping his deck of cards against the table. "Go on. You don't think that it might have impacts that could affect us all? I don't know the exact limits of a caged wisp's power, but it can't be good for the pijavice to have it. They could disrupt everything in this city. We need to know what their goal is. Short of trying to confront the pijavice ourselves, which my men are not at all equipped to do, the only way I see available for getting that information is through you. You've intercepted one of their acquisitions. Now you need to find out what they're planning. I can admit my own restraints. I don't have the resources to do anything about this. The pijavice I feed information to are too paranoid to let any slip back to me. What I can do is make sure *you* realize the stakes."

No matter what Bazil sneered, it didn't take much imagination to think of the damage a pijavica could cause paired with the power of a wisp. Even if the pijavice couldn't utilize the wisp without being sabotaged in some way, as Domek had been at first, their combined lack of regard for human life was a danger in itself. If anyone Domek had met had the silver tongue needed to manipulate the wisp, however, it was Ora. "I see your point. If there are other pijavice bringing wisps into the city, we need to know. But they wouldn't tell me anything."

"Luckily," Bazil said, "in this case we can skip over the pijavice and go directly to the source."

"You think my wisp is involved with this?" Domek asked. He shook his head. "The wisps aren't willing coconspirators. The jars are vodník magic. The wisps are trapped to the will of the holder."

"Then if the pijavica offered their freedom in exchange for cooperation, is it so far-fetched to imagine the two groups working together? Wisps are contrary creatures, but they make their own choices. If you're ensnared by one in the woods, they're as likely to take you to safety as drown you in the bog. You're sure it won't betray you?"

Domek hesitated. He didn't know whether the pijavica had already been summoning Kája for days or weeks before Domek had found them. Could they have already been partners? Was Kája biding its time until it could go back to the pijavice? Perhaps last night's encounter with the poltergeist had been orchestrated by Ora and Kája together.

"Ask it what its old master was planning," Bazil suggested. "Threaten it with silver, if you must, assuming it shares the same weakness as other spirits. Make it tell you what it knows. Don't waste more time. Go and summon it now."

Domek frowned. "I don't have it with me, you know."

"I'm a gambler, remember? I can tell when someone has something precious in their bag," Bazil said, nodding toward the satchel Domek had left tightly secured over his chest. "I have private rooms if you'd like to summon your wisp here."

"Which I'm sure include a dozen peepholes for you to spy through," Domek said.

Bazil shrugged. "I'm a curious man."

"I appreciate the offer, but I'll pursue this on my own. You've given me what I wanted."

"We could help each other."

"I have a team. If I need help, I know who to go to."

Bazil leaned back in his chair. "I've given you more information in the last half-hour than you've found on your own in days," he pointed out. "And I know more. I know the address the jars have been shipped to."

Domek stilled. "Where is it?"

"Use that team of yours and figure it out yourself," Bazil said. "You're sure you don't need me, and I certainly don't need a condescending oaf who tripped into this. We've met and my curiosity is satisfied. Good luck on your own."

"If you really want to save Prague, you'll tell me anyway."

Bazil just shook his head and pointed to the door. "I'll be watching you, Domek Myska. There are countless lives resting on your shoulders. Don't let your pride be humanity's downfall." He flashed a bright grin. "No pressure, of course."

True to her word, Ora let Lina sleep in past midday. It was strange to pass the morning without her. Nedda was in the kitchen with Mila—Ora could hear them gossiping from a floor away. She could go bother them, but they deserved time without their mistress hovering. She could have summoned Hackett for an impromptu ride around town, but she decided that he deserved a break as well. He was probably still cleaning the blood off the interior of the carriage. Ora's attempts to keep him from her secret would be damaged now. She would need to feign vapors in front of him soon to make up for her lack of fear last night. He had worked for her for years, weathering her eccentricities with a stoic face, but some things were too suspicious to overlook.

She rattled around the large house, pacing from room to room. None of her books could hold her attention, though she picked up more than a dozen to flip through. The words slipped past her gaze like raindrops, insubstantial.

The welt on her stomach ached.

She should have closed the door between them the moment she had learned that Domek was a lamplighter. His departure was a blessing in disguise. Her recklessness had nearly gotten her killed. No soft lips and broad hands and gentleness were worth that threat.

To occupy herself, Ora put together a house of cards using two decks, balancing them precariously on the tea table in the sitting room. The structure arched overhead, mathematically precise.

From the front of the house, the doorbell rang. At least now it was daylight. Darina had left after their short conversation. As with all pijavice, she needed no sleep, and had professed an urge to explore the ways Prague had changed since her last mission inside its walls. Ora was not comfortable with Darina wandering the city, but it was a relief to have her on her side for once.

Mila would answer the door in Lina's stead, but she was less prepared to handle the array of visitors. Ora stood up, brushing the edge of the table with her knee. The house of cards collapsed, scattering across the floor in faded green and red and yellow like fall leaves. She sniffed the air, and then relaxed slightly. This guest was no threat to her household.

Mila showed Sokol into the room. After making sure everyone was settled, Mila went to make tea in the kitchen. Sokol picked up one of the fallen cards before sitting in his usual chair. "Sorry for dropping in unannounced," he said, flipping the card between his fingers.

"You know, I believe this is the first time I've seen you during daylight hours," Ora said. "I thought you were nocturnal."

"No rest for the wicked, or for those of us who work in government," Sokol said.

"Should I make a joke about not knowing the difference?"

He shrugged. "I'll consider it said. I got your note."

She had sent Mila out with a note after Alena had left about what she had learned from Czernin. So much had happened since then she had nearly forgotten. "And?"

Leaning forward, elbows on his knees, he said, "I looked through our files and found some more research on the Zizkovs. They've been mostly small time to us as well, since they focus more on controlling other pijavice than trying to take a bite of human Prague. They're involved with smuggling the same sort of things that any human smuggling ring would be interested in, mostly imported artifacts. This new rumor is the only thing that's really worried us."

"But you did have a file on them," Ora said. She recalled Czernin's casual accusation that Sokol was using her. "Why send me out to talk to Lord Czernin if you already knew all that?"

"Everything we have is by humans, for humans," Sokol explained. "Most of the time, that's all we care about. What the pijavice are doing *to humans*. This 'cure' is out of our expertise."

"I told you going to see Czernin was ill-advised," Ora said. "Yesterday was a disaster. Lina and I could have been killed. Are you this reckless with every member of your team?"

"If I wanted you on our team, I'd ask," Sokol said. He flipped the card in his hands with enough force that it slipped, skidding to hit Ora's shoe. The *Unter* looked away at the acorn dropping from his hand, falling into the duplicate frame mirrored below.

The card was nearly as old as Ora, the remnant of a deck mostly destroyed decades earlier. A relic. "Czernin is supposed to know everything. He should have had more information."

"I found out last night that he didn't give me more information because he's *involved*, Sokol, and now he knows we're looking into it."

"He's involved? How? Has he been in touch with Mayer?"

"I don't know the details, but it was a mistake to make me go talk to him. Now he knows you're looking," Ora said. "I'm finished with this investigation of yours. You've put my household in danger. Fortunately for you, I had a lucky break last night that will let you go find out more on your own." She picked up the envelope Darina had given her and handed it to Sokol. "An invitation to the Zizkov house tonight. They're gathering some pijavice to talk about their dastardly plans. Enjoy."

Sokol opened the invitation and stared at it. It was generic and formal, and only the assurance from Darina hinted that the party may be anything beyond a small friendly gathering. "This is precisely why I need your help. My team are all mortal. I couldn't send them into something like this. You were born to infiltrate parties, Ora. Wear one of your pretty dresses."

"Don't be an ass. This is no simple ball and you know it," Ora said. "You're shoving me into danger because your crack team doesn't know what they're doing. I'm trying to leave the pijavice behind me. It's not who I am anymore. I haven't been for a long time. You know that. You'd have me lie about who I am, pretend I don't have the morals I do, just so I can find you information? Spending time with monsters like Czernin and the Zizkovs is exactly what I fought to leave." She huffed.

"For all I know, you have all the information already and have simply decided once again not to share it with me. I'm starting to wonder if this is what our entire relationship has been about."

"I'd be an idiot not to see your potential," Sokol said.

"I just want to live my life," Ora said. "I'm not hurting anyone by being a neutral party. I never gave you a reason to expect anything else from me."

"You don't like other pijavice, you don't agree with what they do, but you refuse to actually help us at all," Sokol said. "Sorry to be the one to tell you this, my lady, but if you're not helping us, you're helping them. You sit here in your fancy house while innocent people die."

"That's not fair," Ora said, standing up. Sokol rose as well, and she was torn between relief and irritation to see that he didn't seem frightened of her. "I didn't want this. To spend decades under Czernin's thumb, to never see the sun, to outlive everyone I've known. What do I owe *you* for my suffering?"

"This isn't about what you owe me," Sokol said. "This is about who you are, who I thought you were. Think of all the good you could do working for us. What would your husband have wanted you to do? You say he was a good man. Would he want you to sit aside and think only of yourself?"

Ora's mind fractured like glass when struck with the unexpected remark. The memory of her horrible conversation with Alena surged forward again. She stared at him as she struggled to orient herself. "You're bringing my husband into this?"

"Well, it seems you're not concerned about anyone still alive."

"You don't know anything about Franz," she said.

"I know he believed the same thing I do about pijavice. He loved you, but he could see the potential for pain they could cause. If he hadn't, you would have turned him. You've told me about his illness. Most men would do anything to escape that."

Franz's death had been slow, inexorable. His body had betrayed him piece by piece. He had clung to his love for Alena even as he watched his body wilt beside Ora's everlasting strength. When the time came, and Franz's suffering had become too great, Ora had given him the one gift her supernatural strength could offer that he would accept: an easy death.

"You would have given him anything. He must have told you he didn't want to be like you," Sokol continued. Ora's fists clenched so tightly that her freshly grown claws pierced her skin. The blood was sluggish to drip out. "I'm right, aren't I?"

Hands shaking, Ora pointed at the door. "Get out. I can't believe I thought you were my friend."

"We are friends," Sokol argued.

She didn't answer.

He stared at her silently for a long moment. She stared at him, jaw set. "If you change your mind," Sokol said, leaving the envelope on the table on top of the scattered cards. He rapped his knuckles on it and turned away. "See you around, Lady Fischerová."

20

Domek made his way circuitously across the city, checking over his shoulder for the girl or another of Bazil's minions.

How much of what he had said was true? If the pijavice were bringing multiple wisps into the city, perhaps they truly had struck some deal with the spirits for their aid. Was Kája working with them? Was Ora?

Domek walked along the narrow streets, dodging the pedestrians and horse-drawn carriages that cluttered the city in pleasant weather, until he was at Cord's flat. Fortunately, Cord was going to be out until evening. He may have already known about the pijavice, but Domek wasn't going to tell him about the wisp. The situation was dangerous enough as it was.

Ora had met Cord. If she were involved, it would not take long for them to find him. Perhaps it was time to bring the issue to Paluska.

If Bazil was right and the pijavice were supplementing their forces by allying with other supernatural creatures, however, the situation could quickly escalate out of their control. Already, the lamplighters were stretched thin over their territory. There was a reason they focused their energies on the pijavice attacking people in the street rather than the ones hiding behind a mask of humanity. Their authority was limited, and their standing in Prague was of a common worker.

Putting his back against the wall so he could keep an eye on the door—locked, just in case Cord came home early—Domek pulled the jar out of his bag once again. The symbols on his palms tingled when they made contact with the warm clay.

The wisp appeared. The flame, so dim the previous night, had strengthened, though it was not as large as it had been at first. Its fiery form was incongruous in the lush bedroom, like someone had tamed a lightning storm in a museum. Domek remembered his uncle's experiments with matches, including the pack still sitting deep in his bag. How did the wisp's internal fire blaze continuously? What fuel allowed it to survive even when trapped inside an airless jar, and to heal there?

"Did the boy survive?" Kája asked.

Domek leaned back against the wall. If Bazil was right that the wisp was working for the pijavice, its concern for the footman was a quick way to gain Domek's trust. "He did. I want to ask you again about the pijavica I took you from."

"This promises to be an exciting new conversation. We couldn't have done this outside again?"

Domek chewed on his lip. "What did you do for him before I found you? How long had you been under his care?"

"Why don't you ask what you really mean? You still don't

trust me. I've told you before that I wasn't working with him. I don't ally with those who hold me captive."

Domek waved a hand, brushing aside that line of conversation. "What had he instructed you to do before you changed ownership to me?"

"There isn't much to tell," the wisp said. "He summoned me, stared for a bit, and then sent me back."

"That's it? I compelled you to tell the truth."

"That is the truth. He'd found what he wanted. We were on the shore by the vodník's pond where I'd first been captured. There were a dozen smashed jars on the ground."

"Why?"

"Vodníks don't usually catch us. They use their jars to hold the souls of the humans they've drowned. The rest of the jars were not like mine—there was no magic inside. The pijavica just said, 'I found one,' to someone else I didn't see. Then he told me he was my new master before sending me right back into the jar. As though I were a slave. Though, since he had the jar, I suppose I was."

"He didn't seem surprised at all to find you?"

"Excited, but not surprised."

That confirmed Bazil's claim that the pijavice had found other wisps. How many wisps had already been smuggled into the city? "We think that pijavice are bringing wisps into Prague. More than just you. We're trying to figure out why. Does your power increase when you work with other wisps?"

"Not that I know of. We don't work well together. Even if we did, we're not a stack of firewood that grows stronger when used at once. Maybe they're collectors. People have always hoarded power to be admired."

"You think they're gathering wisps to, what, gloat that they can?" Domek questioned. It seemed a benign hobby for the bloodsuckers, but the address Kája had mentioned was on Kampa Island, close to the river on the west bank in a neighborhood growing more expensive by the day. Perhaps spending resources on collecting soul jars was the sort of activity the wealthy did for pleasure.

"Hoarding slaves as a status symbol has been a human trait since the beginning of time, living or dead," Kája said. "Pijavice tend to focus on the type of slave with blood for them to drink, but this isn't a surprising turn of events. They're just as interested in power as the rest of you."

Domek nodded thoughtfully. He lifted the jar, ready to return the wisp inside. He hesitated. "If they offered, would you join sides with a pijavica?"

"There are no offers with that jar."

"What if they offered your freedom? Would you work with them against humans?"

Kája considered the question more seriously than Domek had expected. "Freedom means not having to follow someone else's instructions. In that type of deal, I would still be in servitude. I wouldn't give up one set of chains for another, even if they were gilded. But they would not free me," it said. "It would not help their cause. It's slavery that makes our magic malleable to an outsider. Once freed, I'd only be as useful as I wanted to be. And I've always been contrary."

"You helped me last night."

"It was not an order. I offered. It was the right thing to do." Kája's form flickered. "If you want to thank me... Take me outside."

"What?"

"This small room," Kája said, "is mind-numbing. The inside of the jar is even worse. I want to see the stars."

"That's all?" Domek was suspicious. Was there some power the wisp would gain from being outside? The invitation to the opera had seemed benign at first as well. Surely Domek was missing some trick.

"Isn't that enough? I wasn't always a wisp, you know. I miss the sky."

"What were you before?"

"A witch."

Domek blinked. "You were human?"

"All souls leave the body at death. Normal humans can get stuck as ghosts—insubstantial, invisible to anyone without their own magic. Powerful witches create powerful spirits, and not all of us make it to the afterlife."

"I didn't know that was possible."

"Not many do. You're still determined to keep me in here, knowing that?"

Domek hesitated. "Even if you used to be a human, you're a spirit now. You're powerful, and you said yourself that you're contrary. How do I know you won't hurt someone if I freed you?"

"Witches are powerful in life, but death breaks the bonds of flesh and magnifies our powers. I'm not more than I was in life, just unfettered. You'd have to trust me like you'd trust a human. Like you trusted me last night."

Domek hesitated.

There was a sound of frustration from the wisp, a noise that would have been a sigh from something with a throat. Domek realized how much the wisp's lost humanity explained—the personality, the opinions. Domek couldn't see the wisp as an 'it' in that light. "If you're determined to keep me enslaved, at least take me outside. You said yourself that it's a simple request."

Domek hesitated. His instincts trusted that the wisp was telling the truth. He had weakened himself saving the footman the night before, though Domek would never had thought to ask.

"You asked if I'd ever work with you," Kája said suddenly, before Domek could find an answer. "This is why the answer is no. You have all the power here. I have, what, a tricky tongue and an insubstantial form? Surely you're man enough to be confident that you can handle me. You can grant me one request."

There was a knock on the door. "Mister Myska? You have an urgent message."

"Back in the jar," Domek hissed to Kája.

He disappeared without fanfare. It looked like defeat.

Domek opened the door to Cord's butler, Hollas. He peered curiously past Domek into the room. "Do you have company? I thought I heard another voice."

"No," Domek said. "Who sent this?"

"There was a messenger boy. He insisted it get to you immediately."

Domek accepted the envelope, and Hollas did not linger to chat. Frowning, Domek tore open the letter.

It was from Anton, though they had just seen each other that morning. The letter had clearly been jotted down quickly, with ink blotches on the edges.

Webber is dead.

The words swam in front of his eyes. Domek pressed a hand to his chest, trying to find the breath that had vanished.

Assisting Abrahams with unknown disturbance. Details uncertain. Family has been told. Funeral tomorrow, 2PM.

Come see Paluska. He still needs to speak with you.

Death was a part of the job. Lamplighters knew that any night could be their last, and watched innocents die when they failed. It still gutted Domek every time. He had just seen Webber at the guildhall. Two days ago, Webber had been laughing with Anton and Abrahams about Domek's love life. Now, he was gone.

Dear God, Abrahams would be devastated. The two had been best friends for years, and had been together in the end.

Was this what his mother's cards had been warning him would happen?

Domek looked at the inert jar still sitting on the floor. There was more to discuss with Kája, but today, he had other responsibilities.

Over the years, Domek had become a regular at Mesto Tavern, a rowdy pub that stayed open as long as the moon was up. It sat just outside the Jewish Quarter, near the opera house. Inside, he was greeted by the heavy, warm smells of ale, sausages, and tobacco smoke. On cool nights, the tavern was warm and inviting, full and boisterous. Clientele came to the Mesto fresh off the river boats, looking to spend the night in good company, or from the gambling halls—either to enjoy a windfall or use their last coins to drown their sorrows.

This afternoon, walking in from the warm spring day, the tavern seemed stifling. Domek nodded toward the barmaid, Thea, who gave him a small wave in return. As expected, Abrahams was sitting at the bar, staring down into a glass of red wine.

Domek slid onto the stool beside him. Words failed him, and he folded his hands on the counter.

Without prompting, Thea pulled him a glass of pilsner. The amber liquid seemed dull in the dark tavern, the white foam a jarring spot of brightness.

"*L'chayim*," Abrahams said wryly, clicking their glasses together.

"I'm so sorry, Abrahams," Domek said after taking the required sip from his beer.

He grunted and took another sip of his wine.

They drank in silence. Domek could barely taste the pilsner, its light taste overshadowed by the heavy atmosphere. Webber would have laughed at them for the melancholy. He had never been able to dwell, and had hated long silences. Abrahams and Domek had always been more comfortable with the quiet than Webber or Anton, who filled every space with chatter.

Domek finished two beers while Abrahams nursed his single glass of red wine. Thea, intuitive as she was, brought them a plate of beer cheese. Domek tipped a splash of his pilsner onto the plate and mashed it together with the soft cheese, onions, and paprika. He smeared the cheese onto a slice of rye and slid it in front of Abrahams.

Abrahams took it, stared at the traditional bar food, and then set it back down. "I've never seen anything like it, Myska." He shook his head. "It was supposed to be an easy job. Webber helped me in the Jewish Quarter whenever I needed the extra set of hands. We're spread too thin there, but he was always happy to help and then convince my mother to make him dinner. He's seen what we deal with there. The buildings are decrepit, rundown. It's a nesting ground for all sorts of demons. Opening the ghetto helped some of us leave, but it's still the most dangerous neighborhood in Prague. You know they've been talking about renovating it?"

Domek hummed.

"Going to tear down our homes and build new places for goyim to move into. For now, we're stuck living in cramped conditions, preyed on by monsters. But Webber was always willing to help. Someone complained that they had been hearing strange sounds from inside their walls. They said they had thought they had a rat infestation, before they started hearing the voice. Mad muttering, stuttering. I thought they had a ghost, but their pet dog went missing."

Thea had gone to help another customer, so Domek guessed quietly, "Pijavica."

"That's what we thought. That some recently turned monster had gotten itself wedged in their cellar and was driving itself mad. It's happened before."

The change from mortal into the bloodthirsty monsters was fraught, even before the family massacres started. Some pijavice never left behind that early madness, and the ones that remained on the streets to hunt embraced it.

When the lamplighters knew a pijavica's daytime position, they didn't wait until night, and the height of its power, to destroy it. If there was a way to find the creature and break a shaft of sunlight into its hiding space, the problem would be solved with no risk. Too many of them hid deep in the tunnels where sunlight could not pierce, creating an impenetrable domain.

"The people in my neighborhood know that they can call me with strange occurrences. I've helped clean out a number of real rat infestations looking for the more sinister kind, but they're always grateful. Webber and I sent the family away, and then found the abandoned, alternate entrance to the cellar the creature must have used to get down there. We waited outside and listened. We were careful. It had a human voice, male. Muttering some nonsense about never going back somewhere. We waited until the sun was at the perfect angle this morning, and then threw open the door." He traced a line of condensation on the countertop. "Myska, it looked like a human. It was dressed in rags. It blinked against the sunlight, but survived its touch."

Domek frowned. Very few of the demons they hunted could exist in direct sunlight, requiring the shadows to mask the sins of their souls. Vodníks and wisps were examples Domek knew, as well as some ghosts, but it was a rare ability among the monsters.

"There are humans afflicted by madness that makes them seem monsters. We were going to escort it out, find it some help. But when it saw us, its face split open like a pijavica's and it launched at us." Abrahams's hand clenched into a fist. "Webber was smart. Even when we thought it was a human, he didn't drop his stake. He stabbed it through the heart before it could touch us. Myska, it didn't *die*. What type of demon looks like a pijavica, but is immune to hawthorn and sunlight?"

"I don't know," Domek breathed. Abrahams's tale was fantastical, a horror story to a lamplighter.

"I scrambled for my silver dagger—not many things can survive without their heads—but it already had Webber by then." He bowed his head. "By the time I killed it, it was too late. Webber was dead. Then, it fell apart into ash. There's not even a body to prove my story."

"Prove your story?" Domek repeated.

"Paluska told me that grief had rattled my mind. He warned me not to tell any of the other lamplighters. He's worried I'm going to start a panic. Maybe I should—I can't let anyone else be caught by surprise." He huffed. "You know Paluska has never trusted me."

"He's from a different era," Domek said, the words feeling stilted on his tongue.

"The era where Jewish people weren't citizens and they had to defend their neighborhood on their own," Abrahams said. "The old hunters, the ones before the gas lamps, wouldn't have let me fight beside them. Even my death would not have been good enough for them. Men like Paluska are still not sure I'm not one of the demons they're supposed to be protecting this city against." Abrahams knocked his fist against the table. "He's not the only one in our group, much less in all of Prague."

Domek shook his head. "They don't deserve you."

"I know. But this job isn't one we do for the glory. You just have to keep saving people and hope they see you're human too. And in the end, save them even when they don't," Abrahams said.

Domek nodded and sipped from his beer.

"Webber knew no one would know how he might die," Abrahams mused. "But he never would have believed that Paluska would be the one to bury it. I'll find out what that thing was and stop this from happening again."

"I'll be there with you," Domek promised.

21

There were few doors Ora hesitated to walk through.

All of Prague was open to her. With enough money and confidence, Ora was welcome most places. The ones she wasn't, she entered anyway. She had strode into more than one gentlemen's club, and watched with amusement as the staff attempted to find the words to eject a lady who refused to take their gentle hints. Her fine clothes were out of place in the less wealthy areas of the city, but if she smiled brightly and tipped well, no one would turn her away.

She nearly ran away from Alena Nováková's door.

In just the last few days, she had stormed back into the palace of her nightmares and then slept with a man who killed her kind for a living. Speaking to one frail, elderly woman should have been nothing. Instead, Ora found her hands shaking as she finally rapped on the door.

The butler led her through a series of halls toward the sitting room. After Alena's husband had died, she had covered the dark woods and dull patterns he had insisted upon with layers of delicate lace and embroidery. It was the way Alena lived—with her gentle touch, she could transform even the most dull or unwelcoming things under her glow.

"Ora," Alena said, putting down her book when she saw her. She let her reading glasses dangle from a chain at her neck. "I didn't expect to see you again." She waved the butler away, but kept a tight grip on the chair's arm with her other hand.

"Alena," Ora said, ignoring the seat in favor of pacing. The windows in the room were shuttered against the night outside, but Ora didn't do more than pull her cloak's hood off her head. Its weight was a comfort, a blanket and promise of a quick exit at once. She hesitated under Alena's cautious gaze, and finally said, "I didn't mean to tell you like that."

"You resent me. You resented me for years. And I was a fool who thought we were sisters."

"We *are* sisters," Ora said.

Alena was still shaking her head. "I imposed myself into your life because I believed that was what you wanted, even when you avoided me. This is only your fourth time to my home. Four times in ten years. I used to believe I was clever, but I was blind in this." Her jaw worked, stretching her parchment skin. "You'll have to forgive me."

"After a century away, I came back to Prague. The city I was born in, the city where I met my death, the city where I fought men trying to protect innocent people and killed them. I traveled the world to stay away from these city walls. But I came back, and I've been here ten years, which is longer than I spent anywhere but Mělník. People are starting to notice that I haven't aged. Have you not wondered why I'm here?"

"I don't know," Alena said faintly.

"For you," Ora said. "I moved here to be near you, even though I can barely stand it. I moved in down the street from you, but seeing you *hurt*. I wanted you near me, even if all I could think about was losing you too. Franz's death broke my heart. You're my sister, and my only living tie to my time with him. I loved you so much that the thought of losing you made me never want to see you again. I was angry before. What I told you wasn't the whole story. I told Franz about the bloodline curse, but *neither* of us could fathom hurting you. It was never a decision, Alena."

Alena hesitated, and then pointed firmly at the chair. "You should sit down."

"Should I?" Even Ora was not sure how the conversation would go on.

"I feel my age," Alena said shortly. "I don't want to stare up at you while we talk. It will hurt my neck."

Ora sat. Alena's scent had soaked into the house as though she had spilled the essence of herself onto the worn cushions and rugs: lavender and plums and dust. She leaned into the chair, memorizing the smell.

"You've been hiding from me for so long that you don't even know the person you claim you'll be missing," Alena said finally.

The blow landed like hawthorn inside Ora's chest. "I was heartbroken," she protested.

"So was I. And you chose for us to both be heartbroken and alone," Alena said. She sighed. "My husband and I didn't have the same type of relationship that you and Franz had, but his loss left me wishing I could numb my emotions too. For me, that lasted a few months, but you've always been on a different time scale than us."

"I am good at numbing myself," Ora said bitterly. "There was nothing Franz hated more than when I disengaged. He didn't care that I was flirtatious with everyone I met, or that I liked intellectual debates, or any of the other things that would have horrified another man about a woman. The only thing that bothered him was when I was so disillusioned by how much I'd seen that I stopped caring. And for the last ten years, I've cared about *nothing*. And I hate myself for it. If I act the way I did before I met him, then I'm saying that his part in my life was a blip."

"You're not disengaged because you don't care—it's because you care too much, and you've refused to let yourself truly feel it. You avoided me, you kept all your new friends at a distance, but you couldn't move away from Prague and couldn't stop yourself from making those friends. You're still the woman I first met."

Ora shook her head. "I can't go back to how I was with Franz. There is no Franz to go back to. Our life in Mělník was idyllic, but it was only ever him who could make me live somewhere so *quiet* and feel content. I don't know who I am after him."

"You told me once that it was a flaw of your kind to stagnate. Don't let yourself get stuck in your grief."

Ora thought of Czernin alone in his palace in the countryside, drenched in the blood of the past. "Franz once gave me a pocket watch to prove that no matter how long I live, time will keep moving with me. As though that were a good thing."

"He was right. You're going to have a long life after Franz and I are both gone."

"Every death *hurts*, Alena. Every one. I'm tired of watching them happen."

"Regret makes the pain worse, and you'll regret this," Alena said, gesturing between them. "You can't love me from afar. I'm here, Ora. If you want to be here, it's not too late." She took a shaky breath, and there were tears in her eyes. "You are the only sister I've ever had."

"I'm sorry," Ora said.

"Can you stay tonight? I don't sleep like I used to, and since you don't sleep at all, you can keep me company. We could talk."

"I will. As long as I can," Ora said. "But then there's something I have to do."

Shadows stretched over Prague like fingers grasping for gold, scraping away the last bits of sunlight. Night was seeping in.

As the sun set, the warmth of the spring day was swept away in favor of a sharp briskness that shocked the back of the throat with every inhale. The sun's hold over the city was still tenuous after the long winter, and the cold was eager to roll back in.

There was a crackle in the air—despite the nearly clear skies, Domek thought a storm might have been approaching. After trading his shift with another lamplighter, he had trekked upriver to a secluded spot under a tree bursting with foliage. The Vltava swirled at his feet. He sat on the twisted roots of the tree, waving a hand to shoo away the ducks that swam up, hoping for bread. The Provisional Theater sat proud on the opposite bank, and a line of orange tiles and copper domes led toward where Charles Bridge stretched over the river. Boats floated past, preparing to make their trades at one of the river ports.

After one last glance to make sure he was out of sight of any passersby, Domek said, "Kája? Come out."

The wisp appeared beside him. "What now?"

Domek leaned back on his hands, feeling the cool dirt beneath his palms, and nodded toward the sunset. "The stars will be out soon."

"What do you need?"

Domek didn't answer. Words had always failed him, and apologies were the most difficult of all. Instead, he looked toward the horizon and took a deep breath of the evening air.

The wisp's fiery orb flickered. He moved around Domek's still form, exploring the small alcove.

Then, finally, he settled. The fire still crackled, but with the slow, steady effect of a candle instead of a wildfire.

In silence, they watched the sun dip below the Vltava, leaving a canvas of bright orange and purple streaking the sky. The colors were riotous after a day of cloud coverage, a vibrant performance that few noticed. As the sunset faded, stars began to appear overhead, peeking through the darkness. The crescent moon cupped the sky, bright and distant.

"I used to live there," Kája said suddenly.

"Where?" Domek asked.

"The castle."

Domek looked at the wisp. Beyond it, the castle loomed on the hill. "In the castle? You lived in Prague? I thought the vodník caught you in the woods."

"It's a long story."

Domek didn't answer. With the skewed balance of power between them, it felt wrong to say anything to force the question. Their quiet truce on the riverbank felt delicate, something small and fragile that a single wrong move could shatter.

"My wife and I were both servants for the emperor. We were

both witches, and he had us use our power to help around the castle. He collected witches and alchemists alike for his whim, but he underutilized our powers. We could have changed his rule, but he had us in attendance for the prestige. He was awed by magic, and thought our presence in his castle made him seem more elite."

"Which emperor was this?"

"Rudolf II."

Domek bit back a gasp. If he was remembering correctly, Rudolf II had died at the start of the seventeenth century—more than two hundred years ago.

The stifled noise didn't escape Kája. "Has it been so very long, then? I've lost track over the years. The passing of seasons does not matter when you can't feel—and I don't know how many years I lost to the vodník underwater.

"Emperor Rudolf came to Prague from Vienna because he imagined this city would spare him from his dark melancholy, but he was still an anxious, angry bastard. He thought if he surrounded himself enough with magic that it would bring him joy. My wife and I weren't the only witches in his employ, and he also brought astronomers, artists, philosophers, and alchemists to live in his court. He met with scholars and politicians and rabbis. He filled entire rooms with talismans he thought would protect him from death, as though if those existed we wouldn't have kept them for ourselves. He had silver musical instruments, casts of animal bodies covered in gold, miniatures of ships and buildings, horns and claws from beasts across the world, and more clocks than every church in the city combined. That was the first place I saw a vodník's soul jar. At the time, I thought it was a curiosity, but barely gave it a second look. The work paid well, and the castle was a good place to live. We should have known it wouldn't last.

"Rudolf was paranoid. He kept his gold locked up in chests to the point that sometimes those of us who lived in the castle ran out of food. He let his pets roam the halls—several people were mauled by a half-starved lion. At one point, he started hallucinating, and thought one of us had cursed him. Maybe someone did—he would have deserved it. It all got worse after the golem incident. A creature made of clay from the Vltava went on a rampage. It was built to protect the Jewish ghetto, but there was a tragic misstep. Dozens were killed before it was handled. Rudolf was certain the next incident would end his life, and became much stricter.

"In the end, Rudolf's younger brother, Matthias, brought an army to the gates and locked Rudolf in the castle until he handed over the crown. Matthias hated witches. He didn't trust us, even from the start. He ordered a purge of Rudolf's magic aides from the castle. He took Rudolf's paranoia and used it as an excuse to execute us all as traitors. I managed to convince the others to pretend that my wife was nothing more than an innocent woman, and that I alone of the two of us had any power. It was easier than it should have been. The soldiers couldn't imagine fearing a woman. She was furious with me, but I couldn't let her sacrifice herself with me when the purge started."

There was a long pause. Domek didn't dare speak. The stars were a silent vigil overhead.

Finally, Kája continued, "They cut off my head. That wasn't common—hanging was easier, but I suppose they didn't trust it to take with us. They had us all in a line in the central courtyard. By the time I got to the front, the block was almost black with blood. I saw my wife in the courtyard, watching. I think she was going to use magic to try to save me, or to throw herself under the executioner's blade too. So I cast a spell to silence her with my final words. She was always so strong, so clever, and in my last action I took that away. It would have faded when I died, but it was enough to stop her from dying with me. I don't know if she ever forgave me."

Domek thought it was unfair that in his current form, the wisp couldn't shed any tears. There was so much grief in the disembodied voice.

"Death is…disorienting. I don't know how long I wandered on instinct before I came back to myself. By that point, I was deep in the woods, and I couldn't gather my senses to get out. It was difficult to access my mind in this form, as a being of pure energy. It wasn't until the vodník contained me that I regained my sense of self. At that point, I was in a jar and under several feet of water, so the only thing I could use my mind for was regret."

"I'm sorry," Domek said quietly. Kája had been a human walking the same streets Domek now guarded, and now he was trapped by magic to serve Domek's will. The idea sat bitter on his tongue.

"I suppose servitude in Prague was my destiny. At least this time I have nothing to lose."

"At the end of all of this," Domek said quietly, "I'll set you free."

"I don't believe you," Kája said, almost friendly in his mildness. "If you were going to do it, you'd do it now."

"I can't yet. We still need to find out why the pijavice found you and brought you here. Without you, I won't know where to look. I need you to help me find someone tonight. But I swear to you, in the morning, I'll free you."

Kája didn't answer. They stayed by the river until Domek's hands began to ache from the cold ground and roots below them. Stars covered the sky now, nearly as bright as the lamps and buildings being lit on the opposite bank. In the opera house, the performance would be just beginning. Domek recalled the melody from the first aria, the one that had swept him into a new world.

22

The address on the invitation from Darina was distressingly near Ora's own house. How long had the Zizkovs been festering in her neighborhood without her knowledge?

Kampa Island was a small section of Malá Strana, cut off from the rest by the Devil's Stream, which moved lazily between houses and under the bridges and watermills. Many of the resident artisans needed the power the water brought for their craft, but the beauty of the area had drawn in many wealthier residents as well. The façade of the Zizkov house was painted the pale blue of a spring sky, and there was a terrace on the second floor crowned with two marble statues. It faced a small square, with one side of the house facing the larger street and the other forming part of the line of walls that framed the stream.

The trees that lined the square had recently sprouted leaves, small green buds that smelled of new beginnings. It was approaching eleven, and the weather had been clear for the last several hours. A small pink bridge crossed over the Devil's Stream from the square.

From this side of the Vltava, the castle on the hill loomed like a sentinel, casting the city in its shadow. The night sky, still free of the recent rainstorms, was swathed with the wisps of clouds that spread like errant paint strokes over the moon.

If Czernin's estate whispered of old money, the Zizkov family's house screamed of new. They may have retained the name from their old haunt, but the family had upgraded homes to one of the poshest areas of town. The entrance hall was full of imported luxuries: vases from the Far East, furs and ivory from African animals, and silk drapes along the walls. Every surface was a new texture, simultaneously inviting the viewer to indulge and warning them that they weren't worthy.

It was nauseatingly gaudy.

She focused on her surroundings, taking note of everything. She couldn't let her relief over Alena's forgiveness soften her tonight. She had enemies all around, and she couldn't risk distraction.

The air stank of spoiled blood.

She displayed her invitation to a doorman. He was human and wearing an unfashionably low collar that displayed the array of needle marks on his neck. "Welcome, madam. Everyone is gathering in the parlor. Go through the entrance on the right." He gestured, but made no move to follow her. It was a sign of the Zizkovs' new money that their staff was so poorly trained. Clearly, the human had been hired for what was in his veins rather than his head. In this case, his unprofessional attitude would help her. Ora needed the chance to snoop around before she met with the rest of the guests.

She paused a step into the room as the door clicked shut behind her. This was no reception suite—the circular room had been cleared of all furniture. There were scratches on the walls as though it had been a cage for one of the big cats whose fur decorated the entry hall.

There was a shift to her left. Ora barely had time to turn toward it before she was tackled to the ground. From the scent and strength, she identified her assailant as another pijavica. Someone must have already identified her as a spy. Though her gown restricted her movement, Ora recovered quickly and rolled with the tackle, using her attacker's momentum against him. She ended up pinning him to the ground, staring down through her loosened hair. The other pijavica was shirtless, revealing scars from before his transformation. He was muscled like a dockworker, not a soft lord who would have owned a house such as this.

He smirked, and then shoved her so hard that she not only flew off him, but skidded halfway across the room. He got to his feet and prowled toward her. She met him halfway in a blur. Ora hadn't fought so hard just to keep her feet in decades, not since she had been jumped by a pair of pijavice in Singapore. Her training, courtesy of Czernin and others around the world, had gone to rust after years of easy living.

Not wasting her breath on talking, she ducked, jumped, spun, and scratched as quickly as she could. Her opponent seemed like he was barely exerting himself, blocking her hits and returning his own as though they were playing a game. If she didn't do something soon, her energy would wear out and leave her clumsy. Letting him toss her across the room, she used the extra few seconds before he closed the distance to jump up and tear one of the curtain rods from the wall. A heavy drape hung from it, but that wasn't what she needed. Snapping the bar over her knee, she tossed one half and the fabric aside and pointed the jagged end toward her attacker.

"Not hawthorn, but I bet I can make it hurt," Ora said, crouching slightly.

The man stepped forward, unfazed, but halted when the door at the other end of the room opened. "That's enough, Crane."

Crane turned around, straightening from his fighting position. "We were having fun."

The newcomer, a posh blond man dressed in dove gray coattails, clicked his tongue. "There will be at least two more guests for you to enjoy. Come through."

"Good fight," Crane told her.

Keeping her curtain rod between them, Ora slipped past him and walked out with the new pijavica. Once the door was closed, she twirled the curtain rod around her fingers. "What was that about?" she demanded.

"Just a little test," he said. "This gathering is exclusively for a certain caliber of person."

"Surely you could sniff out any mortals without needing that setup," Ora said.

"We're not just looking to weed out humans," the blond man said. "We're looking for the best. If someone fails, we sweep the floor and hope the next guest is better suited. I'm pleased you were. The last two didn't make it through."

"What a kind way to greet your guests," Ora said tightly.

"Kindness has never quite been a factor I'm concerned with," he said. "This is an exclusive gathering. I'm Hans Mayer, leader of this family. We only want potential allies here. No untrained gutter rats. Who are you? I don't remember giving you an invitation."

"Olga Filová. My friend gave me hers—Darina Belanova. From Lord Czernin's family," Ora said, pointedly brushing dust from her torn sleeve.

"She told us about you, Lady Filová," Mayer said, leading her from the room.

There were around a dozen pijavice scattered in the parlor. From the ripped gowns and cravats around the room, everyone had gotten the same welcome as Ora. "Get settled," Mayer instructed. "We'll be along once everyone has arrived."

He left the same way he'd come, no doubt to watch Crane attack another unsuspecting guest. Ora looked around the room at the small gathering and straightened her spine. This would be the true test.

"You're sure this is where she is?" Domek asked, peering at the blue house from the end of the bridge.

The wisp floated beside him. At Domek's request, he had dimmed his flame to that of a gas lamp. Anyone looking too closely would notice the strange, unattached light, but thus far they had stayed away from prying eyes.

"Quite," Kája told him.

The curtains of the house were all tightly closed, which could have simply indicated a desire for privacy. Ora was his only firm lead in this entire mess, and if he was wrong about her, he would need to find another approach to solve the mystery of why pijavice were hunting Kája and other wisps across Europe.

And every minute he wasted also delayed his mission to find the monster that had killed Webber.

Domek spoke softly and urgently. "I need to get inside. Can you help me?"

"I can make you invisible to anyone looking," Kája said. "No smell, no visuals, no sound. Unless you run into something, no one will detect you."

It made sense. In stories, wisps floated in and out of visibility when they lured their victims into danger. "Do it."

"It's done."

Domek looked down at his arms skeptically. He could still see himself. "Are you sure?"

"I can make you invisible to yourself as well," Kája suggested. "Or to me. Would you like me to make you disappear entirely?"

"No," Domek said quickly. "No."

"I used this spell when I was alive," Kája said unexpectedly. "I was antisocial, and preferred to avoid attention. My wife laughed at me for it. It's disorienting the first time."

Domek did not know how to respond, so he only nodded. "Stay with me, invisible as well. I might need you again," he said, peeking at the house again. A hack out front had just disgorged two more people, a tall black couple in well-tailored clothes. Was their gait supernaturally graceful, or was paranoia simply rampant in Domek's mind? Taking a deep breath, Domek strolled across the street as confidently as he dared. The newcomers didn't turn to look at him, even when he walked directly past them.

"You're not using the front door?" Kája asked, keeping pace beside him. "What was the point of my spell?"

"We're taking the servant's entrance," Domek said. He didn't want to see Ora until he had to.

At the nondescript side door, he only had to wait a few minutes before a maid walked out, carrying a dustpan. "I deserve a raise for having to sweep this up," she muttered to herself. Though she stepped within a hairsbreadth of Domek, she didn't even glance at him. "No one warned me I'd have to deal with *remains.*" She emptied a pile of ash onto the ground.

"Someone killed a pijavica here," Domek said, frowning. As Kája had promised, the maid didn't flinch when he spoke.

That settled the question of whether this were some benign gathering of Ora's friends. Had someone else in the lamplighters known there would be pijavice there that night and set up a lure? Or were pijavice killing each other?

The thought that it could have been Ora in that dustpan disturbed him, but he pushed his reaction to the side.

"Come on," Kája said. "We should go through now. This way we don't have to try to open it ourselves. *You* can't go through doors."

Domek followed him inside to a bustling kitchen, or what had once been a kitchen. The space now appeared to be a dressing room.

"Tell me this was not all a ploy to play Peeping Tom," Kája commented dryly. "You acted like you were on some noble crusade."

"I'm not..." Domek said, averting his eyes to the ceiling. "What are they doing?"

The women were dressed in—or in the process of putting on—sleeveless dresses, revealing their necks, shoulders, and décolletage. The men had foregone shirts all together. They were chatting and bickering as though it was perfectly normal to change in a kitchen. Two women were helping another secure her hair in an elaborate up-do, while another used a small hand mirror to apply lip color.

"I'm not sure about this," one of the women said. She was one of the youngest of the group, barely out of girlhood.

"You're about to earn more than you'd make in a month scrubbing dishes," another said, nudging her with a hip.

"It *is* the kitchen," Kája explained. "They're putting together dinner."

23

There were two creatures particularly adept at thoroughly ignoring those around them: cats and pijavice. It was a defensive tactic: removing oneself from a situation through poise and disdain rather than having to give up a room. Looking around the parlor, one would think that every battle-ragged pijavica there had deliberately chosen to rip their own clothes and then stand along the walls, engrossed in examining one of the Zizkovs' many artifacts. The room's array of plush chairs and cushions on the floors were untouched.

Ora walked over to one of the women, an aristocratic brunette in a ruffled yellow gown. One sleeve had been torn off, but she wore it confidently. She had sharp cheekbones and heavy eyelashes that made her look tired. "Hello," Ora greeted. "Quite the welcome, wasn't it?"

The woman looked her over disdainfully. "Quite," she said.

Ora maintained her companionable expression. Despite her

aloof air, Ora pegged her as recently transformed. She was trying too hard.

"I'm Olga Filová," Ora said.

The woman hesitated before answering. "Lady R," she said.

With a conspiratorial smile, Ora said, "Not comfortable mentioning your real name?"

"I'm not sure I should be here. If I leave, I don't want this to follow me."

Ora leaned in slightly closer. "How did the Zizkovs approach you with this invitation, if you're so reluctant to reveal yourself to other pijavice? You're clearly not someone looking to make friends."

"They know I'm skeptical about joining any group," Lady R said. "I'm on casual terms with one of their newer members. He knew when he gave them my name that I wasn't convinced, but the Zizkovs promised a show tonight that would change my mind. They want some new family members. I was bored, so, here I am."

The pijavice in attendance all seemed as new as Lady R. Would Czernin's name mean anything to them, or set Ora apart as different? "They said the same to me."

Lady R glanced around, obviously aware everyone would be able to overhear them, and then added, "I didn't expect them to be so…common. Did you see the foyer?"

"Dreadful," Ora agreed, matching her disdainful tone. "If I don't join their family, maybe I'll at least offer the name of my decorator."

Another pair of pijavice stumbled in looking as worse for wear as the rest of the room. Crane, finally donning a shirt, and Mayer both followed after. From the parlor's other door, three more entered. Lady R sent a flirtatious wave at one of the men. Five members in total. From all the whispers and drama, Ora had expected more. The guests outnumbered the hosts twice over.

There was only one woman in the Zizkov family, a brunette who was more striking than beautiful, with a hawkish nose and dark eyes. In a lush green gown covered in ribbons and ruffles, she was dressed to impress. Like the house itself, the effect was too deliberate to be effective. Lady R nudged Ora, her studied lack of expression as clear as a snide remark.

One of the two new men looked familiar, but Ora couldn't place him. His hair was the color of a wheat field touched by fall's first frost, and he had a lush mustache settled above plump lips. He scanned the room, giving Ora a glimpse of familiar pale green eyes. She ducked so that she was hidden behind Lady R. She *did* know him.

Czernin had told her Mayer was turning local intellectuals. Ora hadn't thought to wonder if it had been anyone in her circles.

His name was Jakob Weintraub, and he had been a professor of chemistry at Charles University a decade ago, just after Ora had returned to Prague. They had met at a salon, and he had flirted with her well into the night. She'd enjoyed his cleverness, but his arrogance had gotten tiring. Back then, he'd been human.

If he spotted her, he'd recognize her. Using her true name would have made them suspicious, but the lie would paint her as a target. She should have watched the house before she had made her plan.

Mayer cleared his throat, drawing everyone's attention. "Welcome, ladies and gentlemen. Thank you all for coming tonight. We apologize for how you were greeted. You can't blame us for being careful." There was a tangible coolness in the room. No one appeared amused. "To make up for it, we'd like to provide a meal before we begin our meeting. We've brought in a variety of options. Please, help yourselves."

The doors opened again, and a line of humans entered the room. There were more of them than the pijavice, at least twenty. Though they were mostly women, there were some men, and they were all unusually attractive. Every single one had a bare neck. With practiced ease, they each selected a floor cushion and knelt down. Each cushion was within easy reach of a chair or couch. Like dinner plates.

One of the guests, a pijavica with pale eyes and a low ponytail, stepped forward. "You can't be serious," he hissed. "This is too obvious."

Other than those who were sworn members of a pijavica's household staff, humans were kept oblivious to the existence of pijavice. The man didn't mention Czernin or another of the old guard by name, but everyone knew who kept the pijavice restricted to dark alleys. It wasn't men like Sokol or Domek, but their own kind.

Though Darina had told her that Czernin had approved their experiments, Ora doubted even at his most mad that he would approve of this. Czernin had carefully crafted a system over centuries that allowed him to live in his palace without stirring the locals into a terrified mob.

Then again, he seemed to have lost that long-held control. Perhaps this was another sign of his decline.

Mayer waved off the man's complaint. "All tonight's entertainment is being well compensated. And you can imagine the penalty for anyone breathing a word of this outside the room."

Ora's hands fisted in the folds of her gown. The Zizkov family was out of control. Killing their own guests, bringing in humans for a blood orgy in the middle of the city—even if the rumors of the 'cure' turned out to be nothing, the family needed to be ended immediately. The first wouldn't draw censure from Sokol's team, but the latter was inexcusable on all fronts. Either he was telling the truth and the score of humans would be back on the streets to whisper about the monsters on Kampa Island, or he was lying...and there would be a massacre at the end of the night.

"Please, enjoy."

Lady R, having apparently accepted Ora as her companion for the evening, nudged her to sit on a small couch near the edge of the room. "It'd be rude to refuse," Lady R said. Her pupils were already dilated and her pretty red lips widened to reveal her layer of secret teeth. Was this what Domek had seen when he had looked at Ora? A monster in a lady's dress?

Ora sat down on the couch and placed one hand on the closest human's neck.

Domek and Kája slipped through the pijavice's house, invisible as promised. After they emerged from the disturbing scene in the kitchen, they discovered an ornately decorated house. Vases, furs, trinkets—it was like entering a museum. Domek could not have afforded a single decoration, even if he had saved everything he'd made.

"Can wisps create money?" Domek asked Kája. "If these are the pijavice who found you in the vodník's pond, could they have worked with the wisps to build this house?"

"You're invisible. You could steal every expensive item in this building and no one would know until they checked their empty pedestals," Kája pointed out. "With control of a wisp, anyone could become a rich man."

Domek hummed and moved forward.

Near the front of the house, he heard voices muffled by the walls.

"Any reason why we're avoiding the room where everyone is?" Kája asked as Domek approached the grand staircase, which was made of dark wood and lined with gold filigree.

"I'd rather see what they're keeping secret."

A door opened and a butler emerged into the entrance hall, carrying a stack of white towels. He must have been human. There was sweat on his brow. Domek froze with one foot on the stairs, but the man did not look at them. Instead, he bustled on toward the back of the house, leaving them alone again.

"You don't trust my magic?" Kája asked, already floating ahead up the stairs.

"Can you blame me?" Domek muttered, following him. He had been right—it was disconcerting to have to trust you were invisible, though the world seemed the same.

Outside of the opulent ground floor, the house was less extravagant. Though the building materials were still as fine as those Domek had seen at the opera house, the hallways upstairs were more sparsely decorated. It was easier to walk here without the constant threat of knocking over some expensive vase that would have the entire nest hunting him.

On the first floor, Domek found a storage room stacked high with wooden boxes. Moving carefully, and conscious of the supernaturally sharp ears downstairs, he lifted the lid of the first.

Sifting through a bundle of straw, he expected to find one of the vodník jars Bazil had warned him had been smuggled into Prague.

Instead, he found rows of metal tins. They were unmarked, but a quick sniff confirmed that they were filled with opium. In another crate, he found empty glass vials still packaged with the maker's wax, unopened. A third had copper tubing, the type he had seen in Imrich's apartment. Were these crates a random amalgamation of a trading business, or part of some larger scheme? The latter two crates seemed more appropriate for an alchemist than a wealthy trader.

"Can you look inside these crates?" he asked Kája. "Are you able to tell if there are any vodník jars here?"

Kája floated quickly through the room, his orange glow passing in and out of the various boxes incorporeally. Though the flames brushed the wooden frames and straw packaging within, nothing caught fire. Kája returned to his side. "If they are keeping any, they aren't here."

Perhaps...perhaps there were pijavice who lived as humans. If Ora was the woman he had first thought, her friends could also be pijavice living within mortal laws. The human meals downstairs may have known precisely what they were being paid to do. There were prostitutes for all tastes. Though drinking human blood was repugnant, if the victims were compensated well and survived the encounter, could Domek let Ora live?

In the next room, Domek froze in the doorway. Any idea of a cabal of benign pijavice was dashed to pieces.

The stench, hidden by the previously closed door, was unmistakable. In his time as a lamplighter, he had uncovered a dozen pijavica nests in and under Prague. The stink of their victims haunted his dreams.

Bones, stripped clumsily of their flesh and belongings, were stacked in the corners of the room. Empty boxes sat in the middle, already lined with straw. Despite the expensive trappings of the house, despite Ora's smiles, this was still the lair of monsters. "Are they planning on shipping them somewhere?" Domek wondered.

"They have no yard for burials, and I'd imagine throwing them in the stream would be suspicious," Kája said, hovering in front of an abandoned skull.

Domek's stomach churned with anger. "We'll get them their justice," he said, closing the door on the macabre discovery.

The staircase to the top level was a simple, narrow spiral twisting upward like a storm cloud. The ceiling of the second floor was cramped where the slanted roof cut downward, making the walls close in on them.

In addition to a collection of small bedrooms—which must have belonged to the house staff, as pijavice needed no sleep—they found a long, narrow office. A heavy wooden desk stacked with papers sat near the door, and the walls were covered with maps. Some were country maps, outlining all of Europe and beyond, but most focused in on various regions of the nearby countryside. Metal pins had been stuck throughout, labeled with small scraps of paper featuring miniscule handwriting.

"Kája, I need your light," Domek said, drawing the wisp from where he had been exploring the far end of the room. He plucked one of the scraps of paper from a pin, revealing that the mark was directly over a small pond in the Black Forest. With the bright flame of Kája's core, he was able to read the cramped handwriting. *Empty.*

He returned the slip of paper and picked another, this one pinned to the middle of a tributary of the Morava River toward the west. *One vodník. Five soul jars, four occupied. No wisps.*

There was no longer space for uncertainty. Ora was one of the pijavice who had found Kája.

"These are all the places they've been searching for wisps captured by vodníks," Domek realized. He blinked at the vast map. It stretched far across the Empire. "They must have been searching for years."

"From this house, they seem to have enough money to not need to do all the searching themselves," Kája pointed out. "I wonder where they found me."

"You don't know?"

"I was wandering for so long before the vodník caught me, I lost track of where I was. I was in an unfamiliar forest. In a hundred years of drifting, I could have been anywhere." Kája was silent for a contemplative moment while Domek continued checking the different scraps of paper. Between the wavering light and the sloppy handwriting, they were difficult to decipher. "How many of us have they found? It must be like striking gold—the exact combination of finding a vodník who managed to capture a wisp in one of its jars would be almost impossible. Each step is rare by itself."

"Most of these mark failures," Domek said, sifting through a few more. "It's no wonder they've been trying so hard to get you back from me. They can't have found very many."

Domek abandoned the maps to examine the stacks of papers. Most were shipping logs from various boats, with high numbers in the payment columns. "Would having a wisp on their side help them find others?" he mused.

"Unlikely. If they're only trying to find wisps that have already been captured, everything they're looking for would be underwater inside a vodník's lair. Without the jar to protect our essences, going underwater to try to detect another spirit would be suicide," Kája said. "That's why the ones who found me had so many smashed jars with them. They'd been checking them one by one."

There was a worn leather journal under the loose sheets of paper. The notes inside were even less legible than on the map. Domek doubted their author could even read them—some words were just rows of erratic loops, and none of the accents seemed connected to any specific letter. He pulled out a few words—*light*, *silver*, and *death* all started with the same distinctive 's'—but the context was incomprehensible.

"The wisps aren't up here," Domek said, giving up and shutting the book. "We haven't seen a single jar or freed wisp floating around. If they've been gathering them—where are they? Could they be hiding from us the way we are from them?"

"It depends on the spirit. I'm powerful, stronger than most. At least, I assume so—I was in life. My illusions would likely overpower theirs. I believe I would know if there were any wisps nearby, and I'm sure there are not."

Domek looked around the attic. "Do you think this building has a cellar?"

"It's likely," Kája said.

"Can you check?"

Silently, Kája sunk through the floor. It was eerily quiet while Domek waited, alert for any sign the monsters gathered below had noticed their presence. Kája returned quickly from his reconnaissance. "There is. I've found the door."

"Lead on," Domek said.

They crept down the two staircases until they reached a door in a narrow hallway near the front entrance. After making sure the hallway was clear, they slipped inside the unlocked door. The cellar was dark and damp, and a cold wall of air made Domek shiver. The blackness consumed the wooden steps midway down, cloaking the rest of the cellar. With Kája's light, Domek carefully descended into a single open room.

Most of Prague's underground was left over from the ancient city centuries ago that had resided by the Vltava. The small river stones covering the floor and the pale stone walls were a familiar sight; less so were the chains. Blood coated the cuffs dangling from the walls, thick and black with age.

Domek inspected the chains while Kája hovered across the room. In the center was a long table full of beakers, copper tubing, and what looked like a portable distillery. If the pijavice were selling their own homemade drugs, like that opium from upstairs, they might have used their cellar to dilute and experiment with tinctures. Ora must have been putting her scientific interest to use for her nest. "Don't touch anything," he instructed.

Beneath the blood, the chains were coated with ash, likely hawthorn. Thick mesh gloves hung on the wall nearby so that the residents could manipulate the poisoned metal without being burned themselves. Between these and the ashes the maid had tossed out earlier, Domek was growing more confused. The house was crawling with pijavice. Why did it seem like so many of their victims were also pijavice? Where did the wisps the nest had so clearly been searching for fit in, and where could they be?

There was another door in the corner of the room, at the base of a short, steep set of stairs. Domek went over and pressed his ear to it to make sure that no pijavice were waiting nearby. It was as silent as the rest of the basement. He opened it, hoping to find the chamber where they'd hidden the soul jars, but the door led down to a dark underground tunnel, which disappeared around a bend ahead.

He closed the door, shaking his head. "I don't understand it. The wisps aren't here."

"No. They're not," Kája said. For the first time since Domek had met him, the wisp sounded truly unnerved.

The distillery was of unusual design. There was a section to boil and separate the layers from the raw substance, pipes that could be used to draw out the different levels, and a winding tube that dripped into a final container. There were pliers and scalpels on the far side of the table, more likely used on the victims they kept in those chains than in any experiments. From their luster, they seemed crafted of silver rather than the standard steel. The pijavice clearly had more money than they knew what to do with.

Finally, Domek noticed the pile of clay jars abandoned on the floor. Some were shattered into large pieces, their intricately carved curves shadowed in the dim light.

Kája wasn't looking down there, though.

One of the vials at the center of the table was full. The liquid inside shimmered slightly and had a rainbow sheen, like it had been touched by oil.

"What is that?" Domek asked.

"This is the last spirit they took," he said. His voice wavered like his flames. "I can feel her energy. There's still power here, even though it's been poisoned and diluted."

"*That's* a wisp?" Was the essence in the vial what Kája would look like if his fire were snuffed? It seemed too small, too lifeless.

"It was. They killed her and then tore her into pieces. No soul should look like this." Kája looked around the room. "They aren't teaming up with my people. This is a slaughterhouse."

24

"Stay very still," Ora whispered into the human's ear. The woman at her feet was young, no more than fourteen. Her small breasts were pushed up by a tight corset and there was dark lip color swiped across her mouth. She seemed fragile and innocent, kneeling in a room full of pijavice. Her pulse beat wildly in her pale, bare throat. Cradling her head was like holding a rabbit in her palm: delicate, fragile, powerless. Had the Zizkovs warned the evening's entertainment just what they were going to be subjected to?

The Zizkov family watched as the guests enjoyed their meals. Mayer and Crane remained beside the door, conversing quietly. It was a display of power—all of these bodies were spare, selected for their guests. No one in the family needed to consume the free blood to survive. Some of the humans remained untouched, sitting still as statues, and Ora was relieved, even though her performance would have been easier had Mayer and Crane been distracted.

Glancing around to make sure that the other pijavice were indulging, Ora used a sharpened nail to prick the girl's neck. The fresh human blood smelled fantastic, raw and wild. Ora inhaled deeply. Then, she pressed a chaste kiss on the skin above it, using her thumb to wipe away the blood. She smeared her wet thumb on her bottom lip and then sat up. The girl shuddered.

Beside her, Lady R was drinking deeply. There were ways to drain blood painlessly, but either Lady R had never learned or didn't bother. Despite her aggressive handling, the man at her feet appeared dazed and lost. Even with the prick of three-dozen sharp teeth in his neck, he was on the verge of falling asleep. The soporific in Lady R's fangs was taking effect.

After a few more minutes, Mayer called their attention away from their meals. A pijavica reluctant to stop had to be nudged by Crane. He hissed before realizing who it was and sat back. Crane loomed over him while Mayer talked.

Lady R rehinged her jaw and used a handkerchief to clean her lips, dabbing them as though she were at a tea party rather than a human buffet.

"Thank you all for being here tonight," Mayer said. "The Zizkov family is looking to expand. The nocturnal citizens of Prague have been complacent for too long, and we're planning on revolutionizing the city. The old ones—they don't realize how much more there is to take from the world. We do."

"Hear, hear!" said one of the guests, tapping long fingernails against the shoulder of his human companion.

Mayer spared him a short smile. "I was turned only two years ago, but I know that the pijavica population is stagnant. They want to keep us in the shadows. We're stronger than humans. We have the potential to be the most powerful beings on the planet if we just seize the opportunity. Our family is just the group to take that chance. I have the vision." He pointed around the room as he spoke. "Crane is the only other original member of the Zizkov family left. A boxer in his mortal days, he is one of the strongest pijavice I've ever met. Besides him, I created our team myself." He moved to the cluster of the other three pijavice. "Ajka, Weintraub, and Byre are revolutionizing science as we know it. They were geniuses in their mortal days, and now they have no limits.

"Our kind has enormous strength. The only thing standing between us and complete domination are a few small restrictions. Sunlight. Hawthorn. And we've found a way around them."

It was just as Darina had said—they were attempting to learn a way to eradicate their weaknesses. From Mayer and his pack of newly turned pijavice, the idea sounded like a child dreaming of a green sky.

There was some laughter in the room, but most of the guests were silent, listening to Mayer. "We started our tests on lesser pijavice," he said, "but most weren't strong enough to survive the process. The ones that did were mad. Their minds were too weak. Our scientists realized that to get powerful results, we needed to focus on powerful pijavice." He smirked. "That's why you're here."

"I don't recall volunteering for experimentation," Ora murmured to Lady R, but her companion didn't respond. She was still staring at the bloody wounds on her meal's neck.

Other guests seemed to agree with Ora. "Perhaps your failure is because you're trying something that can't be done," said another pijavica.

"Oh, it can be done. We had hoped to do more experimentation, but our timeline was…altered. We've lost three of our friends this week at the hands of weak mortals. The time for waiting was over, despite the protests of my more scientifically minded colleagues." He nodded to Weintraub. "The five of us took the serum earlier today. We watched the sunset for the first time in years."

The room immediately broke into whispers. Lady R's eyes were wide and alert for the first time that night. "Is that possible?" she asked softly, awe in her voice.

Ora understood. The sunset. It had been centuries since she had seen her last. She remembered a sky of impossible colors. She would have done anything to see it again.

"Of course, you're all clever people," Mayer continued. "You won't believe a claim like this without proof. Ajka, bring it to me." He gestured to the woman, who stepped forward. When she pulled aside a cloth to reveal a hawthorn stake, those closest recoiled. Deliberately, she grasped the poisonous wood with her bare hand before handing it over to Mayer. Neither of them should have been able to hold onto the stake, not without leaving a permanent burn on their flesh. She had seen a jagged mark on Darina's chest, just at one of her lower ribs, where a hunter had failed to drive a stake into her heart. Though she had not died from the wound, the hawthorn poison left her permanently scarred, the only mark on her immortal body.

Ora wondered if the welt on her own ribs from Domek's stake would mar her forever.

Mayer held up the stake for everyone to see, and then deliberately pressed it to his shaved cheek. He dragged the sharp end over his skin, leaving a thin line of bright red. He must have fed recently, for the blood from his veins was fresh enough to drip down his jaw before the wound healed itself. "Hawthorn can't hurt me anymore," he said, and then threw the stake into the center of the room, near Ora's shoes. The rest of the pijavice stared down at it as though it were the snake in the Garden of Eden, a threat and temptation in one.

"What's the offer? How do we get your cure?" asked a lean man in a blue waistcoat, leaning forward. His fangs were extended, but he spoke around them with the skill of long practice.

"It's simple. Join us. We're bringing pijavice into the light. We're starting with the worthy—our cure is limited, for the moment. You'll be the start of a movement that will change the world. Tonight is the beginning of a new era."

It was no wonder that Sokol had been terrified of the idea of pijavice finding immunity to their only limitations. Without being chained to the darkness or vulnerable to the humans' stakes, there would be nothing to stop pijavice from sweeping over human society.

But Ora wouldn't take advantage of the power. She could take their cure, and keep her own morals. She could attend daytime concerts in the Old Town Square. She could finally learn why Franz had ridden his horse for hours in the meadows while she read inside. She could explore the world again and see every bit in the glow of sunlight, rather than the haze of shadows.

"I'm not interested in being part of your experiments," said the pijavica who had protested the feast of humans.

He had had the restraint not to touch the human he'd been presented with at all, leaving her one of the few still aware of what was happening around her. Unlike Ora's, who had taken her whispered instructions to heart, she was looking around the room in obvious horror.

"You said you were turned only two years ago," the protestor continued, climbing to his feet. "You're a child. I have patience. If your experiments work, I'll still be here in fifty years. We'll talk then."

"There's no progress without risk."

"That's a mortal mentality." He looked around at the others. "We've survived because we can outlast the reckless fools who grasp every meal they can find in the gutters. Don't fall for his pretty words when they only have a day's worth of proof."

It happened in a flash. For such a large man, Crane moved with quiet stealth. One moment, the pijavica was giving his speech. The next, his head was torn from his neck, and his body exploded into dust.

The girl at their feet screamed, and was met with the same treatment. On a human, the result was far bloodier.

"Any other objections?" Mayer asked.

The room was silent.

"Wonderful. Welcome to the Zizkov family."

Ora smiled when Mayer looked around the room at everyone's expressions. Were any others masking their true reactions, or had they all been swayed by the promise of invincibility?

She couldn't lie to herself. It was a tempting offer. If Crane hadn't killed the girl, she might have let them cure her.

But these were not the kind of people she was willing to owe a debt.

"If you're all sated, we can get started. Our laboratory is in our cellar." He gestured for them to rise. "Leave your meals behind; we'll handle them." After everything the humans had heard, Ora doubted they would be getting their promised payment.

"We're starting tonight?" a woman, dark-skinned and elegant, asked. "Now?"

"All this talk of waiting. This is why the pijavice have been stuck for so long. Be bold, my lady," Mayer said. "Besides, secrecy is vital until we make our move. We can't have anyone leaving and telling tales before morning." He smiled. "No one leaves this house without the cure in their veins."

Domek inspected the tools on the table again through a new lens. The delicate machinery, the glimmering liquid, the silver tools—they all seemed grotesque. "How?" he asked.

"I don't know. This shouldn't be possible. What they're doing here, it's unnatural." Kája turned to Domek. "They're using the soul's magic *separate* from its source. They pulled out everything they could and discarded the remains. Look at this silver. They found the only thing that could hurt us and *used* it. They...*exsanguinated* this spirit."

"This looks like science," Domek said. "The woman we tracked here often attends scientific lectures. She has the mind for this. And, apparently, the cruelty." A footstep creaked against a floorboard upstairs, knocking Domek from his thoughts. "We need to leave."

"We need to find out more," Kája argued. "Look at these syringes. Look around the room. They've been taking this and injecting it *into pijavice*. How are they doing this? Why? Is it working? How many spirits have they already destroyed? The greed behind this... It's unfathomable."

"I want to know more too, but if they've already killed the other wisps they've brought in, we might not be safe here,"

Domek said. "We don't know what kind of power this gives them. You said wisps could see through your magic."

"They were already slaves," Kája continued as though he hadn't spoken. "If they were trapped in these vodník jars, there wouldn't have been a way for them to fight back." There was another thud from upstairs. Kája drifted toward the stairs. "These pijavice deserve death."

"I agree, but if we're going to shut this down, we need to be thorough. They've been one step ahead of me this entire time. We need to make sure we stop all of it. We need to figure out if they have any other wisps in transit or already here. If we step in too early, they might get away."

"We could kill everyone here and then pursue the others," Kája said. "I have all the time in the world to hunt them down, if you didn't stop me."

"What we need is more information," Domek said. "There are at least a dozen pijavice upstairs, and some of them might have unknown extra powers. You and I can't beat them alone."

"Coward."

"You nearly depleted your energy just healing the boy last night. You could not kill the number of pijavice we can hear upstairs, and any who escape could continue the experiments." Domek took a deep breath. "Whatever they're doing here, it's dangerous to your people *and* mine. I want this to stop as much as you do."

"We could try. Together. This is your profession."

"I've fought three pijavice at once and only barely won," Domek told him. "Even with your help, a dozen is too many. I would almost certainly be killed."

"Those are odds I'm willing to chance."

"You're forgetting that if I die, you go back in your jar until the next person stumbles upon you," he pointed out. "If that happens, they might not be as interested in stopping those pijavice as I am."

"I wouldn't let a thing like your death stop my vengeance," Kája responded, but his determination was fading. After a long beat of silence, he asked, "What's your plan?"

"We go to the other lamplighters," Domek said. "We use their resources and finish this. They've destroyed a hundred nests like this."

"The lamplighters? The organization you've been dancing around since you found me?" Kája asked. "You wouldn't trust them with me. Why trust them with this?"

"This is bigger than any situation I've ever faced," Domek said. "I need their help. Now that you're on our side, we will focus on the real threat instead of fighting among ourselves for your jar. I'll explain that you're not the enemy—these pijavice are. At the end of this, I'll free you, and we won't need to argue over who controls your powers." He paused, and added, "You'll know that if you betray us, you won't get your revenge."

"It's not revenge. This will be justice."

Domek nodded. "I'm with you," he promised. He picked up the vial from the table. It was warm to the touch. "I want to take this with us," he said. "If we do, though, they'll know someone was in here. Can you replace the serum with something different in this vial and put the real serum in here?" he asked, pointing to a smaller, tear-drop vial.

"And I'm to trust you won't use it?" Kája asked.

"Could a human even survive something like this?"

"It would probably kill you. Or give you powers beyond your dreaming. No one has ever done this before. Men are reckless when they have something powerful in their grasp, and you're a curious man."

"I promise I won't use it. I don't want to leave it here for them, and I don't want to destroy it entirely, not until we learn more."

There was a flicker in the air, and the tear-drop vial was slowly filled with the silver liquid. On the table, the original vial was refilled by something else, a shade darker. Domek tucked the horrid serum into his bag. "If we leave them this machine, they'll just find more of us to mutilate," Kája said.

Domek examined the machinery. "A distillery shouldn't be able to do this," he said thoughtfully, tracing a coil with one finger.

Kája was giving the silver instruments on the table a wide berth. "Those could do a lot," he said. "No spirit could survive under the bite of that much pure silver."

"This is more than science—it's alchemy. There must be something extra, beyond the silver, that makes this possible." He opened a small panel, and peered inside. "Aha!" He grabbed one of the chainmail gloves from the table and then plucked out a piece of obsidian. Though the stone was polished to a shine, its edges were raw and ragged, as though it had just been carved from the ground. "It must be this. It's the only thing that doesn't fit. It must be filtering the magical energies." He put it alongside the serum in his satchel. "There. Now they won't have the serum or the way to make more."

"If leaving prevents me from getting justice for the souls that have been destroyed in this hell, I will hold you accountable."

"So will I," Domek said quietly.

Ora smoothed her skirts, tugging at a thread dangling from the ripped fabric near the floor until most of the other pijavice had filed out of the room. Carefully, she put her hands to her hair, held up a limp red curl, and frowned at it.

Her delay was only partially effective. Most of the Zizkovs' guests had followed the scientists out, but Mayer, Crane, and the woman, Ajka, remained. They watched her closely, a pack of wolves regarding a deer. Mayer raised his eyebrows and tilted his head toward the door.

If she went into the cellar, she would have no chance of escape. If she was going to get out without letting them put their cure in her veins, she had to go now.

"Now I feel guilty that I took Darina's invitation," she said with a small laugh. "I'm sure she would have wanted to be part of this first test."

"You'll be able to walk back to her through the daylight and show her our success."

Ora tugged at her curls again, pouting. "Sorry, I just wish I could look more put-together for something so momentous."

Crane scoffed, and Mayer's expression became indulgent. "Come along," he prompted. "That will not matter."

She gave them another pleasant, vacant smile, and then turned and sprinted toward the far wall.

The woman reacted first, having been the least convinced by her innocent façade. Ajka lunged forward, but tripped over the dazed victims still sitting on cushions around the room. Ora had mapped the room while she had delayed, and didn't hesitate.

Some pijavice carved their window frames from hawthorn to keep out their enemies. Ora hoped that the Zizkovs hadn't thought so far ahead.

"Crane, get her!" Mayer shouted, but anything else he said was hidden by the sound of glass shattering around her.

The glass raked against her skin, leaving thin scratches across her arms, but she was out.

Ora fell down, down, into the stream, the water crashing over her head. She fought against the heavy fabric of her skirts, wishing she had the air to swear. Disoriented by her fight with Crane, she had believed the room to be facing the side street.

Crane leaped through the window after her, twisting to avoid the jagged shards of glass. He dove toward her, and she swam desperately to escape. Using one clawed hand to shred the front of her skirts so that the fabric wouldn't get in her way, she kicked toward the bridge. From the sound behind her, Crane was close on her heels. Her driver, Hackett, was waiting in the adjoining square, pre-warned that she might need a quick getaway.

She just had to reach him first.

When she found the grate under the bridge, she scrambled up the metal rungs and then dug her claws into the brick wall and crawled up the rest of the way, leaving punctures in the stone. She flung herself over the pink wall of the bridge, and started to run. Her slick heels twisted beneath her, and she braced herself against the opposite wall, nearly toppling over into the water mill beyond. She was nearly across the bridge when Crane grabbed her around the waist and hauled her backward. He slammed her against the wall hard enough that the plaster dented beneath her.

"We were excited to offer you membership," Crane said into her ear. "You've been taught how to use your strength, and you're older than you seem. You could have been an asset. But Darina does not know her friends as well as she thought. Shame I have to kill you."

"You disgust me," Ora said. She let her weight drop, leaving his hands grasping at nothing. She moved quickly, fueled by fear, reaching into the single remaining sodden pocket of her dress. She jabbed the spike of the hawthorn stake she had grabbed off the floor during the earlier distraction into his heart. Her claws had ripped open her gloves earlier, and even that light contact with the wood felt like holding fire.

Though her aim had been true, Crane just winced and stepped back rather than dissolving into dust. He pulled the stake from his chest, slick with blood from a recent meal, and threw it to the ground. "Idiot girl," he said as the wound healed. "I'm not a normal pijavica anymore. You can't fight me."

"Girl? I'm older than your grandmother," Ora snarled.

She tried to lunge away when he attacked again, but he was stronger and faster. He had been going easy on her during their earlier brawl, and she had barely managed to keep her feet then. Her power had always been her mind, not her body.

Using one arm and his body weight to pin her against the bridge wall again, Crane's other hand came to rest against her neck. He moved casually, easily—he knew he had nothing to fear from Ora.

Of all the ways for her to die after more than two centuries of survival, she had never predicted being beheaded on a beautiful bridge only blocks away from her home.

She spat in his face, but he just smiled. He closed his eyes and

302

breathed in her scent, enjoying her fear. She slipped a bare leg between his and then twisted, trying to knock him off-balance. He stumbled, and she lurched toward freedom, but then he leaned into her with even more weight. With the water soaking his clothing and the natural chill of the pijavice, it was as though a statue were crushing her. She tried everything she knew, twisting and snapping and clawing the way she'd escaped a hundred men seeking to end her life, but this time, she was stuck. Her sedentary life had made her soft, weak, and now she would die.

He opened his mouth, jaw unhinging to gape and display his row of needle-sharp teeth. He met her eyes, and then lowered his mouth toward her bared neck. She might survive having her throat torn out, but she was sure he would finish her off before she could heal. He was playing with her, drawing out the inevitable.

There was a crack in the night air, a loud sound that echoed across the stream. A gunshot.

Blood sprayed from the nicked vein in Crane's neck. It was warm against her face, too warm to have been in the pijavica's veins for long. He dropped her, stumbling sideways, but the wound was already closing.

Ora turned to face her rescuer, half-expecting to see Domek. It was her driver, Hackett. Of course. Domek would have just as soon shot her as Crane.

Pale and wide-eyed, Hackett looked between the smoking gun in his hand and Crane's healed wound.

"Run!" Ora ordered.

Hackett, recovering quickly, shot Crane again, this time in the chest. At such close range, the bullet made Crane rock backward with the force, but the wound healed just as easily.

Hissing, Crane lunged at Hackett, using one hand to grab the gun and push it away while the other reached for Hackett's neck. Then, Crane jolted back, desperately shaking the hand that had grasped the revolver's barrel. He hissed again, this time in pain.

Hackett shot him a third time.

Ora slipped behind Crane during the commotion. Her hands moved with delicate precision, like a musician testing the untuned strings of a violin. She slid them into place along Crane's neck, which, though healed, was still smeared with blood.

Crane tensed a moment too late. She twisted her hands sharply, snapping his neck. Without his spine to slow her, she jerked her hands again to decapitate him.

"Not as smooth as when you did it, but I haven't had the practice," she snarled at the pile of dust on the ground. "Let's see you heal from that."

"Lady Fischerová?" Hackett breathed.

She looked down at her hands. Her claws were still out. She could feel the extension of her jaw, her fangs exposed to the night air. She swallowed with difficulty, and her face reverted to normal. Revenge for that poor human girl and the brave outspoken pijavica had been satisfying for those heady few seconds, but now she felt ill. She'd torn his head off. Did Judith feel this way after her bloody decapitation of Holofernes? Or even during?

Clenching her fists, she turned to her driver. The gun was still in his shaking hands. "Please don't shoot me," she said. "I can explain all of this."

"I'm not sure I want you to," he said, looking down at the pile of ash and clothing that had been Crane.

"What *is* that made of?" Ora asked, staring at the glinting gun. Crane had not flinched from a bullet wound or a stake to the heart, but this weapon had hurt him.

"Iron alloy," Hackett said. He did not make a move to lower it.

"That's not iron," Ora said, pointing to the decorative filigree on the revolver's barrel and handle.

"Silver, I think. It was a gift," Hackett said. He swallowed. "You're trying to distract me."

"No matter what you saw tonight, you know me," Ora said, keeping her hands raised. "I'm just the same old Lady Fischerová."

"You're a demon."

"Hackett," she said, taking a step toward him, hand outstretched.

A gunshot cracked. A bullet slammed into her shoulder. She was knocked back against the bridge railing again. She stared down at the hole in her skin, revealed by the torn sleeve. Her body's attempts to heal her burnt hand had drained her, and she had not been able to replenish with enough flesh and blood. Her wound did not heal as Crane's had; instead, dark blood dripped sluggishly from the hole. The lifeblood of a pijavica was borrowed from other creatures, propelling them forward through immortality.

"I always knew you were strange," Hackett snarled, "but this is far worse than the spoiled rich bitch I assumed."

"Hackett," she breathed. Her driver had been quiet, but she had never noticed this level of simmering hatred beneath his bland expressions. She reached up to feel the bullet wound, but left her hand hovering above it. It would not kill her, but she could still feel pain. Perhaps it was not as ferocious as it might have been for a human, but she had never been *shot* before.

"Stay back," Hackett said, walking back toward the carriage without turning from her. As painful as the bullet had been, the gun was no true threat to her. If she wanted to overtake Hackett and drive away herself, she could.

She didn't. The disgust in his eyes held her in place.

"You can't leave me here," she pleaded, glancing back toward the bridge. At this angle, the Zizkov house was out of view, but her enemies were close.

He just shook his head and retreated into the carriage. He whipped the horses into a quick trot away, wheels rattling on the cobblestones.

She rubbed her hands over her face, but she knew she had no time to grieve her driver's disgust. The Zizkovs trusted Crane to be their muscle, but would realize soon that he had lost the fight. Would they consider that the gunshots could have been aimed at him? They posed little threat to a pijavica in full health. She had to run. She needed to find help. The Zizkovs needed to be stopped tonight.

She pulled her heeled boots off and flung them into the stream. They were lost in the dark waters in an instant. Freed from the trappings of society, Ora sprinted across the square. She started up the street toward the castle, then looked down at her dress, dark with river water and blood, and shredded into strips that clung to her legs. Her bare feet were pale on the cobblestones.

Perhaps a stop home first was in order after all.

25

They made it safely back through the kitchen door thanks to some sort of commotion toward the front of the house that kept the pijavice occupied, and began walking toward Paluska's house. Though there were still a few hacks on the street, despite the late hour, Domek couldn't imagine sitting down. Overhead, the stars were gone, overtaken by a ripple of dark storm clouds.

They walked in silence for several blocks, taking a twisting route until they reached Charles Bridge. It was well past midnight, and most of the city's residents were tucked away in their homes until dawn.

Once they crossed the river, they emerged into the streets surrounding the Old Town Square, which were some of the widest in the city. Domek kept to the side streets. The vial he was carrying in his satchel was undeniably dangerous, and walking under the towers of Týn Church with it seemed like asking for trouble.

"I appreciate your agreeing to help me," Kája said quietly.

"As I said, this issue involves humans as well."

"You could have sent me back into the jar as soon as you'd gotten the information you needed," Kája said. "You didn't need to keep me here beside you."

"You're the expert on what this serum could do," Domek said. "Besides, my battle is your battle too. You deserve the chance to fight back when someone attacks your own."

"I don't know many other spirits," Kája admitted. "But that in there was wrong. We're not meant to be caged. I thought that was the worst possible fate until what we saw tonight." His light, still invisible to passersby, flickered. "The pijavice are playing a dangerous game. Infusing another being with witch magic is like…attempting to shake hands with a bolt of lightning. It takes a vodník to contain our energy. Attempting to put our untamped power in a physical form without our will to control it… I would have said that it was suicide."

"Even for a pijavica?"

"Especially for a pijavica," Kája said. "They're more powerful than most humans because they lack the functions of life. They subsist on the energy—the blood—of other creatures and simply continue to exist. When witches die, we become wisps or other powerful spirits. Only normal humans become pijavice. They shouldn't survive this."

"We don't know if they've succeeded yet," he said. "They've been trying to get you back. They still need you. Maybe they haven't finished their experiments. From the look of that cellar, they've already killed several pijavice trying."

"If it wouldn't mean more senseless deaths and mutilations of innocent slaves, I'd be happy to see the pijavice waste through their entire race trying to conquer this," Kája said.

"We'll find another way to make them pay," Domek reassured him.

It took less than fifteen minutes for Ora to run through the alleys from Kampa Island back to her own house. The short distance had aided her, but had alarming implications for her safety against the family. No one had followed her, but she would not be safe for long. Rather than wake and alarm Lina, Ora managed to wipe off the worst of the mud and pull on one of her simpler dresses on her own. She rolled her aching shoulder to test its range of movement, and chose boots that would not slow her down.

She waited on her front step for a minute before she left again, expecting Darina to emerge and laugh at her misfortune. She would be delighted to learn that the 'dull social function' she had pawned off on Ora had ended up nearly killing her. However, she was left alone in the silent and cold night.

From there, it was another ten minutes up the hill to the government office where she'd met Sokol yesterday. The narrow street was quiet this late, and storm clouds had swept in from the west. So far, there was no sign of pursuit. If fleeing with the information of their cure had not been enough, killing one of their members would undoubtedly put Ora on their list of targets as soon as they were ready to storm the daylight world. Though they did not know her true name, she doubted that would save her for long.

She needed Sokol's help. If his resources were as extensive as he had claimed, the humans could wipe out the family by dawn and neutralize the threat, sparing Ora and the rest of the world from the invulnerable pijavice. If they moved quickly enough, they may even be able to prevent the conversion of the dozen new recruits.

If she hadn't seen the proof, she would have said the entire situation was ludicrous. No matter which school of thought one adhered to—the one that explained away the creation of pijavice with science, the one that traced their curse back to Lilith, or one of the others—there was no force on the planet that should have been powerful enough to change the face of reality. What science or magic could they be using to do that? How had they lost their vulnerability to hawthorn and sunlight, and why had it seemingly given them a weakness to silver? Silver was the weapon for spirits, the incorporeal remnants of human souls. Pijavice remained in their bodies—they should have been immune.

Even if Ora was right about Crane's reaction to the silver, pijavice able to brazen the light of day would make them nigh unstoppable. It was no wonder Czernin had emerged from his self-imposed retirement to support their experimentation. With the Zizkovs' cure and Czernin's mind for tactics, they would be unbeatable. Humanity was ill-prepared for a daytime predator, and once the secret was out in the world, it would be impossible to take back. The family needed to be stopped tonight.

But Ora remained furious that Sokol had used her husband's death to manipulate her. How long had he been waiting for an opening to pull her into his fight? She undeniably was on the side of humanity against the Zizkovs—she simply wasn't sure if Sokol was on *her* side.

Ora took a deep breath and entered the building.

Sokol's office was on the ground floor of the building near the rear. Ora slipped through the dark hallways quietly. Everyone outside of Sokol's ministry would likely be home at the late hour, but government employees could be testy. When she knocked on his door, it took him nearly a minute to finally answer.

"I didn't expect to see you tonight," he said, leaning against the doorframe. He was wearing a pair of wire glasses, delicate on his strong face. It was strange to remember that he worked at a desk.

"I went to the gathering."

"Come in," he said, and closed the door behind her. "You did?"

"It was a trap," Ora said.

"Are you all right?" He stepped close as though to check her for injury. She had chosen a dress in a dark navy fabric to hide the blood still sluggishly dripping from her wounds. "Why are you wet?"

Ora skipped back. "Don't worry; I escaped. No thanks to you."

"If they managed to do this to you, they would have killed my men," Sokol said. His quick retort hung in the space between them. "I would not have encouraged you to go if I had known it was a trap."

"I believe you, of course," Ora said, waving a hand and sighing. "Even if you *have* been using me for years, at least I can be sure that you wanted me alive."

"Did they know who you were?"

Ora shook her head. "They're looking for recruits. Walking through that door was considered volunteering." She summarized the events of the night, including the demonstration Mayer had done of their miraculous cure. As she spoke, Sokol's expression darkened.

"You're sure it wasn't a trick? They've truly found a cure?"

"I stabbed one of them myself with a stake. I know hawthorn when I feel it. He didn't even flinch."

"This is bad," Sokol said. She snorted at the understatement. "If more of them take this cure, we'll lose our only advantages in this fight. It needs to be destroyed."

"That's why I'm here," Ora said. "Can your ministry do it?"

Sokol hesitated. "You can't do it on your own?"

"They nearly caught me tonight, Sokol. I almost died. It's clear that doesn't matter to you, but there's only so much I can do, even when I'm willing to help. They have at least a dozen members now, and none of them will be vulnerable to our usual weaknesses by morning. I've been on this planet for…a long time, but I've never seen something like that."

"Bringing the ministry into this is not a good idea."

"Sokol, you work for the emperor. Isn't this the entire point of your operation? This is what you're paid to do. Stop trying to trick me into doing the heavy lifting."

"Well…" Sokol said. Ora narrowed her eyes. Sokol never prevaricated. "I've been having trouble mustering the support we need." Ora waved her hand, prompting him to continue, "Not everyone in the government is informed that pijavice are a real threat. I'm fighting with the police for members and resources, and not everyone in charge of budgeting understands why I need them. The emperor is still taking away some of our strongest men for his wars. My team's job is to gather information, but the lamplighters are the ones following up on the ground level."

"So you don't actually do anything," Ora simplified.

"I've been trying to build this team for years," Sokol said. "So far, Válka is the only one I trust. The rest are bureaucratic, retired to our ministry because they weren't of use to the emperor in any other capacity. We're fighting an uphill battle.

Until we find evidence that more support is vital to the country's safety, we have to make do."

Ora folded her arms. "Evidence has been acquired."

"They're old and skeptical. The word of a pijavica won't do much. That's part of the reason I never asked for your help before."

"But these are desperate times," Ora said. "If there were ever a time to challenge them, it's now. You have to trust me."

"I do trust you," he said.

She raised her eyebrows. "Don't treat me like an idiot, Sokol. You know better."

"Do you want me to apologize for using every tool I can find?" he asked.

"I'd rather you didn't see me as a tool at all," Ora snapped.

"Don't take it like that," he said, rolling his eyes. "I never lied to you. You're my friend, but I'm trying to save this city."

"You used my dead husband to make me do what you wanted," she hissed. "What kind of friend is that?"

"The kind without nearly enough resources for the job he has to do. The kind whose own masters are his biggest hindrance. The kind that sees your potential being wasted on literary salons and gambling dens," Sokol said. "You've tried to stay out of this fight, but it's here. If those monsters find a cure, you'll be affected too. It's not time for you to sit back."

"Your ministry can't sit back either," Ora said. "You're worried that they won't listen to the word of a pijavica? I promise you I can convince them that the threat is real."

"This won't go well."

She brushed a wet curl from her face and grinned at him. "Aren't those your favorite type of plans?"

26

Domek knocked on Paluska's front door. Returning to the lamplighter leader's narrow townhouse reminded Domek of his last encounter outside. Was Bazil still watching them? If so, the man was well hidden in the shadows and mist.

At least this time Domek felt confident that no pijavice were following him, since Kája was covering their trail from the house. Not that they needed to follow him. They'd ransacked his apartment—they knew who he was.

Then again, though Domek had seen all sorts of records in the nest's office of their smuggling practices, he hadn't seen any information about himself. If they were so desperate to get the wisp back from him, and knew his home address, why hadn't they started gathering other information? Perhaps his date with Ora had been their next step in getting the jar from him. Why hadn't she tried harder? He'd been vulnerable to her a dozen times that night.

"Stay quiet, if you can," Domek instructed Kája as they waited for the elderly valet to open the door. "They're not going to be eager to hear what you have to say. I warned my boss about your silver tongue."

"Of course," Kája said. "When I can."

Domek was about to argue when the door finally creaked open, revealing...

"Anton?" Domek asked, surprised.

"Good. You're finally here. We've been waiting."

"You and Paluska? Is this where you've been staying since the break-in?"

Anton nodded, still standing in the doorframe. "He has spare rooms. I agreed to help him with some work in exchange for temporary board. Keeping Prague safe is not a weekday job, you know. He's been helping me train with a sword," he said, puffing up with pride.

"I didn't realize this was where you were," Domek said.

"You could have stayed too," Anton said. "Did you get my note?"

Domek nodded. "I did. Webber will be missed."

Anton's jaw worked, tense and angry. "I told you to come here."

"Abrahams needed me more than you did," Domek said flatly. "I need to talk to Paluska. Is he still awake?"

Anton nodded and stood aside, allowing him to enter. He led him to Paluska's office where they found the lamplighter leader examining a pile of maps and documents. He put them aside and stood up. "Hello again, Myska."

"Sir," Domek said. "There's been an update with the...issue I came to you about the other day. Can we talk?"

Paluska gestured for him to continue, but Domek glanced over at Anton uncertainly. As much as he trusted his roommate, they had agreed to keep as few people informed as possible. Paluska cleared his throat. "Anton has proven to be a faithful lamplighter," he said. "I believe that he'll know the right way to use this information."

Domek nodded. "Kája," he instructed. "Let them see you."

Though Domek's vision did not change, Paluska and Anton both looked instantly to the light floating beside him. "Am I wrong in thinking that this is the wisp?" Paluska asked. "If anyone should be dismissed from this conversation, I believe this is it."

"We're working together," Domek said. "What I have to say concerns Kája as much as it does us. I trust him."

"Forgive me if I'm more skeptical," Paluska said.

Domek pulled the jar from his bag, but then hesitated. Not only did Domek want Kája's input for the conversation, it seemed cruel to isolate him after what he'd just witnessed. Instead, he set the jar on the floor at his feet. "Do not harm anyone in this room, no matter the provocation. That's an order," he told Kája. Turning back to Paluska, he asked, "Is that enough?"

"I suppose it will have to be," Paluska said.

Domek briefed them on what they had found in the nest's basement, the strange tools and materials, and the conclusion Kája had drawn about the nature of the serum. "We don't know what they're doing with it," Domek said, "but it can't be good. We need to stop them from getting their hands on any more wisps. I broke their machine, but that won't stop them forever." He pulled the obsidian shard from his pocket and set it on Paluska's desk. "This was the key component in their machine."

"Infusing pijavica blood with magic," Paluska said, tapping his fingers methodically on his desk. "I wouldn't have thought of it. It's brilliant."

"It's dangerous," Domek corrected. "I was talking to Kája, and he said that—"

"At what point did you switch from telling me not to trust the wisp to believing every lie it tells you?" Paluska asked.

Leaning on the wall by the desk, Anton added, "I thought you were smarter than this, Myska."

"The wisps are the victims here," Domek said.

"The pijavice are on to something, and this creature is trying to keep you in the dark. It's been manipulating you for days. You've been keeping secrets from us."

"I was trying to keep us all safe," Domek said.

"You were trying to keep it for yourself," Paluska said. "You claimed that you had left it behind the night you came to see me, but I know you had it with you."

"No, I…"

Anton spoke up again. "The lamplighters come first. You lost sight of that in your selfishness."

"Domek…" Kája said quietly.

Domek ignored them both. "I should have been honest, but it didn't seem right to pass Kája along to a new master. The responsibility for seeing this through is mine. I couldn't guarantee what would happen outside of my care. That's not what matters right now. Wait—how did you know I had the wisp with me?"

"After you came to me that night, I went to talk to the expert on these mysteries—Imrich. He was very irritated that you did not bring this to him. As an alchemist, he understood the value of the trapped wisp, and was the one who encouraged me to take it from you before you could do any more damage. He told me that you've been a disappointing apprentice. You have no right to take responsibility of a creature like this." Paluska shook his head. "I should have guessed that you were lying about having it with you, but it took searching your apartment to be sure."

"Anton," Domek said, the clues coming together with disturbing clarity in his mind. "*You* tore apart our apartment."

"Paluska knew you were hiding something. Why else would you refuse to hand over the wisp?" Anton asked. "I was worried you'd guessed, when you disappeared afterward."

"Luckily, that doesn't matter now," Paluska said.

This was getting dire. Domek looked down for the jar, but found that it was in Anton's hands. He had snatched it from Domek's feet while he'd been distracted. Anton tossed the jar across the desk and Paluska caught it neatly.

Domek lurched forward. "Kája, get—"

He gasped, the words disappearing on his tongue with the sudden burst of pain. His hands started to burn as fiercely as they had the first time he had touched the jar. His palms glowed for an instant before fading, leaving his skin clear of the binding symbols. Across the table, Paluska's hands ignited as he opened the jar.

"Wisp," Paluska said. "You have a new master."

"You can't do this," Domek said.

At his side, Kája was very still.

Paluska was unimpressed. "I believe I am plenty up to the task to keep this new monster in line. Wisp, be careful to obey me. I have enough silver here to kill a dozen of you," he said, nodding to his wall of weapons. "Immobilize your old master. If he moves, I'll have you kill him."

A length of red silk appeared and coiled around his wrists. Domek tugged against it, but he was bound fast. Though the fabric looked delicate, it was impossible to tear through. "I thought you were better than this," Domek snarled. "Why are you doing this?"

"This is a war," Paluska said. "A war we've been only scraping by in for decades, always one night away from defeat from the encroaching darkness. It's my duty to turn the tide. It's time for our fight to end. At dawn, you'll see the world you've been helping me build. I'm going to have the wisp summon every monster in Prague and bring them out to face the sunlight, right in the center of the Old Town Square. We'll cleanse this world and start fresh. We deserve to see the new beginning come."

"He's not that powerful," Domek said.

"Imrich has an idea for amplifying its powers. He's been experimenting for the last few days to prepare, but could tell he was missing a key element to convert the power." Paluska picked up the obsidian piece. "This will complete his machine. With the wisp, I'll be able to actualize what I've always wanted to do. The machine will drain every bit of its power for my command. I can make it bigger than it has ever been, guided entirely by my orders, and we'll end this war."

Domek remembered the way Kája had nearly flickered out after trying to save the footman. "He won't survive that."

"Then an extra monster dies."

"He's not a monster."

"It's an ancient, powerful demon that's been deceiving you for days. There's no humanity in that thing," Paluska said.

"He used to *be* a human! A witch."

"Pijavice start as human as well. And a witch? You know better than to trust them. With what Anton told me about your mother, I should have known you'd be soft." Domek glared at Anton. He had shared his mother's past with his old friend in confidence. Anton looked pale. "You don't have what it takes to finish things. I do. I'll use every last drop of this wisp's power to finally bring peace to Prague—to the entire world."

"But—"

"Wisp, gag him." A loop of silk appeared and wrapped around his head, jerking tight across his mouth and then tying off behind his head. Before he could protest, more silk filled his mouth, threatening to choke him. "You don't know the things I've seen, Myska. I can stop…everything. The world is going to change. You could have been a part of it. You should have handed the wisp over when I asked." Paluska nodded to Anton. "Search him."

Avoiding Domek's gaze, Anton took his satchel and then patted down his pockets. He set his stakes out of reach, and then pulled out the rainbow-tinted glass container of wisp essence. He held it up.

"Liquid magic," Paluska breathed, taking the vial. He held it to the light to examine it, and then slid it in his own pocket. "Of course you would take this and hide it from us as well. You don't understand the resources you have. Anton, we need to go collect Imrich and his machine. We do this tonight."

Anton nodded and, not looking at Domek, left the room.

"Wisp, put Myska inside the cell in the basement. Lock the door and then return here."

In a sudden rush of movement, Domek found himself standing in a stone room. He blinked, disoriented. The only light in the room was Kája's form, which was painfully bright against the darkness. The silk ties fell from Domek's limbs into a bundle like fresh blood on the stone floor, and he spat the piece from his mouth. There was a small window, too high and narrow for anything larger than a sparrow to slip through. Trapped underground, the smell of raw power that rippled from Kája's flames was nearly overwhelming.

"You can't help them," Domek said desperately, mouth dry from the gag. "You have to try to resist."

"I have a new master now. I can't choose not to work for him. I told you not to trust this to someone else. You took away my chance at revenge," Kája said.

"This wasn't my fault!"

"No, nothing is, is it? You were cursed to be the one to kill my last master, chaining you unwillingly to me. You were forced to keep summoning me, even after you had decided to resist the temptation. I told you I was a soul, but you had to keep using my powers. You were tricked into trusting the wrong people. You're the victim in all of this, aren't you?" Kája scoffed. "You're incapable of taking responsibility."

"I kept you because I was *trying* to be responsible," Domek said. "I trusted myself more than I trusted anyone else."

"You kept me because you finally had power, and you couldn't bring yourself to give it up. You wanted to prove yourself."

Domek stepped forward. "What other option did I have? I didn't trust anyone else to do the right thing with you. I suppose I could have thrown you to the bottom of the Vltava; I thought about it."

"You could have set me free," Kája responded, voice unexpectedly quiet.

Wincing, Domek stuttered, "I…"

"I suppose you were too selfless and noble for that," Kája said. In a blink, he was on the other side of the door. The lock clicked into place with a resounding thunk, and then the wisp was gone.

27

When Sokol had spoken about the ministry in charge of monitoring monster activity in the emperor's domain, Ora had always pictured a serious, authoritative group of the city's best and brightest. As an insider, Ora knew that the threat was real and eternal. Though Czernin and the other Czech pijavice masters mostly stayed away from Prague and its dirty, crowded streets, bubáks and the less powerful pijavice were pushing back at the government's initiatives to make the city safer. The lamplighters were a smart first step, but they were spread thin across Prague. The Ministry of Security, responsible for all of old Bohemia under Austrian-Hungarian rule, should have been keeping rigorous watch to supplement that work.

Instead, what Ora found when she entered the room in which Sokol had gathered his peers was an eclectic mix of those too elderly, stubborn, or unpredictable to work in other parts of the emperor's service. In the lavishly decorated space, surrounded by ancient wooden statues and a high ceiling woven with golden chains, they seemed small and weak.

Válka sat in a corner of the room, keeping an eye on everyone gathered. With the scar on his cheek and his tense posture, he looked like a wolf locked in a pen full of bleating sheep. Though the ministry worked on nocturnal issues, everyone but Sokol worked during the day, so the men were grumbling among themselves as they settled into their chairs. One, a plump middle-aged man with thinning hair and a permanent wrinkle in his brow, sat in the center of the room. From what Sokol had told her, he was the one to impress. The chairman, he had been assigned to run the ministry, though he spent most of his time focused on his duties at the War Office. Beside him was a man with a hard glint in his eye that might have impressed Ora if he hadn't been bent with old age. He must have been ex-military, aged out of active duty. The third was a young, reedy man with glasses so thick that his eyes were magnified.

"This is the team assembled to protect Prague from threats in the night?" Ora asked Sokol. They were standing by the door, waiting for the room to settle. "They look like the men whose wives drag them to the opera."

"In addition to my personal team, we have access to police reinforcements and the lamplighters as needed," Sokol told her.

"And who decides when it's needed? That man?" she asked, tilting her head toward the ministry leader. "He doesn't look like he'd know a sound military decision if it smacked him in the face. Your government does realize you'll be fighting for your lives on the streets, does it not?"

"Why do you only align yourself with Prague when you like what we're doing?" Sokol asked.

Ora ignored that. "It's no wonder you had to send me to beg for information from Czernin," she continued. "I can't imagine you have much success here."

Sokol frowned at her. "Despite appearances, we do good work. We have a vast network of information. My team is highly specialized. I asked for your help to reach into a group we can't access."

"You mean the pijavice," Ora said. "The entire race you're here to stop."

Ignoring her, Sokol stepped forward. "Thank you all for coming out at such a late hour, but it was urgent."

"Your message said as much, but was otherwise frustratingly vague," the supervisor said. "What is all this about? Who is your guest?"

"Ora, this is Lord Nosek, from the War Office. Beside him is Major Zaba, 75th Regiment. The other one is an archivist, Jaroslav Kundera. And, of course, you already know Válka."

"She shouldn't be here," Válka said softly. "Sorry, my lady, but it's true."

Ora spared him a small smile. "Hello, Válka. No offense taken."

"Everyone, this is Lady Ora Fischerová."

Zaba straightened immediately. "You don't mean the lady pijavica in Malá Strana?"

"You have a file on me?" Ora asked Sokol.

"Of course we do," Sokol said, unabashed.

She sniffed. "All good things, I hope."

"You can't bring a pijavica to a ministry meeting!" Nosek declared. "Sokol, this is quite improper. I can't stand for it."

"I wouldn't have, but she insisted," Sokol said.

"Well, if she *insisted*," Major Zaba drawled.

Ora interrupted. "I did. There's something you all need to know." She told them about Sokol's request for her to look into the rumors of the cure. From their reactions, it was clear that Sokol had gone behind their collective backs from the beginning, aside from Válka, to get her help. She pushed on despite the interruptions, getting to the heart of the matter—namely that the Zizkov family had found a source of immunity from sunlight and hawthorn. She described Mayer's demonstration with the stake, her own skin prickling at the memory.

The room was silent after she finished. Nosek's ruddy face paled. Major Zaba crossed his arms. "That goes against everything we understand about monsters. That can't be possible."

"It is," Sokol told him. "Ora saw it."

"Have *you* seen it?"

"No," Sokol said. "I wasn't there, but I trust her report. We need to take this seriously. If pijavice break the daylight laws, but keep their strength and bloodlust, we'll lose this war faster than you can blink."

"We're trusting her report of this nonsense? She has a thousand reasons to lie to us," Nosek argued, pointing at Ora, who smiled back, gritting her teeth. If they'd met in a salon, he'd be scraping the ground for her favor.

Sokol folded his arms. He had stayed beside her while she briefed the room in a silent show of support. "She went there at my request. I trust her."

Despite their recent arguments, his tone was solemn and unwavering.

"I'm not sure I appreciate you operating behind my back, Sokol," Nosek continued. "You put this operation at risk by taking Lady Fischerová into your confidence. What if she's working with Mayer and the nest to mislead us?"

"Nothing in her file suggests that she would betray us," Major Zaba said.

"*She* is right here," Ora said. "I understand that you don't trust me. However, this isn't an issue that should be debated in committee. I'm sure Sokol feels terribly"—she knew full well Sokol had never felt a lick of guilt in his life—"about working with me without consulting you, but he was just trying to do what is best for this city. Your people are in danger. Right at this moment, pijavice are being given the ability to walk into sunlight."

Sokol stepped forward. "She's right. We can't afford to let things play out anymore. Swift action is needed."

Nosek said, "From her descriptions, if they're accurate, Mayer was able to take in a dozen more members tonight. Why would we risk Czech soldiers against those odds?"

"We'll bring in the lamplighters," Sokol said. "They have experience fighting pijavice, and there should be enough of them to win against any number."

What would Domek say if he were ordered to work with her by his own ministry?

"I prefer not to trust Kuba Paluska with any delicate information that I could possibly keep to myself," Major Zaba said. "Leave him to do the groundwork, but I won't bring him into something like this until we can't help it. He would use it to ruin us. I served with him for years. He's a selfish, conniving bastard—if you'll pardon my language, my lady." Nosek gave him a betrayed look and he added, "What? Pijavica or not, she *is* a lady."

"I wouldn't be willing to send anyone in there without a proper briefing about what they might find," Válka said quietly.

There were shadows in his eyes, the scars of a lifetime at war.

"We'll need to discuss this further before we take any action," Nosek said.

"We need *decisive* action."

"This isn't the army anymore, Lieutenant Sokol. We don't have the resources to throw cannon fodder at our enemies."

Sokol stiffened, glaring at Nosek. "We are fighting a war here. You've seen the reports, you've seen what pijavice can do to our people even when they have some vulnerabilities. If they're loose in the daylight, the casualties will only grow. We can't let that happen. We have to finish this tonight."

Major Zaba cleared his throat. "If you want the military approach, try listening to your commanding officers."

"I still don't believe it's possible. Mayer was never that smart," Nosek protested.

Slowly, Ora turned to him. "You all speak as though you know him," she realized.

There was a tense silence in the room.

"Why would your ministry know a pijavica family head?"

"We don't owe you an explanation," Nosek spluttered.

She turned to Sokol. She enjoyed playing parlor games with him because, even with her attuned senses picking up his heartrate, she could never see through his bluffs. He looked at her impassively, as though unaware of any guidance he could offer to the conversation.

Everyone she had spoken to had emphasized Mayer's meteoric entry into pijavica politics. Most of the newly turned were so mad with bloodlust and unsettled by their new circumstances that they could barely form a coherent thought, much less overtake and restructure a family. Darina had implied that Czernin had been the one to nudge Mayer toward his experiments, but why pick Mayer? There were many pijavice more established than him to encourage toward experimenting for the cure. Unless, of course, Mayer had had access to information even Czernin did not have.

"He was one of you," Ora realized. The room became a statue garden, unmoving. She shook her head. "This likely isn't even the first time this has happened, is it? You have an underpaid ministry of mortals spending their days staring through the window at pijavice. We live on while your members slowly die. Most of you, hopefully, realize the benefits are not worth the price. Mayer clearly did—he wanted our immortality, not our curses. I'm sure he started making this plan to find a cure before he ever found a pijavica to convert him."

"He stole a stack of old maps and journals from the archives and disappeared one day," Sokol admitted. When Nosek scowled at him, he said, "She already knows. There's no reason to keep it a secret now."

"If Vienna finds out…" Nosek said.

"That's why you've been pretending you couldn't see the Zizkovs," Ora said. "You thought that if you ignored the issue, it would never be tracked back to your negligence. My God, do you not screen your candidates?"

"It's too late to undo what Mayer did, but we can't continue to ignore it," Sokol said. "You heard what Ora saw tonight. We can't sit back while Mayer brings the pijavice into the daylight. We'll have no chance after that. We have to act tonight."

Major Zaba slammed his fist on the table. "We're not going into a situation with only a pijavica's word on what we'll find, and you're to stop going behind our backs and doing things

your own way. You were ordered not to draw attention to this."
He pointed at Sokol. "This sort of insubordination was exactly
what we should have noticed in Mayer. Don't make us do to you
what we should have done to him."

Sokol looked at Válka for support, but his fellow soldier sat
with a tight jaw and a level stare.

"You're all so determined to hide your mistakes that you'd
rather they set off an avalanche than to risk any implication,"
Ora said. "You disgust me."

"Bold words from a demon," Nosek said. "You're both
dismissed. We'll hear no more of your lies. And Lady
Fischerová—you'll not want to come back to this building, or
there will be consequences."

Ora quivered with fury, and growled low in her chest when
Sokol took her arm.

"Ora," he murmured. "We need to leave."

She hesitated for one more moment. In another life, she
would have bathed the room red. Finally, she nodded and let
him lead her from the room.

As they left, Nosek said, "This meeting is adjourned. Everyone
go back to bed, and try not to call any more midnight sessions."

Válka caught up with them by the door. "You should have told
me you were thinking of bringing her," he hissed to Sokol, ushering
them down the hall and around the corner so they would not be
overheard. The rest of the ministry was shuffling toward the front
of the building, seeming content with their decision. Cowards.

"Things were moving quickly," Sokol replied. "There was no
time for delay."

"Or you knew that I would tell you it was foolish to ask them
to believe a pijavica's word."

"Both of you are to blame in this!" Ora snapped, jabbing at Válka's face. "You were one of the ones who talked me into this!"

"I know that," Válka said, pushing her finger aside, "but they don't. And we're going to keep it that way. This was supposed to stay quiet, an information-gathering mission only. I needed to know more about Mayer's plans."

"You knew I was cleaning up your team's messes, and neither of you thought to warn me," Ora said. "You let me go fumbling in the dark without even the Zizkov name, much less the information that he used to be on the ministry."

"If Vienna loses trust in our ministry, that's the end of Prague as we know it," Válka said. "We don't have the political power we once had. We'll lose what's left of our authority if it comes out that Mayer was one of us. Sokol is your friend, Lady Fischerová, but you're not part of this team. You haven't had to fight to protect Prague from the shadows while the rest of the world is moving on."

"She is now," Sokol said. "You have to believe her. We need to act without the ministry's approval. We have to stop the Zizkovs tonight."

"There is protocol for a reason," Válka pointed out. He stared at Sokol like he could see through him. "You understand that, don't you? It's better to let the enemy build some strength than it is to rush forward and lose everything. I swear I'm not going to let the rest of the ministry keep pretending this isn't happening. We'll force their hand. We'll get more information, gather our forces, and then we'll handle this together."

"That's not fast enough."

"It will have to be," Válka said. He patted Sokol on the shoulder, but the other man didn't react. Válka looked at Ora.

"Thank you for your help, Lady Fischerová. Sokol, take her home. She's done enough for us tonight."

"This is a mistake," Sokol said.

"But one we'll live to solve tomorrow."

Válka left them alone in the hallway.

Instead of escorting her outside, Sokol pulled her into a side room and shut the door. It was a smaller meeting chamber with an elaborate mural along the back wall depicting Jan Hus accepting his decree of execution. The revered martyr stared toward the ceiling at the heaven which had not helped him escape his death.

Sokol rested his forehead against the door for a moment, cursing unintelligibly to himself. When he turned back to Ora, his face—lined like the battlefield trenches he had fought in—was solemn. "I wanted to tell you."

"You put me in danger to help hide your masters' dirty secret," Ora snarled.

"I trust you more than I trust them," Sokol said. "I had to keep their secrets, but I knew you would be able to help. You didn't need my restrictions. Now you see what I've had to deal with." He pounded his fist against the door. "The close-minded men in there might not have agreed to help, but they don't control me, no matter how much they like to think they do. I still want to try to stop the nest tonight. Mayer is my responsibility."

Ora frowned, imagining her friend facing down a dozen like Crane. "You need the ministry's support, like Válka said. It would be suicide to go in alone, especially for a human."

"I know. Will you help me?" No cajoling or guilt. Just a question from one friend to another. Could Ora walk away after what she'd seen, leaving Sokol to die and the family to take over the daylight?

"We'll be outmatched," she warned him. "Embarrassingly so. It still might be suicide."

"I'm used to that."

"Why am I not surprised?" She nodded to herself, remembering the terrible scenes she'd seen at the Zizkovs' house that night. "I can't sit by and let them win. I'll do what I can. I've certainly never let panels of old men tell me what to do before." She grinned up at him, fierce. "Between the two of us, we could at least take some of them down with us."

"I wasn't sure you would agree," Sokol admitted.

She crossed her arms. "Did you think I would storm away and handle this on my own? Think again, Sokol. You're a fool, but we're in this together now. You pulled me into this fight, and you'll see it through with me to the end. Besides," she added, "I knew you were a fool when I became your friend."

"I knew I could trust you," he said, with more softness in his voice than she had expected.

He took a step closer to her, and she realized just how small the room was. Sokol was a large man, towering over her in height and bulk. There was a look in his eyes that she recognized, one that she had seen there before but had never expected him to follow through on. After all, he knew just what she was: a pijavica, the enemy. That should have weighed out any physical attraction he had for her.

She had entertained the thought before. She had eyes, and her type these days tended toward his tall, muscular bulk. He was gruff, brash, and inconsiderate, but he would provide her with an exciting night. They'd danced around this for years. She'd always thought she would take him up on some fun if he ever offered.

However, when Sokol leaned forward and brushed his lips against hers, she found herself stepping back.

Even though Domek had left hating her, she found she could no longer imagine kissing anyone but him.

Domek, who had seen who she was and hated her. Domek, who was kind and charming, who flushed when she spoke to him as though he couldn't believe she was giving him her attention. Domek, who listened to music like it was stealing his soul.

For a long moment, Sokol stood in front of her, assessing her. From his pained expression, perhaps he had not been looking only for a physical collision. Then, he pulled back and turned away.

"I'm sorry," she said after a beat of silence. She'd learned that was what one said when they wanted to preserve a friendship after an awkward encounter. She didn't want to lose Sokol.

"Never apologize," Sokol said gruffly. She watched his shoulders rise with a deep breath, and then he faced her again. She wondered how much it cost him to hold his easy smile in place. They were so similar. "You're right. The two of us against an invincible nest of pijavice. They won't stand a chance."

"Perhaps we can ask them to send your head back to the useless pigs here so we can have the last laugh," Ora said. "I'd say we should add some of my dust, but I know how you humans are. All of us look alike to you."

He chuckled, and the lingering tension between them broke like a wave onto the shore.

"I'm not planning on dying tonight. It will be harder to beat them without hawthorn on our side," he continued, "but you said one died after you decapitated it. We have a chance if we can find a way to behead the lot. They're not invincible, not entirely."

"Beheading a pijavica is difficult to do, especially if you don't have our strength. Luckily, I don't believe that's our only chance. I think whatever cure they're using gives them a new weakness. I'm not positive, but it's worth trying, if we're dashing toward death together," she said. "Tell me you have some silver weapons around here."

28

For an hour, Domek paced the small cell, searching for a way out. He had to escape. What was Paluska doing now? Had he already retrieved Imrich for the alchemical experiment they planned to use to kill Kája?

He had to stop them. He was the only one who could.

Or was that the same arrogance that Kája had accused him of?

Domek had been so certain of his own righteousness that he had ignored every warning the wisp had given him. Kája had told him that all humans were convinced that they were special. Domek had been sure that he was an exception to that rule. Instead, he'd kept the wisp's powers secret and close. He'd believed that his hands were the only ones capable of resisting the wisp's lure.

Instead, he'd summoned the spirit whenever he'd needed help, dragged them both into the middle of the nest's territory, and then walked them directly into a trap at Paluska's house. Kája had been right to be furious.

Domek stopped and picked up one of the fallen red ribbons Kája had left behind. They were as soft as clouds in his hands. He stretched the satin as he thought, twisting it around one of his palms. Instantly, the ribbon tightened into place, wrapping around his hand with a life of its own.

Domek swore and quickly yanked at it with his free hand, and the ribbon loosened and fell again. Had Kája created these, or conjured them from somewhere else? How did they still contain his magic when he was across the city? There was still so much he didn't know about the wisp. Now he may never know.

Domek was furious at himself. This was his fault. In addition to his arrogance, he had been so *blind* to his brothers in the night watch. Anton had been spending all his time in extra training sessions, and Domek had never stopped to wonder what he was learning from Paluska. Domek had accused everyone but the real culprit of ransacking his apartment, when he'd told Paluska directly only hours before that he'd hidden the container there. Who else but Paluska and Anton would have known where Domek lived? Even Ora had never known that. When Domek had left the destroyed apartment, Anton had tried to find him again. Domek had thought he'd gone to talk to Cord out of concern, but that hadn't been it at all—he'd wanted to keep an eye on Domek's movements.

Domek had thought discovering that Ora Fischerová was a pijavica would be the biggest betrayal of his life. It wasn't even the biggest betrayal of his week.

His mother's cards had seen more than he could have ever expected. Would he have ten swords in his back by the end of the month?

"Fuck," he muttered, dragging his hands through his hair.

"I wanted to check on how things are going, but I think that answers the question."

Domek turned and looked up. Through the small window on the back wall, he could see a familiar face, barely illuminated by the candle in his cell. "Bazil?" he said. "What are you doing here?"

The proprietor of The Pigeon Hole frowned. "Where's the wisp? What did you do?"

"It's a long story. How did you find me? I need you to get me out of here."

"I had people watching the house, and a few other points around the city. There's something in the air tonight. Things are building. My girl said she overheard Kuba Paluska leaving with another lamplighter, talking about how to deal with you. She followed for a bit before she lost them. At least you won't be in this cell long. Some people wait at St. Wenceslas Prison for years before they finally meet their end. You're one of the lucky ones. You won't live past dawn."

"They're going to kill me?" Somehow, despite everything else, he hadn't thought they would kill one of their own.

"Once they're sure you're not hiding any more information," Bazil agreed. "Did you lose the wisp?"

"Paluska took it. They tricked me," Domek said through gritted teeth.

Bazil hummed. "Still feeling confident in your ability to judge people's character?"

"Are you going to help me, or not?"

"Why? From what I heard, you made some mistakes and trusted the wrong people. It happens. I don't want to piss off the man with an entire organization of lamplighters hanging on his every word."

"You said they're going to kill me," Domek said.

"I did. It happens," Bazil said. "You don't respect me. You just need me."

"I'm sorry," Domek said.

"I'll bet you are."

"Will you help me now?"

"Is that why you apologized?" Bazil rearranged himself to sit on the street outside, his back pressed against Domek's small window. "Your friend lives in a nice area," he mused. "Someone like me poking around the entrances is going to set off alarms. I'll end up in St. Wenceslas myself before I can blink. I didn't live this long by sacrificing myself for strangers."

"Listen," Domek said, "they're doing something dangerous, and they're not the only ones. There's another group, a nest, that's experimenting with wisps. There are threats on every side, and I'm the only one who knows it."

"Don't let the information die with you. Tell me what's happening."

Domek couldn't trust him. He catered to pijavice in his club, and seemed to have no plans to stage a jailbreak. But he was right—if Domek died in the morning, no one would know the dangers to Prague. And, after all, there was little chance Bazil could make the situation *worse*. Quickly, Domek summarized his discoveries of the night, from the Zizkovs' experiments to Paluska's plan to drain Kája's power. Out loud, the situation seemed insurmountable. Only Domek cared about Kája's survival, and the nest unchecked could devastate the city. "And there's nothing I can do from in here. I need you to let me out."

Bazil swore quietly. "I never should have left this to the

lamplighters." His boots scuffed on the cobblestones overhead as he stood up.

"Did you just come here to taunt me?" Domek waited for a beat, and then asked, "Bazil?"

There was no answer. He had left.

Domek kicked the wall and swore. Why had he thought Bazil would save him? He worked with pijavice, and Domek had shunned his help. He would probably sleep well with the image of Domek in a cell to keep him company. He could use the information he'd learned to keep his people safe, and leave Prague to suffer. And what else had Domek expected? He had done nothing but trust the wrong people.

It felt fitting, in hindsight, for Domek to end up imprisoned.

For days now, he had been toting Kája around in a small clay jar, only letting him out when he needed his help. From the way he had reacted to being forced back inside the container, Domek wondered if he experienced some level of the same mind-numbing discomfort when trapped. Kája used to be a man, and Domek had contained him like a slave.

Domek deserved this.

Metal rasped against metal, and then the cell door creaked open. Bazil smirked at him, dangling a set of keys on his fingers. "Somebody's looking out for you. These were right in the open. You might have even been able to reach them if you'd realized. Lucky."

"I suppose I was due some," Domek said. Or maybe the person who had locked him in had wanted to leave him a way out. The question was—why? Was it possible Kája had faith in him, despite everything? "Thank you, Bazil. I won't forget this."

Bazil just shrugged and threw the keys back onto the hook, making them swing around wildly. "Where to next?"

Domek shook his head. "You're not coming with me."

"You don't seem to be able to handle it on your own. If you want something done right..."

"What about your people? You said you have contacts across the city. What could you do alone to help?"

"Break you out of a cell, for one. My spies are children, mostly," he said. "I wouldn't bring them into this. They observe only. The others aren't the type you trust with powerful spirits—a lesson you could have learned earlier."

"I don't trust *you* with powerful spirits." He jogged toward the stairs, Bazil on his heels. "I've already been fooled too many times this night. Thank you for saving me, but I have to finish this on my own. It was my mistake. I'm going to end it."

"You're just one man, and you've already been imprisoned by your own people. I'm the only person in this town who isn't working toward your death, buddy," Bazil said. "Do you know how much I've done to help you? I could have sold your secrets and made a pretty coin for it. I have a contact who would kill to know what you've been doing."

"You said you have pijavice in your clubs. Are you working with the Zizkovs?"

"No," Bazil snapped. "I've told you before that I was watching them too. I'm on retainer for a rich pijavica out in the country. I give him the information I want him to have, and keep him in the dark when it suits me. He would have been very interested in you, but I protected you and your little wisp."

"You're a spy for the pijavice and you expect that to make me trust you? I believe that you've helped me, but you've helped yourself more. When you play both sides, you hurt everyone."

"I have my reasons."

"I'm tired of hidden motives."

Bazil threw up his hands. "Fine. I had no desire to die tonight anyway. God forbid I beg you to let me throw myself on a blade for your mistakes."

"If you want to do something useful, get those child spies of yours out of the city before dawn," Domek said. He opened the front door for Bazil.

"I hope you finish this before you get yourself killed," Bazil said, standing at the threshold. "I'd hate for my work to have gone to waste. You're putting the fate of Prague on your shoulders. Broad as they are, I doubt they can bear it."

The night was approaching its end. Clocks across the city had just struck four in the morning. At this hour, Prague's streets were nearly empty. There were the bakers, up early to start kneading their bread for their morning customers. The worst drunks were stumbling home after seeking oblivion despite the risk of falling into the Vltava or being dragged into an alley by a hungry pijavica or dark-eyed robber. The hoofbeats of the few horse-drawn carriages echoed against the tall buildings. Other than those few sparks of motion, the streets were deserted. Life had paused in the riverside city, taking this lull to breathe and resettle before it started again.

With Hackett and her carriage long gone, Ora and Sokol found the last hack for hire still on the road so late. The driver stared down at them with a leer—her, in her finery, and him, out of uniform—but let them in when Ora waved a handful of zlatý banknotes at him. "To Kampa Island," she said.

The heavy clouds that had been swirling overhead for hours finally broke open, sending a rush of rain sweeping across the streets. Within moments, the water escalated from a mist into a downpour, cold with the lingering bite of winter.

"In, in," the driver said, and Sokol slammed the door behind them.

Inside, Ora rubbed absently at her neck, staring out of the carriage window at the downpour. This truly would be a suicide mission. Crane was dead, but the other four members of the family were still alive—along with the dozen they had just recruited. Ora had nearly died just fighting Crane, and they were likely all now empowered by the cure.

At her side, Sokol was methodically examining the daggers and stakes that bristled from holsters on his torso and thighs. Ora could feel from the bite in the air that every weapon in his collection was tipped with hawthorn or silver. He was prepared no matter whether the pijavice had been cured or not. Hopefully Ora had correctly interpreted Crane's reaction to Hackett's silver-embossed gun.

"Where did your team get all those?" she asked finally, breaking the silence. The collection was not even the extent she had spied in the ministry's armory, though the aura of hawthorn had forced her to stand outside the door while Sokol had armed himself. As Sokol had said, if his team wasn't allowed to help him tonight, their weapons would do no one any good sitting behind a locked door in a government office. "From what I heard in there, your budget does not cover nearly that amount of silver."

"Every piece of silver that's been confiscated by the local government in the last three decades has been filtered over into our department," Sokol said.

"I'm sure all the political prisoners would be glad to know their silver teapots were put to good use," Ora said dryly.

"Run me through what to expect in the house," Sokol said. "We'll be in their territory. We need to take them by surprise, not give them an opportunity to plan. Mayer is a slippery bastard. Hopefully they won't be expecting you to come back tonight."

"They have around a dozen new pijavica recruits. If luck is on our side, they'll be too busy giving them the cure to notice our arrival," Ora said. "It takes days for the pijavica poison to convert a human. Hopefully the reversal process takes some time as well."

"We should hope so," Sokol said darkly. "We're not enough to take on that many."

"Love the optimism," Ora said.

"I've looked death in the eyes before," Sokol said. "So have you."

Ora sighed and moved on to brief him on the family members she'd met.

Despite the chaos Ora had encountered earlier that night, the square in front of the Zizkovs' house was as quiet and empty as the rest of the city. The windows were all covered by heavy drapes. Any glass that had shattered with her leap had fallen into the stream, swept away by the water.

"Do you think we'll be too obvious if we bring an umbrella?" Ora asked as the carriage driver pulled to a stop. She patted the navy skirt of her replacement dress, lamenting her sodden and shredded red gown from the beginning of the night. It had been better suited to grand missions.

Sokol chuckled. "I can always trust you to think of the creature comforts." He glanced out the window again, where the rain crashed against the street, and then said, "If they're going to notice us, they'll notice us. Might as well be as dry as we can."

Ora gave the hack driver an extra stack of banknotes to wait out of sight, in case they needed a quick escape. If they did not make it out of the family's clutches, the driver would certainly grow bored and leave. Sokol and Ora crept across the cobblestones to the house, pressing close to one another beneath Ora's steel-ribbed umbrella. Skirting the front door, they found a side entrance. After Ora listened at the door to make sure that no one was lurking inside, Sokol methodically picked the lock with practiced ease.

Once they were inside the dark, empty kitchen, umbrella carefully set aside, Ora took a deep breath, keeping her lips parted so the scents from the house could hit her tongue. "The humans are all gone," she murmured to Sokol. From the heavy scent of blood, thick and cloying, they hadn't left alive. "I can't smell the family, but..." She paused, listened. "There are voices downstairs. Underground."

"Of course," Sokol muttered.

"That might mean they're still in the middle of administering the cure. We could still have time."

The garishly luxurious decorations of the house seemed more ominous in the dark. No candles were lit—without guests to impress, the pijavice in residence didn't need light. Ora led the way, with Sokol close behind. He kept one hand on her shoulder, trusting her to get him through the darkness.

The door to the cellar was open, and Ora could hear voices from downstairs.

"How did this happen?" demanded Mayer, his lowborn accent thick with rage. "This is the version of the serum we used on ourselves—it should have worked. We planned for weeks to get these new recruits, and half of them have been wiped out in one night!"

Half of the pijavice were dead? What had happened here after she had left?

Carefully, Ora and Sokol took the stairs into the cellar. Behind her, Sokol took his hand from her shoulder to ready his weapons.

The remaining four members of the family were clustered around a table in the center of a small chamber. As Mayer had said, there were several clumps of abandoned clothing scattered around the room where other pijavice had fallen. What could have killed so many?

There were still five pijavice hanging from chains on the walls around the room, most looking too shell-shocked to protest. The outlier, Lady R, was snarling ferally and rocking against her chains. "*This* is what you wanted us to volunteer for, Byre?" she hissed, barely coherent. "You tried to kill us all!"

The family ignored her.

"This isn't the serum I made," said Weintraub, the scientist Ora had recognized earlier, carefully sniffing a glass vial streaked with the remains of something iridescent. "This is pure poison—I can smell hawthorn *and* silver in here. How did this get here? Who injected the subjects without noticing it had been tampered with? This could kill any one of us."

The brunette woman, Ajka, who had changed from her frilly dress from that evening into a more serious long skirt and soot-stained work shirt, sneered. "Of course. My apologies. I should have made sure the serum in our personal laboratory hadn't been *replaced with poison!*"

"This is wisp magic," Mayer said, taking the vial. "A transformation spell like this is something only the most powerful witch could do."

"How?" Weintraub asked. "All our wisps are dead."

"Apart from the one that was taken from Baj," the woman said. "You think it could have been here?"

Ora didn't know what they were talking about, but their impassioned debate was a perfect distraction. She glanced back to nod at Sokol, who was on the stair above her, and then she burst into the room.

It had been decades since Ora had seriously battled another pijavica, excluding her fight with Crane earlier that night. When she had lived with Czernin, she had learned how to use her claws and teeth to rend and tear. In between the lazy, indulgent weeks in his estate, there were short, brutal grabs for power among his followers that always ended in dust.

Since then, Ora had lived a softer life, first of exploration, then briefly of love, and then of a soft haze of grief. Her days in the past decade had been full of masquerades and university lectures, with no room for the harsh blur of violence.

If she'd had the choice, she would have gone for Mayer first, to cut the head from the snake, but he was at the far end of the table from her. Instead, she attacked the one closest to the stairs, Byre, who was standing back to avoid the confrontation between the other three. It was the work of an instant. She moved across the room with supernatural speed and thrust one of Sokol's silver daggers into the pijavica's heart. There was a beat, and then the body turned to dust in her grasp.

She wanted to crow with triumph. She had been right; their cure, whatever it was, had given them a weakness to silver. Perhaps this fight wasn't doomed.

Unfortunately, her element of surprise only lasted so long.

Weintraub, hearing the soft sound of a body dissipating, turned and lunged toward her without hesitation. He threw her against the closest wall. A sliver of bare skin above her glove brushed against one of the chains hanging there, and she hissed. It was smothered with hawthorn poison. Her fangs grew in response to the pain, clogging her mouth.

Before the other two could turn on Ora as well, Sokol charged from the stairwell and slashed his dagger at the woman. For a human, he moved quickly, and she had to dodge to avoid the bite of silver.

Ora scrambled to her feet, and was immediately forced to duck a blow from Weintraub. She slashed his chest with her claws before a knee to her stomach threw her against the wall again.

"Lady Ora Fischerová," Weintraub said, finally recognizing her. "In hindsight, I suppose I should have realized you were a pijavica. You always seemed...above the rest of us."

"I was above you," Ora panted, regaining her stance. She was slowed by her injuries, fighting against the pain. "But not because I'm a pijavica."

"What are you doing here, fighting against us? Mayer told us that your friend was the one who opened his eyes to this path. You care about knowledge. You should be *begging* to join us," Weintraub said.

"I'm here because you've been killing innocent people, and you're planning on killing more," Ora snapped. "You're out of control."

He scoffed and stepped back. Behind him, Sokol was fighting both Ajka and Mayer. Ora tried to dart past Weintraub to help him, but Weintraub grabbed her and they fell heavily to the floor. They grappled, neither able to get a grip. Weintraub hadn't been the most impressive human, so Ora hadn't expected him to put up much of a fight, but he had clearly been trained by Crane. He used his pijavica speed and strength to their full advantage, and Ora found herself outmatched.

Finally, he knocked her head hard against the stone floor and, while she lay there dazed, scrabbled for something on the table. Ora, recovering fast, lunged to snap his neck, but had to scramble backward when he spun toward her, aiming a gleaming syringe at her face. It was half-full of a dark substance with a strange, rainbow sheen, and smelled of ash and slick metal.

"We learned the hard way tonight that one drop of this is enough to kill a pijavica within minutes," Weintraub said, holding the syringe like a dagger and feinting toward her, forcing her back toward the wall. "It burns you from the inside out until you finally—painfully—turn to ash when it hits your heart. You're sure you'd not rather hear our proposal?"

"If you're as longwinded now as you were when you were a professor, we'd be here all night."

Snarling, Weintraub lunged toward her with the needle. She ducked under his arm and elbowed him in the jaw. He stumbled backward, struggling to regain his balance while avoiding jabbing himself.

"No!" Mayer snarled across the room.

Ora glanced over—the woman was gone, a dust pile on the floor. Sokol was wielding a dagger in one hand and a stake in the other. His right sleeve was bloody, and there was a scratch beside one eyebrow, but he seemed otherwise unharmed from the fight so far. "Regretting your betrayal yet?" Sokol taunted. His smile was vicious.

Her distraction nearly cost her life.

As she turned back to Weintraub, she almost met the syringe

with her eye. She fell backward, barely avoiding it, and hit the floor hard. He bore down on her, but she rolled to the side. Instead of fleeing, she grabbed his elbow and yanked him down.

Glass shattered with a sharp crack against the stone floor. Frantically, Weintraub pushed himself to his knees, desperately shaking his hands, but it was too late. The glass, covered in the hawthorn and silver serum, had sliced into his palms, infecting him.

There was a pained grunt across the room, and Ora's head snapped up.

Sokol fell, white-faced, clutching his stomach around the hilt of one of his own daggers. Mayer was standing over him with a wide mouth of glinting, sharp teeth. "You always were a fool, Sokol."

Ora lunged forward, but was pulled short by a hand on her ankle. Weintraub had snared her in a clawed grip, his skin already turning gray from the silver working through his body. If she hadn't been wearing her sturdiest boots, the glass shards from his hand would have pierced her skin too. She kicked him in the head, sending him flying backward. Before he even hit the far wall, the silver poison reached his heart, and he exploded into dust.

A door at the back of the room slammed shut. Mayer was gone.

Scrambling to her feet, Ora sprinted across the room and slid to the floor beside Sokol. The dagger was buried to the hilt just below his ribs. Had it pierced his stomach? His lungs? Using her claws, she tore a swath of fabric from her skirts and bundled the cloth against his torso, careful not to jar the blade. It was a horrifying echo of her fight to save the footman last night. How many men would bleed over her hands during her long life? He blinked up at her, the muscle in his jaw jumping as he clenched his teeth. "What are you doing?" he growled. "Go after him."

"And leave you to die?" Ora demanded, pressing down harder against the wound. The smell of blood was raw in the air, preventing her from retracting her fangs. Her body would not calm. There was so much. Too much.

"Ora," he said, and his voice was more serious than she'd ever heard from him. "I'm dying anyway. Mayer knows how to make the cure. If he gets away, he can make more."

"Shut up and let me take care of you," she said.

The scent of oncoming death roused two of the chained pijavice. One screamed, a piercing, feral sound. The chains burned their skin with every movement.

She could hear every thud of Sokol's familiar heartbeat. His own lifeforce was killing him, each beat keeping him alive while bringing him closer to death as blood pulsed from the wound.

"Hold this," she told him, pressing his hands against the makeshift bandage. Carefully, she slid her hands under his shoulders and knees and prepared to lift him.

"Don't move me," he said. "It's too late. It was my own dagger, remember?" He coughed weakly. "I know when it's hit home."

"No," Ora snarled. "Don't you dare."

His chest spasmed. "When will you learn that you can't control everything?" he asked her. He reached a blood-stained hand toward her face, but let it fall before he touched her.

"When will you start listening to me?" she shot back, voice shaking. "I'll call Dr. Roth. He'll save you."

"Ora, listen," Sokol said. His breathing was growing more and more unsteady, faltering and wincing. "You have to end this. I should have seen what Mayer was becoming. He's too dangerous. This was worth it if you…finish this tonight."

"I will," she promised him. "Sokol, I…"

"I know," he told her. His eyes were wide, pained. "Remember me. Please. You…" He winced, tried to find his next word, but it was lost on his final exhalation.

He stilled, and his eyes lost their desperate focus on her face. Ora had seen death before. More times than she could count. But she would never forget this.

"You can't. Not yet," she demanded, but he didn't respond. He was gone, his body empty of the spirit that had laughed with her, sparred with her, inspired her.

Ora hunched over his still body, her shoulders shaking. She had no tears to spill. She'd lost the ability with her life, but her body remembered. The grief needed to escape her, needed an outlet, but all she could do was keen quietly. "No," she murmured, and put her forehead against his chest.

She stayed there, pressed close to the fading heat of Sokol's body. There were things she needed to do. A mission that needed to be finished. But Sokol was dead. He deserved another moment of her endless life.

Suddenly, the cold, bitter bite of hawthorn-laced metal pressed against the side of her neck. "Back away from him."

With the smell of Sokol's blood overwhelming her nose and the screaming and clanging chains from the pijavice on the walls covering all noise, Ora hadn't noticed someone else enter the room. She took a slow breath.

Metal. Honey. A tang of chemicals. "Domek," she breathed.

29

Domek, holding his sword firmly beside Ora's neck, wondered why he hadn't simply stabbed her as soon as he'd found her at the heart of the crime. He had taken the hawthorn-coated blade when he hadn't been able to find his confiscated stakes in his abandoned bag in Paluska's office, but he was painfully aware how untrained he was with the weapon. Without the element of surprise, he'd have little hope of beating a pijavica with it.

This was the woman who had invited him to the opera, the woman he had taken to bed last night. But he had never truly known her, had he? She had hidden her true nature from him as easily as Paluska had.

Her voice, quiet and raspy, tugged at the thread inside him that still cared for her.

"Lady Fischerová," he said. "This ends here. These experiments, the wisps you've hurt—it all ends."

"I'm not behind this," she said, fierce and strained. Her dress, dark blue and sophisticated, had been torn to shreds. Frills and ribbons hung loose, revealing a white silk slip underneath. "I didn't do this."

"Right," Domek said. His loyalty had already nearly gotten him killed tonight, and Ora was far deadlier than Anton or Paluska. "Let this man go." He peered over her shoulder and realized that the man was still. There were no wounds in his neck, but a bloodied dagger protruded from his stomach.

"It doesn't matter. He's already dead," Ora said, confirming his suspicions. "It's over. It's all over."

"What happened here?" The lab had been wrecked since he had been in it only hours before. In addition to the screaming pijavice chained to the walls, there were shattered beakers, spilled liquids, and several piles of abandoned, dust-covered clothing.

"We... My partner and I, we killed the family for what they were doing here. We knew it was a risk when we came, but we had to try. They... They were stronger than us. So much stronger." She bowed her head, heedless of the blade to her throat, to look at the man on the floor.

There was immeasurable grief in her voice, broken and empty.

Another trick? When he had escaped Paluska's house, he had been faced with a choice: go after Paluska to retrieve Kája, or follow through on the promise he'd made to Kája to get revenge on the nest. He had wanted to rescue Kája from his new master, but the wisp would have never forgiven him for that choice. Kája had made his desires clear—he wanted these experiments on his kin ended. And Domek had, finally, listened to Kája.

If Ora was the scientist behind the experimentation, he'd be betraying Kája once again by letting her walk away.

If she was telling the truth, he would be killing an innocent, grieving woman.

"You have the knowledge to create monstrosities like this. You spend half your time at Charles University," Domek said. "Humans have never appreciated your mind. The pijavice here did. They gave you an outlet for that cleverness of yours."

"For someone who thinks so lowly of me, you think quite highly of me. My skills have never been with experimentation. You would have been better suited to these strange experiments than I. I'm just clever enough to land myself and my friends in trouble. I thought to play spy and then hero tonight, and failed at both."

"The evidence all points to you."

"I suppose it does. Maybe this was where I was always going to end up. I've started too late to make a difference. To save anyone." She put a bloodied hand on the dead man's forehead. "I should have left it to you. Promise me you'll stop this." She pointed toward a door at the edge of the room without turning. "Their leader, Mayer, he escaped down the tunnel. Find him. Kill him. Make it hurt."

"How do I know you're not lying?" he asked, his grip so tight on the sword hilt that his arm trembled.

She sighed. "You don't. Do what you must, if it will free you to go destroy Mayer. I've lived too long as it is."

He hesitated for another moment, and then slid the sword back into its sheath and stood up. "We'll find him together."

She turned around, blinking up at him. Her mouth was distended by fangs. Her hands were red with blood, just as they had been when she had desperately tried to help him save the footman the night before. "Why?"

"Most guilty people don't ask for death." He nodded to the fallen man. "He was your friend?"

"He was an utter bastard," Ora said with a harsh laugh. "And one of my dearest friends." She stood up. "I should go hunt Mayer. Maybe he won't have gotten far." She looked back down at the still form of her partner. "But I can't leave him here."

"I can find Mayer."

"Then I hope that's silver and not only tipped with hawthorn," she said, nodding toward his sword. "Otherwise, it won't work."

"He's not a pijavica?"

"He is—and more. They've taken a cure, something that makes them immune to hawthorn and sunlight. Silver is their only weakness now." She shook her head. "I wouldn't even be able to catch up with him now. I'm injured, and he's enhanced. And if I can't outrun him, you certainly can't. He'll be gone by now."

A pijavica that could walk in the daylight. One that could not be killed by hawthorn. The serum made from the dissected wisp had made the monster that had killed Webber. Abrahams had been right—it *was* a pijavica, but warped beyond their understanding.

Domek looked to the tunnel, and then glanced around the room again. "I have an idea. If I can work quickly enough, I might be able to stop Mayer—there are some deaths nothing can survive, and either way, we can't leave this lab for anyone to find. Take care of your friend. I will finish things here."

Carefully, she scooped up the body, as easily as picking up a child. She was so much stronger than she looked. "I promised him I would end this," she told Domek.

"We will," he assured her.

She nodded and turned toward the steps.

"Wait," he said. She glanced back over her shoulder to him, her face solemn and drawn. "The things the pijavice were doing here, that was only the start. Someone else got hold of...what they were experimenting with. He'll be going after the pijavice first. Be careful."

She blinked at him. "How can this person use the cure to kill us?"

"It's complicated, but you're in danger," Domek said. "He's reckless, and he doesn't understand the power he's using."

"You know where this man is?"

Domek nodded.

She hesitated, and then stepped toward the stairs. "I need to take care of Sokol. Do what you need to down here." After a beat, she said, "These pijavice in the chains, they hurt innocent people tonight. Destroy them all." Then, she was gone.

Three of the five dangling pijavice were awake. Though they were all, like Ora, dressed in posh, urban clothing, they were snarling and growling. They were lashing against their chains, and their eyes were locked on the staircase where they'd last seen the blood-covered body.

Domek ignored them and started to examine the lab equipment that was still intact on the center table. After all his years working with his uncle, he was more of a tinkerer than a scientist. The Zizkovs, as Ora had called them, had technology more sophisticated than the run-down gadgets in Zacharias's shop. Still, he understood how things fit together. He knew tubes and chemicals and standardized reactions, not betrayal and mystery. This, he could do.

Sniffing some vials, he cranked a dial to send a liquid flowing through the bronze piping that looped over the table, and then added a second to it. Carefully, he used the butt of his sword to break off a valve, letting the resulting gas mixture loose in the air.

He opened the door that led into the tunnels, and then threw a second container of his caustic mixture down it. It smashed in the dirt, swirling and hissing.

He needed to move quickly. His hands were shaking slightly as he jogged over to the stairs. He looked back over the basement once more, though the gases were already rising to sting his nose. The cruel, delicate machine that had ripped apart the remains of the wisps' spirits glinted on the table. The pijavice dangling around the room hissed at him, still lurching against their chains.

Ora had told him to destroy the remaining pijavice, that they had blood on their claws from that very night. This house had evil seeping through the cracks in the floorboards. There was nothing worth saving.

He took the stairs two at a time, fumbling into his bag as he went to pull out the gifts he'd gotten from his uncle. He dropped a scarf as he went, but left it abandoned on the wooden steps.

Fortunately, when Anton had taken his supplies, he hadn't noticed the extra matches tucked in the pockets of the bag. Carefully, he struck one matchstick against the strip of phosphorous. The chemicals dragged against the ragged red surface. Fire burst into life at the tip of the wooden stick, crackling unfettered and burning its way toward his fingers.

Deftly, Domek flicked the match down, sending the small flame spiraling over the steps. Before it could land in the heavy gases Domek had flooded into the cellar, he slammed the door and sprinted toward the front entrance.

The explosion, when it caught, was momentous. The floorboards under Domek's feet seemed to lurch with the force of it, the sound shattering the air around him. He nearly fell through the front door when he reached it, heart pounding in his ears.

He stumbled onto the front lawn in the pouring rain, his boots slapping on the slick, muddy grass. He turned around at the street to look back at the house. The explosion had been mostly contained to the cellar, as he had hoped, but he could see fire crackling in the sitting room. The nest's lush décor blackened and shriveled under the flames.

As the flames licked toward the window, the heavy rain hissed against them through the broken glass, beating them back. He hoped it was enough to prevent it from spreading through the entire neighborhood.

Perhaps the fire would make it to the top floor before the rain could beat it into charcoal. The maps and papers up there could still be dangerous in the wrong hands, even if the nest and machinery were destroyed.

Ora stepped up beside him, watching the house burn. She had gotten an umbrella from somewhere, and held it partially over his head as well. Her blue dress was stained dark with the man, Sokol's, blood.

"Incineration. Bold choice. Let's hope the bastard couldn't outrun the explosion."

"If he did, we'll hunt him down. He won't get away with this. What did you do with...?"

"I paid our hack to deliver him to my house. Lina will see that he's...taken care of. The driver was not happy, but has been warned that any deviation on his part will not end well for him." In the light of the fire, she seemed a warrior queen.

"Why not go with him yourself?"

"I've been alive long enough to know that there's nothing to be done for the dead but follow their last wishes. Sokol's soul will move on. It has to." She seemed to be convincing herself as much as Domek. For Ora, death had not been the end. Those who died without settling their debts were cursed to live on in mangled forms, like the screaming White Lady, the lost wisps, and the bloodthirsty pijavice. "If you're going after someone who stole the family's research and is planning on using it, I want to help stop them. If you would accept the help. I'm ending Mayer's legacy tonight. He'll be wiped from this earth."

Domek took a deep breath. If he was wrong to trust Ora, he might be leading a pijavica straight to the last wisp, but Paluska had already gotten the better of him once that night. He had a potential ally, and he couldn't bring himself to doubt the grief and fury in her eyes. He couldn't turn her away. "Then let's end this."

"Come. The storm will have scared away any remaining hacks, and I seem to have sent mine away. We'll have to walk."

Despite the blows she'd taken while fighting Weintraub, Ora walked without a limp. She would heal by next week, and until then, she could ignore the bruised bones, the headache, the sun-blackened hand, the gunshot wound, the blood the rain hadn't washed from her hands...and the empty space in her heart where Sokol had once resided.

Her mind wanted action, to rend and tear the world apart until Sokol's task was completed. Her body craved blood to fill her veins and repair some of the recent damage. If she'd been home, she would have gone to the cellar to drink some of the cow's blood they'd gotten from the butcher yesterday. Instead, she was on the empty streets of Prague, ignoring the steady pulse of Domek Myska's heartbeat beside her. They were pressed close under the umbrella, which he held high over their heads.

It had been decades since Ora had partaken from a human. When she'd left Czernin, she'd continued to dine upon human blood on occasion, though she had never killed to find it. She'd left that behind with Czernin. Money built up over time, and with enough of that, one could find people willing to do just about anything. Then, she'd met Franz, and the very idea of acting as a predator to man's prey repelled her. She'd known if she'd asked, her husband would have let her take blood from him. She never asked.

The cravings didn't disappear over the years, no matter how determined she was to never slip. Instead, it was knowing how disgusted she would be with herself afterward that made human flesh almost unappetizing. She'd gone once to a meeting in a church on the edge of town for a group of people all struggling to resist drink. Only once, and she'd used a false name. For everyone there, the feeling was much the same. Knowing the consequences and hating the action didn't quite ruin the allure of their poison of choice.

No matter how much her body ached for the warm blood beside her, she ignored it.

As they walked, Domek explained what they were heading into. While she had been luring him into opera dates, the lamplighter had been having a horrible week. Days ago, the source of the cure had fallen into his hands, and he'd been hounded by people on all sides for it since, including, of all things, a White Lady.

The story, strange as it was, had the benefit of distracting her. She had a task now, a mission to complete. Sokol would have shouted at her if she let his death interfere with it. Mayer existed because of Sokol's masters, and hers. The ministry had given him the resources, and Czernin had pushed him into action. It was her responsibility to end it.

"This mysterious cure," Ora said thoughtfully, "this thing—the source of Mayer's research *and* your friend Paluska's power—what is it? I've been trying to deduce it from your story, but I can't imagine anything that could do what you claim it could do. Weintraub, the Zizkovs' lead scientist, was college-educated. He was a prodigy of chemistry and alchemy, but he was never creative. He shouldn't have been able to make something so revolutionary. Even with Mayer to lead them, this type of energy should be decades away."

"After everything I told you, can't you see that the fewer people who know about it, the better?"

"I understand that you still don't trust me," Ora said. "But if I'm going to help you tonight, I need to at least know what we're looking for. Is it a plant, a flower? Has it already been made into a serum like I saw in the cellar? Can we destroy it at the source?"

Domek was silent. She felt his eyes on her. He had always been quiet and difficult to read, but she knew he was judging whether or not to trust her.

Did she deserve his confidence? He'd been betrayed twofold tonight by those he saw as allies. She was one of his enemies. He could use her tonight, but she doubted she'd be able to regain his trust fully. Did she even want it? For months, she had been flirting with a lamplighter, someone who would have killed her in a heartbeat if they'd run across each other in another circumstance. His people never gave hers the benefit of the doubt.

Except Sokol. He had known her nature, accepted it, and still had trusted her as a friend and ally. From the disgust on Domek's face when he'd found out what she was the night before, she doubted he could ever do the same.

They stepped onto Charles Bridge. The Vltava flowed as dark as the sky overhead, punctured by the driving rain. The sound of rushing water was as loud as drums.

"I know you have no reason to believe me, but I swear that I won't use the Zizkovs' secret for my own ends," Ora said. "I'm not interested in power. Not in that way. I know what you think of pijavice."

"I don't know what I think anymore. Tell me; how did you become one?"

"I died when I was twenty-five. Or, more accurately, I let a man kill me when I was twenty-five. I know you're not much older than twenty-five yourself, but it feels as though I was so very young. So foolish. I drank his blood, and the pijavica poison keeps me in stasis."

"Is that how all pijavice are made?"

She shrugged. "The energy of our blood is what makes us what we are. Some take it from a master. Others pull themselves from their own graves, and the poison comes directly from the hate in their hearts. It takes a lot of power and hatred to make a pijavica from nothing. They're much rarer than those of us who are made. It's easier to convince a young girl that immortality is a gift."

At the center of the bridge, Domek sighed. In the distance, the many spires of Prague peeked over the skyline, leading them onward. "Did you know that will-o'-the-wisps are the souls of witches?" Apparently, he was deciding to trust her.

"I've seen some wisps, but never spoken to them. The witches I've known were never my friends, but none had the kind of power you're talking about."

Domek explained the wisp's magic to her, sketching out a magical soul unfettered by the constraints of life, honed by the will of an enslaver. In all her travels, from England to Russia to India, she had never encountered anything like it. There were always other monsters lurking in the night, but Ora had been young and interested only in herself. Pijavice were her death and rebirth, and she had little time for the other perversions of the human soul. She hadn't known something this powerful lurked in the fiery flashes floating in her periphery. When had Mayer learned of the wisps' power? That must have been the secret he had uncovered in the ministry's archives, the one which had pushed him into action.

"This wisp, Kája. You think he'll help your Paluska?" Ora asked.

"He won't have a choice. Paluska has the jar, which means he has the vodník's power to control him. He's going to use some sort of device to drain his power completely." Domek looked away. "I should have let him go. He asked, before, but I could only think of stopping the pijavice."

Ora shook her head. "You know, I believe your friend Kája was lucky to land in your care." Domek glanced over at her, frowning. "There aren't many who could resist the temptation of unlimited power. It fell directly into your hands, and your only thought was on how to keep everyone safe."

"It wasn't my only thought," Domek admitted, gaze on the horizon. In the darkness and rain, the sky was nearly indistinguishable from the river.

"Your only action, then," Ora said, "which is the most important part."

Domek was silent as they passed under the dark tower at the east end of the bridge. It loomed over them, the pointed spires on top standing like flags blazing on a parapet. St. Salvador Church greeted them on the other side, pale as a ghost. After two hundred years spent isolated at Lord Czernin's estate and then exploring the rest of the world, the familiar streets of Prague sometimes seemed to have barely changed. She knew they had—in her time, the four areas of the city had not yet been combined into one. But at night, far from the encroaching steam engines and new structures, the solid heart of Prague made even Ora's long life seem ephemeral.

To Prague, Sokol's life and death would be as a blink.

"How did you become involved in this? Not just finding the wisp. Why are you a lamplighter, Domek Myska?" Ora asked, pushing down her grief. "You're thoughtful, introspective—not the kind to look for glory on the dark streets of Prague."

"If I was searching for glory, becoming a lamplighter would have been a poor move. Our actions are mostly hidden."

"That doesn't mean it's not there. Most of the hunters I've met have been looking for proof of their own power. It's a source of pride for them to kill their predators, even if no one ever knows." She glanced over at him. "That doesn't seem like your style."

"I've only ever wanted to protect people," Domek said. "Since I was a little boy, that was my only dream."

"Most little boys dream of pretty women and horse races."

He shrugged. "Not in my area of town," he said. "Certainly not in my flat." They walked in silence for a long moment. "I've seen what happens when someone with power goes unchecked. When someone who thinks their need, their anger, their power is more important than someone else's right to live. Not every victim can stand up for themselves. Even before I knew about the pijavice, I knew that there are women and children who need help, who can't fight for themselves. Sometimes, it takes someone else stepping in on the victims' behalf to make things right. I grew up big, and I made myself strong. I became the kind of person who could help."

What had Domek's childhood been like for him to grow that understanding of the world so young? So many like him, boys who grew up as victims and then found power later, fell into the same patterns as their abusers. It was always easier to protect oneself than find a way to protect others. "You're a good man," Ora said.

"I did what anyone would do," Domek said.

Ora couldn't stop her choked laugh. "Domek, I've been alive for a very long time. I have more power from one night than most humans can build in years of training. Since then, I've experienced more than one lifetime's share of suffering. Would you like to know my reaction to it?" She didn't give him the chance to respond. "Asking how I could protect myself next time." Shaking her head, she said, "Your pain made you selfless. Mine just made me more selfish."

"You stopped the Zizkovs tonight."

"I was cajoled into it," Ora said bluntly. "Sokol—my friend— he needed a favor. I wouldn't have volunteered for any of this. I had to be pushed every step of the way."

"You're coming with me now," Domek said, not wavering.

She sighed and looked back at the castle looming on the hill behind them. The storm made the night nearly impenetrable, but she knew dawn would be on its way soon. "I suppose I am."

30

Domek and Ora entered the Old Town Square from the south, passing alongside the Old Town Hall and its orloj, the ancient clock that tracked the sun, moon, months, and astronomical positions. Its intricate surface, gold and orange and turquoise, was muted by the darkness.

Domek's mother had once told him that if the clock ever fell to disuse, Prague would be cursed. She'd warned him that a ghost would appear, crouching above the clock and nodding at passing citizens to confirm the city's fate. The clock was polished and well-kept, but Domek half-expected to see the White Lady appear on its roof to scream her silent fury anyway. After the night he'd had, it seemed as though the world should have been falling to pieces.

Buildings walled the square in, limiting the entrances to a few key points. To a hunter's eye, it was the perfect trap. The creatures Paluska would summon to the center would have to fight to flee as the sun started to rise. If Paluska could successfully amplify Kája's magic, he would kill every creature in Prague in the morning light. It was everything Domek had once wanted. He hoped he was in time to stop it.

Domek looked upward, but the tower at the top of the Old Town Hall was dark. There should have been watchmen on guard duty, an offshoot of the lamplighter group. From there, the guards could alert the town if a fire began to crackle through the old wooden buildings, or a foreign army invaded.

The clock arms split the face as they passed, silently marking six in the morning. The clock would not chime again until nine, when more of the city was awake. Its silence tonight felt like censure of the activities happening in its square.

Anton and Paluska were standing with Imrich at the base of the Marian column in the square between Týn Church and the Old Town Hall. The column was near the center of the square, built to thank the Virgin Mary for the Czech victory in the Thirty Years' War. During the day, its shadow could be used to check the time, but at night the soaring, intricately carved column was simply a guardian for the square. At the top, fifteen meters overhead, the Virgin Mary looked down on them, her face wreathed in shadow.

Imrich was fiddling with a machine resting on the steps of the column, a bundle of gears and brass piping that seemed too heavy for the three of them to have carried across town. To one side, standing impatiently at the base of the column, Paluska was tied to the contraption by a bronze circlet stuck along his scalp. Kája illuminated the scene, trapped in the center of the machine in a glass ball. His flames crackled and licked at the edges, his size not dampened despite the fact the orb seemed entirely sealed against oxygen.

When the figures at the base of the column finally noticed Ora and Domek striding across the open square toward them, Anton stepped forward in front of the other two and reached for his weapons. Domek's stakes lined his belt.

Paluska held out a hand to stop Anton. "Myska," he greeted, voice clear and loud over the pounding rain. "This is a surprise. Have you changed your mind?" His eyes were cold.

Anton, Paluska, Ora, and Domek stared at each other. Of all of them, only Ora seemed comfortable. If it hadn't been for the heavy tension in the air, and her ruined clothes—growing more ruined by the second—she might have been at a literary salon, waiting for the next speaker to start.

"Who's this?" Anton asked, nodding to Ora.

"Ora Fischerová," she said. "And you are?"

Anton started and looked at her again. "*This* is Lady Fischerová?" When Domek stared at him, Anton seemed to remember again that they had fallen on opposing sides. He grimaced and fell silent.

Domek ignored them. "Kája, they're dead. They're dead. The nest that was experimenting on your brothers is gone, and so is their research."

"Dead?" Paluska repeated. "You've been busy tonight."

Kája didn't react. Had Domek made the wrong choice in pursuing the Zizkovs instead of going directly to save the wisp, or was Kája hiding his reaction because of their company? Or was whatever energy the machine was draining already in progress?

"Myska, you fool," Imrich said, leaving one hand on his machine as he surveyed the newcomers. Though the brass and wires were slick with the rain, Imrich did not seem concerned by the water. "Your arrogance knows no bounds. You keep the wisp to yourself, and then bring a lady into this?"

"More than just a lady," Ora said, and her smile split too wide for a human face.

"Pijavica," Paluska spat.

"Paluska, you can't do this," Domek pressed. "Using Kája in that machine makes you as bad as the monsters. He's not a tool for you to use and destroy. We can find a better way to do this."

Paluska held up his hands. His palms gleamed silver in Kája's light, covered in the intricate scars that Domek's hands were now missing. "You'll find that I can do whatever I want," he said. "Wisp—"

"Don't," interrupted Imrich. "Don't use its power while it's in the machine. You'll dilute the energies."

Paluska stopped, jaw clenching white. Instead, he just said, "Unlike you, who hid it away, I've been running tests with Imrich all night. The power is even more than I expected. With Imrich's machine here, I can stretch that power even further. I'll be able to do anything."

"If pity won't move you, what about self-preservation? What happens if your machine frees him? Do you think he'll spare you after what you're trying?"

Paluska raised his eyebrows. "I thought you trusted that thing."

Domek looked at Kája as he spoke, stroking the soft fabric of the ribbons inside his jacket pocket Kája had used to imprison him. The ribbons he had slipped free from inside his cell, only to find the keys hanging within reach. "If Kája decided to lash back and punish all those who have been keeping him captive and using his powers for their own ends, I couldn't blame him. I never earned his loyalty, even when I had the chance. I wish I had."

"I don't need its loyalty—I won't need it at all as of dawn," Paluska told him. "According to Imrich's calculations, the wisp will dissipate after the machine is finished. It will serve its purpose."

"Those are some very naughty plans," Ora purred. Even without her hunting teeth and claws extended, it was astounding Domek had never noticed Ora was a predator. There was a gleam in her eye that said she knew she was the most powerful being in the square, and that she thrived on that knowledge. "It takes a strong man to kill an enslaved being."

"Silence, pijavica. You would use it too, if you had the chance. You're as bad as it is. That's why there will be a pijavica purge come dawn," Paluska said. "I doubt you'll survive long enough to die that way, though."

"Pijavice are not all the same," Domek told him. "You don't understand. What we've learned about pijavice was wrong. They're not all mindless beasts. They were once human, the same as Kája. They can choose to defy their nature."

"This is becoming a habit for you, isn't it, Domek? Befriending monsters?" Anton said, shaking his head.

"Apparently," Domek returned coldly.

"I am not wrong about the pijavice," Paluska said. "I haven't shared all the complexities of the supernatural with the lamplighters. What does their origin matter to you? Having you engage in moral debates while you're on patrol would waste our time. You knew what you needed to know."

"You didn't think we should get to make that choice?"

"Of course not," Paluska said. "I'm not interested in philosophical debates with grunts on the front lines. You were my soldier, Myska, not my equal. If you'd followed my orders when I gave them, you wouldn't be in this position." Domek's hands clenched into fists. How long had he blindly followed this man? "Generals make the difficult decisions," Paluska continued. "You may not understand it, but my plan is what matters. I'm going to make a decisive strike with the new day, and it will change this city."

"And you sent the watchmen away because you're proud of yourself?" Domek asked, gesturing back to the dark tower.

"After tonight, none of us will be needed."

That was enough conversation. Paluska would not be swayed by words, and Domek couldn't let him destroy Kája.

Domek drew the sword he'd taken from Paluska's office and lunged forward, but Anton met him before he got near the machine, striking at him with Domek's own hawthorn stakes. Domek ducked out of the way, attempting and failing to use the sword to knock one of the stakes from Anton's hand.

As his roommate, Domek had always thought of Anton as a lazy fighter, but it was quickly clear that his extra training sessions with Paluska had made an impact. Domek had never trained with anything larger than a dagger, and Anton was in his element. He was fast and deliberate with his movements, grazing Domek's shoulder with the stake Domek himself had whittled into a sharp point last week.

Inexorably, he pushed Domek back, away from the column.

"Dawn is close. Begin the process," Paluska instructed the alchemist, placing the circlet on his head. Imrich pulled a lever, and the machine whirred to life.

While Domek and the other young lamplighter grappled, Ora kept her attention on the two remaining men. Domek had explained some of the complicated lamplighter dynamics on their approach to the square. She flexed her hands and tilted her head, willing her claws to burst forward and her human teeth to retract in favor of her second set. She opened her mouth, letting the wide gash of her extended lips reveal the needle-like teeth below.

Imrich and Paluska seemed unimpressed by her display.

She shrugged and darted forward. She expected Paluska to try to stop her. He was the leader of the lamplighters, and had undoubtedly fought many of her kind before. He might even be able to beat her. But if she could get him fighting for his life instead of draining the essence from Domek's wisp, she could delay his plan long enough to stop it.

Instead, he stayed beside the pulsing machine while the old man stepped forward to meet her. He hobbled on ancient, sore muscles down the steps. If he thought she would balk from incapacitating an old man, he would be disappointed. Tonight, she'd lost a friend who had stuck by her side against his own people. Stopping a monster would not faze her.

She moved with superhuman speed, prepared to knock him out without killing him. When she stepped within arm's length, though, he reached out and touched her chest with one frail, old hand.

There was a loud, violent crackle, and Ora was sent flying backward. Her skin felt hot and painful, centered on her collarbone where he had struck her. She reached up to feel the wound, but there was no damage to her skin. She looked up at Imrich, who was smiling.

"What was that?" she asked through battered lungs.

He held up his hand to reveal a small rod. A wire snaked back from its end toward the machine. "The legends say hawthorn is the only force that can harm a pijavica, but I knew that couldn't be true. You're undead, but not stone. Fire can destroy anything—even your kind. I knew there would be something else we could harness against you. I had a theory, which you have kindly proven. Electricity."

Ora, from her hours spent reading at the university library and attending lectures from guest scientists, knew the basics of electricity, but also that the technology for harnessing lightning was still infantile. Who was this man Domek had been apprenticed to?

He didn't wait for her to recover her feet. He approached her with that same slow, steady pace, and leaned down to shock her again. The caged lightning jolted through her, pain searing through to the tips of her hair.

"The future is coming, Lady Fischerová," Imrich said. "I've worked my entire life toward a breakthrough like the ones we're exploring tonight. Where we can't use your power, we'll destroy it. Monsters will be banished from the world in the light of electricity. Darkness is your domain. When we conquer it, only humanity will remain."

"Monsters come *from* humanity," Ora spat.

"Then we'll destroy them as they're born," Imrich said, and electrocuted her again.

She screamed.

Domek dodged another swipe from Anton, narrowly avoiding the tip of the stake. Anton had gotten in several cuts, leaving blood dripping into his right eye from a slice in his brow. In contrast, Domek was clumsy and slow with the sword. With the added weight of his injuries, he telegraphed each motion enough for Anton to dodge him easily.

"You know this isn't right," Domek snarled, stumbling backward. Anton was still pushing him away from the column, where Paluska was draining Kája and Ora had collided with Imrich. "Are you really prepared to live with killing the human soul that's up there? With wiping out every pijavica at once?"

"You should be cheering for us," Anton snarled. "You were my *brother*, Domek."

"How could I cheer for this?"

"We're doing what we always wanted. We're ending this war."

"You don't understand what you're doing. What has Paluska told you?" Domek said, barely dodging a sharp jab of a stake. "He's lying to you, Anton. He's manipulating you."

Anton's thrusts were becoming erratic, his jaw clenched with fury. He was shepherding Domek, keeping him away from the column. "Paluska is a good leader. He noticed me. He's helped me. You've *always* thought I was stupid."

Domek tried to swipe at Anton's arm with the sword, but its heft was unwieldy in his hands, and the other man was easily able to duck out of the way. Anton had the advantage, but he was not moving in for the kill. Perhaps Domek could still reach him. "I never thought you were stupid," he said.

"Don't lie to me." He lunged forward. Domek tried to parry the blow with the sword, but he was a moment too slow. The stake drove into the flesh of Domek's upper arm, sending a flood of pain through him. He shouted, dropping the sword with a clatter to the wet cobblestones and falling to his knees. The agony was too intense to try to lift his right arm again, and he had no chance of wielding the sword with his left.

Domek stared up at his roommate, clutching the wound. "I heard you were planning to kill me in the morning," he spat. "Is that really what you want? When did Paluska become more important to you than me? I've been by your side for years. What about Evka? What about the promise we made after that?"

Anton hesitated, the bloody stake still held at the ready. His eyes were wild.

"What has Paluska done for you but lead you into this?"

"He helped me," he said, readjusting his grip on the weapon. "He's the only one who could help me. After…" He stopped talking, gaze distant. Something had changed inside his friend. Domek had been too focused on his own troubles to notice, but there had been a weight on Anton's shoulders for months now.

"What *happened*, Anton?"

"I thought he was a monster," he blurted. "He jumped out at me while I was on patrol. It was raining. The stake was already in my hand. It hit his heart and he died. No dust—just a human bleeding out on the street. Paluska understood. We have a difficult job."

"Anton… You should have told me."

"You think you're so noble," Anton spat. "So much better than everyone else. Now look at you. You're fucking our enemy! You're betraying everything we knew."

"Ora isn't the enemy."

"No," Anton said, eyes blazing. "I guess I am."

A scream pierced the square, feminine and feral at once.

Anton jolted and looked back, and Domek lunged forward to collide with his knees, sending him sprawling onto the cobblestones. They fell heavily, rain splashing around them.

They grappled messily, desperate hands searching for leverage. Despite his injured arm, Domek had the advantage of sheer heft. He threw his weight into his movements, pressing Anton into the mud.

Domek knelt over him, legs pinning Anton's to the ground. "You're a traitor," Anton snarled, trying to free himself.

"Better that than a murderer," Domek growled, and then punched Anton across the face. His left arm was not as strong as his right, but the blow collided all the same. After years of fighting stone-skinned pijavice, it was strange to feel flesh give under his knuckles. The hit knocked Anton's head against the cobblestones, and his eyes grew unfocused.

Domek raised his fist again, and then stopped. The punch had cut open Anton's lip, and the blood was mixing with the rain, diluting and washing onto the ground. He was staring up at Domek with rage and hurt, as though he expected Domek to beat him to death.

Gritting his teeth, Domek reached into his pocket and pulled out one of Kája's red ribbons. Moving as quickly as he could through the pain without letting Anton gain enough leverage to get up, he looped the ribbon around one of Anton's wrists. It pulled tight without his help, latching on. The bright red silk stood out against the mud and dirt like a wound. Using the loose end as a leash, he jerked the wrist across Anton's body. As Domek had hoped, the ribbon leaped to do its job, lassoing Anton's other wrist and pinning them together.

"What is this?" Anton demanded. His arms flexed as he tried to pull himself free, but the ribbons were deceptively strong.

Domek ignored him, pulling out the second ribbon and turning to get Anton's feet. Keeping his injured arm close to his chest, Domek used the other to pin one of Anton's boots and wrap it with the last ribbon. When he turned to the other, Anton kicked out with it, managing to catch Domek in the stomach. The air rushed from him, but the blow was too glancing to do any damage. Breathing through his nose with difficulty, Domek wrestled the second foot into place.

When both Anton's hands and feet were bound, Domek fell back onto the cobblestones. His hands splashed in the mud, jarring his injured arm.

"You can't leave me like this," Anton shouted, twisting on the ground.

Domek clamored to his feet. "I can't kill you. Maybe I don't have your conviction," he said, the last word coming out like a snarl. "Stay down, Anton."

Without waiting for a response, he raced back to the column, wiping the blood from his eyes with his left hand as he went, his right arm cradled close to his chest.

On the cobblestones, Ora lay in a crumpled heap at Imrich's feet, but Domek didn't deviate from his race for Paluska. Unless Ora was dust, she would survive. Kája didn't have that long. The wires connecting Paluska with the globe containing the wisp were quivering with the power of the current racing through them, and Kája's glow was flickering like a heartbeat.

The machine seemed complicated. If he'd had time, Domek was sure he could have figured out how to disable it. He didn't have time, so he gathered as much speed as he could get on the slick marble and tackled Paluska instead, digging his shoulder into Paluska's torso. The circlet tore from his head as they both landed heavily on the column's marble steps, and the delicate machine rocked dangerously.

Domek panted, trying to pin Paluska, but the other man had been fighting for longer than Domek had been alive, and Domek had been slowed by his brawl with Anton. The leader of the lamplighters moved with brutal skill, slamming Domek's head against the column's base. Still, Domek fought blindly, determined to keep Paluska away from the machine. He shoved Paluska hard, sending him tripping down the steps and sprawling onto the ground.

Domek turned back to the machine to find that Imrich had taken Paluska's place, and was fitting the circlet to his own head.

"You're an arrogant little fool," Imrich said, "but your stubbornness won't stop me. You could have joined us."

"Imrich, don't—" Domek started, but Paluska punched him in the jaw before he could finish the sentence. It was Domek's turn to fall down the steps, and he landed heavily. His head cracked against the stone, and the world spun around him. The breath had been knocked from his lungs, and it was all he could do to roll and look up at Imrich manipulating the machine holding Kája.

The wisp's fire flickered, as though it were being peeled away from its center. "Let's turn up the speed of this process, shall we?" Imrich said, maneuvering a lever.

Paluska strode slowly down the steps toward Domek, languid lethality in every motion. Anton had been going easy on Domek, not truly wanting to hurt him. Paluska appeared ready to kill him.

"Don't," Domek panted, reaching toward Imrich.

Ora, suddenly, appeared at the base of the column. She had recovered from whatever Imrich had done to her, and—ignoring the complicated mess of wires—snatched the simple clay jar from the base of the machine. He stared at her, transfixed. Her dress was torn and mussed, her beautiful face split for the row of sharp fangs. She was stunning, slender and powerful as a snake, bright-eyed and fierce.

The last thing Domek saw before Paluska's boot connected with his head was her palms beginning to glow.

Flame scorched Ora's hands, branding her with the sigils on the outside of the vodník's jar. She screamed—it was worse than the lightning, worse than the bullet wound. Then, the pain receded, and the wisp was hers.

"Kája," she called. "Back in your jar."

No machine could overpower the wisp's focused magic. In a blink, Kája was free of the glass globe. He streamed into the jar in Ora's hands, whirling and sparking. As soon as he was inside, Ora secured the lid, and the only light left illuminating the square were the lamps along the edges.

Then, there was another light.

A pale woman appeared in their midst, her pristine white gown glowing as though bathed in a full moon that wasn't there. If her sudden appearance hadn't been enough of a clue that she was no human, she was floating well off the ground. She looked at the tableau, and her mouth opened in a vicious, silent scream.

Hearing Domek's story of the White Lady had not prepared her for encountering it face-to-face. Ora had known that there was a White Lady haunting Prague. She had been in the castle since Ora had been born, a rumor and myth that had always seemed like part of Prague's mystery. The being in front of her now was very real, and very angry.

Ora tensed, clutching the jar to her chest, but the White Lady did not attack her. Instead, it darted forward nearly too fast to see and grabbed Imrich with pale fingers. In one quick motion, she jerked him free of the circlet connecting him to his hellish machine and held him aloft.

They were at the base of the column, only a meter from its grand center, and the White Lady threw Imrich back against it with enough force that something cracked loudly.

Between bone and marble, Ora had a theory what it was.

The old man didn't move again.

Paluska, still standing over Domek's limp form, pulled a glass vial of something iridescent from his jacket pocket. The family's lost cure. "I don't need the wisp," he said, voice nearly frantic. "I'll take back Prague myself." In a swift motion, he uncapped the vial and drank. He blinked. When his eyes opened, they were glowing.

He gasped, and the sound seemed to echo in the square. He lifted his hand and snapped. A ball of fire hovered over his palm, flickering and crackling without any fuel apart from Paluska's magic. The serum had worked.

The White Lady turned to him, still silently screaming. He twisted his wrist and flung the fire toward the spirit. It glanced through her incorporeal chest, slamming into the building behind her. She darted toward him, fast as a shooting star, but the wisp's magic had made him quicker than any human.

The White Lady collided with him, and then jolted backward. Face a mask of pain, she put a hand to her side. Bright white light was seeping from a hole in her dress, illuminating the column.

Paluska held up a gleaming silver dagger. "I can feel its burn now," he said. "It's like ice."

The White Lady snarled at him silently, still on her feet.

With the feral grin of a wolf, he lunged to meet her.

Ora watched them fight for a moment, but had no plans to step in the middle. She didn't trust the White Lady to know the difference between friend and foe.

Instead, keeping Kája's jar close to her chest, she raced toward Domek. She knelt beside him and put her hand on his chest. He was breathing, but she could smell the iron tang of his blood hot in the air. Carefully, Ora cupped Domek's head and lifted it off the ground.

"Domek," she murmured, listening to the rushing pulse of blood under his skin. "Domek, wake up." He didn't move.

She glanced back at Paluska's swift and brutal fight with the White Lady. They were evenly matched—the White Lady was more powerful, but now Paluska was enhanced as well, and he was accustomed to fighting a stronger opponent. More gashes of light were pouring from the White Lady's form, but Paluska was bleeding from both nostrils. The White Lady threw him into the flat façade of the building in front of Týn Church, cracking the plaster, but he was on his feet again in an instant.

"Domek, I'm not losing anyone else tonight."

He did not stir.

"Damn it, we have to go! If you don't get up, I'm going to carry you out of this square like a fair maiden," she snarled quietly. Furiously, she pressed a kiss against his lips. For a moment, he was still limp, unmoving, but he finally shifted under her.

He blinked and stared up at her. "Ora?" He reached up, a hand hovering by her cheek.

"It's me," she said, relief choking her for a moment. "The situation is getting out of control. We need to get out of here.

I have your friend." She nodded beside them, where she'd set the jar.

Domek looked over, already gaining some of the energy that had drained away with his blood. "We can't leave," he said. "That machine…"

"The alchemist is dead. Your White Lady showed up. She seems to be fighting on our side—for now."

"What happened to Paluska?" he asked, clearly noticing the lamplighter leader's enhanced speed.

"He drank the cure."

"*Drank* it…?"

"Come on. We have to go."

"The lamplighters could figure out how to use that machine without Imrich. Just let me…" He sat up with Ora's help, and then climbed to his feet. He stumbled only once, but Ora's hand on his elbow steadied him. "Keep Kája safe. I'll take care of it."

Ora ignored him, as he should have expected. After she helped him walk the final few meters to the abandoned copper machine, she set herself at the foot of the steps between him and the dueling figures, Kája's jar held close. She crouched slightly, ready to defend him with claws and teeth if necessary. There was an alarmingly large gash on Paluska's forehead, but it healed as Domek watched. He was beyond human now. Would he have taken the serum if he had known it had created the monster that had killed Webber? Or was he too obsessed with power to care?

Standing in front of the machine, Domek was only steps away from Imrich's crumpled form. He focused on what was in front of him. Without the wisp inside lighting its tangle of wires, Imrich's dark machine seemed spindly and nonthreatening. Domek had always loved the careful precision of gears and mechanics, but this machine was poison. It was difficult to believe that Imrich had found a way to drain a soul of its power and transfer it to another, destroying the very essence of what had once been a human being. Nothing should have been able to erase the last traces of a soul from the earth.

He examined it carefully, noting the key components in the faint light of the lamps around the square. Shaking the haziness from his head, he deftly removed the obsidian shard from the pijavice's distillery, which now connected the globe to the rest of the machine. Imrich had not been satisfied with the pijavice's magics. Domek frowned and unspooled a raven's beak from a tangle of wire, disconnected a string of copper from the rest, and then stepped back to examine the machine. Without someone mechanically minded like Domek or Imrich to help them fill in the missing pieces, no one would know how to recreate the machine's effects now.

Still, just in case.

Careful not to lose his uneasy balance, Domek leaned back and kicked the machine off the bottom step. It arced through the air, and then crashed on the ground, shattering the delicate machinery on the wet cobblestones below. Wires and gears launched free, covering the stones in glinting metal fragments. The noise echoed off the building façades like a gunshot.

Paluska whirled to look at the column, his eyes bright across the square. His head twitched, a strange, birdlike motion, too fast for a human. "Myska!" he roared, and lunged toward them. Ora braced herself between them and hissed, high and threatening.

The White Lady jolted to intercept him again, but stumbled, pressing a hand to an injury in her chest. Her light was dimming. Her eyes seemed drawn like a magnet to the jar in Ora's hands. With another silent scream that contorted her face, she vanished into the night.

Left alone, Paluska and Ora collided in a blur of movement. They were both slowed by their injuries, and Ora was still hampered by the jar in her grasp. She dug her claws into his chest and slammed him into the ground, but he planted his feet into her stomach and sent her flying backward. She rolled, curled in on herself to keep the jar protected.

The distraction gave Domek enough time to limp down from the steps. His body was screaming for him to rest, but there was no time. As Paluska twisted to look at him, Domek stomped hard on his wrist, making the silver dagger clatter to the cobblestones.

"Traitor," Paluska snarled.

A fist slammed into Domek's calf like a train, and he fell to his knees. Gasping, he grabbed the dagger. With the speed of nearly ten years of training, he whirled and aimed it at Paluska.

His old leader jerked to attack him, but stopped when the blade pressed against his throat. The metal left a welt on the muddy skin.

Paluska panted, half-crouched on the wet ground.

"Look what you've become," Domek said. "You're what we always fought to stop."

"You're the one working with a pijavica," he snarled.

"You've become a monster to fight the monsters. And I'm not talking about the powers."

"After everything, you…" Paluska shuddered, the full body motion of a dog attempting to shake off water. Instead of water droplets, he sent a shower of sparks into the night. "There's a voice," Paluska said softly. "Inside me. I can't..." Paluska scrubbed a hand over his eyes, and then ran it through his hair before tugging at the strands.

"The wisp. Why did you drink that? You have another soul inside you. It's killing you," Domek demanded.

Paluska twitched. It was grotesque, as though he were attempting to shake free of his own skin.

"Kill him," Ora said from behind him. "It's too late for him."

"You have the power," Domek told Paluska. "Surely you can put yourself back to normal. You're stronger than this."

Paluska looked up at him with pained eyes, and reached out a shaking hand.

Domek nodded and grasped it. "We can still stop this."

Paluska surged upward. In one swift movement, he grabbed the dagger from Domek's loose grip and jammed it into his chest. The breath was knocked from Domek's lungs as a lightning-sharp pain lanced through him. "That's always been your problem, Myska," Paluska said, twisting the blade deeper. "You're naïve."

Ora appeared behind Paluska, pulling him off Domek and flinging him aside. Paluska skidded, but then clamored to his feet. His teeth were bared in hideous triumph. The dagger bounced across the ground, dark with Domek's blood.

Domek tried to stand, to help, but fell back to the ground. The pain was blinding. He blinked against the rain, praying for Ora's survival. She was the only one who could end this.

Ora snatched up the dagger and was on top of Paluska in a moment. He slammed a fist into her ribs, but she only backhanded him hard enough for the sound to echo across the square. There was no more banter, no more bright smiles. Moving with astonishing speed, she dragged the blade across Paluska's throat.

Blood sprayed from the wound, and the skin around the gash turned gray.

Paluska's face became a mask of horror just before his body turned to black ash in a swirl of fire. Ora lurched backward as the flame that consumed him grew taller and wider than his body, dancing in a spiral like an explosion that ate itself with every blossom. An ouroboros, the flame circled in to consume itself, and then vanished.

Black ash floated to the ground, and was washed away by the rain.

31

Ora tossed the dagger aside and ran back to Domek.

It was a cruel mockery of the scene with Sokol only hours before.

"No, no, Domek," she said. She pressed down against his chest, but the blade had caused more damage when it had ripped free. She could hear the blood gurgling in his lungs.

"You did it," he croaked.

Overhead, the rain stopped as quickly as it had started, leaving the square in surreal silence. Dawn was close now. The sky over the square was washed with gray at the edges.

"Hush," she said. "Don't talk."

"I'm sorry. I made…so many mistakes."

"You tried. That's more than most can say."

He coughed, and blood specked his lips. His breath rattled.

Ora was so damn tired of watching men die.

She stood up. "Don't leave…" Domek whispered, but she

ignored him.

She raced to the side of the column where she had left the jar and picked it up. Its ridges slotted against the new scars on her hands. "Kája," she shouted. "Come out now."

The wisp appeared silently beside her, flickering like a candle.

"Ora, no," Domek whispered, watching them with pain-clouded eyes.

"Can you save him?" she demanded. "Can you help him?"

"They drained me of my power," the wisp said, its voice a wavering rasp that had once been human. "I'm weak."

"Damn it," Ora choked through gritted teeth. Despair clawed at her throat. After everything they had gone through that night, she would still lose him.

"But he came back for me. I'll try," Kája said, drifting toward the fallen form. "Give me the order."

"Kája," Ora whispered. "Save him."

The wisp floated over Domek's chest, bathing him in a soft, warm glow. Under the light, it was clear how deep the blade had gone. The flesh was mangled, and dark blood pooled beneath him. Domek was no longer moving, staring with glazed eyes at the clouds overhead.

There was a long moment of stillness. The light pulsed, but the wound remained raw and ugly.

Then, slowly, so slowly, his flesh began to knit back together. When a pijavica healed, they pulled the life from the flesh they consumed to revert their bodies to their original state. The wisp seemed to speed up time. The wound scabbed over before her eyes, and then the scabs were shed for thick scar tissue.

The wisp's light faded slowly, like a setting sun.

"Stop him before he dies," Domek said. His voice was clear now, his lungs working steadily.

"Stop. You've done enough."

Kája floated back, flame shivering. "He should survive. I...fixed the internal damage f-first."

"You didn't have to do that." Domek addressed the wisp, heaving himself into a sitting position. "Thank you, Kája."

"I..." The wisp flickered, for a moment seeming like no more than the blaze at the tip of a match.

"He needs to go back in the jar. It will let him heal," Domek said. "Right?"

"Yes," Kája murmured.

Ora gave the order, and the small fire flowed back into the jar. "He wanted to save you."

"Thank you for helping him." He rubbed at his healed chest. "I thought that was the end."

"That's one powerful creature." She held out the jar. "You should have this back."

"I'll take it, but I don't want to be his master again. It's time for me to stop making the decisions. I'm going to ask Kája what he wants me to do once he's had time to heal. The wisps have been the victims from the beginning."

"They have a lot of power," Ora said mildly.

"So do you," Domek said.

The protector of the innocent. Somehow, Domek's designation of his enemies and friends had shifted, and she was grateful she'd seemed to end on the latter side. "Either way, take it back for now. I don't have much longer tonight. Dawn is near."

She helped him to his feet, and then Domek took the jar. Though she knew it hurt when his palms glowed, he didn't flinch against the searing pain. Her own scars faded as though they had never been. He tucked the jar into his bag and held it tightly to his side.

Anton had broken free of his restraints and approached the column cautiously. Ora sneered at him, showing her fangs. He wasn't paying her much attention. His voice was barely a croak when he said, "Domek. Are you okay? I saw you go down…"

"He will be."

He stared at her mouth, eyes wide. She realized that her battle fangs were still extended.

"You're not going to be an idiot, are you?" Domek asked him. He held a hand over where the wound had been in his chest, as though feeling the phantom pain.

"What happened to Paluska?"

He shook his head. "He drank the serum I took from the nest. Anton, you had to realize that Paluska's plan was mad."

"He was trying to change the world," Anton said quietly.

"He saw power, and he couldn't resist using it. He's been manipulating you."

"We needed strong, decisive action. We were finally going to be doing something, instead of fighting every night. He's been telling me for months that I could follow in his footsteps." He looked down at the ash smeared across the cobblestones. "I'm not sure I want to anymore."

"Go home, Anton," Domek said. "We can fix what Paluska broke. Don't make it worse. It's not too late for you."

Anton nodded once. Domek frowned after him as he crossed the empty square alone.

Ora cleared her throat once he was out of earshot. "This would have been a good opportunity for you to set yourself up as the next leader of the lamplighters. That boy is desperate for someone to follow. You don't have a political bone in your body, do you?"

"I don't want to be in charge," Domek said. "After all of this, I'm wondering whether our system is spoiled from the start. There has to be a better way. Someone who understands the shades of gray, and can make sure the lamplighters do too."

Ora hummed. "I might know a candidate." She looked at the ashes, barely visible against the mud. "What a disgusting man," she said.

"The sun will be up any moment. What will you do?"

She glanced at him. He was still adjusting to the knowledge that she was a pijavica, but from his expression, the reminder that she couldn't experience the sun didn't bother him. "There's a tunnel entrance nearby. The Old Town is full of them. I'll use it to get somewhere safe for the day. I might not be able to make it home from here, but I'll hole up somewhere." He collected his fallen sword, wincing at its weight, and followed her out of the square.

"Can I help?" Domek asked.

"Once I'm somewhere safe, I'll have a note sent to Lina for her to have someone collect me," Ora told him. In the early morning, the main streets around the square were starting to see more activity. Most of those out were bakers and maids, up before the rest of the city to get everything in order. An older man gave them a second look as he passed, and she realized that after a night of fighting, her gown had been torn to ribbons. Again. She gave him a reassuring smile, which didn't seem to alleviate his confusion. "I'm used to the hassles of daylight," she continued. "The old underground sits beneath our feet. I've learned every tunnel and nook, like most pijavice do."

"I've been down there. It's not pleasant," Domek said.

"It keeps us off your streets," Ora said. They reached the side of the Old Town Hall, and the door that would lead downward. The city staff tried to keep it locked, but had not found any bars strong enough to keep out a determined pijavica. Hopefully the storm earlier had been short enough not to flood the tunnels. As she didn't need to breathe, a waterlogged tunnel was more of an inconvenience than an impediment, but Ora wanted to get dry as soon as possible. "Consider it a gift. It keeps most of the monsters out of sight. You can avoid those of us who are just trying to get by."

Domek turned to her. "What if I don't want to avoid certain ones? I haven't forgotten waking up to a kiss earlier. And you did help save my life. Does it mean you have forgiven me for how I reacted last night?"

It seemed he truly was *not* bothered by her monstrous pijavica form any longer. She had always known there was more to Domek Myska than his humble appearance. Smirking, she said, "I suppose I could find mercy in my heart, if you had a way to make it up to me. I—"

She saw his eyes widen just as she felt a shift in the air behind her. She turned, already ducking. Hands snatched the empty space where her head had been, but before she could react, her attacker followed up with a sharp knee to her chest. There was enough force behind the blow to send her flying backward. She landed on the cobblestones, the breath punched from her battered lungs. Snarling against the pain, she scrambled into a crouch, teeth and claws emerging with enough force to rip her skin.

Mayer was on the dark, pre-dawn street in front of them. Half of his face had been scorched in the tunnel explosion, leaving his skin blackened and blistered. With his pijavica regeneration speed, he would not have so much as a scar within the fortnight, as long as he consumed a few pints of blood. His clothes had fared even worse, leaving him in the tattered rags of a once posh outfit.

"You," he snarled, pointing at Ora. "You ruined everything. You destroyed my research, everything I had built."

Ora's entire body was tense, still as a gargoyle. This was the monster who had killed Sokol, who had fallen to Czernin's charms and betrayed his humanity. The grief she had been holding at bay suddenly threatened to overwhelm her, drag her into its depths.

Domek, standing between them, didn't run. "You've lost. Leave now."

"You're a fool. The lamplighters have always been blind soldiers. The secret of immortality was right in front of you and you wasted your time trying to eradicate it," Mayer said.

Pain had a distinctive scent, sour and bright as lemon. It lanced through the air as Domek lifted his sword with a shaking hand. Kája clearly had not been able to heal all of Domek's injuries. Blood dripped from his arm. "Your experiments killed a friend of mine." He tilted his head toward the center of the square, not taking his eyes from the scorched monster. "And pushed several more to their own deaths."

Mayer glanced at Ora. "Let's see if this one dies as easily as Sokol did."

Finally, the painful grip of grief released her, and she gratefully accepted the flood of fury in its place. "Sokol was twice the man you've ever been," Ora spat. "Domek is mine. You won't touch him."

She leaped forward and tackled him to the ground. Her body screamed with protest, the myriad injuries of the week joining forces to slow her down. She fought against the locked muscles and clawed him across the face. It was a weak hit, especially since she was forced to use her non-blackened left hand, but her nails met the flesh mangled by the explosion and he hissed up at her.

She lashed out with her fangs, aiming for his neck, but a set of claws latched onto her shoulder and pushed her back. His fingers dug into the bullet hole Hackett had left in her skin. The world seemed to shrink to that glowing spot of pain. She groaned when Mayer used the grip to toss her aside. She skidded across the muddy cobblestones, wheezing. She fought to her hands and knees, and collapsed back down when her shoulder protested the weight.

Mayer leaped to follow her, but Domek stepped between them. He held the sword in one hand, keeping the jar cradled to his chest. "You fight to protect a pijavica," Mayer said, swaying in the gray morning and watching Domek through narrowed eyes. "The lamplighter and the monster. And you both thought *I* was corrupting the natural order."

"How many wisps did you kill in your experiments?" Domek challenged.

Ora fought to find her feet, hissing against the pain lancing through her body. Mayer may have been distracted by Domek's posturing, but she could see his unsteadiness. The sword lolled in his grip, too heavy for a single hand.

"As many as I had to," Mayer said. He lunged forward, mouth agape. Poison glinted from dozens of needle-sharp teeth.

Ora raced to intercept him. Using her full weight, she grabbed Mayer's collar and jerked his gaping jaws to the side.

They snapped closed beside her ear with the force of a rabid dog.

Domek's swing was wide, clumsy, but the silver sword met Mayer's side. The pijavica screamed with pain as the precious metal burned his skin. Ora danced backward, away from the hawthorn-stained weapon, but Mayer turned into it, backhanding Domek across the face.

He stumbled and fell to the ground, abandoning the hilt of the sword to curl around the jar and protect Kája. He groaned, sagging against the mud.

Mayer swore and tugged the sword from his side, tossing it to the cobblestones. The blade was stained with blood, but the blow had not reached any of Mayer's vital organs. With enough time, even a wound from silver would heal. He was injured, but so were they. The fight was nearly over—Ora simply wasn't sure who would win.

Limping, Ora scooped up the sword and stood over Domek. She winced when the hawthorn rubbed onto the weapon singed her palms, but she held tight.

Mayer clutched his side, palm dark with blood. "Why did she send you to me? Everything was going to plan before you showed up," he lamented, staring at the silver sword and panting. "I never should have trusted her."

Then, a figure melted from the shadows behind Mayer.

Someone shoved him forward onto Ora's waiting sword. She was clumsy with the weapon, out of practice and weak, but she used both hands to jab it up past his ribs and into his blackened heart. "For Sokol," she snarled into his stunned face.

With a sigh, his body turned to ash, and his tattered clothes fell to the cobblestones. Ora let the poison sword fall with them.

His attacker stood revealed, illuminated by the pre-dawn glow. "You're welcome," Darina said mildly. The pijavica clapped her hands, sending a cloud of dust spiraling in the morning air.

"A friend of yours?" Domek asked, levering himself to his feet. There was a bruise already blossoming across the left half of his face from Mayer's blow. Though Darina appeared human in the dim light, her strength would have betrayed her true nature to the lamplighter.

Darina ignored Domek. Her attention, as always, was on Ora.

"In a sense," Ora said.

"I just saved you," Darina pointed out.

"At the last minute, as always," Ora said, shaking her head. "You've missed a hell of a night, Darina."

"From the look of the two of you, I'm glad I wasn't here. I haven't seen you look this ragged since we took down those rebels in Hostavice."

"Domek, this is Darina. We were in the same family. She's the one who warned me about the Zizkovs. She put me on their doorstep. Without her, you'd have been on your own tonight."

"Then we're lucky to have you," Domek said.

"Your timing really is astounding, Darina. Five minutes earlier and you might have seen a real fight. There were strange happenings tonight." Ora frowned. "Astounding timing. Darina…why was Mayer talking about you?"

"Hm?"

"He said he shouldn't have trusted *her*. You told me Czernin was the one who pushed Mayer into this plan. But Czernin isn't here… *He's* not the one who handed me an invitation to Mayer's house."

"You know Czernin doesn't leave his palace. I've been his liaison with the new family. That's why I'm here, remember?"

"Impressive that you appeared as soon as Mayer mentioned you. Almost like you were waiting for the right moment. We had the same teacher, Darina. I know you were blending in the shadows, watching. But why not help me earlier? What happened to us being on the same team? We nearly *died* out there."

"If you couldn't handle a couple of humans, then I don't want you on my team."

"No, no, I guess you wouldn't. That's what this whole thing has been about, hasn't it? To see who would win and to ally yourself with the right team?"

"Ora," Domek said quietly.

She held up a hand. "Czernin has never been interested in experimentation. He doesn't want a new world order. He hasn't looked outside his palace in decades. But you...you've been looking for a way to get away from him. You wanted to enter the scene with a splash, didn't you?"

Darina laughed and shook her head. "I didn't think you'd realize. You've always been so dazzled by Czernin. You still think he's the center of the universe. You and Czernin, you're both stuck in the past. He's lost his mind, and you think he's the puppet master behind every mildly interesting thing that happens in the world. You always were a beautiful idiot."

"How did you even meet Mayer?" Ora asked. Was she close enough to Domek to save him if Darina attacked him? Ora was weak from fighting, and Darina had always been fast. "I thought you've been trapped with Czernin since I left."

"He came to Czernin's estate when he was still mortal. The ministry liked to keep tabs on Czernin, and it made Czernin feel relevant. I could tell from that one's simpering that all he wanted was to become one of us. We talked, and he confided the clever idea he had been researching. It seemed an experiment worth trying. I've been keeping an eye on it from a distance, but your conversation with Czernin made me a bit worried."

"Why pretend to be on my side at all?" Ora asked, gesturing to Mayer's fallen clothes. "Why help me?"

"He already lost. You nearly killed him. His entire family is gone. Why waste my time with him? I was hoping you'd win, you know."

"Of course," Ora repeated dryly.

"You were sticking your nose where it didn't belong. Someone needed to test Mayer's mettle. I'm not interested in weak allies. If the cure had worked, you would have been in the first group to experience it. Imagine it. Feeling the sun again." She looked toward the horizon, stained with the oncoming sunrise. "You would have thanked me, in the end."

"That's not why you sent me to that house tonight."

"Not only that," Darina admitted, turning back to her. "I wanted to see if Mayer was more than talk. He's been overselling his research to me for years now. If he was taken down by you and your little lover then the cure can't have worked. He was on his last legs this morning. I don't waste my time with failures. Though, I wish you hadn't blown up the damn place. There might have been some ideas left to salvage," Darina said. "Ah well. There will be others."

Ora did not let the conversation linger on the cure. Better to let Darina believe it had failed. "Mayer killed a good man tonight," she said. "You let that happen."

"Mayer made his own choices," Darina said. "I was his shepherd, not his queen. If I had taken control of the family sooner, maybe they wouldn't all be dead now."

"And that poltergeist in the alley," Ora realized. "That timing was too perfect to be real. How did you arrange that?"

"Stomp on the right grave for a bit, dangle some bait, wait for an idiot to walk alone in the dark. It wasn't so hard."

Ora sneered. "You're as bad as Czernin."

"Czernin, Czernin," Darina mocked. "This was supposed to be my moment, you know. To find my allies and leave him behind for good. Leaving him was always going to be a risk. I wanted to wait until I had the perfect opportunity. He's probably looking for me already—if he cares to."

"He'll kill you."

"He hasn't killed you yet. And it's not too late for me to find that ally." She searched Ora's face. "He doesn't matter anymore. Let him waste away in his little palace. We're about to cross into another century. Mortals are coming up with ways to kill each other far worse than anything we could do. Times are changing. If we don't change with them, the shadows will disappear and take us with them."

"Maybe they should."

"You don't believe that. Everything I did, I did to save all of us. You have to see where things are heading. There isn't space for us in this world anymore, Ora. We have to adapt."

"You don't have to change for the worse. You don't have to end up like Czernin," Ora insisted. Her hands throbbed with pain as she clenched them into fists. Angry blisters coated one palm. The other, still blackened from its time in the sun, had been stripped nearly to the bone.

Darina tracked the movement. "We were always going to end like this, weren't we? Are you going to try to kill me now, Ora?"

They stared at each other in the lightening square, frozen as the world moved around them.

Darina's reckless meddling had helped Mayer along the path that killed Sokol. She and Domek had both nearly followed him. The night had been awash with blood from beginning to end.

Ora wanted no more.

"No," Ora said finally. "Leave Prague, Darina. You think you're beyond Czernin's influence? Everything you've done has been to measure yourself against him. You don't have to do that. You could be free."

"You were always soft inside," Darina said.

"It's not softness," Ora said. "Think about which of us has managed to make her own life. You've already left the palace. If he finds you, he finds you. You say I'm obsessed with him? You've made your entire escape about him. That's not the way—trust me."

"You're not better than me," she snapped.

"Prove it. Leave Prague. Make a new life. Leave Czernin and all this behind." Ora stared at her oldest enemy, her sometimes friend.

Darina was shaking, the movement barely visible in the dawn light. Domek was stiff beside her. She hoped he would not go for the fallen blade. With his lingering injuries, he would have no chance of harming Darina, and Ora was not prepared for another fight this night. She couldn't watch him die again.

Finally, Darina looked away. "I don't need to prove myself to you. And I don't need you. Keep your dying city and mortal pets."

"Lovely. I'll escort you to the walls." Ora turned and put a hand on Domek's uninjured arm. "The sun is almost up. We need to go underground," she told him. "You'll take care of the last of the business?"

He nodded. "I will. Be careful." He watched Darina cautiously.

Ora glanced up at the sky. The horizon was painted hues of pink and lavender, with a line of ominous, beautiful orange just at the base of the eastern sky. The temptation to stay out and watch the sun finally cross into view was as strong as ever, but she ignored it. She led Darina to the door in the Old Town Hall and snapped the lock with a twist of her fingers.

"Go on," Ora said, nodding to the dark stairs leading down.

Darina paused, looking between her and Domek. "I like this one," she commented. "Try not to kill him."

Ora scowled and shoved her between the shoulder blades, and Darina went laughing down the stairs. Once she was sure the other pijavica was moving into the tunnels, she turned back to Domek. "I'll make sure she leaves the city."

"Are you sure this is the right decision?"

"No. I'm not. But she and I have history. She deserves the chance I had. There's a way to come back from the worst. And if she can't—well, we'll be here. We've faced worse than her tonight."

"Will you be safe with her? You're still hurt."

"I can handle this. I promise. Keep a hold of your friend," Ora said, nodding to the clay jar, "and I'll watch mine."

Domek nodded, far too solemn for her taste. "I trust you."

"Everyone's first mistake. Smile, Domek," she said, giving him a quick wink. The gesture didn't hurt as much as she'd expected, after the losses of the night. "We won."

Charles Bridge at dawn was empty, free of the crowds that would take over the Old Town as the day aged. The Vltava reflected the multihued sunrise in both directions, refracting gray, then yellow, then orange as the sun stretched its first rays over the horizon. The statues that lined the bridge were mostly black with age, but there were golden accents and patches of bronze where passersby rubbed the saints for luck that glinted in the morning light.

To Domek's left, the castle on the hill watched over the city, and the spires of the churches stretched skyward all around him. Prague was coming to life. He took a deep breath, remembering Ora's last words to him. They'd won—but it wasn't over.

He hoped she had made the right choice about the strange female pijavica who had nudged Mayer into his horrible experiments, but Domek had his own responsibilities.

He peeled his stiff fingers from the jar, taking a moment to appreciate the clay's intricate design. Then, he opened the lid. "Kája," Domek said.

Then, as though he'd been there all along, Kája was floating beside him while he looked over the river.

"Myska," he said.

"I didn't have the chance to tell you earlier. Paluska is dead," Domek said. "So is the alchemist."

"Luckily for you. He was asking me questions all night before he shoved me into that glass orb. He seemed to believe that you were collateral he couldn't risk keeping alive. It would have been a bloody dawn. It still could be. What is your plan now, Domek Myska?"

"The nest's experiments have been destroyed, along with their research. They've all been killed, and there's no one left to continue their project. Everyone who was threatening wisps in this city is gone," Domek told him. "My work is done. Tell me what you want."

"What I want?"

"I know you helped me escape Paluska's cell. You left the keys in plain view. And you could have let me die tonight, but you risked yourself to save me," Domek said. "It was inevitable that we started as enemies. I enslaved you simply by meeting you. You never had any responsibility to help me, or to trust me. But in the end, you did. I owe you."

"I told you that I wanted to stop the nest. When you escaped, you did just that," Kája said. "You could have—maybe you *should* have—run and protected yourself. You did as I asked you, and then you came for me. To save me from your own friends."

"It was my fault you were stuck with a new master, one who saw you as a tool in his arsenal. I couldn't leave you."

"Most would have."

Domek shook his head. "Not me." He took a deep breath. There was a breeze coming down the Vltava against their backs, carrying the morning scents of baking bread and fires burning. "Is there anything else you want to do before I free you?"

Kája turned to him. "No. You'd truly do it?" he asked. "I won't be as strong. You'll lose access to my power."

"I never wanted it," Domek said.

"You've always wanted power. The power to protect yourself, the power to protect the people you love, the power to protect an entire city."

"Then, I never wanted power at the cost of someone else's freedom," Domek corrected. "Nothing you can offer me is worth what you'd suffer for it. You've done enough." He examined the jar in his hands. "Tell me how to do it."

"That's the easiest part," he said. "Break the jar."

Domek put the jar on the bridge's cobblestones. "Not just yet," he said, straightening back up.

"Why not?"

"Someone has been waiting for you. They've been too scared to get close when you were outside the jar, but I thought, maybe after everything…"

Domek felt her before he saw her. He turned. The White Lady was standing behind them. The wounds from Paluska's blade were still blazing, and she was as blurred as a dream. In the pre-dawn light, she seemed less horrifying. She wasn't screaming now. Her dark eyes were locked on the wisp, her face a mask of longing.

"Isa," Kája said, crackling voice barely louder than the breeze.

She was silent. She held out a hand toward the flames.

"She was your wife," Domek said. "Wasn't she?"

"She was a powerful witch. There are many things that can happen to a soul when it dies. Pure power becomes a wisp. Pure hate a pijavica. And pure grief…" There was a heavy pause. "All this time, I wandered alone. I thought she'd moved on. But she was here, waiting for me."

She held out her other hand, reaching to him with both now. She beckoned him toward her.

"Do it now," Kája said quietly.

Domek did. He lifted his foot and smashed the jar. The pottery shattered under his foot, a loud crack in the quiet morning.

When Paluska had fallen into ashes, Domek had thought it was beautiful, in a tragic, horrifying manner. It was nothing compared to this. Together with her love again, the grief binding the White Lady to her form broke. At the same moment, Kája and the White Lady melted away into a shower of bright, crystalline lights. The sparks spread and scattered, spiraling together and apart and together again.

Some kicked and sparked around Domek for another few moments, while the rest faded into the sky. One quick breeze later, which ruffled Domek's hair with cool air as it passed, the lights were gone.

Domek stayed alone on the bridge for a while longer, watching the sunrise over the Old Town. It was a beautiful, clear morning. Carts clattered past him along the bridge, and bells clanged deeper into the city.

Finally, he straightened. He smiled up at the sky, and then scooped up the clay shards, leaned over the railing, and let them fall from his fingers.

The carved clay pieces glinted in the rising sun, and then disappeared with a quiet splash into the Vltava.

EPILOGUE

The dinner spread out in front of them was lusher than any Domek had seen before he'd started spending his time with Lady Ora Fischerová. After he'd moved out of Anton's apartment and found a smaller, private space of his own, he had eaten breads and cheeses for most of his meals, or gone to his mother's to share her hearty goulash. On this table, there was roasted duck covered with plum sauce, meat pies made with wild boar and gravy, and piles of fresh vegetables, paired with several bottles of wine and pitchers of beer.

The table was an eclectic mix of company. Domek sat beside Válka. The scarred soldier had previously worked with the mysterious ministry that organized the efforts against the monsters, but he had quit after Sokol's death in the spring. Instead, at Ora's prodding, Válka had taken over Paluska's role as leader of the lamplighters.

The transition into Válka's leadership had been smoother

than anyone could have hoped, considering the circumstances.

To Domek's surprise, Anton had been one of the first to welcome Válka when he'd been reassigned from the War Office. He had kept quiet about the truth of what happened that night in the Old Town Square, and some of his brash charm had been subdued in the aftermath. Though hesitant to attach himself to another commander, Anton had told the other lamplighters that new leadership was the way forward after Paluska's death. In contrast to the charismatic Paluska, Válka was as quiet and serious as he was skilled and deadly. The lamplighters were still kept separate from the broader workings of the government, but Válka's influence brought a level of discipline—and respect— the lamplighters had been craving.

Abrahams was sitting by Válka's side. Webber's loss had been difficult for all the lamplighters, but Abrahams had been left the most bereft. With Anton still kept at arm's length, Domek had spent more time with Abrahams, and had found a steadfast friend in the Jewish man. Unlike Paluska, Válka saw Abrahams's value, and had assigned additional lamplighters to the Jewish Quarter to help control the monsters within its borders.

On Domek's other side was Ora, who was engaged talking to Cord. After their first meeting in the museum, Cord and Ora had gotten along alarmingly well. When they were together in a room, they tended to outshine any other comers.

Tonight, they were both speaking so quickly that it gave Domek a headache to try to listen in. The conversation bounced as quickly as their words, sending them darting from topic to topic and sentence to sentence like deer bounding from danger.

Noticing his attention, Ora reached over and patted Domek's forearm without taking her eyes off Cord. Domek held her hand and squeezed it for a moment before returning his attention to Válka.

After dinner, they retreated to the sitting room at the front of the house, nursing their glasses of wine—or blood—and chatting. It was late into the night. Domek had come after his dusk to midnight shift, and dinner had been served after one in the morning. Sometimes, they held the parties before Domek's shifts started, but tonight, the mood was languorous, with nowhere for any of them to be until late the next day.

At the first such gathering, he had been worried that he would be outclassed by Ora's idea of a casual dinner party, but his fears had been quickly alleviated. The food was extravagant, but Ora never compared her coffers to those of her guests. She had money and influence, and she chose to spend it on her friends. Domek's brief flirtation with shame had quickly given way to appreciation when he'd seen how she glowed when the house was full of guests.

Ora was in her element in a group. She was the glue that bound them together; with her quick smile and quicker tongue, she swept them all into her orbit.

"How was Alena?" Domek asked Ora quietly when they finally had a moment alone, tucked at the side of the room. Cord was telling some story to Abrahams with animated hand gestures. Though he enjoyed her parties, extended time with any group tended to exhaust Domek. He needed occasional breaks from the pressure, but over the last few months, as he and Ora had grown closer, her company had become as healing as being alone.

She smiled at him, leaning close. In public, they kept a respectable distance, if only for Domek's sensibilities, but among their friends, Ora never resisted her instincts to reach out to him. Domek leaned into her touches, returning them in his own small ways. "She was sorry to miss this. I invited her, but she said it was far past her bedtime. Otherwise, I'm sure she'd love to be charming this menagerie of men."

"How is she doing?" Domek had met Ora's sister-in-law a few weeks earlier. He had never seen her so nervous, apart from when Domek had taken her to meet his mother. She had told Domek about her first husband, and had warned him that his sister might see Domek as an interloper, despite the years that had passed. Instead, Alena had been delighted to meet Ora's new romantic interest.

Ora shrugged. "She's having a good week. She's feeling stronger for the moment."

"I'm sure she was grateful that you visited," Domek said.

"It's not as hard now, when I know I won't be coming back to an empty house," Ora admitted. Domek spent most evenings before work there, when she wasn't visiting him across the city. "Is that wrong of me?"

"You know I could never judge you for being happy," Domek pointed out. He'd gotten over his fear of living up to the memory of her husband quickly. Lord Franz Fischer had spent many blissful decades with Ora that Domek would never know. Ora was still there, though, and now Domek was the one with the chance to bring her happiness. His only plan was to live up to the task.

"I wish Sokol were here. He would have loved this," Ora said, looking over the room.

"I'm sorry I never got to meet him."

"You would have driven each other up the wall," she said fondly. "It would have been a sight to see."

"Ora," Cord called from across the room. "We need you to settle an argument."

"I do love to argue," Ora said to Domek with a bright smile. "Will you help?"

Domek shook his head. "I'm going to grab another bottle of wine," he said, and slipped out of the room.

He refilled his glass and took it up to the balcony on the second level. It was a balmy night now that summer had come to Prague, the air heavy with the scents of green leaves, sweat, fish, and stone. Over the years, the smell of the city had become as familiar to Domek as its churches.

It was difficult for all of them to remember the ones they had lost. The absences were as loud as the presences. His mother's cards had been right—there had been death in his life, too much, and endless change.

He had not seen Kája again since he had set him free those months ago. Had the wisp and his wife finally broken from the ties that bound them to earth, or were their spirits still in the city? What of those who had been lost during the fight? No ending seemed truly final in Prague.

Glancing over the street, swirling the wine in his hand, he saw an unexpected figure leaning against a lamppost on the opposite side. It was Bazil, his face half-shadowed by a top hat.

He caught Domek watching him from the balcony and gave him a jaunty wave before sauntering over. "Domek Myska," he called up, voice just loud enough to carry. "It's good to see you. I'm glad you survived our last business."

"What are you doing here? Did Lord Czernin send you?" Domek asked, not smiling back. After telling Ora about the gambler, it had been obvious to them both that Bazil's mysterious pijavica lord in the countryside had been Ora's old master.

"You're not quite as ignorant as you were when we first met, are you?"

"I've been wondering for weeks why you saved me," Domek said. "I know Czernin would not have wanted me alive."

"He never knew about you—not from me, at least. I never truly worked for him, you know. I gave him some information only when it benefited both of us, but he didn't hold my strings. I led him on a merry dance for a few years. He never confirmed my reports, so I could make sure he only knew what I wanted him to know. But he's gone off the rails since his last pet left. He's more engaged than he's been in a long time. He's curious again. It's dangerous."

"I warned you about playing two sides."

"You won't be so self-righteous when I'm the only person who can warn you if he decides to make a move. It's good to have an eye on your enemy. But I'm not here about Czernin tonight."

"Then why are you here? What business could you have with this house?"

Bazil crossed his arms, seeming casual despite the strangeness of their positions. "Surely you've guessed by now. Why do you think I was following you in the first place? I told you—Czernin didn't know who you were. You were a nobody lamplighter. He wouldn't have known to have you trailed."

Bazil had seen Domek's first test with Kája, before even the second set of pijavice had found him. Why had he been there? Domek had been so wrapped up in the chaos that he hadn't questioned it. "If it wasn't on Czernin's orders, why did you do it?"

"It was for your own good," Bazil said. "A friend of mine was worried about you patrolling on your own. You're reckless for such a slow man. I had some time, so I did him the favor of trailing you myself. It only got more interesting when I realized what you possessed."

Domek frowned. "What friend was worried about me?"

Bazil cleared his throat. "Cord speaks highly of you. I didn't want him to lose someone he cares about when I could do something about it."

"*Cord?*" Domek repeated in shock. Then, seeing Bazil's expression—which was somewhere between smug and soft— he said, "Tell me you're not the unsavory human he told me he was seeing."

Bazil raised his eyebrows. "Is that how he described me? Either way, rest assured I'm not here to spy on you tonight. I'm meeting with Cord after dinner, but arrived early. I thought I'd keep an eye out while he has his fun. I'll take a walk around the block while you finish your brooding, shall I?"

"I'm not brooding," Domek contradicted, but Bazil was already heading off, hands in his pockets.

Cord and Bazil. He'd hoped his friend had better taste than getting romantically involved with a thief and a gambler. Then again, if the man was willing to divide his resources to look after the people who made Cord happy, perhaps Domek could look past his career for Cord's sake.

Domek brushed his hair from his eyes. Hot air hung heavily over the city, despite the late hour. In the morning, those who went out would bake in the sun's heat, though the occasional breeze from the Vltava would give them a moment's respite.

As though his thoughts had summoned it, a wind drifted over the balcony. It tugged at his sleeves and rustled the pages of the book Ora had left by the railing, dancing lightly. The wind brushed his skin with a fresh kiss of coolness from the river.

Though the skies were clear, the scent of a storm lingered in the air.

ACKNOWLEDGEMENTS

There are so many people who helped make this book in your hands a reality. I'm grateful for everyone, but special thanks need to be given:

To my agent, Michael Carr. What a gift we got to meet in the city that started it all!

To the brilliant staff at Titan Books. To my editorial team, Craig Leyenaar and Natasha Qureshi. To Polly Grice, Katharine Carroll, Laura Price, Julia Lloyd, Lydia Gittins, Julia Bradley, Filippos Rempoutzakos, and all the others who work behind the scenes.

To my friends. To Anna, Katherine, Lu, and Shae. To my Charmanders and my FYA ladies. Around you, I've never felt afraid to be my fullest self, and I'm so grateful for that.

Finally, to my family. To Clint, who demonstrates kindness in every action. To Jenna, who brings joy into every room. To Paul, who loves adventure as much as I do. To Emily, my roommate, travel partner, and biggest cheerleader. To my dad, who encouraged me to chase my dreams. To my mom, whose loyalty, love, and compassion I'm lucky to have in my life. I love you all so much.

A NOTE ON THE AUTHOR

Nicole Jarvis has been writing stories as long as she can remember. After graduating with degrees in English and Italian from Emory University, Nicole moved to New York City to work in publishing. She lives in Manhattan with two cats named after children's book characters.

www.nicolejarvisbooks.com

For more fantastic fiction, author events,
exclusive excerpts, competitions, limited editions and more

VISIT OUR WEBSITE
titanbooks.com

LIKE US ON FACEBOOK
facebook.com/titanbooks

FOLLOW US ON TWITTER AND INSTAGRAM
@TitanBooks

EMAIL US
readerfeedback@titanemail.com